White and Other Tales of Ruin

Other books by Tim Lebbon:

Novels:
Mesmer
Hush (with Gavin Williams)
Naming of Parts
Face
The Nature of the Balance
Until She Sleeps
Dusk (forthcoming from Night Shade Books)
Dawn (forthcoming from Night Shade Books)

Collections:
Faith in the Flesh
As The Sun Goes Down

White and Other Tales of Ruin

by
Tim
Lebbon

with an introduction
by Jack Ketchum

NIGHT SHADE BOOKS
San Francisco & Portland

First Edition

ISBN
1-892389-34-7 (Trade Paper)
1-892389-30-4 (Hardcover)
1-892389-31-2 (Limited Edition)

Night Shade Books
http://www.nightshadebooks.com

For Jason, Jeremy & Ben, who are not bleak.

Contents

1
Introduction by Jack Ketchum

7
White

65
From Bad Flesh

121
Hell

195
The First Law

251
The Origin of Truth

277
Mannequin Man and the Plastic Bitch

337
Story Notes

Introduction
by Jack Ketchum

You like a good opening, don't you?

Sure you do.

Me, I insist on it. I do a first paragraph test. You don't pass it, you're a goner. I open the book or the story and read the first paragraph and if it works for me, if it engages me, I go on — if it doesn't, no purchase, or if I already own the thing it gets shelved forever. To do a reversal on Hippocrates, Art may be long, but Life is short. And of books, there are aplenty.

An author doesn't necessarily have to send me racing breathless out of the gate. Not necessary. A leisurely pace is fine too. Though if a writer and I are going for a little stroll together, it had better be a pretty nice day.

So how about this for an opening paragraph? It's from Tim Lebbon's "The Origin of Truth."

They were stuck in a traffic jam. There was nowhere they could go. They couldn't help but see the melting man.

Melting man? Okay, Tim, you got me.

Or this, from "White" — which won the British Fantasy Award, by the way.

We found the first body two days before Christmas.

Yeah, I know, I know — that's an opening line. But sometimes the opening line is the opening paragraph, right? And if it's a good one it'll do just fine to set the writer and me along on our mutual paths together. Of course, if the writer pulls that particular gambit, he's got to have a decent follow-up. Like...

Charley had been out gathering sticks to dry for tinder. She had worked her way through the wild garden and down toward the cliffs, scooping snow from beneath and around bushes and bagging whatever dead twigs she found there. There were no signs, she said. No disturbances in the virgin surface of the snow; no tracks; no warning. Nothing to prepare her for the scene of bloody devastation she stumbled across.

I don't know about you but that sets my foot a-tappin' too.

And a final one, on a quieter note. To seduce you into thinking you're taking one of those little strolls I mentioned.

Della is the only person I listen to. I hear the views of others, weigh the significance of their opinions; but Della is wise, Della is good. Sometimes, I think she's one step removed from everyone else.

I'm in again. *Della is wise, Della is good.* I want to know who Della is. And dammit, I'm gonna find out.

So why's a good opening so important?

Because paying attention to the initial steps, figuring the texture, getting the rhythms right, deciding if you want something simple or complex, how much you want to reveal or merely hint at, is the mark of a real writer — the first sign you as reader get that maybe, just maybe, *this* time you're in luck, you've got the honest-to-god real thing and you're not in the hands of some hack.

Lebbon clues you in right away.

Fear not, reader, I have something to offer you.

Part of what he's offering is fear. But that's beside the point.

A few years back a bunch of us old fart horror writers were maundering over our beers and scotches at some bar at some Con or other, wringing our hands and asking ourselves, *where the hell the were all the kids?* Where were the new crop of horror writers? The new blood, the ones who'd take up the mantle? Where were the goddamn kids? We were kids once. We could remember that, some of us.

But we were in our forties, fifties now. And from what we could see, with a few exceptions we could name thank god, most of the younger writers in their twenties and even thirties just weren't doing their homework. The stuff we were seeing was sloppy, underbaked. Either derivative as hell or — worse — wholly ignorant of our own particular canon or maybe of *any* canon at all, of what had come before. They were either reading a handful of people and aping them shamelessly or else they seemed to be barely reading period, and thought that a vampire who *doesn't* burn up under direct sunlight was the bees knees in originality. They seemed to lack the real ambition of any true novelist or storyteller — to be doing something fresh and honest, human and exciting. A lot of what we were seeing was just plain *phoney.*

Not to mention heartless. Not to mention without meaning.

Real characters, real folks you could care about in real difficulty were getting hard to come by.

As I say, we did a lot of hand-wringing and gnashing of teeth that evening. And yes, there were a few people we could point to who were doing really interesting stuff on a consistent basis but damn, they were few, and most of them were already in their thirties. Proto-Old Farts like us.

Tim was all of about twenty-six, twenty-seven at the time.

I didn't even know he existed. Wish I had.

It would have gone a long way toward setting our minds at ease.

Because he was out there — while we were sitting there drinking — doing what you're supposed to do. Plugging along, doing his goddamn homework, experimenting, feeling, putting that feeling down on paper. Even getting published now and then.

Working at getting it right.

I didn't exactly dive right in to Tim's stuff. I tiptoed first. *Then* I dove.

Tim and I first met at World Horror in Seattle. He was good company. Smart, funny and — well, you know those Brits, they can be so charming you forget all about King George and that they once owned half the world. I wasn't familiar with his writing, though. Then at some point he asked me if I'd like a copy of his short story collection, *As the Sun Goes Down*. I have more unread books in my closet than Burger Hut has burger huts but I make it a point never to turn one down. Especially if it's written by somebody I already like.

But liking the writer doesn't necessarily mean you'll like the work and to be honest, often I'm disappointed. That damn unforgiving first paragraph rears its ugly head or else there's just not enough *there* there, if you know what I mean. So as usual, I approached Tim's stuff with hope but also with some trepidation. I'll just read a story, I thought. Just one. Check it out.

I'm in the middle of reading *Gotham* anyway. Only about a thousand pages to go.

The next day and only a third of the way into *As the Sun Goes Down*, *Gotham* was in a holding pattern over Kennedy and I was asking people, *have you heard of this guy Lebbon?*

And by the time I finished it, I was writing him a fan letter.

I told him the story I've just told you about us writers sitting around complaining and then said, in part, *these stories are amazing. It's utterly accomplished stuff. I'd pay the cover price for the novella alone or*

"Endangered Species in C Minor" for that matter... you are not just a hell of a storyteller, which you are. And it's not just that your prose is lucid and clean and sometimes downright beautiful. What you do so well that so many others fail to do... is to make me care about your characters — even the ones who are not so very nice. No plot-over-people bullshit here. You have the true gift of compassion, Tim, and it shines through everywhere... you write not just from the mind but from the heart and that's sort of rare in our sub-species of writer, y'know? Especially one of your age... congratulations on this book, and thanks very much for handing it to me. I know I'll be visiting your good deep well again before too long....

Which obviously turned out to be true, since here I am.

But I meant every word of it. *Sun*... blew me away. And what I said is true of the volume you hold in your hands as well. These stories are meant to chill you, to hurt you, and they will. But they'll do so for the right reasons. They'll do so because of the people. The plots here are all to one degree or another apocalyptic. In each one all hell's broken loose, something terrible has happened and something in the world is winding down.

But that doesn't mean the human spirit's winding down. Far from it. That's where the stories get their teeth from and why they hurt.

Some hurt right from the opening.

A really good writer pays attention to his openings because he knows he needs to engage you. Then once engaged, he wants a wedding. It's not the 'til-death-do-us-part variety exactly. The wedding consists of your mind and his in fine and special intimacy for the duration of the story, long or short. Like any good bridegroom, in exchange for this intimacy he promises certain things. He will not insult your intelligence. He will not betray you with cheap tricks just to force you to follow in his direction. And most importantly, he will honor your heart.

Tim keeps his promises.

And he's young. He's only just begun.

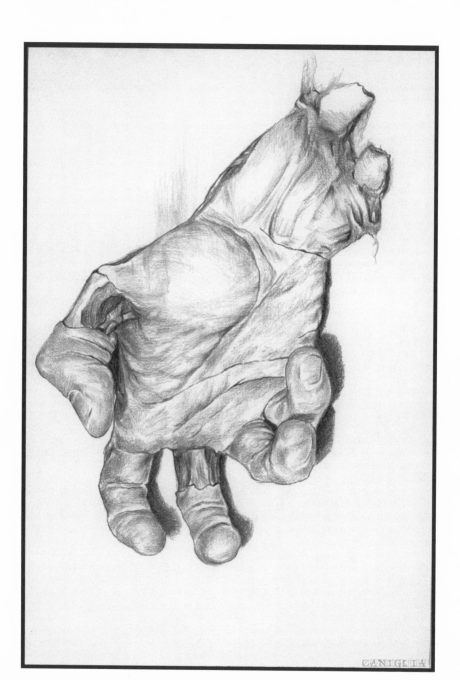

White

one

the color of blood

We found the first body two days before Christmas.

Charley had been out gathering sticks to dry for tinder. She had worked her way through the wild garden and down toward the cliffs, scooping snow from beneath and around bushes and bagging whatever dead twigs she found there. There were no signs, she said. No disturbances in the virgin surface of the snow; no tracks; no warning. Nothing to prepare her for the scene of bloody devastation she stumbled across.

She had rounded a big boulder and seen the red splash in the snow which was all that remained of a human being. The shock froze her comprehension. The reality of the scene struggled to imprint itself on her mind. Then, slowly, what she was looking at finally registered.

She ran back screaming. She'd only recognized her boyfriend by what was left of his shoes.

We were in the dining room trying to make sense of the last few weeks when Charley came bursting in. We spent a lot of time doing that: talking together in the big living rooms of the manor; in pairs, crying and sharing warmth; or alone, staring into darkening skies and struggling to discern a meaning in the infinite. I was one of those more usually alone. I'd been an only child and contrary to popular belief, my upbringing had been a nightmare. I always thought my parents blamed me for the fact that they could not have any more children, and instead of enjoying and revelling in my own childhood, I spent those years watching my mother and father mourn the ghosts of unborn offspring. It would have been funny if it were not so sad.

Charley opened the door by falling into it. She slumped to the floor, hair plastered across her forehead, her eyes two bright sparks peering between the knotted strands. Caked snow fell from her boots and speckled the timber floor, dirtied into slush. The first thing I noticed was its pinkish tinge.

The second thing I saw was the blood covering Charley's hands.

"Charley!" Hayden jumped to his feet and almost caught the frantic woman before she hit the deck. He went down with her, sprawling in a sudden puddle of dirt and tears. He saw the blood then and backed away automatically. "Charley?"

"Get some towels," Ellie said, always the pragmatist, "and a fucking gun."

I'd seen people screaming — all my life I'd never forgotten Jayne's final hours — but I had never seen someone actually *beyond* the point of screaming. Charley gasped and clawed at her throat, trying to open it up and let out the pain and the shock trapped within. It was not exertion that had stolen her breath; it was whatever she had seen.

She told us what that was.

I went with Ellie and Brand. Ellie had a shotgun cradled in the crook of her arm, a bobble hat hiding her severely short hair, her face all hard. There was no room in her life for compliments, but right now she was the one person in the manor I'd choose to be with. She'd been all for trying to make it out alone on foot; I was so glad that she eventually decided to stay.

Brand muttered all the way. "Oh fuck, oh shit, what are we doing coming out here? Like those crazy girls in slasher movies, you know? Always chasing the bad guys instead of running from them? Asking to get their throats cut? Oh man...."

In many ways I agreed with him. According to Charley there was little left of Boris to recover, but she could have been wrong. We owed it to him to find out. However harsh the conditions, whatever the likelihood of his murderer — animal or human — still being out here, we could not leave Boris lying dead in the snow. Apply whatever levels of civilization, foolish custom or superiority complex you like, it just wasn't done.

Ellie led the way across the manor's front garden and out onto the coastal road. The whole landscape was hidden beneath snow, like old sheet-covered furniture awaiting the homecoming of long-gone owners. I wondered who would ever make use of this land again — who would be left to bother when the snow did finally melt — but that train of thought led only to depression.

We crossed the flat area of the road, following Charley's earlier footprints in the deep snow; even and distinct on the way out, chaotic on the return journey. As if she'd had something following her.

She had. We all saw what had been chasing her when we slid and clambered down toward the cliffs, veering behind the big rock that signified the beginning of the coastal path. The sight of Boris opened up and spread across the snow had pursued her all the way, and was probably still snapping at her heels now. The smell of his insides slowly cooling under an indifferent sky. The sound of his frozen blood crackling underfoot.

Ellie hefted the gun, holding it waist-high, ready to fire in an instant. Her breath condensed in the air before her, coming slightly faster than moments before. She glanced at the torn-up Boris, then surveyed our surroundings, looking for whoever had done this. East and west along the coast, down toward the cliff edge, up to the lip of rock above us, east and west again; Ellie never looked back down at Boris.

I did. I couldn't keep my eyes off what was left of him. It looked as though something big and powerful had held him up to the rock, scraped and twisted him there for a while, and then calmly taken him apart across the snow-covered path. Spray patterns of blood stood out brighter than their surroundings. Every speck was visible and there were many specks, thousands of them spread across a ten metre area. I tried to find a recognizable part of him, but all that was even vaguely identifiable as human was a hand, stuck to the rock in a mess of frosty blood, fingers curled in like the legs of a dead spider. The wrist was tattered, the bone splintered. It had been snapped, not cut.

Brand pointed out a shoe on its side in the snow. "Fuck, Charley was right. Just his shoes left. Miserable bastard always wore the same shoes."

I'd already seen the shoe. It was still mostly full. Boris had not been a miserable bastard. He was introspective, thoughtful, sensitive, sincere; qualities which Brand would never recognize as anything other than sourness. Brand was as thick as shit and twice as unpleasant.

The silence seemed to press in around me. Silence, and cold, and a raw smell of meat, and the sea chanting from below. I was surrounded by everything.

"Let's get back," I said. Ellie glanced at me and nodded.

"But what about — " Brand started, but Ellie cut in without even looking at him.

"You want to make bloody snowballs, go ahead. There's not

much to take back. We'll maybe come again later. Maybe."

"What did this?" I said, feeling reality start to shimmy past the shock I'd been gripped by for the last couple of minutes. "Just what the hell?"

Ellie backed up to me and glanced at the rock, then both ways along the path. "I don't want to find out just yet," she said.

Later, alone in my room, I would think about exactly what Ellie had meant. *I don't want to find out just yet,* she had said, implying that the perpetrator of Boris's demise would be revealed to us soon. I'd hardly known Boris, quiet guy that he was, and his fate was just another line in the strange composition of death that had overcome the whole country during the last few weeks.

Charley and I were here in the employment of the Department of the Environment. Our brief was to keep a check on the radiation levels in the Atlantic Drift, since things had gone to shit in South America and the dirty reactors began to melt down in Brazil. It was a bad job with hardly any pay, but it gave us somewhere to live. The others had tagged along for differing reasons; friends and lovers of friends, all taking the opportunity to get away from things for a while and chill out in the wilds of Cornwall.

But then things went to shit here as well. On TV, minutes before it had ceased broadcasting for good, someone called it the ruin.

Then it had started to snow.

Hayden had taken Charley upstairs, still trying to quell her hysteria. We had no medicines other than aspirin and cough mixtures, but there were a hundred bottles of wine in the cellar. It seemed that Hayden had already poured most of a bottle down Charley's throat by the time the three of us arrived back at the manor. Not a good idea, I thought — I could hardly imagine what ghosts a drunken Charley would see, what terrors her alcohol-induced dreams held in store for her once she was finally left on her own — but it was not my place to say.

Brand stormed in and with his usual subtlety painted a picture of what we'd seen. "Boris's guts were just everywhere, hanging on the rock, spread over the snow. Melted in, like they were still hot when he was being cut up. What the fuck would do that? Eh? Just what the fuck?"

"Who did it?" Rosalie, our resident paranoid, asked.

I shrugged. "Can't say."

"Why not?"

"Not won't," I said, "can't. Can't tell. There's not too much left to tell by, as Brand has so eloquently revealed."

Ellie stood before the open fire and held out her hands, palms up, as if asking for something. A touch of emotion, I mused, but then my thoughts were often cruel.

"Ellie?" Rosalie demanded an answer.

Ellie shrugged. "We can rule out suicide." Nobody responded.

I went through to the kitchen and opened the back door. We were keeping our beers on a shelf in the rear conservatory now that the electricity had gone off. There was a generator, but not enough fuel to run it for more than an hour every day. We agreed that hot water was a priority for that meager time, so the fridge was now extinct.

I surveyed my choice: Stella; a few final cans of Caffreys; Boddingtons. That had been Jayne's favorite. She'd drunk it in pints, inevitably doing a bad impression of some mustachioed actor after the first creamy sip. I could still see her sparkling eyes as she tried to think of someone new.... I grabbed a Caffreys and shut the back door, and it was as the latch clicked home that I started to shake.

I'd seen a dead man five minutes ago, a man I'd been talking to the previous evening, drinking with, chatting about what the hell had happened to the world, making inebriated plans of escape, knowing all the time that the snow had us trapped here like chickens surrounded by a fiery moat. Boris had been quiet but thoughtful, the most intelligent person here at the manor. It had been his idea to lock the doors to many of the rooms because we never used them, and any heat we managed to generate should be kept in the rooms we did use. He had suggested a long walk as the snow had begun in earnest and it had been our prevarication and, I admit, our arguing that had kept us here long enough for it to matter. By the time Boris had persuaded us to make a go of it, the snow was three feet deep. Five miles and we'd be dead. Maximum. The nearest village was ten miles away.

He was dead. Something had taken him apart, torn him up, ripped him to pieces. I was certain that there had been no cutting involved as Brand had suggested. And yes, his bits did look melted into the snow. Still hot when they struck the surface, blooding it in death. Still alive and beating as they were taken out.

I sat at the kitchen table and held my head in my hands. Jayne had said that this would hold all the good thoughts in and let the bad ones seep through your fingers, and sometimes it seemed to work. Now it was just a comfort, like the hands of a lover kneading hope into flaccid muscles, or fear from tense ones.

It could not work this time. I had seen a dead man. And there was nothing we could do about it. We should be telling someone, but over the past few months any sense of "relevant authorities" had fast faded away, just as Jayne had two years before; faded away to agony, then confusion, and then to nothing. Nobody knew what had killed her. Growths on her chest and stomach. Bad blood. Life.

I tried to open the can but my fingers were too cold to slip under the ring-pull. I became frustrated, then angry, and eventually my temper threw the can to the floor. It struck the flagstones and one edge split, sending a fine yellowish spray of beer across the old kitchen cupboards. I cried out at the waste. It was a feeling I was becoming more than used to.

"Hey," Ellie said. She put one hand on my shoulder and removed it before I could shrug her away. "They're saying we should tell someone."

"Who?" I turned to look at her, unashamed of my tears. Ellie was a hard bitch. Maybe they made me more of a person than she.

She raised one eyebrow and pursed her lips. "Brand thinks the army. Rosalie thinks the Fairy Underground."

I scoffed. "Fairy-fucking-Underground. Stupid cow."

"She can't help being like that. You ask me, it makes her more suited to how it's all turning out."

"And how's that, exactly?" I hated Ellie sometimes, all her stronger-than-thou talk and steely eyes. But she was also the person I respected the most in our pathetic little group. Now that Boris had gone.

"Well," she said, "for a start, take a look at how we're all reacting to this. Shocked, maybe. Horrified. But it's almost like it was expected."

"It's all been going to shit...." I said, but I did not need to continue. We had all known that we were not immune to the rot settling across society, nature, the world. Eventually it would find us. We just had not known when.

"There is the question of who did it," she said quietly.

"Or what."

She nodded. "Or what."

For now, we left it at that.

"How's Charley?"

"I was just going to see," Ellie said. "Coming?"

I nodded and followed her from the room. The beer had stopped spraying and now fizzled into sticky rivulets where the flags joined.

I was still thirsty.

Charley looked bad. She was drunk, that was obvious, and she had been sick down herself, and she had wet herself. Hayden was in the process of trying to mop up the mess when we knocked and entered.

"How is she?" Ellie asked pointlessly.

"How do you think?" He did not even glance at us as he tried to hold onto the babbling, crying, laughing and puking Charley.

"Maybe you shouldn't have given her so much to drink," Ellie said. Hayden sent her daggers but did not reply.

Charley struggled suddenly in his arms, ranting and shouting at the shaded candles in the corners of the room.

"What's that?" I said. "What's she saying?" For some reason it sounded important, like a solution to a problem encoded by grief.

"She's been saying some stuff," Hayden said loudly, so we could hear above Charley's slurred cries. "Stuff about Boris. Seeing angels in the snow. She says his angels came to get him."

"Some angels," Ellie muttered.

"You go down," Hayden said, "I'll stay here with her." He wanted us gone, that much was obvious, so we did not disappoint him.

Downstairs, Brand and Rosalie were hanging around the mobile phone. It had sat on the mantelpiece for the last three weeks like a gun without bullets, ugly and useless. Every now and then someone would try it, receiving only a crackling nothing in response. Random numbers, recalled numbers, numbers held in the phone's memory, all came to naught. Gradually it was tried less — every unsuccessful attempt had been more depressing.

"What?" I said.

"Trying to call someone," Brand said. "Police. Someone."

"So they can come to take fingerprints?" Ellie flopped into one of the old armchairs and began picking at its upholstery, widening a hole she'd been plucking at for days. "Any replies?"

Brand shook his head.

"We've got to do something," Rosalie said, "we can't just sit here while Boris is lying dead out there."

Ellie said nothing. The telephone hissed its amusement. Rosalie looked to me. "There's nothing we can do," I said. "Really, there's not much to collect up. If we did bring his... bits... back here, what would we do?"

"Bury..." Rosalie began.

"Three feet of snow? Frozen ground?"

"And the things," Brand said. The phone cackled again and he turned it off.

"What things?"

Brand looked around our small group. "The things Boris said he'd seen."

Boris had mentioned nothing to me. In our long, drunken talks, he had never talked of any angels in the snow. Upstairs, I'd thought that it was simply Charley drunk and mad with grief, but now Brand had said it too I had the distinct feeling I was missing out on something. I was irked, and upset at feeling irked.

"Things?" Rosalie said, and I closed my eyes. *Oh fuck, don't tell her*, I willed at Brand. She'd regale us with stories of secret societies and messages in the clouds, disease-makers who were wiping out the inept and the crippled, the barren and the intellectually inadequate. Jayne had been sterile, so we'd never had kids. The last thing I needed was another one of Rosalie's mad ravings about how my wife had died, why she'd died, who had killed her.

Luckily, Brand seemed of like mind. Maybe the joint he'd lit up had stewed him into silence at last. He turned to the fire and stared into its dying depths, sitting on the edge of the seat as if wondering whether or not to feed it some more. The stack of logs was running low.

"Things?" Rosalie said again, nothing if not persistent.

"No things," I said. "Nothing." I left the room before it all flared up.

In the kitchen I opened another can, carefully this time, and poured it into a tall glass. I stared into creamy depths as bubbles passed up and down. It took a couple of minutes for the drink to settle, and in that time I had recalled Jayne's face, her body, the best times we'd had together. At my first sip, a tear replenished the glass.

That night I heard doors opening and closing as someone wandered between beds. I was too tired to care who.

The next morning I half expected it to be all better. I had the bitter taste of dread in my mouth when I woke up, but also a vague idea that all the bad stuff could only have happened in nightmares. As I dressed — two shirts, a heavy pullover, a jacket — I wondered what awaited me beyond my bedroom door.

In the kitchen Charley was swigging from a fat mug of tea. It steamed so much, it seemed liable to burn whatever it touched. Her lips were red-raw, as were her eyes. She clutched the cup tightly, knuckles white, thumbs twisted into the handle. She looked as though she wanted to never let it go.

I had a sinking feeling in my stomach when I saw her. I glanced out of the window and saw the landscape of snow, added to yet again the previous night, bloated flakes still fluttering down to reinforce the barricade against our escape. Somewhere out there, Boris's parts were frozen memories hidden under a new layer.

"Okay?" I said quietly.

Charley looked up at me as if I'd farted at her mother's funeral. "Of course I'm not okay," she said, enunciating each word carefully. "And what do you care?"

I sat at the table opposite her, yawning, rubbing hands through my greasy hair, generally trying to disperse the remnants of sleep. There was a pot of tea on the table and I took a spare mug and poured a steaming brew. Charley watched my every move. I was aware of her eyes upon me, but I tried not to let it show. The cup shook, I could barely grab a spoon. I'd seen her boyfriend splashed across the snow, I felt terrible about it, but then I realized that she'd seen the same scene. How bad must she be feeling?

"We have to do something," she said.

"Charley — "

"We can't just sit here. We have to go. Boris needs a funeral. We have to go and find someone, get out of this God-forsaken place. There must be someone near, able to help, someone to look after us? I need someone to look after me."

The statement was phrased as a question, but I ventured no answer.

"Look," she said, "we have to get out. Don't you see?" She let go of her mug and clasped my hands; hers were hot and sweaty. "The village, we can get there, I know we can."

"No, Charley," I said, but I did not have a chance to finish my sentence *(there's no way out, we tried, and didn't you see the television reports weeks ago?)* before Ellie marched into the room. She paused when she saw Charley, then went to the cupboard and poured herself a bowl of cereal. She used water. We'd run out of milk a week ago.

"There's no telephone," she said, spooning some soggy corn flakes into her mouth. "No television, save some flickering pictures most of us don't want to see. Or believe. There's no radio, other than the occasional foreign channel. Rosie says she speaks French. She's heard them talking of 'the doom.' That's how she translates it, though I think it sounds more like 'the ruin.' The nearest village is ten miles away. We have no motorized transport that will even get out of the garage. To walk it would be suicide." She crunched her limp breakfast, mixing in more sugar to give some taste.

Charley did not reply. She knew what Ellie was saying, but tears were her only answer.

"So we're here until the snow melts," I said. Ellie really was a straight bitch. Not a glimmer of concern for Charley, not a word of comfort.

Ellie looked at me and stopped chewing for a moment. "I think until it does melt, we're protected." She had a way of coming out with ideas that both enraged me, and scared the living shit out of me at the same time.

Charley could only cry.

Later, three of us decided to try to get out. In moments of stress, panic and mourning, logic holds no sway.

I said I'd go with Brand and Charley. It was one of the most foolish decisions I've ever made, but seeing Charley's eyes as she sat in the kitchen on her own, thinking about her slaughtered boy-friend, listening to Ellie go on about how hopeless it all was... I could not say no. And in truth, I was as desperate to leave as anyone.

It was almost ten in the morning when we set out.

Ellie was right, I knew that even then. Her face as she watched us struggle across the garden should have brought me back straight away: she thought I was a fool. She was the last person in the world I wanted to appear foolish in front of, but still there was that nagging feeling in my heart that pushed me on — a mixture of desire to help Charley and a hopeless feeling that by staying here, we were simply waiting for death to catch us up.

It seemed to have laid its shroud over the rest of the world already. Weeks ago the television had shown some dreadful sights: people falling ill and dying in their thousands; food riots in Lon-don; a nuclear exchange between Greece and Turkey. More, lots more, all of it bad. We'd known something was coming — things had been falling apart for years — but once it began it was a cu-mulative effect, speeding from a steady trickle toward decline, to a raging torrent. *We're better off where we are*, Boris had said to me. It was ironic that because of him, we were leaving.

I carried the shotgun. Brand had an air pistol, though I'd barely trust him with a sharpened stick. As well as being loud and brash, he spent most of his time doped to the eyeballs. If there was any trouble, I'd be watching out for him as much as anything else.

Something had killed Boris and whatever it was, animal or human, it was still out there in the snow. Moved on, hopefully, now it had fed. But then again perhaps not. It did not dissuade us from trying.

The snow in the manor garden was almost a meter deep. The three of us had botched together snowshoes of varying effectiveness. Brand wore two snapped-off lengths of picture frame on each foot, which seemed to act more as knives to slice down through the snow than anything else. He was tenaciously pompous; he struggled with his mistake rather than admitting it. Charley had used two frying pans with their handles snapped off, and she seemed to be making good headway. My own creations consisted of circles of mounted canvas cut from the redundant artwork in the manor. Old owners of the estate stared up at me through the snow as I repeatedly stepped on their faces.

By the time we reached the end of the driveway and turned to see Ellie and Hayden watching us, I was sweating and exhausted. We had traveled about fifty meters.

Across the road lay the cliff path leading to Boris's dismembered corpse. Charley glanced that way, perhaps wishing to look down upon her boyfriend one more time.

"Come on," I said, clasping her elbow and heading away. She offered no resistance.

The road was apparent as a slightly lower, smoother plain of snow between the two hedged banks on either side. Everything was glaring white, and we were all wearing sunglasses to prevent snow blindness. We could see far along the coast from here as the bay swept around toward the east, the craggy cliffs spotted white where snow had drifted onto ledges, an occasional lonely seabird diving to the sea and returning empty-beaked to sing a mournful song for company. In places the snow was cantilevered out over the edge of the cliff, a deadly trap should any of us stray that way. The sea itself surged against the rocks below, but it broke no spray. The usual roar of the waters crashing into the earth, slowly eroding it away and reclaiming it, had changed. It was now more of a grind as tons of slushy ice replaced the usual white horses, not yet forming a solid barrier over the water but still thick enough to temper the waves. In a way it was sad; a huge beast winding down in old age.

I watched as a cormorant plunged down through the chunky ice and failed to break surface again. It was as if it were committing suicide. Who was I to say it was not?

"How far?" Brand asked yet again.

"Ten miles," I said.

"I'm knackered." He had already lit up a joint and he took long, hard pulls on it. I could hear its tip sizzling in the crisp morning air.

"We've come about three hundred meters," I said, and Brand shut up.

It was difficult to talk; we needed all our breath for the effort of walking. Sometimes the snowshoes worked, especially where the surface of the snow had frozen the previous night. Other times we plunged straight in up to our thighs and we had to hold our arms out for balance as we hauled our legs out, just to let them sink in again a step along. The rucksacks did not help. We each carried food, water and dry clothing, and Brand especially seemed to be having trouble with his.

The sky was a clear blue. The sun rose ahead of us as if mocking the frozen landscape. Some days it started like this, but the snow never seemed to melt. I had almost forgotten what the ground below it looked like; it seemed that the snow had been here forever. When it began our spirits had soared, like a bunch of school kids waking to find the landscape had changed overnight. Charley and I had still gone down to the sea to take our readings, and when we returned there was a snowman in the garden wearing one of her bras and a pair of my briefs. A snowball fight had ensued, during which Brand became a little too aggressive for his own good. We'd ganged up on him and pelted him with snow compacted to ice until he shouted and yelped. We were cold and wet and bruised, but we did not stop laughing for hours.

We'd all dried out in front of the open fire in the huge living room. Rosalie had stripped to her knickers and danced to music on the radio. She was a bit of a sixties throwback, Rosalie, and she didn't seem to realize what her little display did to cosseted people like me. I watched happily enough.

Later, we sat around the fire and told ghost stories. Boris was still with us then, of course, and he came up with the best one which had us all cowering behind casual expressions. He told us of a man who could not see, hear or speak, but who knew of the ghosts around him. His life was silent and senseless save for the day his mother died. Then he cried and shouted and raged at the darkness, before curling up and dying himself. His world opened up then, and he no longer felt alone, but whoever he tried to speak to could only fear or loathe him. The living could never make friends with the dead. And death had made him more silent than ever.

None of us would admit it, but we were all scared shitless as we went to bed that night. As usual, doors opened and footsteps padded along corridors. And, as usual, my door remained shut and I slept alone.

Days later the snow was too thick to be enjoyable. It became risky to go outside, and as the woodpile started to dwindle and the radio and television broadcasts turned more grim, we realized that we were becoming trapped. A few of us had tried to get to the village, but it was a half-hearted attempt and we'd returned once we were tired. We figured we'd traveled about two miles along the coast. We had seen no one.

As the days passed and the snow thickened, the atmosphere did likewise with a palpable sense of panic. A week ago, Boris had pointed out that there were no plane trails anymore.

This, our second attempt to reach the village, felt more like life and death. Before Boris had been killed we'd felt confined, but it also gave a sense of protection from the things going on in the world. Now there was a feeling that if we could not get out, worse things would happen to us where we were.

I remembered Jayne as she lay dying from the unknown disease. I had been useless, helpless, hopeless, praying to a God I had long ignored to grant us a kind fate. I refused to sit back and go the same way. I would not go gentle. Fuck fate.

"What was that?"

Brand stopped and tugged the little pistol from his belt. It was stark black against the pure white snow.

"What?"

He nodded. "Over there." I followed his gaze and looked up the sloping hillside. To our right the sea sighed against the base of the cliffs. To our left — the direction Brand was now facing — snowfields led up a gentle slope towards the moors several miles inland. It was a rocky, craggy landscape, and some rocks had managed to hold off the drifts. They peered out darkly here and there, like the faces of drowning men going under for the final time.

"What?" I said again, exasperated. I'd slipped the shotgun off my shoulder and held it waist-high. My finger twitched on the trigger guard. Images of Boris's remains sharpened my senses. I did not want to end up like that.

"I saw something moving. Something white."

"Some snow, perhaps?" Charley said bitterly.

"Something running across the snow," he said, frowning as he concentrated on the middle-distance. The smoke from his joint mingled with his condensing breath.

We stood that way for a minute or two, steaming sweat like smoke signals of exhaustion. I tried taking off my glasses to look, but the glare was too much. I glanced sideways at Charley. She'd pulled a big old revolver from her rucksack and held it with both hands. Her lips were pulled back from her teeth in a feral grimace. She really wanted to use that gun.

I saw nothing. "Could have been a cat. Or a seagull flying low."

"Could have been." Brand shoved the pistol back into his belt and reached around for his water canteen. He tipped it to his lips and cursed. "Frozen!"

"Give it a shake," I said. I knew it would do no good but it may shut him up for a while. "Charley, what's the time?" I had a watch but I wanted to talk to Charley, keep her involved with the present, keep her here. I had started to realize not only what a stupid idea this was, but what an even more idiotic step it had been letting Charley come along. If she wasn't here for revenge, she was blind with grief. I could not see her eyes behind her sunglasses.

"Nearly midday." She was hoisting her rucksack back onto her shoulders, never taking her eyes from the snowscape sloping slowly up and away from us. "What do you think it was?"

I shrugged. "Brand seeing things. Too much wacky baccy."

We set off again. Charley was in the lead, I followed close behind and Brand stumbled along at the rear. It was eerily silent around us, the snow muffling our gasps and puffs, the constant grumble of the sea soon blending into the background as much as it ever did. There was a sort of white noise in my ears: blood pumping; breath ebbing and flowing; snow crunching underfoot. They merged into one whisper, eschewing all outside noise, almost soporific in rhythm. I coughed to break the spell.

"What the hell do we do when we get to the village?" Brand said.

"Send back help," Charley stated slowly, enunciating each word as if to a naïve young child.

"But what if the village is like everywhere else we've seen or heard about on TV?"

Charley was silent for a while. So was I. A collage of images tumbled through my mind, hateful and hurtful and sharper because of that. Hazy scenes from the last day of television broadcasts we had watched: loaded ships leaving docks and sailing off to some nebulous sanctuary abroad; shootings in the streets, bodies in the gutters, dogs sniffing at open wounds; an airship, drifting over the hills in some vague attempt to offer hope.

"Don't be stupid," I said.

"Even if it is, there will be help there," Charley said quietly.

"Like hell." Brand lit up another joint. It was cold, we were risking our lives, there may very well be something in the snow itching to attack us… but at that moment I wanted nothing more than to take a long haul on Brand's pot, and let casual oblivion anesthetize my fears.

An hour later we found the car.

By my figuring we had come about three miles. We were all but exhausted. My legs ached, knee joints stiff and hot as if on fire.

The road had started a slow curve to the left, heading inland from the coast toward the distant village. Its path had become less distinct, the hedges having sunk slowly into the ground until there was really nothing to distinguish the path from the fields of snow on either side. We had been walking the last half hour on memory alone.

The car was almost completely buried by snow, only one side of the windscreen and the iced-up aerial still visible. There was no sign of the route it had taken; whatever tracks it had made were long since obliterated by the blizzards. As we approached the snow started again, fat flakes drifting lazily down and landing on the icy surface of last night's fall.

"Do not drive unless absolutely necessary," Brand said. Charley and I ignored him. We unslung our rucksacks and approached the buried shape, all of us keeping hold of our weapons. I meant to ask Charley where she'd got hold of the revolver — whether she'd had it with her when we both came here to test the sea and write environmental reports which would never be read — but now did not seem the time. I had no wish to seem judgmental or patronizing.

As I reached out to knock some of the frozen snow from the windscreen a flight of seagulls cawed and took off from nearby. They had been all but invisible against the snow, but there were at least thirty of them lifting as one, calling loudly as they twirled over our heads and then headed out to sea.

We all shouted out in shock. Charley stumbled sideways as she tried to bring her gun to bear and fell on her back. Brand screeched like a kid, then let off a pop with his air pistol to hide his embarrassment. The pellet found no target. The birds ignored us after the initial fly-past, and they slowly merged with the hazy distance. The new snow shower brought the horizon in close.

"Shit," Charley muttered.

"Yeah." Brand reloaded his pistol without looking at either of us, then rooted around for the joint he'd dropped when he screamed.

Charley and I went back to knocking the snow away, using our gloved hands to make tracks down the windscreen and across the bonnet. "I think it's a Ford," I said uselessly. "Maybe an old Mondeo." Jayne and I had owned a Mondeo when we'd been court-ing. Many was the time we had parked in some shaded woodland or beside units on the local industrial estate, wound down the windows and made love as the cool night air looked on. We'd broken down once while I was driving her home; it had made us two hours late and her father had come close to beating me sense-less. It was only the oil on my hands that had convinced him of our story.

I closed my eyes.

"Can't see anything," Charley said, jerking me back to cold real-ity. "Windscreen's frozen up on the inside."

"Take us ages to clear the doors."

"What do you want to do that for?" Brand said. "Dead car, probably full of dead people."

"Dead people may have guns and food and fuel," I said. "Go-ing to give us a hand?"

Brand glanced at the dark windshield, the contents of the car hidden by ice and shadowed by the weight of snow surrounding it. He sat gently on his rucksack, and when he saw it would take his weight without sinking in the snow, he re-lit his joint and stared out to sea. I wondered whether he'd even notice if we left him there.

"We could uncover the passenger door," Charley said. "Driver's side is stuck fast in the drift, take us hours."

We both set about trying to shift snow away from the car. "Keep your eyes open," I said to Brand. He just nodded and watched the sea lift and drop its thickening ice floes. I used the shotgun as a crutch to lift myself onto the bonnet, and from there to the covered roof.

"What?" Charley said. I ignored her, turning a slow circle, try-ing to pick out any movement against the fields of white. To the west lay the manor, a couple of miles away and long since hidden by creases in the landscape. To the north the ground still rose steadily away from the sea, rocks protruding here and there along with an occasional clump of trees hardy enough to survive Atlantic storms. Nothing moved. The shower was turning quickly into a storm and I felt suddenly afraid. The manor was at least three miles behind us; the village seven miles ahead. We were in the middle, three weak humans slowly freezing as nature freaked out and threw weeks of snow and ice at us. And here we were, convinced we could defeat it, certain in our own puny minds that we were the rulers here, we called the shots. However much we polluted and contaminated, I knew, we would never call the shots. Nature may let us live within it, but in the end it would purge and clean itself. And whether there would be room for us in the new world....

Perhaps this was the first stage of that cleansing. While civilization slaughtered itself, disease and extremes of weather took advantage of our distraction to pick off the weak.

"We should get back," I said.

"But the village — "

"Charley, it's almost two. It'll start getting dark in two hours, maximum. We can't travel in the dark; we might walk right by the village, or stumble onto one of those ice overhangs at the cliff edge. Brand here may get so doped he thinks we're ghosts and shoot us with his popgun."

"Hey!"

"But Boris...." Charley said. "He's... we need help. To bury him. We need to tell someone."

I climbed carefully down from the car roof and landed in the snow beside her. "We'll take a look in the car. Then we should get back. It'll help no one if we freeze to death out here."

"I'm not cold," she said defiantly.

"That's because you're moving, you're working. When you walk you sweat and you'll stay warm. When we have to stop — and eventually we will — you'll stop moving. Your sweat will freeze, and so will you. We'll all freeze. They'll find us in the thaw, you and me huddled up for warmth, Brand with a frozen reefer still in his gob."

Charley smiled, Brand scowled. Both expressions pleased me.

"The door's frozen shut," she said.

"I'll use my key." I punched at the glass with the butt of the shotgun. After three attempts the glass shattered and I used my gloved hands to clear it all away. I caught a waft of something foul and stale. Charley stepped back with a slight groan. Brand was oblivious.

We peered inside the car, leaning forward so that the weak light could filter in around us.

There was a dead man in the driver's seat. He was frozen solid, hunched up under several blankets, only his eyes and nose visible. Icicles hung from both. His eyelids were still open. On the dashboard a candle had burnt down to nothing more than a puddle of wax, imitating the ice as it dripped forever toward the floor. The scene was so still it was eerie, like a painting so lifelike that textures and shapes could be felt. I noticed the driver's door handle was jammed open, though the door had not budged against the snowdrift burying that side of the car. At the end he had obviously attempted to get out. I shuddered as I tried to imagine this man's lonely death. It was the second body I'd seen in two days.

"Well?" Brand called from behind us.

"Your drug supplier," Charley said. "Car's full of snow."

I snorted, pleased to hear the humor, but when I looked at her she seemed as sad and forlorn as ever. "Maybe we should see if he brought us anything useful," she said, and I nodded.

Charley was smaller than me so she said she'd go. I went to protest but she was already wriggling through the shattered window, and a minute later she'd thrown out everything loose she could find. She came back out without looking at me.

There was a rucksack half full of canned foods; a petrol can with a swill of fuel in the bottom; a novel frozen at page ninety; some plastic bottles filled with piss and split by the ice; a rifle, but no ammunition; a smaller rucksack with wallet, some papers, an electronic credit card; a photo wallet frozen shut; a plastic bag full of shit; a screwed-up newspaper as hard as wood.

Everything was frozen.

"Let's go," I said. Brand and Charley took a couple of items each and shouldered their rucksacks. I picked up the rifle. We took everything except the shit and piss.

It took us four hours to get back to the manor. Three times on the way Brand said he'd seen something bounding through the snow — a stag, he said, big and white with sparkling antlers — and we dropped everything and went into a defensive huddle. But nothing ever materialized from the worsening storm, even though our imaginations painted all sorts of horrors behind and beyond the snowflakes. If there were anything out there, it kept itself well hidden.

The light was fast fading as we arrived back. Our tracks had been all but covered, and it was only later that I realized how staggeringly lucky we'd been to even find our way home. Perhaps something was on our side, guiding us, steering us back to the manor. Perhaps it was the change in nature taking us home, preparing us for what was to come next.

It was the last favor we were granted.

Hayden cooked us some soup as the others huddled around the fire, listening to our story and trying so hard not to show their disappointment. Brand kept chiming in about the things he'd seen in the snow. Even Ellie's face held the taint of fading hope.

"Boris's angels?" Rosalie suggested. "He *may* have seen angels, you know. They're not averse to steering things their way, when it suits them." Nobody answered.

Charley was crying again, shivering by the fire. Rosalie had wrapped her in blankets and now hugged her close.

"The gun looks okay." Ellie said. She'd sat at the table and stripped and oiled the rifle, listening to us all as we talked. She illustrated the fact by pointing it at the wall and squeezing the trigger a few times. *Click click click.* There was no ammunition for it.

"What about the body?" Rosalie asked. "Did you see who it was?"

I frowned. "What do you mean?"

"Well, if it was someone coming along the road toward the manor, maybe one of us knew him." We were all motionless save for Ellie, who still rooted through the contents of the car. She'd already put the newspaper on the floor so that it could dry out, in the hope of being able to read at least some of it. We'd made out the date: one week ago. The television had stopped showing pictures two weeks ago. There was a week of history in there, if only we could save it.

"He was frozen stiff," I said. "We didn't get a good look… and anyway, who'd be coming here? And why? Maybe it was a good job — "

Ellie gasped. There was a tearing sound as she peeled apart more pages of the photo wallet and gasped again, this time struggling to draw in a breath afterwards.

"Ellie?"

She did not answer. The others had turned to her but she seemed not to notice. She saw nothing, other than the photographs in her hand. She stared at them for an endless few seconds, eyes moist yet unreadable in the glittering fire light. Then she scraped the chair back across the polished floor, crumpled the photo's into her back pocket and walked quickly from the room.

I followed, glancing at the others to indicate that they should stay where they were. None of them argued. Ellie was already halfway up the long staircase by the time I entered the hallway, but it was not until the final stair that she stopped, turned and answered my soft calling.

"My husband," she said, "Jack. I haven't seen him for two years." A tear ran icily down her cheek. "We never really made it, you know?" She looked at the wall beside her, as though she could stare straight through and discern logic and truth in the blanked-out landscape beyond. "He was coming here. For me. To find me."

There was nothing I could say. Ellie seemed to forget I was there and she mumbled the next few words to herself. Then she turned and disappeared from view along the upstairs corridor, shadow dancing in the light of disturbed candles.

Back in the living room I told the others that Ellie was all right, she had gone to bed, she was tired and cold and as human as the rest of us. I did not let on about her dead husband, I figured it was really none of their business. Charley glared at me with bloodshot eyes, and I was sure she'd figured it out. Brand flicked bits of carrot from his soup into the fire and watched them sizzle to nothing.

We went to bed soon after. Alone in my room I sat at the window for a long time, huddled in clothes and blankets, staring out at the moonlit brightness of the snow drifts and the fat flakes still falling. I tried to imagine Ellie's estranged husband struggling to steer the car through deepening snow, the radiator clogging in the drift it had buried its nose in, splitting, gushing boiling water and steaming instantly into an ice trap. Sitting there, perhaps not knowing just how near he was, thinking of his wife and how much he needed to see her. And I tried to imagine what desperate events must have driven him to do such a thing, though I did not think too hard.

A door opened and closed quietly, footsteps, another door slipped open to allow a guest entry. I wondered who was sharing a bed tonight.

I saw Jayne, naked and beautiful in the snow, bearing no sign of the illness that had killed her. She beckoned me, drawing me nearer, and at last a door was opening for me as well, a shape coming into the room, white material floating around its hips, or perhaps they were limbs, membranous and thin....

My eyes snapped open and I sat up on the bed. I was still dressed from the night before. Dawn streamed in the window and my candle had burnt down to nothing.

Ellie stood next to the bed. Her eyes were red-rimmed and swollen. I tried to pretend I had not noticed.

"Happy Christmas," she said. "Come on. Brand's dead."

Brand was lying just beyond the smashed conservatory doors behind the kitchen. There was a small courtyard area here, protected somewhat by an overhanging roof so that the snow was only about knee-deep. Most of it was red. A drift had already edged its way into the conservatory, and the beer cans on the shelf had frozen and split. No more beer.

He had been punctured by countless holes, each the width of a thumb, all of them clogged with hardened blood. One eye stared hopefully out to the hidden horizon, the other was absent. His hair was also missing; it looked like he'd been scalped. There were bits of him all around — a finger here, a splash of brain there — but he was less mutilated than Boris had been. At least we could see that this smudge in the snow had once been Brand.

Hayden was standing next to him, posing daintily in an effort to avoid stepping in the blood. It was a lost cause. "What the hell was he doing out here?" he asked in disgust.

"I heard doors opening last night," I said. "Maybe he came for a walk. Or a smoke."

"The door was mine," Rosalie said softly. She had appeared behind us and nudged in between Ellie and me. She wore a long, creased shirt. Brand's shirt, I noticed. "Brand was with me until three o'clock this morning. Then he left to go back to his own room, said he was feeling ill. We thought perhaps you shouldn't know about us." Her eyes were wide in an effort not to cry. "We thought everyone would laugh."

Nobody answered. Nobody laughed. Rosalie looked at Brand with more shock than sadness, and I wondered just how often he'd opened her door in the night. The insane, unfair notion that she may even be relieved flashed across my mind, one of those awful thoughts you try to expunge but which hangs around like a guilty secret.

"Maybe we should go inside," I said to Rosalie, but she gave me such an icy glare that I turned away, looking at Brand's shattered body rather than her piercing eyes.

"I'm a big girl now," she said. I could hear her rapid breathing as she tried to contain the disgust and shock at what she saw. I wondered if she'd ever seen a dead body. Most people had, nowadays.

Charley was nowhere to be seen. "I didn't wake her," Ellie

said when I queried. "She had enough to handle yesterday. I thought she shouldn't really see this. No need."

And you? I thought, noticing Ellie's puffy eyes, the gauntness of her face, her hands fisting open and closed at her sides. *Are you all right? Did you have enough to handle yesterday?*

"What the hell do we do with him?" Hayden asked. He was still standing closer to Brand than the rest of us, hugging himself to try to preserve some of the warmth from sleep. "I mean, Boris was all over the place, from what I hear. But Brand... we have to do something. Bury him, or something. It's Christmas, for God's sake."

"The ground's like iron," I protested.

"So we take it in turns digging," Rosalie said quietly.

"It'll take us — "

"Then I'll do it myself." She walked out into the blooded snow and shattered glass in bare feet, bent over Brand's body and grabbed under each armpit as if to lift him. She was naked beneath the shirt. Hayden stared in frank fascination. I turned away, embarrassed for myself more than for Rosalie.

"Wait," Ellie sighed. "Rosalie, wait. Let's all dress properly, then we'll come and bury him. Rosalie." The girl stood and smoothed Brand's shirt down over her thighs, perhaps realizing what she had put on display. She looked up at the sky and caught the morning's first snowflake on her nose.

"Snowing," she said. "Just for a fucking change."

We went inside. Hayden remained in the kitchen with the outside door shut and bolted while the rest of us went upstairs to dress, wake Charley and tell her the grim Yule tidings. Once Rosalie's door had closed I followed Ellie along to her room. She opened her door for me and invited me in, obviously knowing I needed to talk.

Her place was a mess. Perhaps, I thought, she was so busy being strong and mysterious that she had no time for tidying up. Clothes were strewn across the floor, a false covering like the snow outside. Used plates were piled next to her bed, those at the bottom already blurred with mold, the uppermost still showing the remains of the meal we'd had before Boris had been killed. Spaghetti bolognaise, I recalled, to Hayden's own recipe, rich and tangy with tinned tomatoes, strong with garlic, the helpings massive. Somewhere out there Boris's last meal lay frozen in the snow, half digested, torn from his guts —

I snorted and closed my eyes. Another terrible thought that

wouldn't go away.

"Brand really saw things in the snow, didn't he?" Ellie asked.

"Yes, he was pretty sure. At least, *a* thing. He said it was like a stag, except white. It was bounding along next to us, he said. We stopped a few times but I'm certain I never saw anything. Don't think Charley did, either." I made space on Ellie's bed and sat down. "Why?"

Ellie walked to the window and opened the curtains. The snowstorm had started in earnest, and although her window faced the Atlantic all we could see was a sea of white. She rested her forehead on the cold glass, her breath misting, fading, misting again. "I've seen something too," she said.

Ellie. Seeing things in the snow. Ellie was the nearest we had to a leader, though none of us had ever wanted one. She was strong, if distant. Intelligent, if a little straight with it. She'd never been much of a laugh, even before things had turned to shit, and her dogged conservatism in someone so young annoyed me no end.

Ellie, seeing things in the snow.

I could not bring myself to believe it. I did not want to. If I did accept it then there really were things out there, because Ellie did not lie, and she was not prone to fanciful journeys of the imagination.

"What something?" I asked at last, fearing it a question I would never wish to be answered. But I could not simply ignore it. I could not sit here and listen to Ellie opening up, then stand and walk away. Not with Boris frozen out there, not with Brand still cooling into the landscape.

She rocked her head against the glass. "Don't know. Something white. So how did I see it?" She turned from the window, stared at me, crossed her arms. "From this window," she said. "Two days ago. Just before Charley found Boris. Something flitting across the snow like a bird, except it left faint tracks. As big as a fox, perhaps, but it had more legs. Certainly not a deer."

"Or one of Boris's angels?"

She shook her head and smiled, but there was no humor there. There rarely was. "Don't tell anyone," she said. "I don't want anyone to know. But! We will have to be careful. Take the guns when we try to bury Brand. A couple of us keep a lookout while the others dig. Though I doubt we'll even get through the snow."

"You and guns," I said perplexed. I didn't know how to word what I was trying to ask.

Ellie smiled wryly. "Me and guns. I hate guns."

I stared at her, saying nothing, using silence to pose the next question.

"I have a history," she said. And that was all.

Later, downstairs in the kitchen, Charley told us what she'd managed to read in the paper from the frozen car. In the week since we'd picked up the last TV signal and the paper was printed, things had gone from bad to worse. The illness that had killed my Jayne was claiming millions across the globe. The USA blamed Iraq. Russia blamed China. Blame continued to waste lives. There was civil unrest and shootings in the streets, mass burials at sea, martial law, air strikes, food shortages... the words melded into one another as Rosalie recited the reports.

Hayden was trying to cook mince pies without the mince. He was using stewed apples instead, and the kitchen stank sickeningly sweet. None of us felt particularly festive.

Outside, in the heavy snow that even now was attempting to drift in and cover Brand, we were all twitchy. Whoever or — now more likely — whatever had done this could still be around. Guns were held at the ready.

We wrapped him in an old sheet and enclosed this in torn black plastic bags until there was no white or red showing. Ellie and I dragged him around the corner of the house to where there were some old flowers beds. We started to dig where we remembered them to be, but when we got through the snow the ground was too hard. In the end we left him on the surface of the frozen earth and covered the hole back in with snow, mumbling about burying him when the thaw came. The whole process had an unsettling sense of permanence.

As if the snow would never melt.

Later, staring from the dining room window as Hayden brought in a platter of old vegetables as our Christmas feast, I saw something big and white skimming across the surface of the snow. It moved too quickly for me to make it out properly, but I was certain I saw wings.

I turned away from the window, glanced at Ellie and said nothing.

two
the color of fear

During the final few days of Jayne's life I had felt completely hemmed in. Not only physically trapped within our home — and more often the bedroom where she lay — but also mentally hindered. It was a feeling I hated, felt guilty about and tried desperately to relieve, but it was always there.

I stayed, holding her hand for hour after terrible hour, our palms fused by sweat, her face pasty and contorted by agonies I could barely imagine. Sometimes she would be conscious and alert, sitting up in bed and listening as I read to her, smiling at the humorous parts, trying to ignore the sad ones. She would ask me questions about how things were in the outside world, and I would lie and tell her they were getting better. There was no need to add to her misery. Other times she would be a shadow of her old self, a grey stain on the bed with liquid limbs and weak bowels, a screaming thing with bloody growths sprouting across her skin and pumping their venom inward with uncontrollable, unstoppable tenacity. At these times I would talk truthfully and tell her the reality of things, that the world was going to shit and she would be much better off when she left it.

Even then I did not tell her the complete truth: that I wished I were going with her. Just in case she could still hear.

Wherever I went during those final few days I was under assault, besieged by images of Jayne, thoughts of her impending death, vague ideas of what would happen after she had gone. I tried to fill the landscape of time laid out before me, but Jayne never figured and so the landscape was bare. She was my whole world; without her I could picture nothing to live for. My mind was never free although sometimes, when a doctor found time to visit our house and *tut* and sigh over Jayne's wasting body, I would go for a walk. Mostly she barely knew the doctor was there, for which I was grateful. There was nothing he could do. I would not be able to bear even the faintest glimmer of hope in her eyes.

I strolled through the park opposite our house, staying to the paths so that I did not risk stepping on discarded needles or stumbling across suicides decaying slowly back to nature. The trees were as beautiful as ever, huge emeralds against the grimly polluted sky. Somehow they bled the taint of humanity from their systems. They adapted, changed, and our arrival had really done little to halt their progress. A few years of poisons and disease, perhaps. A shaping of the landscape upon which we projected an idea of control. But when we were all dead and gone our industrial disease on the planet would be little more than a few twisted, corrupted rings in the lifetime of the oldest trees. I wished we could adapt so well.

When Jayne died there was no sense of release. My grief was as great as if she'd been killed at the height of health, her slow decline doing nothing to prepare me for the dread that enveloped me at the moment of her last strangled sigh. Still I was under siege, this time by death. The certainty of its black fingers rested on my shoulders day and night, long past the hour of Jayne's hurried burial in a local football ground alongside a thousand others. I would turn around sometimes and try to see past it, make out some ray of hope in a stranger's gaze. But there was always the blackness bearing down on me, clouding my vision and the gaze of others, promising doom soon.

It's ironic that it was not death that truly scared me, but living. Without Jayne the world was nothing but an empty, dying place.

Then I had come here, an old manor on the rugged South West coast. I'd thought that solitude — a distance between me and the terrible place the world was slowly becoming — would be a balm to my suffering. In reality it was little more than a placebo and realizing that negated it. I felt more trapped than ever.

The morning after Brand's death and botched burial — Boxing Day — I sat at my bedroom window and watched nature laying siege. The snow hugged the landscape like a funeral shroud in negative. The coast was hidden by the cliffs, but I could see the sea further out. There was something that I thought at first to be an iceberg and it took me a few minutes to figure out what it really was; the upturned hull of a big boat. A ferry, perhaps, or one of the huge cruise liners being used to ship people south, away from blighted Britain to the false promise of Australia. I was glad I could not see any more detail. I wondered what we would find washed up in the rock pools that morning, were Charley and I to venture down to the sea.

If I stared hard at the snowbanks, the fields of virgin white, the humped shadows that were our ruined and hidden cars, I could see no sign of movement. An occasional shadow passed across the snow, though it could have been from a bird flying in front of the sun. But if I relaxed my gaze, tried not to concentrate too hard, lowered my eyelids, then I could see them. Sometimes they skimmed low and fast over the snow, twisting like sea serpents or Chinese dragons and throwing up a fine mist of flakes behind them. At other times they lay still and watchful, fading into the background if I looked directly at them until one shadow looked much like the next, but could be so different.

I wanted to talk about them. I wanted to ask Ellie just what the hell they were, because I knew that she had seen them too. I wanted to know what was happening and why it was happening to us. But I had some mad idea that to mention them would make them real, like ghosts in the cupboard and slithering wet things beneath the bed. Best ignore them and they would go away.

I counted a dozen white shapes that morning.

"Anyone dead today?" Rosalie asked.

The statement shocked me, made me wonder just what sort of relationship she and Brand had had, but we all ignored her. No need to aggravate an argument.

Charley sat close to Rosalie, as if a sharing of grief would halve it. Hayden was cooking up bacon and bagels long past their sell-by date. Ellie had not yet come downstairs. She'd been stalking the manor all night, and now we were up she was washing and changing.

"What do we do today?" Charley asked. "Are we going to try to get away again? Get to the village for help?"

I sighed and went to say something, but the thought of those things out in the snow kept me quiet. Nobody else spoke, and the silence was the only answer required.

We ate our stale breakfast, drank tea clotted with powdered milk, listened to the silence outside. It had snowed again in the night and our tracks from the day before had been obliterated. Standing at the sink to wash up I stared through the window, and it was like looking upon the same day as yesterday, the day before, and the day before that; no signs of our presence existed. All footprints had vanished, all echoes of voices swallowed by the snow, shadows covered with another six inches and frozen like corpses in a glacier. I wondered what patterns and traces the snow would hold this evening, when darkness closed in to wipe us away once more.

"We have to tell someone," Charley said. "Something's happening, we should tell someone. We have to do something, we can't just...." She trailed off, staring into a cooling cup of tea, perhaps remembering a time before all this had begun, or imagining she could remember. "This is crazy."

"It's God," Rosalie said.

"Huh?" Hayden was already peeling wrinkled old vegetables ready for lunch, constantly busy, always doing something to keep his mind off everything else. I wondered how much really went on behind his fringed brow, how much theorizing he did while he was boiling, how much nostalgia he wallowed in as familiar cooking smells settled into his clothes.

"It's God, fucking us over one more time. Crazy, as Charley says. God and crazy are synonymous."

"Rosie," I said, knowing she hated the shortened name, "if it's not constructive, don't bother. None of this will bring — "

"Anything is more constructive than sod-all, which is what you lot have got to say this morning. We wake up one morning without one of us dead, and you're all tongue-tied. Bored? Is that it?"

"Rosalie, why — "

"Shut it, Charley. You more than anyone should be thinking about all this. Wondering why the hell we came here a few weeks ago to escape all the shit, and now we've landed right in the middle of it. Right up to our armpits. Drowning in it. Maybe one of us is a Jonah and it's followed — "

"And you think it's God?" I said. I knew that asking the question would give her open opportunity to rant, but in a way I felt she was right, we did need to talk. Sitting here stewing in our own thoughts could not help anyone.

"Oh yes, it's His Holiness," she nodded, "sitting on his pedestal of lost souls, playing around one day and deciding, hmm, maybe I'll have some fun today, been a year since a decent earthquake, a few months since the last big volcano eruption. Soooo, what can I do?"

Ellie appeared then, sat at the table and poured a cup of cold tea that looked like sewer water. Her appearance did nothing to mar Rosalie's flow.

"I know, he says, I'll nudge things to one side, turn them slightly askew, give the world a gasp before I've cleaned my teeth. Just a little, not so that anyone will notice for a while. Get them paranoid. Get them looking over their shoulders at each other. See how the wrinkly pink bastards deal with that one!"

"Why would He do that?" Hayden said.

Rosalie stood and put on a deep voice. "Forget me, will they? I'll show them. Turn over and open your legs, humanity, for I shall root you up the arse."

"Just shut up!" Charley screeched. The kitchen went ringingly quiet, even Rosalie sitting slowly down. "You're full of this sort of shit, Rosie. Always telling us how we're being controlled, manipulated. Who by? Ever seen anyone? There's a hidden agenda behind everything for you, isn't there? If there's no toilet paper after you've had a crap you'd blame it on the global dirty-arse conspiracy!"

Hysteria hung silently in the room. The urge to cry grabbed me, but also a yearning to laugh out loud. The air was heavy with held breaths and barely restrained comments, thick with the potential for violence.

"So," Ellie said at last, her voice little more than a whisper, "let's hear some truths."

"What?" Rosalie obviously expected an extension of her foolish monologue. Ellie, however, cut her down.

"Well, for starters has anyone else seen things in the snow?" Heads shook. My own shook as well. I wondered who else was lying with me. "Anyone seen anything strange out there at all?" she continued. "Maybe not the things Brand and Boris saw, but something else?" Again, shaken heads. An uncomfortable shuffling from Hayden as he stirred something on the gas cooker.

"I saw God looking down on us," Rosalie said quietly, "with blood in his eyes." She did not continue or elaborate, did not go off on one of her rants. I think that's why her strange comment stayed with me.

"Right," said Ellie, "then may I make a suggestion. Firstly, there's no point trying to get to the village. The snow's even deeper than it was yesterday, it's colder, and freezing to death for the sake of it will achieve nothing. If we did manage to find help, Boris and Brand are long past it." She paused, waiting for assent.

"Fair enough," Charley said quietly. "Yeah, you're right."

"Secondly, we need to make sure the manor is secure. We need to protect ourselves from whatever got at Brand and Boris. There are a dozen rooms on the ground floor; we only use two or three of them. Check the others. Make sure windows are locked and storm shutters are bolted. Make sure French doors aren't loose or liable to break open at the slightest... breeze, or whatever."

"What do you think the things out there are?" Hayden asked. "Lock pickers?"

Ellie glanced at his back, looked at me, shrugged. "No," she said, "I don't think so. But there's no use being complacent. We can't try to make it out, so we should do the most we can here. The snow can't last forever, and when it finally melts we'll go to the village then. Agreed?"

Heads nodded.

"If the village is still there," Rosalie cut in. "If everyone isn't dead. If the disease hasn't wiped out most of the country. If a war doesn't start somewhere in the meantime."

"Yes," Ellie sighed impatiently, "if all those things don't happen." She nodded at me. "We'll do the two rooms at the back. The rest of you check the others. There are some tools in the big cupboard under the stairs, some nails and hammers if you need them, a crowbar too. And if you think you need timber to nail across windows... if it'll make you feel any better... tear up some floorboards in the dining room. They're hardwood, they're strong."

"Oh, let battle commence!" Rosalie cried. She stood quickly, her chair falling onto its back, and stalked from the room with a swish of her long skirts. Charley followed.

Ellie and I went to the rear of the manor. In the first of the large rooms the snow had drifted up against the windows to cut out any view or light from outside. For an instant it seemed as if nothing existed beyond the glass and I wondered if that was the case, then why were we trying to protect ourselves?

Against nothing.

"What do you think is out there?" I asked.

"Have you seen anything?"

I paused. There was something, but nothing I could easily identify or put a name to. What I had seen had been way beyond my ken, white shadows apparent against whiteness. "No," I said, "nothing."

Ellie turned from the window and looked at me in the half-light, and it was obvious that she knew I was lying. "Well, if you do see something, don't tell."

"Why?"

"Boris and Brand told," she said. She did not say any more. They'd seen angels and stags in the snow and they'd talked about it, and now they were dead.

She pushed at one of the window frames. Although the damp timber fragmented at her touch, the snowdrift behind it was as effective as a vault door. We moved on to the next window. The room was noisy with unspoken thoughts, and it was only a matter of time before they made themselves heard.

"You think someone in here has something to do with Brand and Boris," I said.

Ellie sat on one of the wide windowsills and sighed deeply. She ran a hand through her spiky hair and rubbed at her neck. I wondered whether she'd had any sleep at all last night. I wondered whose door had been opening and closing; the prickle of jealousy was crazy under the circumstances. I realized all of a sudden how much Ellie reminded me of Jayne, and I swayed under the sudden barrage of memory.

"Who?" she said. "Rosie? Hayden? Don't be soft."

"But you do, don't you?" I said again.

She nodded. Then shook her head. Shrugged. "I don't bloody know, I'm not Sherlock Holmes. It's just strange that Brand and Boris...." She trailed off, avoiding my eyes.

"I have seen something out there," I said to break the awkward silence. "Something in the snow. Can't say what. Shadows. Fleeting glimpses. Like everything I see is from the corner of my eye."

Ellie stared at me for so long that I thought she'd died there on the windowsill, a victim of my admission, another dead person to throw outside and let freeze until the thaw came and we could do our burying.

"You've seen what I've seen," she said eventually, verbalizing the trust between us. It felt good, but it also felt a little dangerous. A trust like that could alienate the others, not consciously but in our mind's eye. By working and thinking closer together, perhaps we would drive them further away.

We moved to the next window.

"I've known there was something since you found Jack in his car," Ellie said. "He'd never have just sat there and waited to die. He'd have tried to get out, to get here, no matter how dangerous. He wouldn't have sat watching the candle burn down, listening to the wind, feeling his eyes freeze over. It's just not like him to give in."

"So why did he? Why didn't he get out?"

"There was something waiting for him outside the car. Something he was trying to keep away from." She rattled a window, stared at the snow pressed up against the glass. "Something that would make him rather freeze to death than face it."

We moved on to the last window; Ellie reached out to touch the rusted clasp and there was a loud crash. Glass broke, wood struck wood, someone screamed, all from a distance.

We spun around and ran from the room, listening to the shrieks. Two voices now, a man and a woman, the woman's muffled. Somewhere in the manor, someone else was dying.

The reaction to death is sometimes as violent as death itself. Shock throws a cautious coolness over the senses, but your stomach still knots, your skin stings as if the Reaper is glaring at you as well. For a second you live that death, and then shameful relief floods in when you see it's someone else's.

Such were my thoughts as we turned a corner into the main hallway of the manor. Hayden was hammering at the library door, crashing his fists into the wood hard enough to draw blood. "Charley!" he shouted, again and again. "Charley!" The door shook under his assault but it did not budge. Tears streaked his face, dribble strung from chin to chest. The dark old wood of the door sucked up the blood from his split knuckles. "Charley!"

Ellie and I arrived just ahead of Rosalie.

"Hayden!" Rosalie shouted.

"Charley! In there! She went in and locked the door, and there was a crash and she was screaming!"

"Why did she — " Rosalie began, but Ellie shushed us all with one wave of her hand.

Silence. "No screaming now," she said.

Then we heard other noises through the door, faint and tremulous as if picked up from a distance along a bad telephone line. They sounded like chewing; bone snapping; flesh ripping. I could not believe what I was hearing, but at the same time I remembered the bodies of Boris and Brand. Suddenly I did not want to open the door. I wanted to defy whatever it was laying siege to us here by ignoring the results of its actions. Forget Charley, continue checking the windows and doors, deny whoever or whatever it was the satisfaction —

"Charley," I said quietly. She was a small woman, fragile; strong but sensitive. She'd told me once, sitting at the base of the cliffs before it had begun to snow, how she loved to sit and watch the sea. It made her feel safe. It made her feel a part of nature. She'd never hurt anyone. "Charley."

Hayden kicked at the door again and I added my weight, shouldering into the tough old wood, jarring my body painfully with each impact. Ellie did the same and soon we were taking it in turns. The noises continued between each impact — increased in volume if anything — and our assault became more frantic to cover them up.

If the manor had not been so old and decrepit we would never have broken in. The door was probably as old as all of us put together, but its surround had been replaced some time in the past. Softwood painted as hardwood had slowly crumbled in the damp atmosphere and after a minute the door burst in, frame splintering into the coldness of the library.

One of the three big windows had been smashed. Shattered glass and snapped mullions hung crazily from the frame. The cold had already made the room its home, laying a fine sheen of frost across the thousands of books, hiding some of their titles from view as if to conceal whatever tumultuous history they contained. Snow flurried in, hung around for awhile then chose somewhere to settle. It did not melt. Once on the inside, this room was now a part of the outside.

As was Charley.

The area around the broken window was red and Charley had spread. Bits of her hung on the glass like hellish party streamers.

Other parts had melted into the snow outside and turned it pink. Some of her was recognizable — her hair splayed out across the soft whiteness, a hand fisted around a melting clump of ice — other parts had never been seen before, because they'd always been inside.

I leaned over and puked. My vomit cleared a space of frost on the floor so I did it again, moving into the room. My stomach was in agonized spasms but I enjoyed seeing the white sheen vanish, as if I were claiming the room back for a time. Then I went to my knees and tried to forget what I'd seen, shake it from my head, pound it from my temples. I felt hands close around my wrists to stop me from punching myself, but I fell forward and struck my forehead on the cold timber floor. If I could forget, if I could drive the image away, perhaps it would no longer be true.

But there was the smell. And the steam, rising from the open body and misting what glass remained. Charley's last breath.

"Shut the door!" I shouted. "Nail it shut! Quickly!"

Ellie had helped me from the room, and now Hayden was pulling on the broken-in door to try to close it again. Rosalie came back from the dining room with a few splintered floorboards, her face pale, eyes staring somewhere no one else could see.

"Hurry!" I shouted. I felt a distance pressing in around me; the walls receding; the ceiling rising. Voices turned slow and deep, movement became stilted. My stomach heaved again but there was nothing left to bring up. I was the center of everything but it was all leaving me, all sight and sound and scent fleeing my faint. And then, clear and bright, Jayne's laugh broke through. Only once, but I knew it was her.

Something brushed my cheek and gave warmth to my face. My jaw clicked and my head turned to one side, slowly but inexorably. Something white blurred across my vision and my other cheek burst into warmth, and I was glad, the cold was the enemy, the cold brought the snow, which brought the fleeting things I had seen outside, things without a name or, perhaps, things with a million names. Or things with a name I already knew.

The warmth was good.

Ellie's mouth moved slowly and watery rumbles tumbled forth. Her words took shape in my mind, hauling themselves together just as events took on their own speed once more.

"Snap out of it," Ellie said, and slapped me across the face again.

Another sound dragged itself together. I could not identify it, but I knew where it was coming from. The others were staring fearfully at the door; Hayden was still leaning back with both hands around the handle, straining to get as far away as possible without letting go.

Scratching. Sniffing. Something rifling through books, snuffling in long-forgotten corners at dust from long-dead people. A slow regular beat, which could have been footfalls or a heartbeat. I realized it was my own and another sound took its place.

"What...?"

Ellie grabbed the tops of my arms and shook me harshly. "You with us? You back with us now?"

I nodded, closing my eyes at the swimming sensation in my head. Vertical fought with horizontal and won out this time. "Yeah."

"Rosalie," Ellie whispered. "Get more boards. Hayden, keep hold of that handle. Just keep hold." She looked at me. "Hand me the nails as I hold my hand out. Now listen. Once I start banging, it may attract — "

"What are you doing?" I said.

"Nailing the bastards in."

I thought of the shapes I had watched from my bedroom window, the shadows flowing through other shadows, the ease with which they moved, the strength and beauty they exuded as they passed from drift to drift without leaving any trace behind. I laughed. "You think you can keep them in?"

Rosalie turned a fearful face my way. Her eyes were wide, her mouth hanging open as if readying for a scream.

"You think a few nails will stop them — "

"Just shut up," Ellie hissed, and she slapped me around the face once more. This time I was all there, and the slap was a burning sting rather than a warm caress. My head whipped around and by the time I looked up again Ellie was heaving a board against the doors, steadying it with one elbow and weighing a hammer in the other hand.

Only Rosalie looked at me. What I'd said was still plain on her face — the chance that whatever had done these foul things would find their way in, take us apart as it had done to Boris, to Brand and now to Charley. And I could say nothing to comfort her. I shook my head, though I had no idea what message I was trying to convey.

Ellie held out her hand and clicked her fingers. Rosalie passed her a nail.

I stepped forward and pressed the board across the door. We had to tilt it so that each end rested across the frame. There were still secretive sounds from inside, like a fox rummaging through a bin late at night. I tried to imagine the scene in the room now but I could not. My mind would not place what I had seen outside into the library, could not stretch to that feat of imagination. I was glad.

For one terrible second I wanted to see. It would only take a kick at the door, a single heave and the whole room would be open to view, and then I would know whatever was in there for the second before it hit me. Jayne perhaps, a white Jayne from elsewhere, holding out her hands so that I could join her once more, just as she had promised on her deathbed. *I'll be with you again*, she had said, and the words had terrified me and comforted me and kept me going ever since. Sometimes I thought they were all that kept me alive — *I'll be with you again.*

"Jayne...."

Ellie brought the hammer down. The sound was explosive and I felt the impact transmitted through the wood and into my arms. I expected another impact a second later from the opposite way, but instead we heard the sound of something scampering through the already shattered window.

Ellie kept hammering until the board held firm, then she started another, and another. She did not stop until most of the door was covered, nails protruding at crazy angles, splinters under her fingernails, sweat running across her face and staining her armpits.

"Has it gone?" Rosalie asked. "Is it still in there?"

"Is what still in there, precisely?" I muttered.

We all stood that way for awhile, panting with exertion, adrenaline priming us for the chase.

"I think," Ellie said after a while, "we should make some plans."

"What about Charley?" I asked. They all knew what I meant: *we can't just leave her there; we have to do something; she'd do the same for us.*

"Charley's dead," Ellie said, without looking at anyone. "Come on." She headed for the kitchen.

"What happened?" Ellie asked.

Hayden was shaking. "I told you. We were checking the rooms. Charley ran in before me and locked the door, I heard glass breaking and...." He trailed off.

"And?"

"Screams. I heard her screaming. I heard her dying."

The kitchen fell silent as we all recalled the cries, as if they were still echoing around the manor. They meant different things to each of us. For me death always meant Jayne.

"Okay, this is how I see things," Ellie said. "There's a wild animal, or wild animals, out there now."

"What wild animals!" Rosalie scoffed. "Mutant badgers come to eat us up? Hedgehogs gone bad?"

"I don't know, but pray it is animals. If a person has done all this, then they'll be able to get in to us. However fucking goofy crazy, they'll have the intelligence to get in. No way to stop them. Nothing we could do." She patted the shotgun resting across her thighs as if to reassure herself of its presence.

"But what animals — "

"Do you know what's happening everywhere?" Ellie shouted, not just at doubting Rosalie but at us all. "Do you realize that the world's changing? Every day we wake up there's a new world facing us. And every day there're fewer of us left. I mean the big us, the worldwide us, us humans." Her voice became quieter. "How long before one morning, no one wakes up?"

"What has what's happening elsewhere got to do with all this?" I asked, although inside I already had an idea of what Ellie meant. I think maybe I'd known for a while, but now my mind was opening up, my beliefs stretching, levering fantastic truths into place. They fitted; that terrified me.

"I mean, it's all changing. A disease is wiping out millions and no one knows where it came from. Unrest everywhere, shootings, bombings. Nuclear bombs in the Med, for Christ's sake. You've heard what people have called it; it's the Ruin. Capital R, people. The world's gone bad. Maybe what's happening here is just not that unusual anymore."

"That doesn't tell us what they are," Rosalie said. "Doesn't explain why they're here, or where they come from. Doesn't tell us why Charley did what she did."

"Maybe she wanted to be with Boris again," Hayden said.

I simply stared at him. "I've seen them," I said, and Ellie sighed. "I saw them outside last night."

The others looked at me, Rosalie's eyes still full of the fear I had planted there and was even now propagating.

"So what were they?" Rosalie asked. "Ninja seabirds?"

"I don't know." I ignored her sarcasm. "They were white, but they hid in shadows. Animals, they must have been. There are no people like that. But they were canny. They moved only when I wasn't looking straight at them, otherwise they stayed still and... blended in with the snow." Rosalie, I could see, was terrified. The sarcasm was a front. Everything I said scared her more.

"Camouflaged," Hayden said.

"No. They blended in. As if they melted in, but they didn't. I can't really...."

"In China," Rosalie said, "white is the color of death. It's the color of happiness and joy. They wear white at funerals."

Ellie spoke quickly, trying to grab back the conversation. "Right. Let's think of what we're going to do. First, no use trying to get out. Agreed? Good. Second, we limit ourselves to a couple of rooms downstairs, the hallway and staircase area and upstairs. Third, do what we can to block up, nail up, glue up the doors to the other rooms and corridors."

"And then?" Rosalie asked quietly. "Charades?"

Ellie shrugged and smiled. "Why not? It is Christmas time."

I'd never dreamt of a white Christmas. I was cursing Bing fucking Crosby with every gasped breath I could spare.

The air sang with echoing hammer blows, dropped boards and groans as hammers crunched fingernails. I was working with Ellie to board up the rest of the downstairs rooms while Hayden and Rosalie tried to lever up the remaining boards in the dining room. We did the windows first, Ellie standing to one side with the shotgun aiming out while I hammered. It was snowing again and I could see vague shapes hiding behind flakes, dipping in and out of the snow like larking dolphins. I think we all saw them, but none of us ventured to say for sure that they were there. Our imagination was pumped up on what had happened and it had started to paint its own pictures.

We finished one of the living rooms and locked the door behind us. There was an awful sense of finality in the heavy thunk of the tumblers clicking in, a feeling that perhaps we would never go into that room again. I'd lived the last few years telling myself that there was no such thing as never — Jayne was dead and I would certainly see her again, after all — but there was nothing in these rooms that I could ever imagine us needing again. They were mostly designed for luxury, and luxury was a conceit of the contented mind. Over the past few weeks, I had seen contentment vanish forever under the grey cloud of humankind's fall from grace.

None of this seemed to matter now as we closed it all in. I thought I should feel sad, for the symbolism of what we were doing if not for the loss itself. Jayne had told me we would be together again, and then she had died and I had felt trapped ever since by her death and the promise of her final words. If nailing up doors would take me closer to her, then so be it.

In the next room I looked out of the window and saw Jayne striding naked towards me through the snow. Fat flakes landed on her shoulders and did not melt, and by the time she was near enough for me to see the look in her eyes she had collapsed down into a drift, leaving a memory there in her place. Something flitted past the window, sending flakes flying against the wind, bristly fur spiking dead white leaves.

I blinked hard and the snow was just snow once more. I turned and looked at Ellie, but she was concentrating too hard to return my stare. For the first time I could see how scared she was — how her hand clasped so tightly around the shotgun barrel that her knuckles were pearly white, her nails a shiny pink — and I wondered exactly what *she* was seeing out there in the white storm.

By midday we had done what we could. The kitchen, one of the living rooms and the hall and staircase were left open; every other room downstairs was boarded up from the outside in. We'd also covered the windows in those rooms left open, but we left thin viewing ports like horizontal arrow slits in the walls of an old castle. And like the weary defenders of those ancient citadels, we were under siege.

"So what did you all see?" I said as we sat in the kitchen. Nobody denied anything.

"Badgers," Rosalie said. "Big, white, fast. Sliding over the snow like they were on skis. Demon badgers from hell!" She joked, but it was obvious that she was terrified.

"Not badgers," Ellie cut in. "Deer. But wrong. Deer with scales. Or something. All wrong."

"Hayden, what did you see?"

He remained hunched over the cooker, stirring a weak stew of old vegetable and stringy beef. "I didn't see anything."

I went to argue with him but realized he was probably telling the truth. We had all seen something different, why not see nothing at all? Just as unlikely.

"You know," said Ellie, standing at a viewing slot with the snow reflecting sunlight in a band across her face, "we're all seeing white animals. White animals in the snow. So maybe we're seeing nothing at all. Maybe it's our imaginations. Perhaps Hayden is nearer the truth than all of us."

"Boris and the others had pretty strong imaginations, then," said Rosalie, bitter tears animating her eyes.

We were silent once again, stirring our weak milkless tea, all thinking our own thoughts about what was out in the snow. Nobody had asked me what I had seen and I was glad. Last night they were fleeting white shadows, but today I had seen Jayne as well. A Jayne I had known was not really there, even as I watched her coming at me through the snow. *I'll be with you again.*

"In China, white is the color of death," Ellie said. She spoke at the boarded window, never for an instant glancing away. Her hands held onto the shotgun as if it had become one with her body. I wondered what she had been in the past: *I have a history,* she'd said. "White. Happiness and joy."

"It was also the color of mourning for the Victorians," I added.

"And we're in a Victorian manor." Hayden did not turn around as he spoke, but his words sent our imaginations scurrying.

"We're all seeing white animals," Ellie said quietly. "Like white noise. All tones, all frequencies. We're all seeing different things as one."

"Oh," Rosalie whispered, "well that explains a lot."

I thought I could see where Ellie was coming from; at least, I was looking in the right direction. "White noise is used to mask other sounds," I said.

Ellie only nodded.

"There's something else going on here." I sat back in my chair and stared up, trying to divine the truth in the patchwork mold on the kitchen ceiling. "We're not seeing it all."

Ellie glanced away from the window, just for a second. "I don't think we're seeing anything."

Later we found out some more of what was happening. We went to bed; doors opened in the night, footsteps creaked old floorboards. And through the dark the sound of lovemaking drew us all to another, more terrible death.

three
the color of mourning

I had not made love to anyone since Jayne's death. It was months before she died that we last indulged, a bitter, tearful experience when she held a sheet of polythene between our chests and stomachs to prevent her diseased skin touching my own. It did not make for the most romantic of occasions, and afterward she cried herself to sleep as I sat holding her hand and staring into the dark.

After her death I came to the manor; the others came along to find something or escape from something else, and there were secretive noises in the night. The manor was large enough for us to have a room each, but in the darkness doors would open and close again, and every morning the atmosphere at breakfast was different.

My door had never opened and I had opened no doors. There was a lingering guilt over Jayne's death, a sense that I would be betraying her love if I went with someone else. A greater cause of my loneliness was my inherent lack of confidence, a certainty that no one here would be interested in me: I was quiet, introspective, and uninteresting, a fledgling bird devoid of any hope of taking wing with any particular talent. No one would want me.

But none of this could prevent the sense of isolation, subtle jealousy and yearning I felt each time I heard footsteps in the dark. I never heard anything else — the walls were too thick for that, the building too solid — but my imagination filled in the missing parts. Usually, Ellie was the star. And there lay another problem — lusting after a woman I did not even like very much.

The night it all changed for us was the first time I heard someone making love in the manor. The voice was androgynous in its ecstasy, a high keening, dropping off into a prolonged sigh before rising again. I sat up in bed, trying to shake off the remnants of dreams that clung like seaweed to a drowned corpse. Jayne had been there, of course, and something in the snow, and another something which was Jayne and the snow combined. I recalled wallowing in the sharp whiteness and feeling my skin sliced by ice edges, watching the snow grow pink around me, then white again as Jayne came and spread her cleansing touch across the devastation.

The cry came once more, wanton and unhindered by any sense of decorum.

Who? I thought. *Obviously Hayden, but who was he with? Rosalie? Cynical, paranoid, terrified Rosalie?*

Or Ellie?

I hoped Rosalie.

I sat back against the headboard, unable to lie down and ignore the sound. The curtains hung open — I had no reason to close them — and the moonlight revealed that it was snowing once again. I wondered what was out there watching the sleeping manor, listening to the crazy sounds of lust emanating from a building still spattered with the blood and memory of those who had died so recently. I wondered whether the things out there had any understanding of human emotion — the highs, the lows, the tenacious spirit that could sometimes survive even the most downheartening, devastating events — and what they made of the sound they could hear now. Perhaps they thought they were screams of pain. Ecstasy and thoughtless agony often sounded the same.

The sound continued, rising and falling. Added to it now the noise of something thumping rhythmically against a wall.

I thought of the times before Jayne had been ill, before the great decline had really begun, when most of the population still thought humankind could clean up what it had dirtied and repair what it had torn asunder. We'd been married for several years, our love as deep as ever, our lust still refreshing and invigorating. Car seats, cinemas, woodland, even a telephone box, all had been visited by us at some stage, laughing like adolescents, moaning and sighing together, content in familiarity.

And as I sat there remembering my dead wife, something strange happened. I could not identify exactly when the realization hit me, but I was suddenly sure of one thing: the voice I was listening to was Jayne's. She was moaning as someone else in the house made love to her. She had come in from outside, that cold unreal Jayne I had seen so recently, and she had gone to Hayden's room, and now I was being betrayed by someone I had never betrayed, ever.

I shook my head, knowing it was nonsense but certain also that the voice was hers. I was so sure that I stood, dressed and opened my bedroom door without considering the impossibility of what was happening. Reality was controlled by the darkness, not by whatever light I could attempt to throw upon it. I may as well have had my eyes closed.

The landing was lit by several shaded candles in wall brackets, their soft light barely reaching the floor, flickering as breezes came from nowhere. Where the light did touch it showed old carpet, worn by time and faded by countless unknown footfalls. The walls hung with shredded paper, damp and torn like dead skin, the lath and plaster beneath pitted and crumbled. The air was thick with age, heavy with must, redolent with faint hints of hauntings. Where my feet fell I could sense the floor dipping slightly beneath me, though whether this was actuality or a runover from my dream I was unsure.

I could have been walking on snow.

I moved toward Hayden's room and the volume of the sighing and crying increased. I paused one door away, my heart thumping not with exertion but with the thought that Jayne was a dozen steps from me, making love with Hayden, a man I hardly really knew.

Jayne's dead, I told myself, and she cried out once, loud, as she came. Another voice then, sighing and straining, and this one was Jayne as well.

Someone touched my elbow. I gasped and spun around, too shocked to scream. Ellie was there in her nightshirt, bare legs hidden in shadow. She had a strange look in her eye. It may have been the subdued lighting. I went to ask her what she was doing here, but then I realized it was probably the same as me. She'd stayed downstairs last night, unwilling to share a watch duty, insistent that we should all sleep.

I went to tell her that Jayne was in there with Hayden, then I realized how stupid this would sound, how foolish it actually *was*.

At least, I thought, *it's not Ellie in there. Rosalie it must be. At least not Ellie. Certainly not Jayne.*

And Jayne cried out again.

Goosebumps speckled my skin and brought it to life. The hairs on my neck stood to attention, my spine tingled.

"Hayden having a nice time?" someone whispered, and Rosalie stepped up behind Ellie.

I closed my eyes, listening to Jayne's cries. She had once screamed like that in a park, and the keeper had chased us out with his waving torch and throaty shout, the light splaying across our nakedness as we laughed and struggled to gather our clothes around us as we ran.

"Doesn't sound like Hayden to me," Ellie said.

The three of us stood outside Hayden's door for a while, listening to the sounds of lovemaking from within — the cries, the moving bed, the thud of wood against the wall. I felt like an intruder, however much I realized something was very wrong with all of this. Hayden was on his own in there. As we each tried to figure out what we were really hearing, the sounds from within changed. There was not one cry, not two, but many, overlying each other, increasing and expanding until the voice became that of a crowd. The light in the corridor seemed to dim as the crying increased, though it may have been my imagination.

I struggled to make out Jayne's voice and there was a hint of something familiar, a whisper in the cacophony that was so slight as to be little more than an echo of a memory. But still, to me, it was real.

Ellie knelt and peered through the keyhole, and I noticed for the first time that she was carrying her shotgun. She stood quickly and backed away from the door, her mouth opening, eyes widening. "It's Hayden," she said aghast, and then she fired at the door handle and lock.

The explosion tore through the sounds of ecstasy and left them in shreds. They echoed away like streamers in the wind, to be replaced by the lonely moan of a man's voice, pleading not to stop, it was so wonderful so pure so alive...

The door swung open. None of us entered the room. We could not move.

Hayden was on his back on the bed, surrounded by the whites from outside. I had seen them as shadows against the snow, little more than pale phantoms, but here in the room they stood out bright and definite. There were several of them; I could not make out an exact number because they squirmed and twisted against each other, and against Hayden. Diaphanous limbs stretched out and wavered in the air, arms or wings or tentacles, tapping at the bed and the wall and the ceiling, leaving spots of ice like ink on blotting paper wherever they touched.

I could see no real faces but I knew that the things were looking at me.

Their crying and sighing had ceased, but Hayden's continued. He moved quickly and violently, thrusting into the malleable shape that still straddled him, not yet noticing our intrusion even though the shotgun blast still rang in my ears. He continued his penetration, but slowly the white lifted itself away until Hayden's cock flopped back wetly onto his stomach.

He raised his head and looked straight at us between his knees, looked *through* one of the things where it flipped itself easily across the bed. The air stank of sex and something else, something cold and old and rotten, frozen forever and only now experiencing a hint of thaw.

"Oh please...." he said, though whether he spoke to us or the constantly shifting shapes I could not tell.

I tried to focus but the whites were minutely out of phase with my vision, shifting to and fro too quickly for me to concentrate. I thought I saw a face, but it may have been a false splay of shadows thrown as a shape turned and sprang to the floor. I searched for something I knew — an arm kinked slightly from an old break; a breast with a mole near the nipple; a smile turned wryly down at the edges — and I realized I was looking for Jayne. Even in all this mess, I thought she may be here. *I'll be with you again*, she had said.

I almost called her name, but Ellie lifted the shotgun and shattered the moment once more. It barked out once, loud, and everything happened so quickly. One instant the white things were there, smothering Hayden and touching him with their fluid limbs.

The next, the room was empty of all but us humans, moth-eaten curtains fluttering slightly, window invitingly open. And Hayden's face had disappeared into a red mist.

After the shotgun blast there was only the wet sound of Hayden's brains and skull fragments pattering down onto the bedding. His hard-on still glinted in the weak candlelight. His hands each clasped a fistful of blanket. One leg tipped and rested on the sheets clumped around him. His skin was pale, almost white.

Almost.

Rosalie leaned against the wall, dry heaving. Her dress was wet and heavy with puke and the stink of it had found a home in my nostrils. Ellie was busy reloading the shotgun, mumbling and cursing, trying to look anywhere but at the carnage of Hayden's body.

I could not tear my eyes away. I'd never seen anything like this. Brand and Boris and Charley, yes, their torn and tattered corpses had been terrible to behold, but here… I had seen the instant a rounded, functional person had turned into a shattered lump of meat. I'd seen the red splash of Hayden's head as it came apart and hit the wall, big bits ricocheting, the smaller, wetter pieces sticking to the old wallpaper and drawing their dreadful art for all to see. Every detail stood out and demanded my attention, as if the shot had cleared the air and brought light. It seemed red-tinged, the atmosphere itself stained with violence.

Hayden's right hand clasped onto the blanket, opening and closing very slightly, very slowly.

Doesn't feel so cold. Maybe there's a thaw on the way, I thought distractedly, trying perhaps to withdraw somewhere banal and comfortable and familiar….

There was a splash of sperm across his stomach. Blood from his ruined head was running down his neck and chest and mixing with it, dribbling soft and pink onto the bed.

Ten seconds ago he was alive. Now he was dead. Extinguished, just like that.

Where is he? I thought. *Where has he gone?*

"Hayden?" I said.

"He's dead!" Ellie hissed, a little too harshly.

"I can see that." But his hand still moved. Slowly. Slightly.

Something was happening at the window. The curtains were still now, but there was a definite sense of movement in the darkness beyond. I caught it from the corner of my eye as I stared at Hayden.

"Rosalie, go get some boards," Ellie whispered.

"You killed Hayden!" Rosalie spat. She coughed up the remnants of her last meal, and they hung on her chin like wet boils. "You blew his head off! You shot him! What the hell, what's going on, what's happening here. I don't know, I don't know...."

"The things are coming back in," Ellie said. She shouldered the gun, leaned through the door and fired at the window. Stray shot plucked at the curtains. There was a cessation of noise from outside, then a rustling, slipping, sliding. It sounded like something flopping around in snow. "Go and get the boards, you two."

Rosalie stumbled noisily along the corridor toward the staircase.

"You killed him," I said lamely.

"He was fucking them," Ellie shouted. Then, quieter: "I didn't mean to..." She looked at the body on the bed, only briefly but long enough for me to see her eyes narrow and her lips squeeze tight. "He was fucking them. His fault."

"What were they? What the hell, I've never seen any animals like them."

Ellie grabbed my bicep and squeezed hard, eliciting an unconscious yelp. She had fingers like steel nails. "They aren't animals," she said. "They aren't people. Help me with the door."

Her tone invited no response. She aimed the gun at the open window for as long as she could while I pulled the door shut. The shotgun blast had blown the handle away, and I could not see how we would be able to keep it shut should the whites return. We stood that way for awhile, me hunkered down with two fingers through a jagged hole in the door to try to keep it closed, Ellie standing slightly back, aiming the gun at the pocked wood. I wondered whether I'd end up getting shot if the whites chose this moment to climb back into the room and launch themselves at the door....

Banging and cursing marked Rosalie's return. She carried several snapped floor boards, the hammer and nails. I held the boards up, Rosalie nailed, both of us now in Ellie's line of fire. Again I wondered about Ellie and guns, about her history. I was glad when the job was done.

We stepped back from the door and stood there silently, three relative strangers trying to understand and come to terms with what we had seen. But without understanding, coming to terms was impossible. I felt a tear run down my cheek, then another. A sense of breathless panic settled around me, clasping me in cool hands and sending my heart racing.

"What do we do?" I said. "How do we keep those things

out?"

"They won't get through the boarded windows," Rosalie said confidently, doubt so evident in her voice.

I remembered how quickly they had moved, how lithe and alert they had been to virtually dodge the blast from Ellie's shotgun.

I held my breath; the others were doing the same.

Noises. Clambering and a soft whistling at first, then light thuds as something ran around the walls of the room, across the ceiling, bounding from the floor and the furniture. Then tearing, slurping, cracking, as the whites fed on what was left of Hayden.

"Let's go down," Ellie suggested. We were already backing away.

Jayne may be in danger, I thought, recalling her waving to me as she walked naked through the snow. If she was out there, and these things were out there as well, she would be at risk. She may not know, she may be too trusting, she may let them take advantage of her, abuse and molest her —

Hayden had been enjoying it. He was not being raped; if anything, he was doing the raping. Even as he died he'd been spurting ignorant bliss across his stomach.

And Jayne was dead. I repeated this over and over, whispering it, not caring if the others heard, certain that they would take no notice. Jayne was dead. Jayne was dead.

I suddenly knew for certain that the whites could smash in at any time, dodge Ellie's clumsy shooting and tear us to shreds in seconds. They could do it, but they did not. They scratched and tapped at windows, clambered around the house, but they did not break in. Not yet.

They were playing with us. Whether they needed us for food, fun, or revenge, it was nothing but a game.

Ellie was smashing up the kitchen.

She kicked open cupboard doors, swept the contents of shelves onto the floor with the barrel of the shotgun, sifted through them with her feet, then did the same to the next cupboard. At first I thought it was blind rage, fear, dread; then I saw that she was searching for something.

"What?" I asked. "What are you doing?"

"Just a hunch."

"What sort of hunch? Ellie, we should be watching out — "

"There's something moving out there," Rosalie said. She was looking through the slit in the boarded window. There was a band of moonlight across her eyes.

"Here!" Ellie said triumphantly. She knelt and rooted around in the mess on the floor, shoving jars and cans aside, delving into a splash of spilled rice to find a small bottle. "Bastard. The bastard. Oh God, the bastard's been doing it all along."

"There's something out there in the snow," Rosalie said again, louder this time. "It's coming to the manor. It's..." Her voice trailed off and I saw her stiffen, her mouth slightly open.

"Rosalie?" I moved towards her, but she glanced at me and waved me away.

"It's okay," she said. "It's nothing."

"Look." Ellie slammed a bottle down on the table and stood back for us to see.

"A bottle."

Ellie nodded. She looked at me and tilted her head. Waiting for me to see, expecting me to realize what she was trying to say.

"A bottle from Hayden's food cupboard," I said.

She nodded again.

I looked at Rosalie. She was still frozen at the window, hands pressed flat to her thighs, eyes wide and full of the moon. "Rosie?" She only shook her head. Nothing wrong, the gesture said, but it did not look like that. It looked like everything was wrong but she was too afraid to tell us. I went to move her out of the way, look for myself, see what had stolen her tongue.

"Poison," Ellie revealed. I paused, glanced at the bottle on the table. Ellie picked it up and held it in front of a candle, shook it, turned it this way and that. "Poison. Hayden's been cooking for us ever since we've been here. And he's always had this bottle. And a couple of times lately, he's added a little extra to certain meals."

"Brand," I nodded, aghast. "And Boris. But why? They were outside, they were killed by those things — "

"Torn up by those things," Ellie corrected. "Killed in here. Then dragged out."

"By Hayden?"

She shrugged. "Why not? He was fucking the whites."

"But why would he want to… Why did he have something against Boris and Brand? And Charley? An accident, like he said?"

"I guess he gave her a helping hand," Ellie mused, sitting at the table and rubbing her temples. "They both saw something outside. Boris and Brand, they'd both seen things in the snow. They made it known, they told us all about it, and Hayden heard as well. Maybe he felt threatened. Maybe he thought we'd steal his little sex mates." She stared down at the table, at the rings burnt there over the years by hot mugs, the scratches made by endless cutlery. "Maybe they told him to do it."

"Oh, come on!" I felt my eyes go wide like those of a rabbit caught in car headlights.

Ellie shrugged, stood and rested the gun on her shoulder. "Whatever, we've got to protect ourselves. They may be in soon, you saw them up there. They're intelligent. They're — "

"Animals!" I shouted. "They're animals! How could they tell Hayden anything? How could they get in?"

Ellie looked at me, weighing her reply.

"They're white animals, like you said!"

Ellie shook her head. "They're new. They're unique. They're a part of the change."

New. Unique. The words instilled very little hope in me, and Ellie's next comment did more to scare me than anything that had happened up to now.

"They were using Hayden to get rid of us. Now he's gone... well, they've no reason not to do it themselves."

As if on cue, something started to brush up against the outside wall of the house.

"Rosalie!" I shouted. "Step back!"

"It's alright," she said dreamily, "it's only the wind. Nothing there. Nothing to worry about." The sound continued, like soap on sandpaper. It came from beyond the boarded windows but it also seemed to filter through from elsewhere, surrounding us like an audio enemy.

"Ellie," I said, "what can we do?" She seemed to have taken charge so easily that I deferred to her without thinking, assuming she would have a plan with a certainty which was painfully cut down.

"I have no idea." She nursed the shotgun in the crook of her elbow like a baby substitute, and I realized I didn't know her half as well as I thought. Did she have children? I wondered. Where were her family? Where had this level of self-control come from?

"Rosalie," I said carefully, "what are you looking at?" Rosalie was staring through the slit at a moonlit scene none of us could see. Her expression had dropped from scared to melancholy, and I saw a tear trickle down her cheek. She was no longer her old cynical, bitter self. It was as if all her fears had come true and she was content with the fact. "Rosie!" I called again, quietly but firmly.

Rosalie turned to look at us. Reality hit her, but it could not hide the tears. "But he's dead," she said, half-question, half-statement. Before I could ask whom she was talking about, something hit the house.

The sound of smashing glass came from everywhere: behind the boards across the kitchen windows; out in the corridor; muffled crashes from elsewhere in the dark manor. Rosalie stepped back from the slit just as a long, shimmering white limb came in, glassy nails scratching for her face but ripping the air instead.

Ellie stepped forward, thrust the shotgun through the slit and pulled the trigger. There was no cry of pain, no scream, but the limb withdrew.

Something began to batter against the ruined kitchen window, the vibration traveling through the hastily nailed boards, nail heads emerging slowly from the gouged wood after each impact. Ellie fired again, though I could not see what she was shooting at. As she turned to reload she avoided my questioning glance.

"They're coming in!" I shouted.

"Can it!" Ellie said bitterly. She stepped back as a sliver of timber broke away from the edge of one of the boards, clattering to the floor stained with frost. She shouldered the gun and fired twice through the widening gap. White things began to worm their way between the boards; fingers perhaps, but long and thin and more flexible than any I had ever seen. They twisted and felt blindly across the wood... and then wrapped themselves around the exposed nails.

They began to pull.

The nails squealed as they were withdrawn from the wood, one by one.

I hefted the hammer and went at the nails, hitting each of them only once, aiming for those surrounded by cool white digits. As each nail went back in the things around them drew back and squirmed out of sight behind the boards, only to reappear elsewhere. I hammered until my arm ached, resting my left hand against the vibrating timber. Not once did I catch a white digit beneath the hammer, even when I aimed for them specifically. I began to giggle and the sound frightened me. It was the voice of a madman, the utterance of someone looking for his lost mind, and I found that funnier than ever. Every time I hit another nail it reminded me more and more of an old fairground game. Pop the gophers on the head. I wondered what the prize would be tonight.

"What the hell do we do?" I shouted.

Rosalie had stepped away from the windows and now leaned against the kitchen worktop, eyes wide, mouth working slowly in some unknown mantra. I glanced at her between hammer blows and saw her chest rising and falling at an almost impossible speed. She was slipping into shock.

"Where?" I shouted to Ellie over my shoulder.

"The hallway."

"Why?"

"Why not?"

I had no real answer, so I nodded and indicated with a jerk of my head that the other two should go first. Ellie shoved Rosalie ahead of her and stood waiting for me.

I continued bashing with the hammer, but now I had fresh targets. Not only were the slim white limbs nudging aside the boards and working at the nails, but they were also coming through the ventilation bricks at skirting level in the kitchen. They would gain no hold there, I knew; they could never pull their whole body through there. But still I found their presence abhorrent and terrifying, and every third hammer strike was directed at these white monstrosities trying to twist around my ankles.

And at the third missed strike, I knew what they were doing. It was then, also, that I had some true inkling of their intelligence and wiliness. Two digits trapped my leg between them — they were cold and hard, even through my jeans — and they jerked so hard that I felt my skin tearing in their grasp.

I went down and the hammer skittered across the kitchen floor. At the same instant a twisting forest of the things appeared between the boards above me, and in seconds the timber had started to snap and splinter as the onslaught intensified, the attackers now seemingly aware of my predicament. Shards of wood and glass and ice showered down on me, all of them sharp and cutting. And then, looking up, I saw one of the whites appear in the gap above me, framed by broken wood, its own limbs joined by others in their efforts to widen the gap and come in to tear me apart.

Jayne stared down at me. Her face was there but the thing was not her; it was as if her image were projected there, cast onto the pure whiteness of my attacker by memory or circumstance, put there because it knew what the sight would do to me.

I went weak, not because I thought Jayne was there — I knew that I was being fooled — but because her false visage inspired a flood of warm memories through my stunned bones, hitting cold muscles and sending me into a white-hot agony of paused circulation, blood pooling at my extremities, consciousness retreating into the warmer parts of my brain, all thought of escape and salvation and the other three survivors erased by the plain whiteness that invaded from outside, sweeping in through the rent in the wall and promising me a quick, painful death, but only if I no longer struggled, only if I submitted —

The explosion blew away everything but the pain. The thing above me had been so intent upon its imminent kill that it must have missed Ellie, leaning in the kitchen door and shouldering the shotgun.

The thing blew apart. I closed my eyes as I saw it fold up before me, and when I opened them again there was nothing there, not even a shower of dust in the air, no sprinkle of blood, no splash of insides. Whatever it had been it left nothing behind in death.

"Come on!" Ellie hissed, grabbing me under one arm and hauling me across the kitchen floor. I kicked with my feet to help her then finally managed to stand, albeit shakily.

There was now a gaping hole in the boards across the kitchen windows. Weak candlelight bled out and illuminated the falling snow and the shadows behind it. I expected the hole to be filled again in seconds and this time they would pour in, each of them a mimic of Jayne in some terrifying fashion.

"Shut the door," Ellie said calmly. I did so and Rosalie was there with a hammer and nails. We'd run out of broken floor boards, so we simply nailed the door into the frame. It was clumsy and would no doubt prove ineffectual, but it might give us a few more seconds.

But for what? What good would time do us now, other than to extend our agony?

"Now where?" I asked hopelessly. "Now what?" There were sounds all around us; soft thuds from behind the kitchen door, and louder noises from further away. Breaking glass; cracking wood; a gentle rustling, more horrible because they could not be identified. As far as I could see, we really had nowhere to go.

"Upstairs," Ellie said. "The attic. The hatch is outside my room; it's got a loft ladder; as far as I know it's the only way up. Maybe we could hold them off until...."

"Until they go home for tea," Rosalie whispered. I said nothing. There was no use in verbalizing the hopelessness we felt at the moment, because we could see it in each other's eyes. The snow had been here for weeks and maybe now it would be here forever. Along with whatever strangeness it contained.

Ellie checked the bag of cartridges and handed them to me. "Hand these to me," she said. "Six shots left. Then we have to beat them up."

It was dark inside the manor, even though dawn must now be breaking outside. I thanked God that at least we had some candles left... but that got me thinking about God and how He would let this happen, launch these things against us, torture us with the promise of certain death and yet give us these false splashes of hope. I'd spent most of my life thinking that God was indifferent, a passive force holding the big picture together while we acted out our own foolish little plays within it. Now, if He did exist, He could only be a cruel God indeed. And I'd rather there be nothing than a God who found pleasure or entertainment in the discomfort of His creations.

Maybe Rosalie had been right. She had seen God staring down with blood in His eyes.

As we stumbled out into the main hallway I began to cry, gasping out my fears and my grief, and Ellie held me up and whispered into my ear. "Prove Him wrong if you have to. Prove Him wrong. Help me to survive, and prove Him wrong."

I heard Jayne beyond the main front doors, calling my name into the snowbanks, her voice muffled and bland. I paused, confused, and then I even smelled her; apple-blossom shampoo; the sweet scent of her breath. For a few seconds Jayne was there with me and I could all but hold her hand. None of the last few weeks had happened. We were here on a holiday, but there was something wrong and she was in danger outside. I went to open the doors to her, ask her in and help her, assuage whatever fears she had.

I would have reached the doors and opened them if it were not for Ellie striking me on the shoulder with the stock of the shotgun.

"There's nothing out there but those things!" she shouted. I blinked rapidly as reality settled down around me but it was like wrapping paper, only disguising the truth I thought I knew, not dismissing it completely.

The onslaught increased.

Ellie ran up the stairs, shotgun held out before her. I glanced around once, listening to the sounds coming from near and far, all of them noises of siege, each of them promising pain at any second. Rosalie stood at the foot of the stairs doing likewise. Her face was pale and drawn and corpse-like.

"I can't believe Hayden," she said. "He was doing it with them. I can't believe... does Ellie really think he...?"

"I can't believe a second of any of this," I said. "I hear my dead wife." As if ashamed of the admission I lowered my eyes as I walked by Rosalie. "Come on," I said. "We can hold out in the attic."

"I don't think so." Her voice was so sure, so full of conviction, that I thought she was all right. Ironic that a statement of doom should inspire such a feeling, but it was as close to the truth as anything.

I thought Rosalie was all right.

It was only as I reached the top of the stairs that I realized she had not followed me.

I looked out over the ornate old banister, down into the hallway where shadows played and cast false impressions on eyes I could barely trust anyway. At first I thought I was seeing things because Rosalie was not stupid; Rosalie was cynical and bitter, but never stupid. She would not do such a thing.

She stood by the open front doors. How I had not heard her unbolting and opening them I do not know, but there she was, a stark shadow against white fluttering snow, dim daylight parting around her and pouring in. Other things came in too, the whites, slinking across the floor and leaving paw prints of frost wherever they came. Rosalie stood with arms held wide in a welcoming embrace.

She said something as the whites launched at her. I could not hear the individual words but I sensed the tone; she was happy. As if she were greeting someone she had not seen for a very long time.

And then they hit her and took her apart in seconds.

"Run!" I shouted, sprinting along the corridor, chasing Ellie's shadow. In seconds I was right behind her, pushing at her shoulders as if this would make her move faster. "Run! Run! Run!"

She glanced back as she ran. "Where's Rosalie?"

"She opened the door." It was all I needed to say. Ellie turned away and concentrated on negotiating a corner in the corridor.

From behind me I heard the things bursting in all around. Those that had slunk past Rosalie must have broken into rooms from the inside even as others came in from outside, helping each other, crashing through our pathetic barricades by force of cooperation.

I noticed how cold it had become. Frost clung to the walls and the old carpet beneath our feet crunched with each footfall. Candles threw erratic shadows at icicle-encrusted ceilings. I felt ice under my fingernails.

Jayne's voice called out behind me and I slowed, but then I ran on once more, desperate to fight what I so wanted to believe. She'd said we would be together again and now she was calling me... but she was dead, she was dead. Still she called. Still I ran. And then she started to cry because I was not going to her, and I imagined her naked out there in the snow with white things everywhere. I stopped and turned around.

Ellie grabbed my shoulder, spun me and slapped me across the face. It brought tears to my eyes, but it also brought me back to shady reality. "We're here," she said. "Stay with us." Then she looked over my shoulder. Her eyes widened. She brought the gun up so quickly that it smacked into my ribs, and the explosion in the confined corridor felt like a hammer pummelling my ears.

I turned and saw what she had seen. It was like a drift of snow moving down the corridor toward us, rolling across the walls and ceiling, pouring along the floor. Ellie's shot had blown a hole through it, but the whites quickly regrouped and moved forward once more. Long, fine tendrils felt out before them, freezing the corridor seconds before the things passed by. There were no faces or eyes or mouths, but if I looked long enough I could see Jayne rolling naked in there with them, her mouth wide, arms holding whites to her, into her. If I really listened I was sure I would hear her sighs as she fucked them. They had passed from luring to mocking now that we were trapped, but still....

They stopped. The silence was a withheld chuckle.

"Why don't they rush us?" I whispered. Ellie had already pulled down the loft ladder and was waiting to climb up. She reached out and pulled me back, indicating with a nod of her head that I should go first. I reached out for the gun, wanting to give her a chance, but she elbowed me away without taking her eyes off the advancing white mass. "Why don't they...?"

She fired again. The shot tore a hole, but another thing soon filled that hole and stretched out toward us. "I'll shoot you if you stand in my way any more," she said.

I believed her. I handed her two cartridges and scurried up the ladder, trying not to see Jayne where she rolled and writhed, trying not to hear her sighs of ecstasy as the whites did things to her that only I knew she liked.

The instant I made it through the hatch the sounds changed. I heard Ellie squeal as the things rushed, the metallic clack as she slammed the gun shut again, two explosions in quick succession, a wet sound as whites ripped apart. Their charge sounded like a steam train: wood cracked and split; the floorboards were smashed up beneath icy feet; ceilings collapsed. I could not see, but I felt the corridor shattering as they came at Ellie, as if it were suddenly too small to house them all and they were plowing their own way through the manor.

Ellie came up the ladder fast, throwing the shotgun through before hauling herself up after it. I saw a flash of white before she slammed the hatch down and locked it behind her.

"There's no way they can't get up here," I said. "They'll be here in seconds."

Ellie struck a match and lit a pathetic stub of candle. "Last one." She was panting. In the weak light she looked pale and worn out. "Let's see what they decide," she said.

We were in one of four attics in the manor roof. This one was boarded but bare, empty of everything except spiders and dust. Ellie shivered and cried, mumbling about her dead husband Jack frozen in the car. Maybe she heard him. Maybe she'd seen him down there. I found with a twinge of guilt that I could not care less.

"They herded us, didn't they?" I said. I was breathless and aching, but it was similar to the feeling after a good workout; enervated, not exhausted.

Ellie shrugged, then nodded. She moved over to me and took the last couple of cartridges from the bag on my belt. As she broke the gun and removed the spent shells her shoulders hitched. She gasped and dropped the gun.

"What? Ellie?" But she was not hearing me. She stared into old shadows which had not been bathed in light for years, seeing some unknown truths there, her mouth falling open into an expression so unfamiliar on her face that it took me some seconds to place it — a smile. Whatever she saw, whatever she heard, it was something she was happy with.

I almost let her go. In the space of a second, all possibilities flashed across my mind. We were going to die, there was no escape, they would take us singly or all in one go, they would starve us out, the snow would never melt, the whites would change and grow and evolve beneath us, we could do nothing, whatever they were they had won already, they had won when Humankind brought the ruin down upon itself....

Then I leaned over and slapped Ellie across the face. Her head snapped around and she lost her balance, falling onto all fours over the gun.

I heard Jayne's footsteps as she prowled the corridors searching for me, calling my name with increasing exasperation. Her voice was changing from singsong, to monotone, to panicked.

The whites were down there with her, the white animals, all animals, searching and stalking her tender naked body through the freezing manor. I had to help her. I knew what it would mean but at least then we would be together, at least then her last promise to me would have been fulfilled.

Ellie's moan brought me back and for a second I hated her for that. I had been with Jayne and now I was here in some dark, filthy attic with a hundred creatures below trying to find a way to tear me apart. I hated her and I could not help it one little bit.

I moved to one of the sloping rooflights and stared out. I looked for Jayne across the snowscape, but the whites now had other things on their mind. Fooling me was not a priority.

"What do we do?" I asked Ellie, sure even now that she would have an idea, a plan. "How many shots have you got left?"

She looked at me. The candle was too weak to light up her eyes. "Enough." Before I even realized what she was doing she had flipped the shotgun over, wrapped her mouth around the twin barrels, reached down, curved her thumb through the trigger guard and blasted her brains into the air.

It's been over an hour since Ellie killed herself and left me on my own.

In that time snow has been blown into the attic to cover her body from view. Elsewhere it's merely a sprinkling, but Ellie is little more than a white hump on the floor now, the mess of her head a pink splash across the ever-whitening boards.

At first the noise from downstairs was terrific. The whites raged and ran and screamed, and I curled into a ball and tried to prepare myself for them to smash through the hatch and take me apart. I even considered the shotgun... there's one shot left... but Ellie was brave, Ellie was strong. I don't have that strength.

Besides, there's Jayne to think of. She's down there now, I know, because I have not heard a sound for ten minutes. Outside it is snowing heavier than I've ever seen; it must be ten feet deep, and there is no movement whatsoever. Inside, below the hatch and throughout the manor, in rooms sealed and broken open, the whites must be waiting. Here and there, Jayne will be waiting with them. For me. So that I can be with her again.

Soon I will open the hatch, make my way downstairs and out through the front doors. I hope, Jayne, that you will meet me there.

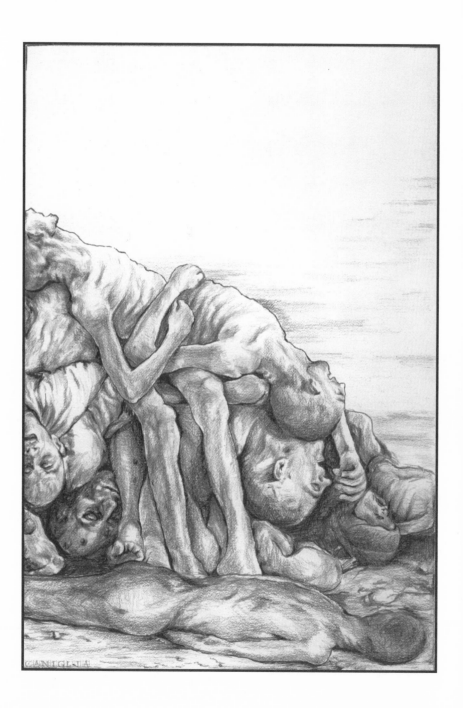

From Bad Flesh

Part One
Bred in the Bone
i

Della is the only person I still listen to. I hear the views of others, weigh the significance of their opinions; but Della is wise, Della is good. Sometimes, I think she's one step removed from everyone else.

She once told me that you can distinguish between truth and lies by the way the speaker tilts their head: slightly to the side, truth; forwards, a lie. It's not effective for everyone, of course. There are professional liars out there who know how to control such noticeable mannerisms, and there are people like Della who spend their time marking these liars. They are the most accomplished deceivers of all. I am sure now that Della spun me more than a few mild deceits in the time I knew her.

There is a pile of bodies heaped against the harbor wall as I step from the gangway and onto the mole. Two or three deep, a hundred meters long, with seagulls darting their heads here and there to lift out moist morsels in their red-tainted beaks. I'd always wondered where that red mark came from, ever since I was a child. Della told me it was tomato sauce from all the chips the gulls used to steal, and I believed her for a while. Then she told me they were natural markings. Now, I know the truth.

"Where do they come from?" I ask the policeman who stands at the bottom of the gangway. He glances over his shoulder at the bodies, as if surprised that I even deigned mention them.

"No worries," he grins through black and missing teeth. "Dead trouble, rioters. Normal, all is normal." He grabs my arm and helps me onto the mole, nodding and never, for one instant, relinquishing eye contact until I tip him.

"Rioters, eh?"

The little man forces a mock expression of disgust, and I actually believe he wants me to smile at his display. "Rioters, wasters, trouble. No more worries." He performs an exaggerated salute, then turns and makes sure my tip is safe in his pocket before helping down the passenger behind me.

I stroll quickly along the dock, sweat already tickling my sides and plastering my wispy hair to my forehead. I try not to look at the pile of corpses, but as I approach the gulls let out a raucous cry and take flight in one frantic cloud. Three young boys run to the corpses and begin levering at them with broom handles, lifting limbs so that they can scour the fingers and wrists of those beneath for signs of jewelry. Evidently they have already been picked clean, because by the time I reach the harbor and hurry by with my breath held, the kids have fled, and the gulls are settling once more.

ii

"There's a guy called String," Della said, handing me another bottle of beer and lobbing a log onto the fire. "He may be able to help." So casual. So matter-of-fact. It was as if she were talking about the weather, rather than my fading life.

"String?" The name intrigued me, and repeating it gave me time to think. He'd been all over the news a few months ago, but then I'd thought nothing of it. At the time I'd had no need of a cure.

Della stared over at me, the light from the fire casting shadows that hid her expression. Calm, I guessed. Content. That was Della all over. She had short hair, which she cut herself, and her clothes consisted of innumerable lengths of thin colored cloth, twisted decoratively around her body and giving her the appearance of an old, psychedelic mummy.

She had no legs. They had been ripped off in a road accident, just at the beginning of the Ruin. She was too stubborn to wear prosthetics.

"Lives in Greece. On one of the islands. Can't remember which." She frowned into the fire, but I did not believe her faulty memory for a moment.

"So what could he do? What does he know?"

Della shrugged, sipping her beer. "Just rumors, that's all I've heard."

I almost cried then. I felt the lump in my throat and my eyes burning and blurring; a mixture of anger and resentment, both at my fellow humans for tearing the world apart, and at Della for her nonchalant approach to my fatal condition.

"I'm pretty fucking far past rumors, now. Look." I lifted my shirt and showed her my chest. The growths were becoming visible, patterns of innocent-looking bumps beneath my skin that spelled death. "Just tell me, Della. I need to know anything."

She looked at my chest with feigned detachment. It was because she hated displays of self-pity rather than because she didn't care. She did care. I knew that.

"His name's String — rumor. He's a witch doctor, of sorts — rumor. Rumor has it he's come up with all kinds of impossible cures. I've not met anyone who's gone to him, but there are lots of stories."

"Like?"

She shrugged, and for the first time I realized what a long shot this was. I was way beyond saving — me and a billion others — but she was giving me this hope to grab onto, clasp to my rotting chest and pray it may give me a cause for the few months left to me.

"A woman with the Sickness eating at her womb. She crawls to him. Five days later, she turns up back home, cured."

"Where was home?"

"London Suburbs. Not the healthiest, wealthiest of places since the Ruin, as I'm sure you know. But String, so they say, doesn't distinguish." Della poked the fire angrily with a long stick. I could see she wanted to give this up, but she was the one who'd started it.

"Which island, Della?"

She did not answer me, nor look at me.

"I'll know if you lie."

She smiled. "No you won't." From the tone of her voice I knew she was going to tell me, so I let her take her own time. She looked up at the corrugated iron roof, the rusted nail holes that let acidic water in, the hungry spread of spider's webs hanging like festive decorations.

"Malakki," she said. "Malakki Town, on the island of Malakki. He's got some sort of a commune in the hills. So rumor has it."

"Thanks, Della. You know I've got to go?" I wondered why she had not mentioned it before. Was it because it was a hopeless long shot? Or perhaps she just did not want to lose me? Maybe she relied on me a lot more than she let me think.

She nodded. I left a week later, but I did not see her again after that night. It was as if we'd said goodbye already, and any further communication would make it all the more painful.

iii

There is a good chance that I will never return from this trip. The lumps on my chest have opened up and are weeping foul-smelling fluid; the first sign of the end. I wear two T-shirts beneath my shirt to soak up the mess.

And if my disease does not kill me, Malakki is always there in the background to complete the job.

The island is awash with a deluge of refugees from the Greek mainland, fleeing the out-of-control rioting that has periodically torn the old country apart since the Ruin. From the harbor I can see the shantytowns covering the hillsides, scatterings of huts and tents and sheets that resemble a rash of boils across the bare slopes. All hint of vegetation has been swept away, stripped by the first few thousand settlers and used for food or fuel for their constant fires. Soil erosion prevents any sort of replanting, if there were those left to consider it. There is a continuous movement of people across the hillsides; from this distance they resemble an intermingling carpet of ants, several lines heading down towards the outskirts of the city.

In the city itself, faceless gangs ebb and flow through the streets, moving aimlessly from one plaza to the next or sitting at the roadside and begging for food. There are hundreds of people in uniform or regulation dress, most of them carrying firearms, many of them obviously not of standard issue. Whether these are regular army and police it is impossible to tell, but the relevance is negligible. The fact is, they seem to be keeping some form of radical order; I can see thin shapes hanging from balconies and street lamps, heads swollen in the fierce heat, necks squeezed impossibly narrow by the ropes. A seagull lands on one of the shapes and sets it swaying, as if instilling life into the bloated corpse. Retribution may be harsh, but there seems to be little trouble in the streets. The fight has gone from these people.

I reach the edge of the harbor and look around, trying to find a place to sit. The boat journey has taken eight days, and in my already weakened state the stress on my body has been immense. Inside I am still fighting. I cannot imagine myself passing away, slipping through the fingers of life like so much sand. I can barely come to terms with the certainty of my bleeding chest, the knowledge of what is inside me, eating away at my future with thoughtless, soulless tenacity. The Sickness is a result of the Ruin, perhaps the cause of it, but for me it is a personal affront. I hate the fact that my destiny is being eroded by a microscopic horror created by someone else.

Over the course of the journey, I have decided not to sit back and accept it. I wonder whether this is what Della intended — that her vague mention of a rumored cure would instil within me a final burst of optimism. Something to keep me buoyant as death circles closer and closer. And that is why I am here, chasing a witch doctor in the withering remains of Europe's paradise.

I see a vacant seat, an old bench looking out over the once-luxurious harbor. I make my way through the jostling crowd and sit down, realizing only then that this position gives me a perfect view of the long heap of corpses against the wall. I wonder if they are there waiting to be shipped out, perhaps dumped into the sea. I muse upon the twisted morals behind their slaughter, try to remember what reason the policeman had been trying to impart to me. Trouble, he had said. Poor bastards.

"You ill?" I had not even noticed the woman sitting beside me until she spoke. I glare at her. She is the picture of health, or as healthy as anyone can be in today's world. Her face is tanned and smooth, her hair long and naturally curled. As for the rest of her, her robustness sets her aside. She is trim, short, athletic looking, but still curved pleasingly around the hips and chest. Her bright expression, however, is one of arrogance. I take an immediate dislike to her.

Apart from anything, it is presumptuous to assume I even want to talk.

"And is it your business?" I ask.

"Might be."

The relevance of the answer eludes me. Thoughts of String are still long-term; in the short term, I have to decide what to do now that I have arrived.

My thoughts are interrupted, however, by the sound that has become so familiar over the years. A swarm of angry bees, amplified a million times; a continuous explosion, ripping the air asunder and filling the gaps with fear; pounding, pulsing, throbbing through the air like sentient lightning. A Lord Ship.

Around me, along the mole and in the plaza facing the harbor, people fall to their knees. The act effectively identifies those who have come to the island recently, for they remain standing, glancing around with a mixture of shock and bewilderment.

"What the hell are they doing?" I gasp in disgust.

There are two men huddled at my feet, their eyes cast downwards and their hands clasped in front of their faces in an attitude of prayer. They are mumbling, and I can hear the fear in their voices even over the rumble from the sky. I nudge the nearest with my foot, and he glances up at me.

"What are you doing? Don't you know what they are? Why don't you try to live for yourself?" The man merely looks at me for a second or two — even then, I'm unsure whether he understands — before remembering what he had been doing. He hits his forehead on the ground, such is his keenness to prostrate himself once more. His voice raises an octave and becomes louder; he is sweating freely, shirt plastered to his back; two ruby drops hit the pavement from his clasped hands where his nails have pierced the skin.

I stand, dumbfounded. "They must be fools! Don't they know?"

"Leave it!" the short woman says.

"What?"

"Leave it! Leave them be! Don't say anymore!" She stands next to me and stares into my eyes, and what I see there convinces me that she knows what she is talking about.

My pride, however, tries one more time: "But don't they know — ?"

She grabs my elbow and begins to lead me through the kneeling crowds. The dirigible has drifted past the edge of the town, pumping out its voiceless message, and now it appears to be heading inland. The hillsides have stilled, the dry ground hidden beneath a carpet of procumbent humanity. I try to resist, but she walks faster, surprising me with her strength. She seems to know where she is going. Within a minute we have scampered into a shaded alleyway and she has dragged me into the shadows, hushing me with a hand over my mouth as I go to protest.

"Watch," she whispers. "Things can get a bit weird around here."

Like a snapshot of life, the entrance to the alley affords us a framed view of what is happening in the streets. As we slump down into the heat, the sound of the airship gradually disappears into the distance. The people begin to rise, gaze cast downward at first, then glancing up, then staring forcefully at the sky as movement becomes the prime motive once more. Voices call out, shouts and songs and screams. Some of the people remain subdued, but these seem to bleed away from the streets immediately. Others seem possessed of a frantic activity, running quietly at first, leaping into the air, rolling across the pitted tarmac, bumping into each other, exchanging silent blows. Within seconds their voices have returned; they scream, curse, fight their neighbor, their friend, their family. Less than three minutes after the first people have risen from their subdued pose, the street is a mass of flailing limbs and struggling bodies. It is repulsive.

"You'd better come with me," the woman says. "Maybe you'll

be safe if you do. Maybe you won't."

"Makes no real difference," I say, feeling the warm reminder of imminent death in my chest.

"Didn't to me when I came here, either," she says. "Does now. Believe me, you want to live."

The declaration provokes a stupefied silence from me. I follow the woman further along the alley, soon finding myself creeping through dusty backstreets where old women huddle under black shawls in doorways like sleeping bats. I can smell the mouth-watering aroma of genuine Greek cooking.

As if identity is an afterthought, the woman turns several minutes later. "I'm Jade, by the way."

"Gabe."

From far away, we hear the first sounds of gunfire. The steady roar of the rioting crowd escalates with the effects of fear and fury, and the crackling of rifle fire continues.

"I'm looking for a man called String." We are hurrying through dusty yellow alleyways. Shots herald the death of a few more rioters. My utterance seems melodramatic, to say the least.

"I know. Why else would you be here?" Jade does not turn around, but I guess that she senses my surprise. I can almost see the satisfied grin on her face. I bet she grins a lot, at other people's misfortune. Her long hair swings between her shoulderblades as she rushes us through the twisting byways. She seems to know her way; either that, or she has me completely fooled.

Someone jumps into our path, a snarling, scruffy man with Sickness growths around his mouth. Jade stumbles to a halt and I walk into her, grabbing her hips to steady us both. The stranger begins shouting, gesticulating wildly, pointing at the air, at his forehead, almost growling as he motions towards me. Jade shakes her head, very definitely, confidently, and the man shouts again. I can see something in his eyes — the glint of madness, the desperation he must feel at the unfairness of things — and smell his degradation in the air; sweat, shit, aromas belonging nowhere near a comfortable, civilized human.

He is mad. He is ruined.

For a couple of seconds, I fear his madness will infect me. Indeed, this seems to be his motive, for he lunges past Jade, hands clawing for my throat.

She punches him in the gut. The movement is smooth and assured. He falls to his knees, gasping for breath and unconsciously adopting the same attitude as the hundreds of people at the harbor minutes before. He leans over until his forehead hits the dusty path, then his whole body shudders as he once again gasps in foul air. A smudge of muck sticks to his sweating forehead as he looks up at us.

"Do we go now?" I ask, but Jade disregards me completely. She whispers to him, indicating me with a derisive nod of her head. In the jumble of conspiratorial words, I hear String mentioned more than once. At each utterance of his name, the grubby man jerks as if given a minor electrical shock. I wonder how a name could invoke such a reaction.

Fear. Respect. From what I know, and what Della told me, these are the two things that String would revel in. One commands the other, both ways, and in the end it does not seem to matter whether he is good or bad.

Jade looks up at me and smiles her confident smile again. "We can go now."

"What did you say to him?" I ask as we pass the man, still kneeling in the dust, eyes apparently staring at some point a few meters behind my head as I pass him.

"We can go now, " Jade repeats, effectively denying me any explanation. I suddenly wonder whether I really want to follow her.

From the harbor — now several hundred yards away by my reckoning — comes a more sustained burst of rifle and machine-gun fire, and then a stunned silence. Jade seems unconcerned.

I wonder how much higher the pile on the harbor will be by morning.

iv

"In here," Jade says. I follow her through a narrow doorway and we feel our way along a twisting, oppressive tunnel. I hear the scampering of tiny feet, and wonder whether they are rats or lizards. When we emerge into the courtyard, I am struck by the sight of beautiful pots of flowers, hanging from every available space on the balconies above us. Then I realize that the flowers are painted onto roughly cut wood, which in turn is nailed to handrails and windowsills. The revelation depresses me enormously.

The buildings rise only three stories, but they seem to lean in close at the top as if the perspective is all wrong. I look up for a few more seconds, but still there is only a small, uneven rectangle of sunlight filtering down from above.

"Is String here?" I ask.

Jade laughs. "Don't flatter yourself, buddy. Did I say I'd decided to take you to him? Hmm? If I did, I've sure forgotten it." She opens a door in one corner of the courtyard and disappears into shadow. I follow and watch in embarrassment as she strips off her shirt and splashes her bare chest and shoulders from a bowl of water.

She glances at me, amused. "Surely you've seen a naked woman before."

I cannot help myself. I stare at her breasts and feel a stirring inside which has been absent for so long. She seems to be doing it on purpose, teasing me, but she excites me. She's arrogant, confident, brash, intriguing... invigorating.

Jade turns away and finishes washing as if I'm not there. She starts to unbuckle her trousers, but I have a sudden twinge in my chest and go out into the courtyard to sit down. A few minutes later she reappears, unperturbed by my sudden bashfulness. She is carrying a bottle of wine in one hand.

I have not tasted wine for months. The last time was that night at Della's, when she told me about String. The last time I saw her. "Wine," I mutter, unable to keep a hint of awe from my voice.

"Ohh, wine," Jade mimics, taking a swig from the bottle. I feel that we should be using glasses, but such luxuries died out during the early years of the Ruin. I gladly take the proffered bottle and drink from it myself. I do not bother to wipe the neck. Jade could have TGD, Numb-Skull, QS... anything. But I'm dying anyway. What's another fatal disease to such as me? It would be like sunburn to an Ebola victim.

"Where are we now?" I ask.

Jade throws me an amused little smile — condescension seems to be her forte — and takes back the bottle. "Globally, we're fucked."

"I meant where are we, here, now. Your place?" I cannot keep the frustration from my voice.

"No, not my place. I don't live anywhere, really. I stayed here for a while when I first came to Malakki, then after..." She trails off, looks away, as if she had almost said something revealing.

"After...?" I prompt. She takes another swig from the bottle and I stare at the new shirt, clinging to her still damp skin like an affectionate parasite. Her nipples are trying to break through. I think of the growths on my own chest, slowly killing me.

"After I went to String, I was going to say." She stares at me, but I sense that she is really looking at something far away.

It hits me all at once. I realize that ever since Jade had led me from the troubled harbor, I have been doing little but complaining and asking questions of a person I do not know. Her avoidance of many of my queries frustrates me, but I did not have to come with her, did I? She had offered her help like a latter-day Samaritan — a breed of person that seems to have all but vanished, swallowed into the gullet of mankind's folly — and I had willingly accepted. She had very probably saved me from a bullet.

With a painful flash of clarity, I imagine my own body on that grotesque heap on the harbor; my pale skin splitting under the sun, gases belching to join the overall smell of the dying town, eyes food for birds and rats and street kids. Diseased or not, the dead are all alike.

I had decided to live. This girl might just help me.

"String cured you?"

Jade gently places the bottle on the stone surround of the lifeless fountain and pops the buttons on her shirt. She slips it from her shoulders and holds it in the crooks of her elbows, her gaze resting calmly on my shocked face.

I stare at her breasts. They are small, pert, the nipples still pink and raised from her recent cold wash. Her skin is pale, but the smoother area between her breasts is paler still, almost white. I feel a twinge in my own diseased chest, then stoop forward to look more closely. All sexual thoughts — teasing my stomach, warming my groin — vanish when I see the scars.

"Do you think I'm attractive?" Jade asks, and there is a note of abandonment in her voice which brings an instant lump to my throat.

"I… yes, I do. But…." I point at her chest, realizing the absurdity of the situation for the first time — an attractive woman, revealing her breasts to me on this hot afternoon, sweat already glistening on the small mounds. And my reaction, to point and gulp my disbelief like someone seeing a dodo for the first time in centuries. But maybe that's what she wants.

"I wasn't a few weeks ago." Jade sighs, lifts her shirt back onto her shoulders and sits on the fountain wall. I see her mouth tense, her face harden, and she reaches for the bottle. But she cannot halt the tears. They are strange, these tears. They clean the grime from her face, but they seem dirty against her skin. Her mouth twists into an expression of rage, yet she seems to be laughing between sobs.

I step towards her and hesitantly hold out my hands. It's a long time since I've held a woman, and I feel clumsy with the gesture. She waves me away and takes another swig of wine, spitting it into the dust when a further spasm of laughter-crying wracks her body.

It takes a few minutes for her to calm down, a time in which I feel more helpless than I have in years. She cries, laughs, drinks some more, but her initial rejection of my offer of comfort has hurt me. I feel foolish, being upset by this denial from a stranger. But I really wanted to help.

"I'm sorry," she says. "I've had a rough few weeks."

"You could have fooled me." I say it quietly but it makes her giggle, and that makes me feel good. After a pause during which a group of old women shuffle through the courtyard, and Jade procures another bottle of wine, I ask the question. "Will you tell me?"

She waves at a fly, wine spilling down the front of her shirt like stale blood. Then she nods. "I've been going to help you since I saw you on the harbor. It's obvious why you're here. Do you have growths?"

I nod. "The Sickness."

"I had it too."

I nod again, glancing at her chest as if I can see the smooth scar through her shirt. "So I guessed."

"And, yes, String cured me." Her American accent has almost vanished. As if she is speaking for everyone.

"He's genuine, then? I'd heard so many stories that I'd begun to think he was a myth. A hope for the new age." I look down at my feet and cringe when a spasm of pain courses through me, as if the Sickness itself can sense a danger to its spread.

"There is no hope after the Ruin," Jade says, though not bitterly. "Not for mankind. There's personal hope, of course. There always will be as long as there's one person alive on the planet. Human nature, animal instinct, survival of the species, no matter what the odds. That's why String does what he does. But mankind was fucked the minute the Ruin set in."

"The crop blight?"

She shakes her head. "Long before that, I reckon. How about the fall of Communism?"

"Why that far back?"

She shrugs. "Just my personal opinion." She looks at the front of my shirt, a glint of concern marking her voice. "You need to see him soon, I think."

I look down and see blood seeping through the material, spreading like ink dots on blotting paper. One of the growths has split and started spewing my life out into the heat, and I have the disturbing feeling that our talk of cures and hope has encouraged it. My personification of the Sickness makes it no easier to accept.

"How does he do it?" I ask. It's the question I have been yearning a positive answer to since the Sickness first struck me.

I see something then, a shadow of an emotion pass across Jade's face. It is only brief, as if a bird had passed across the sun and cast its silhouette down to earth. If I knew her better, I could perhaps discern what that look meant, decipher from her tone of voice what sudden thought had made her blush and twist her hands in her lap.

She tilts her head slightly towards me, and I think of Della. "I don't know," she says. I nod, reach for the wine. Maybe later I can ask her again.

"Will you take me to him?"

"Yes." The answer is abrupt, definite.

"Thank you." I smile and feel a warm glow as my cheer is reflected on her face.

"But first," she says, jumping up, "we eat. Then, we drink some more wine. Then, we sleep."

"Can't we go now?"

She shakes her head, motioning for me to precede her into the building. She slams the door shut behind me and flicks on a light, revealing one large room with bed, fridge, curtained bathroom area and an old computer monitor with a picture of a goldfish glued across its redundant screen.

"Why?"

"It's nearly dark; one." She holds up a finger to count the point. "It's about twenty miles up into the hills; two." Another finger. "People are hungry; three. It's got pretty bad here. Last month they ate two Frenchmen."

I am unsure whether or not she is joking, but the implication of what she has said is so shocking that I can't bring myself to question it. Instead, I sit on the edge of the bed as she goes about preparing some food. She does so in silence, only occasionally humming some vanished tune under her breath. I watch her moving about the room; lithe, confident, her body echoing her surface personality. Underneath, I am sure, there is still a lost person.

We eat. Old salad and a sausage shared between us, but I am ravenous and the food tastes gorgeous. I wonder where I am going to sleep.

v

In the dark, memory fails me.

For a whole minute I believe that the hand caressing my stomach belongs to Della. I cannot bring myself to talk. I fear that this will taint our friendship with jealousy and resentment, but I want it so much, have *always* wanted it. Della must know that. I cannot lie to her, and even lying by omission seems impossible.

I have never mentioned my love for her.

I know I should turn away, but it feels so good. Since the Sickness struck two years ago I have chosen to distance myself from sex with women, taking matters into my own hand. I acted before I was ever turned down, unable to bear the humiliation, preferring voluntary abstinence to enforced sexual solitude.

I sit up, turn away.

"Oh please," a voice whispers, fighting through tears which I can just see as floating, glinting diamonds in the dark. "Oh please, don't reject me. It's been years, so many years. Feel!" A hand grasps my wrist and I remember then where I am, whom I am with. Jade forces my hand to her chest and drags my palm across the smooth scar tissue between her breasts. It is cool, like glass.

"Gone now, it's all gone now." I cannot ally the voice with the feisty, arrogant woman I have known for only several hours. Tears do not suit her. Her beseeching words make me blush in the dark.

"What about me?" Old fears shrink my penis in her hand, sending a flush of heat through my diseased chest. I twist the sheets beneath me, trying to hold back the tears. I feel something touch me, stroke the growths, and I cringe back.

"Okay, it's okay," Jade sooths. "Wait." Her weight leaves the bed and then there is light. She is standing by the door, hand on the light cord, proud and beautiful in her nakedness. The pale white patch on her chest is almost attractive, set against the light tan she has picked up in the last few weeks. She catches my eye, then looks unselfconsciously down my body, eyes resting on my groin and causing a new stirring there.

"Nobody has loved me for years," she says. She is crying again, but her voice is strong and I wonder whether they are really tears of anguish anymore. She comes back to the bed and sinks her head into my lap.

I close my eyes and think of Della. And my overwhelming emotion is a sense of relief that it is Jade here, and not her.

Jade is wild. Our lovemaking is fast and furious, passion-filled and almost violent in its intensity. By the end we are both crying. She remains sitting astride me, wiping tears from my cheeks, and I kiss her salty eyes and whisper that she is beautiful.

"How could you, when...?" I ask, half-pointing to my chest with unwilling fingers.

"You'll be beautiful too, soon," she says. Nobody has ever called me beautiful before. I like it.

In the morning we wake late. Passion seems to have fled with the dark, and although we smile and kiss it feels more as friends.

vi

"String is in the hills." Jade is tightening the straps on her rucksack, checking the lid is screwed onto her water bottle, rubbing sun cream onto her bare legs and arms. She hands me the bottle and I smear my balding scalp with cream.

"How will we get there? Last night you said twenty miles. That's a long way to walk, and I'm not so strong lately."

"Maybe we can hitch a ride with a Lord Ship," she smiles. "Come on."

It is even hotter than the previous day, and before long sweat has pasted my shirt to my sickly body and soaked through to darken the material. I can feel the sun working on my arms and trying to find a way through the cream, and I guess that I'll end up getting horribly burnt whatever measures I take to prevent it.

Jade has changed. She's still the no-nonsense girl I had met the previous day, but she seems somehow more relaxed in my company. There is still an undefined tension, however, a distance that I cannot help but feel sad at.

After last night, I would have hoped for more.

Part Two
The Trappings of the Flesh
i

"Faith is as personal and as private as a thing can be," Della once told me. "If you understand someone's faith, you know their soul. But most people aren't very comfortable with the idea of personal faith. Sometimes, it's just too much effort, too challenging. They have to ascribe to some preordained vision of things, where there are books and preachers and teachers to lead them through the minefield of knowledge. Prophesies tell them what they need to know, words written millennia ago by some holy man drunk on monastery wine and eager to bury his cock in the young girl from the local village. Then they wonder why their faith lets them down so much, and causes so many wars and death and hatred. Simple reason — it's not their faith. It's a ready-made idea of faith. Dehumanized. Just add belief."

It was a hot summer's day, only a couple of years before the Ruin really took hold and threw people back two hundred years into anarchy and poverty. Della sat in a garden chair, reaching over every now and then to snatch a sweet from the table next to her. I was lying on the lawn, mindful of insects and ants, feeling the sun cook my exposed scalp but not really caring. The sunburn would be a brand of the day, a reminder of what Della was telling me. She was a wise woman, and I knew nothing. I loved her.

"You have faith? " she asked. The question surprised me, but I felt I recovered well.

"Of course."

"Good." She said no more. I was afraid that she would ask me where my faith was set. She'd know if I lied, she'd read me like a large-print book held under a magnifying glass. Because in truth, my faith was based solely in her. I wondered whether she really ever knew that.

"You may need it one day."

She did not look at me. She stared into the eye-blue sky, a strange smile on her face. A smile I did not like. She carefully took another sweet from the table without looking at what she was doing. She could just as easily have snatched up a bug.

"Why?" I said, finally.

She glanced down at me, then nodded up at the sky as if the fluffy white clouds could explain everything. "Bad days coming."

Fuck, was she right.

ii

Jade leads me through the warren of alleys and side streets until we emerge onto a main thoroughfare. The rucksack already feels heavy against my shoulders, pressing against my back and slipping my shirt back and forth across damp skin. The cream I had applied is already redundant, and I feel as though my skull is growing ready to split the skin from my head. There's no real protection any more other than staying out of the sun altogether, and skin cancer is the least of my concerns.

The streets are surprisingly quiet, and the few people there are seem to be milling aimlessly rather than actually going places. I see several people who are obviously not Greek. None of them appear sane. They scrabble in the dust for dog-ends, fighting over a few flakes of rough tobacco. Growths have turned their bodies into grotesque parodies of people, walking warts that gibber and leak from various orifices, both natural and disease-given.

I catch up with Jade and walk by her side, her presence giving me a comfortable sense of safety. She's seen all this before, she knows what to expect; she can handle herself.

I wonder whether these people came to be cured.

"They're all wasters," Jade says in answer to my thoughts. The expression reminds me of the uniformed man who had helped me from the boat, the way he had spoken of the piled corpses. "Some of them were given the opportunity, apparently, but they wasted it. Now, they're down to this. They even worship the Lord Ships." She seemed to have slipped into her own personal conversation, excluding me even before I replied. "Strange how we regress so easily."

"But they must know about the Lord Ships?" I say, confusion twisting my voice into a whine.

"Hmm?" Jade looks at me as if she'd forgotten I was there, and a brief pang of resentment stabs at my chest. She wasn't like this last night, not when she was riding me, sweating her lust over me. "Oh, yeah, they know," she says. "That's what I mean. They know the Lord Ships are unmanned; automatons, pilots dead or gone. But they've been here for a while, and I suppose in their state the fears of the locals drive their certainties back out."

We pass a group of young men and women who regard us with a mixture of anger and fear. I can understand what they have to be angry with — aliens in their country, invaders in a world shrinking back to almost tribal roots — but what do they fear?

"Why don't the locals know about the Lord Ships?" I ask.

"Oh, they do. They just choose not to believe it."

I can scarcely credit this myself. The fact that a civilized people can let themselves be controlled by ghosts from the past, willingly prostrating themselves at the feet of dead gods, knowing all the time that their actions are a sham. I ask Jade why this is so. I do not like the answer I receive.

"God is dead," she says. "That's what anyone here will tell you if you ask them. Do you know what these people have been through since the Ruin? Their population was halved by CJD-two; the Turks decided to nuke the north of the island for the hell of it; and at the end, when it all went totally fucking haywire, the Lord Ships condemned them as heathens and witches. Sentenced to death. It was only the fall of the Lord Ships that saved them."

"And now they worship them all the more since they're dead and gone?"

"As I said," Jade confirmed through a sardonic smile, "God is dead. He let them be dragged through hell, now they hate Him for it."

"Do you believe he's still there?" I ask. I surprise myself with my frankness about a subject I feel so confused and cynical about. I have never believed in God. I have my own faith.

"I have my own faith," Jade says quietly.

I think of Della, smile, wonder where she is now, what she's doing. Sitting back and sharing her infinite wisdom with some other sucker, no doubt. A pang of jealousy tickles my insides, but I force it out and tell myself that Della would hate me for it.

"Here we are." Jade has stopped in front of what was obviously once an affluent hotel. Now, it seems exclusively to house street-women between the ages of fifteen and fifty. A dozen of them are sitting in broken chairs on the cracked patio and they appraise me, laughing and jeering, as I step behind Jade. My face colors, but I secretly enjoy the attention. Last night has kick-started my libido.

Jade talks to the women in Greek and waves profuse thanks as she backs away from the hotel. I back away with her, wondering whether it's a ritual of sorts or simple politeness, but the women are laughing again. A dog runs by and nearly trips me up. It's a mangy mutt, but seems well fed. I remember the pile of corpses along the harbor and wonder what it's been feeding on, and any sense of humor quickly flees. The women seem to sense this and stop laughing.

"Follow me," Jade says, somewhat impatiently.

"Where?"

"Bikes." She strides around the corner of the hotel.

In what used to be the swimming pool there are at least a hundred bicycles of all shapes and sizes, ranging from a rusty kiddie's tricycle, to a three-wheeled stainless steel monster that would have set me back a month's salary in the days before the Ruin. I wonder what the owner would want for it now. The bikes fill the pool, a tatty metallic pond of tortured frames, tired tires and accusing spokes. Dust has blown down from the depleted hillsides and formed drifts at the edges of the pool, like frozen waves trying to reclaim it. I see the remains of what I'm sure is a dead dog, buried beneath the network of wheels, handles and pedals. I try to imagine its panic as it realized that the strange, surreal landscape it had slunk into had effectively trapped it. It must have been cooked to death by the relentless sun.

"You Yankee?" says a huge man sitting under an awning.

"No, English," Jade replies instantly. I've already been here long enough to know that there must be a reason for her denying her birth.

"Good. I hate Yankee. Fuckin' killing bastards." Jade nods and smiles, and this seems to secure her in the big man's favor.

"We'd like a couple of bikes, if you have any to spare," she says, unfazed by his vicious outburst.

He laughs, a sound that would have seemed ridiculously over-played had it not been for the machine pistol dangling from his belt. As he bellows his mirth at the sky, I take the opportunity to size him up. He's not just big, he's massive, at least twenty-five stone, all of it sweaty and sickly and grey. He's wearing a pair of Bermuda shorts which are grotesquely too small, cutting into his flesh and stretching out in places like the skin on an overcooked sausage. With each shudder of his body, I fear they will burst. His bare chest is studded with black, oozing growths. I'm amazed at how hearty he seems.

"You want bikes? I have bikes!" He waves his hand at the pool, as if drawing our attention to a fine display of quality antiques. In a way, I think to myself, they are. "But the final question as always, lady: Price?"

"I've got your price," she says, heaving her rucksack from her shoulders. Her loose shirt flaps open and I catch a glimpse of her breasts swinging freely as she bends down. I suddenly fear what this fat man's price will be, and wonder how close I would get before he could unclip the gun from his belt.

"I'll take the shiny trike and the hefty mountain bike," Jade says, pulling a small package from the backpack.

"Hmm, big spending if you want those, little lady," Fat Man says. I hear something I don't like in his voice — it is quieter, more serious — and tense as he stretches his neck in an effort to see down Jade's top. The Sickness picks a bad time to announce its presence to me, jabbing at my chest with white-hot fingertips of pain. I groan and swoon, but pinch a twist of skin on my leg to prevent myself from fainting.

Jade glances back at me and moves off towards Fat Man. She whispers something to him, actually standing on tiptoe so that she can speak into his ear, one hand resting on his pendulous stom-ach. I can barely imagine how she could give him a better chance to grab at her, but he does not. Instead, the grimness of his face falls away under the emergence of an expression so childlike and angelic that I almost laugh out loud.

Jade turns, looks at me, nods towards the pool of bikes. I wonder what the hell she has shown him. I sidle sideways and lean across the heap of metal, grabbing the handlebars of the stainless steel trike and tugging hard.

Within minutes we are away, the Fat Man calling cheerfully after us and telling us to watch out for the fuckin' murdering Yankee.

Jade takes the mountain bike, I'm on the trike. I'm surprised to find it well oiled and maintained, the brakes old but well-adjusted, saddle soft and pliable.

"Two questions," I start, but both are obvious. She eases back until she is pedalling alongside me. We are traveling two abreast along the main road, but there is no motor traffic.

"He hates Americans because the rest of the world does," she says. "We're blamed for it all. The wars. The starvation. The Ruin." She's silent for a moment, and I'm about to ask my second question when she continues. "He should visit the States sometime, see what's left of it." She pedals harder and slips down a gear, motoring on ahead. Her move offers me a pleasing view of her rump, flexing as her legs pump her along the degenerating tarmac.

"Second question," she says, "is what did I give him? Right?" She glances back over her shoulder and I nod. "None of your fucking business." I try to hear a joke in her voice, but there is none. Or if there is, she can hide it well.

We pedal for an hour in silence, Jade leading, me following comfortably on the trike. More than once I think of asking her whether she wants to swap, but my body is stiffening and burning as the infected blood from the growths on my chest surges once more into my veins. One day, a surge like this will kill me. One day soon — perhaps today, riding this bike, my feet describing thousands of circles an hour — black blood will leak from a growth and block an artery, popping a dozen blood vessels at a time until I die. If I'm lucky, it may only take a minute or two.

On the outskirts of the town we pass through the ribbon of huts and tents which go to make up the camps for the un-homed. Eyes follow us on our way, but there is little real interest there. Even the children I see appear old, apathetic and grim instead of lively and playful. We pass a body at the side of the road. A sick fascination forces me to slow down so that I can properly see the dog chewing on its open stomach. There are lizards here, too, darting in and out of the empty eye-sockets to dine on the delicate morsels within.

We pass by. Jade seems unconcerned, but I cannot help but stare out over the sea of torn tents and makeshift hovels. There are families of eight living in one tent; great open ditches full of shit and flies and the discarded bodies of the dead; queues to gather water from a meager stream, the liquid resembling diseased effluent rather than water. Smells assault us physically, the stench clenching my stomach and throat in its acidic grip. But throughout the ten minutes it takes us to pass through the shantytown, Jade does not slow down once. She does not glance to either side. She does not seem to care.

She has seen it all before.

As we leave Malakki Town and head into the surrounding hills, there is a change. I can feel it in the air, a potential of something that I cannot describe or adequately read. Jade senses it too, and she keeps glancing back at me as if afraid I have begun to lag behind. In truth, I feel as energetic and excited as I have for months, a power pumping through my muscles which has more to do with my sense of freedom than the potential cure I am traveling towards.

The new aura of well-being makes me think about the night before: the passion we had for each other, as if love were at a dearth.

There is a gunshot. Jade's bike swerves, then leaves the road, flipping over into the dry ditch. I hear a scream, and for a terrible few seconds I cannot tell whether it is Jade's voice, or my own. Then more gunshots, breaking the air apart like the answer to a silent question.

iii

The hillside is smooth, stripped bare of plant life, topsoil scoured away by the biting winds. Sound travels further here. The gunfire is coming from around a bend in the road ahead. Its executors, and executed, are hidden from sight by an old stone wall.

Jade curses bitterly, trying to untangle her legs from the wreckage of the bicycle. I notice that she is keeping her head down almost without thinking about it, and I wonder how many shootouts she's been witness to. I crawl along the dry ditch, leaving the trike behind, hands reaching out to drag the bike away from her legs. I try to tell her to keep still, but the gunfire has increased to a screaming crescendo and she can only frown at my words.

Eventually, through a combination of her kicking and me pulling, she extracts her legs from the twisted bike. There is a raw gravel burn on her left knee, blood already seeping from a hundred pinpricks in the skin and merging into angry red rivulets. She sucks her palm, spitting out black pellets of stone, sucking again, spitting. I feel queasy watching her, and then the Sickness comes along and sends me into a faint.

The gunshots fade away — either the shooting has finished, or I'm really losing it. I slump in the ditch, Jade staring at me past the splayed fingers of her right hand, palm pressed to her mouth. The last image I see is Jade spitting a mouthful of blood and gravel into the air, and the sun hiding behind clouds like the ghost of an airship.

iv

"About time," the voice says. I open my eyes and grimace as the sun dazzles me. I feel heat on my front, and realize instantly that my shirt has been removed. The sun is slowly cooking the growths on my chest, turning them an angry red as if embarrassed at their nakedness.

"How long...?" is all I can manage.

"Half an hour," Jade says, leaning into view. She tips a water bottle over my face and then splashes more across my body. I flinch, but then sigh with pleasure.

Groggily, I sit up. I realize that the hillside is silent, just as I see the crimson mess of Jade's hand holding the bottle. "Oh Christ, your hand." I reach out, but she withdraws.

"It's all right! Bloody, that's all, looks worse than it is."

She has washed her leg and is wearing what looks like her knickers as an improvised bandage. She looks away from me, as if ashamed of her wounds, and wraps a strip of cloth from her shirt around her hand. It instantly soaks red. She cringes, flexes her hands and draws in an uncomfortable breath.

"How're you feeling?" she asks.

Memory suddenly jerks me upright, instils me with a sense of urgency. "Where are the guns? Who was shooting?"

"Don't worry, while you were doing your Rip Van Winkle they got into a truck and drove off."

"Did they see us?"

"If they had you wouldn't have woken up."

I try to stand, sway, sit down again. "Who were they shooting?"

Jade looks up the gentle hillside, trying to see past the crumbling wall. "Once we get moving again we'll find out."

"So many guns...." I say, trailing off, leaving the obvious unsaid. So many guns, how many people?

We haul the tricycle from the ditch, brushing off the accumulated rubbish of decades. Apart from a twisted spoke or two the machine is undamaged, but that's more than can be said for Jade's bike. It's ruined, all pointing spokes and bent frame, the saddle deformed almost ninety degree out of true. The front wheel is buckled beyond repair, the rear tire flat and shredded. I realize how lucky Jade had been. Torn hand and slashed leg, true; but if the ground had been as unkind to her as it had to her bike, we'd be looking at more than a bit of leaking blood right now.

"You were lucky," I say.

She nods. "Come on, we'd better get a move on."

"Jade."

"What?"

"Why are you so pissed with me?"

She stares at me. I realize how old she looks under the superficial attractiveness, how her eyes never really laugh but bear whatever terrible things she has seen like a brand. I wonder how I would feel if I was cured of the Sickness; I like to think it would give me a new-found energy, a reason to be grateful, a duty to thank life every single day. I know Della would want it like that.

"I'm not pissed at you, Gabe. Oh Christ, it's something you'll know soon enough."

Her words scare me more than I'd like to admit, burrow their way into my thoughts like insubstantial maggots. "What are you leading me to?" I ask, for the first time. Until now, I'd always trusted her implicitly. A stupid reaction for someone I didn't know, maybe, but there had really been no reason to think otherwise. And she seems to know what she is doing, she's streetwise and confident, knows things, like how to get the bikes and how to get me to String. But just what the hell had I really gotten myself into?

"I'm leading you to a man called String. He's a bit of a witch doctor, I suppose you'd say." She punctuates each point with a nod of the head, as if explaining to me the rules of a game instead of the particulars of our current situation. "String can cure people of the Sickness — he cured me," she continues, tapping her chest. "But on the way to where String is, you're likely to see some nasty things. That's just the nature of things — the way things have to be. It doesn't really matter, sometimes it's just got to happen. But the things you see might not be nice. Like what's around that corner."

She waves a hand over her head, then turns and gazes in the direction she indicated, giving me her back to stare at as she continues. "I've been this way once before, remember. I've seen these things already, I've experienced them. The Ruin's a right fucker, but just when you think you've seen everything bad it's got to throw at you, there's something else. But some bad things are good as well." She turns back, and her haunted expression sends a shiver down my spine. "Remember that. There are sayings: Cruel to be kind; Good comes from evil." She bends and sighs as she eases her rucksack onto her shoulders. "I'm not pissed at you. I'm just not looking forward to seeing all the bad stuff again."

"What bad stuff?" Her words have planted the fear of damnation in me, sent an arrow of terror streaking through my veins and pincering my heart between its dozens of heads. "What am I going to see?"

Jade nods at the tricycle, indicating that I should travel on it, then walks on ahead. "Best see for yourself. Up here. Around the corner."

At first, I think it's a stagnant pond. There is a light steam rising from it, though the surface appears uneven and scattered with protruding growths of fungi. Then, I realize what I am really seeing. In a dip in the ground — perhaps where water had once gathered naturally, before the Ruin decimated the atmosphere of the planet — there is a lake of twitching bodies. The movement I had mistaken as ripples on the surface of the water is their dying shivers, translating through the hundreds of corpses as if by electric shock. There *is* a pool, of sorts; the bodies lay in a quagmire of blackened, soupy mud, dust having sucked up the spilled blood and spread under the bodies. The steam rises, like nebulous spirits making their final journey.

But surely there can be no peace here. Not where for every five bodies that lay still there is one still alive, squirming silently in the white-hot agony of approaching death. Not here, where the stark white dead eye of a child stares from an otherwise shattered face. No peace here, where the rich stench of death and dying is a meaty tang in the hot air.

I stop pedalling and the trike drifts to a tired pause in the middle of the road. I cannot begin to estimate the number of bodies. Shock has frozen my mind, the sheer unexpectedness of this sight paralyzing my thoughts.

In the city, yes, I had seen the great mound of corpses along the quay. But there, perversely, it had not seemed obtrusive. Maybe it was the casual way that people had regarded the bodies, barely looking at them, treating them more as a landmark than an object of pity or disgust. In the city, I had been prepared for anything. The Ruin had changed so much and the face of humanity had changed with it, often blending back into ages past like an ill child, retarding in years.

But here, in the country, on a hillside that had once been beautiful, and could be again, the sight is almost surreal with contradictions. The deep blue of the sky, decorated with an occasional cloud cheerful in its fluffiness; and the bloody red mess of open meat, steaming insides, pulsing wounds.

I begin to cry. I cannot help myself and Jade, in her defence, moves away and sits under a tree stripped of life years ago. The tears are warm and heavy in the approaching furnace of midday, streaking the dust from my face and falling like hot blood onto my shirt. They merge with sweat and the leakings from my growths, to form a liquid testament to my wretchedness.

I sit that way for several minutes, willing the tears to stay because they blur my vision and camouflage, however falsely, the sight before me. Then Jade walks over to me and places a hand on my shoulder.

"I don't understand," I say, realizing the stupidity of the statement. Who could possibly claim to understand the insanity of this moment?

But Jade seems to know.

"There are lots of reasons," she says. "Population control, for one. At least half of those you see are children. The others are men and women of a... breeding age. No old people. No ill people."

"But it's just so misguided. So *wrong*. How can anyone think this can help?"

Jade is silent for a moment. She seems to be staring over the bodies, perhaps glimpsing some vague future that lies beyond their steaming deaths, but nearer than we think.

"But it does work," she says, pained. "More food, more medicine, more water. Times have changed since the Ruin, you know."

"I never dreamed...." I cannot finish. I can barely comprehend the terrible truth of what I have seen. On the harbor, the bodies... I suppose I thought that they had died in some natural, acceptable way, and merely been stored or placed there. The gunshots I heard, the shouts, and the riots I had placed in a mental file marked "Disregard." My own tenuous hold on reality, perverted by the Ruin, could never stoop as low as this, and so my mind precluded the possibilities that had been laid out so obviously for me to see.

"I don't believe it," I say. I have stopped crying, but the anguish is even deeper now that the tears have dried. "It's just horrible."

"I'm sorry," Jade says suddenly, "I should have warned you."

I smile up at her where she stands next to the tricycle, reach for her uninjured hand and feel a warm rush of relief when she returns the pressure of my grasp. That means a lot. It helps.

We turn from the terrible sight and I try to crowd the hateful images from my mind. But though I avert my eyes, my senses will not let me forget. I can still smell the unmistakable stink of death. I can almost *taste* it in the air. Either that, or the bitterness of my own impotence is polluting my body as well as my mind. And even as I cycle away, Jade walking beside me, I can hear the sounds from the pool of dead people. The sounds of dying, and corpses deflating. The sounds of the Ruin.

"What will happen to them?" I ask.

"They'll be put to use," Jade says quietly. "Things are too bad now to waste anything."

I cannot ask what she means. I don't wish to know.

v

We travel a further three miles that day, taking it in turns on the tricycle, before exhaustion claims us. I wait by the side of the road while Jade wanders off to find somewhere to camp, trying to find some shade under a shirt stretched across the handlebars. She is gone for nearly half an hour and I am becoming worried, but this does not stop me from falling asleep. When I wake up she is standing there, looking down at me, a strange expression on her face. Yet again I don't know whether to be frightened or excited by this unusual, confident, aggressive woman.

We wheel the trike most of the way, but for the last few hundred paces we have to virtually carry it up the steep gradient. By the time we reach the small plateau she has chosen for our camp we are both exhausted, and sleep claims us before we can erect the shelter.

I wake up from a dream of cool water, innocent nakedness beside a waterfall, greenery and fruit growing all about. Jade is rubbing cream into my bare legs where the sun has found its way through the cotton of my trousers, which I see lying in a heap beside me. Before I am fully awake I see that curious expression in her eyes once more and her hands move quickly up to my groin.

Whatever stresses had been tempering Jade's attitude to me earlier that day seem to have evaporated with the sun. Perhaps it was the tension of knowing what was to come, but feeling unable to tell me beforehand. Maybe the fear that we could have fallen into trouble leaving Malakki Town had distanced her from me; after all, she has been this way before. She is doing all this now as nothing more than a favor for me. Whatever the cause, she seems as happy now as she was last night.

The memories of the day, the trials of the journey thus far, the twinges from my chest cause me to remain limp, even as I watch Jade strip. But she works on me with her hand, her mouth, and soon we are making love under the astonished sky.

We drift towards sleep around midnight. I see a shooting star, but Jade says it is just another falling satellite.

Part Three
The Flight of Birds
i

"I'm older than you think," Della said to me. "It's as if losing my legs provided less of me to age; time can't find me, sometimes, because I'm not whole, I'm a smaller target than most. I'm older than you think."

I almost asked how old, but in reality I did not want to know. Her age was just another enigma which identified her, an unknown that made her even more mysterious and exotic in my eyes. She scratched her stumps as I looked around the overgrown garden. I tried to appear blasé but actually felt so nervous in her presence that I could faint. She was not ashamed of her terrible wounds — seemed to display them as a badge of worldliness, sometimes — but still I hated them. It was extremely disorientating looking at the stumps of legs that should continue on down to the floor. Instead, they were cut short at the edge of the wheelchair. Sometimes, when Della scratched them all night, she drew blood. I tried to get her talking.

"So what happens now?"

It was the start of the Ruin. The Sickness was still to come, lying in wait in some distant African cave like the ghost of a wronged nation ready to exact a chilling, relentless revenge. The first nukes had fallen in the Middle East, and money markets across the globe had crashed the previous month. Britain was already threatening a worldwide ban on trade, import or export. In some areas of the country, martial law had been declared. It was rumored that people were being shot. In London, the army was hanging looters they caught pillaging the pickings of the Numb-Skull plague in the streets; their bloated bodies became home to fattened, less homely pigeons than those that adorned Nelson's column.

Della shrugged, rolled her eyes skyward. "Well, you heard

them, kiddo, telling everyone how good it would be. The Lord Ships are mighty fine and high, ready, they say, to restore to us all that we've lost over the last few years: justice; law; peace; even food. In the process, where do you think the Lords live? What do you reckon they eat?"

"I don't know."

"Somewhere nicer and something better than you, that's where and what." She flinched as her nail caught a fold of skin and opened a cut. A tear of blood formed on the stump and I watched, fascinated, as it grew, swelled and then dropped like a folded petal to the ground. When I looked up, I saw that Della had been watching me watching her.

"But don't you think it'll all work out for us?" I asked, naïve and blindly trusting. "They say it's the answer. 'Government from afar,' they say."

"I think the Lord Ships will last a long time," she mused. She sat back in her chair and stopped worrying her absent legs. I knew the signs — she was warming to the subject, not only because she loved sharing her wisdom with me, but also because it meant she did not hurt herself. At least, for a time.

"At the end of that long time," she continued, "there're going to be a lot less people in the world. I think the Lords'll rule adequately, considering, but they'll also reap any rewards of their labors before anyone else even knows they're there. The worst thing..." She trailed off. This was something that Della never did, she had an angle on everything, an opinion for anyone who would listen. She stared up at the moon where it was emerging from the azure blue of a summer sky. I'm sure that for those few moments she was alone, and she had forgotten how different life had become.

"What's the worst thing, Della?" I asked. Each time we spoke, I remembered her every word, repeated each word to myself like a mantra as I drifted off to sleep. They were precious to me, in a way priceless. Some people — a few — still read the Bible. My bible was the lake of words I remembered from Della.

"The worst thing, kiddo, is that they're going to be gods."

Della sent me away then, complaining about her stumps, saying her legs were aching and she could only ever put the ghosts to sleep when she was alone. I knew what she meant, but sometimes I lay awake at night, imagining a pair of discorporated limbs stumbling unconnected down a straight, dusty road.

I left Della to her thoughts, knowing that I would benefit from them the next time we met. Della was a treasure.

ii

I wake in the night and hear the distant sounds of engines, protesting as if hauling a huge weight up a steep slope. Disembodied lights climb the darkness in the distance, pause for a while and then continue on their journey. Jade does not hear them, or if she does she pays no attention.

I think of the massacre, of the bodies cooling in the night, providing food for whatever wild creatures remained. I huddle closer to Jade, but sleep eludes me. The darkness is haunted by the silvery twinkle of stars, their brightness distracting and surprising at this altitude. Sometime in the night, just before the darkness flees and there is a brief lull in nature to greet the dawn, I hear a faint sound from the south. A wailing, but possessed of many voices; a calling, like the tortured grind of metal on stone. I sit up and listen harder, but then the birds start singing and their song drowns the noise. I am glad.

When Jade wakes up I tell her, but she merely shrugs and smiles. "Another Lord Ship over the town."

"But I didn't hear it coming."

"Sometimes they just drift in from over the sea, then out again. Sometimes, they're as consistent as the tides."

I shake my head. "But they're not manned anymore. The Lords died, or fled."

Jade shrugs. When she has no answer, she shrugs.

She begins to prepare breakfast — a thick, stodgy gruel made from a paste in her bag and powdered milk, a few drops of water added to lighten the load on our stomachs. She looks tired, as if she was the one kept awake by the night, not me.

"I heard engines last night," I say, watching for a reaction. She raises her eyebrows, but she does not look at me. I wonder whether she is beginning to regret her offer of help. I wonder how sane she can really be.

Jade does not speak for the next hour. We eat and wipe our bowls clean, then roll up the sleeping packs ready for transport. I sit for a few minutes on a large rock overlooking the valley we had traveled up the previous day. The Sickness is not too bad today, the pain bearable, the growths only leaking small amounts into my already stained and caked shirt. From my observation point I cannot make out the gully where the bodies lay, nor the dried streambed, not even the wall that had hidden the terrible slaughter from our view. On the horizon, marked more by its haze of smoke than the actual outline of buildings, lies Malakki

Town

Jade taps me on the shoulder and informs me that we should be going. I smile, but she is as unreceptive as before. I begin to fear that she is like this because, just as yesterday morning, there are things to be seen today that she cannot bring herself to talk of. The thought stretches the skin over my scalp with terror, but I cannot bring myself to ask. I try to remember our sex from the night before, but it seems like the memory of another person's story, told long ago.

iii

Around midday I see the first of the birds. It is high up, almost out of sight in the glare of the callous sun. It is circling in a way that induces a vague feeling of disquiet; drifting, around and around, wings steady.

"Look up there," I say. Jade stops and follows my gaze.

"Nearly there," she says.

I feel a jolt which seems to trigger a rush of blood from my chest. I slump on the saddle, slip sideways onto the hot dust of the road. A groan escapes me as the lightheadedness dulls my vision.

"String?" I manage to whisper through the haze of pain.

"Just over that brow," Jade replies. I try to hear pity in her voice, but even my own yearnings cannot paint indifference a different shade. "Come on."

She grabs under my armpits and heaves me back into the trike's saddle. I have no strength to pedal, so she has to push me the final stretch to the top of the small hill. As we reach the summit and look down into the shallow valley beyond, I am dazzled by something in the distance. At first I think it is the sun reflecting from a body of water, and my heart leaps into my chest. Water! A wash! A bath, even! Then, while my eyes adjust to the glare and detail rushes in, I realize how wrong I am.

What I do see is far more fantastic than a deep lake in an area stricken with drought.

There is a small village in the valley. The collection of tents and ramshackle huts seems discordant with my preconceived image of String and his people, but the closer I look the more I can detect a design in the apparent chaos of the scene. The whole layout of the place is pleasing to the eye — not only providing color in a bland land blasted by winds and heat, but also offering a geometry that seems to comfort with its very order.

Around the village is a moat. The sun reflects from something bright, hard edged, many angled. Jade turns to me and truly smiles for just about the first time that day.

"String's lake of glass," she says. I want to ask more, but suddenly feel the urge to find out for myself.

We start down the hillside and are soon approached by two guards. They are carrying guns, ugly squat black cylinders that could spit hundreds of rounds per second. They are both tall, muscular, fit-looking, their skin a healthy tan, clothes neat and presentable. They seem to be wearing what approaches a uniform: thin cotton trousers; khaki shirts buttoned at the wrists and neck to protect from the sun; peaked caps to keep the glare out of their eyes. They are cautious but confident as they stop a dozen steps in front of us and casually place hands on their guns. They regard us with what I can only describe as pity, and I am jolted from the grey haze that pain still holds across my senses.

Pity is the last thing I expect.

"You're Tiarnan, right?" Jade says. The guard on the right tenses, then nods. He steps forward, swinging his gun to bear evenly upon us.

A sense of unease itches at me, tensing my muscles and stiffening my neck. No one knows we're here, I think. No one will miss us. There are a thousand bodies back down the road, what would two more be added to it? More food for the dogs? More human detritus to leak slowly back into the soil, replacing the goodness we've bled from the planet for centuries? I wonder if Della will miss me. I wonder if she ever expected to see me again, once I left that final time. I had the suspicion then — and it still niggles now, even though I've come so far — that she sent me here to give me hope in my final days. She never really believed in what she told me; she did not have any real faith in her words of comfort.

"Jade Kowski?" The guard's expression does not change but there is familiarity in his voice. His gun swings slightly until it's pointing directly at me.

"Hi, Tiarnan. Who's your buddy?"

Tiarnan waves a hand at the other guard. "Oh, that's Wade." He lowers his gun — but Wade, I notice, does not follow suit — and approaches Jade. "What the fuck are you doing back here, girl?" He claps her on the shoulder and ruffles her hair with fatherly affection, though I guess Tiarnan to be younger than Jade by at least half a decade: straggly beard, kid's smile in a face already aged by the sun and the Ruin.

"Brought a friend." Jade nods down at me where I slump weakly on the trike. "String still entertaining?"

Tiarnan shrugs. "When people make it here. Still pretty exclusive, though, y'know?" He looks me over, removing his dusty sunglasses and squinting in the sudden brightness. At first I feel like an exhibit in a museum of dying people, but then I detect the same pity in his eyes that I saw earlier. He glances at my shirt, muddied by the fluids leaking from me. He sees Jade's bandaged hand, notices the bright redness of the scrape on her leg set against the more subtle pink of sunburn.

"Hell, Jade, you sure ain't looking after yourself." He looks across at his companion and some secret signal lowers his gun. "Wade, do me a favor, push our friend here down to the moat. Jade, why not walk with me? You can tell me why you're still in this Godforsaken country after all String did for you."

"You're still here," she says, but Tiarnan laughs and starts off towards the glittering moat.

Wade pushes the Trike — I could have pedalled, but I am tired and in pain and not about to pass up the opportunity of a free ride. When we reach the moat I can see what it really is. I wonder at the work that went into making it; the weeks of traveling to and from towns and deserted villages to collect all the materials; the dedication; the planning. The idea itself is sheer brilliance.

The moat is at least twenty meters across, composed entirely of broken glass. Bottles, windowpanes, bowls, mirrors, windscreens, all smashed down into a sea of sharp, deadly blades. The sun glares from its multifaceted surface and throws up a haze of light, and it is all I can do to keep my eyes open. It is effective as a thick fog at concealing what lies beyond.

I wonder how we will cross, but then I hear the musical crunching of glass cracking and shattering. Before I have a chance to see what is happening, Wade is lifting me from the trike and sitting me gently on a large, flat-bedded vehicle that has crawled across from the other side. Wade and Tiarnan help the other two men on the strange boat as they haul on a rope, dragging it across to the inside of the moat.

"Nearly there," Jade says, bending down over me and blocking out the sun. "You okay?" As if the question gives my body a chance to answer, pain shouts and I fade out. The sun recedes, voices float away, and I fall unconscious to the grinding sound of breaking glass.

iv

"How are you feeling?"

I open my eyes. "Like I'm going to die." It's dusk or I'm indoors. Whichever, the torturous sunlight has abated.

"Well, I'll see what I can do about that." The voice is gentle, low, understated. But there is a power there, a certainty of control, a glaring confidence. Even before I see who has spoken, I know I am talking to String.

I turn my head and there he is, sitting calmly beside my bed, Jade standing behind him and Tiarnan next to her. String is a surprisingly small man — for some reason I had been imagining him huge and powerful — and another surprise is that he is black. It is only now that I realize I have seen no other colored people on Malakki. The world is getting larger.

"I thought Jade, perhaps, would have told you about me?" He is trying not to smile, but there is laughter painted all over his face.

"Only what you can do," I say. I manage to sit up, cringing as the Sickness sends a wave of shivering heat through me.

"It's progressed quickly, hasn't it?" he says. It is more a statement than a question, so I say nothing. "May I?" He reaches for my shirt before I can object and gently pops the couple of remaining buttons. I look down as he bares my chest, and even I recoil in disgust.

String, however, retains his composure. He passes his hand close to the ugly growths and I'm sure I can feel the subtle movement of air. It is comforting. He is frowning, his big eyes so full of a pained compassion that I cannot recognize the look for several seconds. Even Della is more concerned than compassionate, a state that I think is based upon realizm rather than choice.

"It must hurt," he says.

"You bet." But I'm used to the pain, the burning that tears at my chest as if some rabid animal is trapped within, trying to escape. Used to it, but still it tortures me unremittingly, driving blade after blade of discomfort between my joints, into my limbs, piercing my lungs. It's the faints I cannot conquer, the regular grey spells when my body seems to say, *right, that's it, enough for now.* "But the pain won't last forever."

String looks at me, then his face splits into an infectious smile. I feel myself mimicking him, and it appears that Tiarnan was born grinning. I look at Jade. She smiles back at me, but I still don't know her quite well enough to read the expression. I wonder once more whether everything bad has happened, or if there are still terrible things left for me to see.

"That's true, Gabe," he says. "Because I'm going to cure you."

V

An hour later, when I am feeling stronger, String takes me on a walking tour of the village. It is larger than I first thought, stretching back along the course of the shallow valley and into a ravine formed by a small stream. The waters have long gone, but the streambed seems fertile and lush. Vegetables and fruit grow in profusion. I taste my first red-berries in years. String tells me it is the fertilizer they use.

There are hundreds of people here, going about their daily routine with a calm assurance. Some huts serve as meeting places or stores, but most of the people appear to live in tents, either self-serving or abutting old cars, lorries and buses. I see no active motor vehicle of any kind. Some of the residents throw a curious glance my way, but seem to sense why I am here — perhaps it shows in my tired walk, my hopeful eyes. They turn away again, though I cannot tell whether it is from respect or simple disinterest. I wonder how many people like me they see. I ask String, and the answer surprises me more than it really should.

"Most of them *are* people like you. Or they were, until I cured them."

I become more aware of the layout of the colony, and realize that it is far more established and self-sufficient than I first assumed. The glass moat merely encircles the front portion of the village, ending where sudden cliffs rise from the ground and soar towards the sun. The bulk of the dwellings and other buildings exist further into the ravine, sheltered from both the sun, and casually prying eyes, by the sheer cliffs on both sides.

"We've been here a long time," String says. "We've created quite a little oasis here for ourselves. Not just one of food and water, but... well, I like to think of it as an oasis of life, an enclave of what little civilization remains." He smiles sadly, and for the first time I really believe how genuine he is. "Where do you come from?"

The sudden question startles me. "Britain."

"I'm from the Dominican Republic. Ever been there?"

"No, of course not. Isn't that where...?"

String is still staring directly at me, as though he can read the constant unease in my face. "Voodoo? No, that's Haiti. Different country. Though I believe some of my ancestors were Haitians." He leaves it at that, though my query feels unanswered.

"What state is Britain in?" he asks. The change of subject distracts me, and I cannot believe that he does not know. He seems the sort of man who knows everything.

"Britain is dissolving." The word appears unbidden, but it suits perfectly what I am trying to say. "It's regressing. The army has taken control in many places. Rumor has it there is no central government anymore." I think of my last few days there, making my way to Southampton through a countryside ripped apart by flaming villages and sporadic, random battles. At first, I had thought the gunfire was army units taking on looters and thieving parties, but then I saw that they were really fighting each other.

"On my last day there, I saw a woman raped in the street by three men. One after the other. It was terrible. But the worst thing wasn't the crime itself, but the fact that the woman stood up, brushed herself down and walked away. As if she was *used* to it. As if... it was the norm. Isn't that just gruesome?"

"It's a sad new world," String says. We stroll for a few seconds, each lost in our own thoughts, most of them dark. "What of the culture?" he asks

"What do you mean?"

String stops walking, smoothing his shirt. He is not sweating. I am soaked. I wonder whether it is my Sickness bleeding the goodness from me, or whether String is so used to the sun that he no longer perspires. "The culture; the history; tradition. The soul of the place. What of that now?"

I suddenly feel sad. I wish Della was here with us, I am certain that she and String would talk forever and never become bored or disillusioned. "It's gone," I say.

String nods. I am sure he already knew. "I thought so. That cannot happen." He motions for me to follow him and we walk towards the cliff face, passing into the shadow of the mountain. He starts climbing the scree slope without pause, and I suddenly wonder whether he intends to haul himself to the top. I look up, see the thin wedge of blue sky high above, reminding me of that first day in Jade's courtyard.

"Here," he says. I look. String is standing at a split in the rock, a crevasse that could easily be the doorway to a cave. Its entrance looks like a swollen vulva, and I wonder whether it is manmade. I also ponder what is inside, in the womb of the rock, hidden in shadows. As I near String he holds out his hands, halting me.

"Gabe, Jade brought you here. She's a good woman, though I've told her before she should leave this dying place. She's too independent to join us here, more's the pity." He stands framed by the cave entrance; his skin shines in the shadows as if possessed of an inner light. I feel completely insubstantial. "I'm going to cure you. You can be assured of that, though I know that until it's done you probably won't allow yourself to believe me. But I cannot cure everyone. There's not enough medicine for the billion people with the Sickness. And there really aren't that many people who I think deserve curing."

I go to say something, but he waves me down.

"I've already decided that you're worthy. Jade is a good judge of character. But we're only a small community, and we treasure what we have. We have to. Because we have *treasures*. Do you have faith?"

"Yes," I reply without thinking. He has a way of springing questions without warning, the only way to find an honest answer.

"In what?"

I think of Della; not only my utter faith in her goodness and knowledge, but also what she said to me. *If you know someone's faith, you know their soul.... You may need it one day.* "In a friend."

"What's her name?"

"Della." I am not surprised that he knew the sex of my friend, He reminds me of Della in many ways, and *she* would have known.

He asks no more. I feel that I am about to swoon, but String is there before my body can react to the thought. He grabs me around the shoulders, and his touch seems to strengthen me. I have the unsettling certainty that he knows everything about me, understands that my feelings for Della lie way beyond simple friendship or even love. He knows my soul. But I am not worried, I have no fear. I think he deserves to know.

He points to the cave. "I'm going to take you in there, and show you some things. They're things I show everyone I cure, once, but never again. They're precious, you see, and precious things are coveted. Especially in the shit new world we inhabit. And ironically, that's why I'm showing you. So that you know how special what we have here is. So you know that knowledge of good things shouldn't always be shared, because too many bad things can dilute good things. Do you understand?"

I nod. He confuses me, his words twist and turn into obscure, half-seen truths. But I also understand him, fully, and it pleases me to think that there are still the likes of him living on our dying world.

"I can't deny the power there is in me," he says. "You may think I'm some sort of... magician? Witch doctor? I'm none of those things. In the old days, before the Ruin, I may have been called charismatic. But now, I'm a funnel for a power of a more fundamental kind. The real magic, my friend, is here." He stamps on the ground, coughing up a haze of dust around his legs. He squats, grabs a handful of the dried soil and looks at it almost reverently. "The power of the greatest magic flows through my fingers with the dust." The breeze carries trails of dust from his hand and into the cave entrance, like wraiths showing us the way. "The power of Time; the immortality of Gaia."

I feel frightened, but enlivened. The Sickness sends a warm flush into me, but for once my body combats it, cooling the fever as if the atmosphere of the cave already surrounds me. String possesses me with his words, and I feel no repulsion, no desires to flee. My skin tingles with a delicious anticipation. I wonder what is in the cave, and I am sure that it is beyond anything I can imagine.

"This is holy ground, Gabe," String says. "I don't mean religious-holy. I don't care for religion, and have none save my own. Similarly, you have your own faith, and that's how things should be. But this site is powerful. It has a holiness that precedes any form of organized, preached religion. It has the power of Nature. It is the site of a temple, a shrine of rock and dust and water and sky that pays constant, eternal homage to Nature itself. See, up there." He points to the strips of sky between the cliffs.

I look up and see the birds there, circling, drifting on updrafts of warm air from the ravine. I sigh and feel any remaining tension leave me, sucked into the sky by the soporific movement of the birds, swallowed by the sight of their gentle movement.

"The temple is a place of faith, worship of the cosmos. The site of a temple was often ascribed by the flights of birds, their cries, their circling. As if they knew more than man of the powers of creation. And why shouldn't they? Man has long distanced himself from the truth, even though there are those who profess to seek it. He distances himself even more by worshipping gods who suit him, gods who tell him that he is set above the animals, and they are his to lord over. Man has denied Nature. That's why he no longer knows true holiness. But the birds, now. See the birds. They know.

"This is Nature's temple. Come inside. Let me show you wonders."

Part Four
From Bad Flesh
i

We enter a tunnel. It smells damp and musty, the walls sprouting petrified fungi and lank mosses. True darkness never falls before light intrudes from above. It is cool this deep in the rock, and the air seems to possess something more of the climate I am used to: moisture. I breathe in deeply, relishing the coolness on my lungs, hearing String laugh quietly to himself in front of me.

The floors are uneven and the ceiling low enough in places to make me stoop. String is short, so he can walk through normally. A smell reaches us from further in, a waft of something familiar yet long lost carried on warmer currents of air like dragon's breath. I cannot quite place the scent, but I do not feel inclined to ask String. He is going to show me, anyway, and I am almost enjoying the adventurous mystery.

Looking up, I can make out where the light is coming from — natural vent-holes that reach high up to the top of the cliff — and in doing so I miss the abrupt change from tunnel to cave. I stop, stunned by the sheer size of what lays before me.

The cave is massive. I can see that it has been hacked from the rock by crude tools, their marks still peppering the wall and ceiling like the timeless signatures of those who did the deed. It could be recent or ten thousand years old, there is no real way of telling. There are no vents in the ceiling here, but the walls are inlaid with a strange glowing material which gives out a muted light. It looks like glass, feels like metal, and it's warm to the touch as if heated from within. String stands in the center of the space, smiling and staring around as if wallowing in the grandeur of whatever has been achieved here. And just what is that? What is the smell that tickles my memory once more, encourages me to silence, comforts me, conjures a million facts from a million minds other than mine?

"Books," String says. He holds out his arms, indicating the hundreds of boxes stacked around the edges of the cavern. "About two hundred thousand in all. Mainly factual, though some fiction. We want out descendants to know our dreams, don't you think?"

I cannot talk. It is not simply the sight of so many boxes, but the effort that had obviously gone in to bringing them here. And not only that, but the thought and experience and life that has been poured into making every book here. Billions of hours of struggle, work, strife, pained effort in creating, writing, producing and then dragging these books through a dying world to build a library for the future. It is staggering. It is so huge that I can barely comprehend it.

String has a proud glint in his eyes, the look of a father for his adoring children. "Philosophy, biology, psychology, botany; maps, travels books, cultural works, histories; stories, poems, novels, plays; even some religious works — much against my better judgement, but who am I to chose what people will believe in the future?"

"You've got it all here, in your hands," I manage to say at last. The enormity of what is here makes me slur. "You can shape the future from this place." For the first time I am truly frightened of String, this man who Della only vaguely heard of and who now holds my soul, as well as my fate, in the palm of his hand, to do with as he will.

"Not only this place," he says. "And it's not me who will shape it. There will be people in the future — two years, fifty years, who knows — who will feel the time is right. Now... to tell the truth, it's still all in decline. I've merely brought these things together, protected them from the random destruction that's sweeping the globe. It's happened before, you know? The Dark Ages were darker than many people imagine."

"So we're heading for a new Dark Age?"

String sits on one of the boxes, lifts a flap and brings out a book. It is a gardening guide, splashes of forgotten blossoms decorating the cover and catching the strange light from the walls. "Maybe we're already there. But when it's over, I hope it won't take long to get light again. I hope all this will help."

"Who are you?" I ask. The question seems to take him by surprise, and I feel a brief moment of satisfaction that I have tackled him at his own game.

"I'm String. I'm just a lucky man who found something wonderful. I'm doing what I can with it, because... well, just because."

"You found all this?" I say, aghast. "You must have. No man could do all this."

He shakes his head, a wry smile playing across his lips. "Faith can move mountains," he says, and for once I see that the saying can be literal. "I dragged all this here. Some I had with me when I arrived, most of it I went out and recovered. Before it was destroyed."

"I saw them burning books in the streets in England," I say quietly, the memory of the voracious flames eating at my heart. I remember thinking that the fire had always been there, waiting for its chance to pounce on our knowledge and reduce it to so much dust, restrained only by whatever quaint notion of civilization we entertained. In the end, all it took was a little help from us. Wilful self-destruction.

I come to my senses. "So what else is it you want to show me?"

He nods to the far end of the cavern, where another dark tunnel entrance stand inviting us enter. "I found it soon after the crash," he says. "I crawled in here to die. Then I realized I was in a very special place — had the power of life in my hands, quite literally — and the rest just happened."

"Crash?" Disparate shreds of his story seem to be flowing together, images from the last few hours intrude, as if they mean to tell me something before he speaks.

"I was a Lord," he says. "I flew a Lord Ship. As far as I know, I'm the last one left alive." He stands and heads towards the dark mouth. I follow.

ii

"Some people are not what they seem," Della said. It was cold, the chill November winds bringing unseasonable blizzards from the north and coating Britain in a sheen of ice. Thousands would die this winter, freezing, starving, giving in. The national grid had failed completely six months previously. It had been a severe inconvenience then, rather than life threatening. Now, though, as frost found its way into homes and burrowed into previously warm bones, it was mourned more than ever. Only the week before, in Nottingham, an old theater full of people had burned to the ground. They had been huddled around a bonfire on the stage, like a performing troupe acting a play about Neanderthal Man. The heat of their final performance melted the snow in the surrounding streets, and when it refroze the local kids began using it as a skating rink. Surprising, how well children adapt, as if they're a blank on which the reality of the moment can imprint itself.

I handed her a dish of curry from the vat she constantly kept on the go above the gas fire. The smell had permeated the whole house, ground its way into furniture and carpets and Della herself. I loved it; I loved her. I never told her.

"Hmm," she mumbled, "not enough powder. Next time, more powder."

I nodded my assent, hardly able to sit still with the acid that seemed to be eating away my tongue and lips. My chest felt warm. I had seen the discoloration there for the first time the week before, but I still had not told Della. It was as if telling her would confirm my worst fears to myself.

I had been told that the army was seen dumping bodies into a dry outdoor swimming pool and burning them. They'd even rigged up some sort of fuel pump, pouring petrol into the pool through the old water pipes. It meant that none of them had to get too near. I did not want to be one of those dead people, burnt in a pool, bodies boned by flames and whisked into clogged drains.

"Take old Marcus, for instance," she continued. "You know Marcus?"

"The old guy who sits in the park pissing himself?"

"That's right, the scruffy old tramp who lets kids kick him, lies under a bench because he'll only fall off if he sleeps on it, eats grass and dandelions and blackberries and dead dogs." She nodded. "Marcus was a pilot, years before the Ruin. He flew in the Gulf war. Did they teach you about that in school?" I nodded. Della shrugged as if surprised. "What do you think of him now?"

I could only be honest. "He's an old tramp. I suppose... I suppose every tramp is someone. Had a life before they took to the streets. Before, anyway."

Della smiled, wiping her mouth and burping loudly and resonantly. "There you are, you see. I've made you think of him as a man, just by telling you something about him. Before, to you, he was a nobody, a tramp, someone without identity. You never even thought he was human."

I realized how right Della was. I imagined Marcus as a young man with a wife, going on family holidays, proud and arrogant in his pilot's suit, flying helmet under his arm as he posed for the papers. "He's still out there, and he's going to freeze," I said.

Della scoffed. "Marcus'll still be alive when you and I are dead and gone. It's as if he'd adapted for the Ruin before it happened. He's always been ready. His life has always been a ruin." She looked at me across the candlelit room, scratching slowly beneath her chin. A breeze whistled in under the corrugated roof, flickering the candles and making Della shimmer with feigned movement. "What do you think of him now?"

I sighed. "I suppose... well, he's a tramp, but I can appreciate him. He's human."

Della nodded. "Some people aren't what they seem. Some are much more than you think, or at least better than they like to portray themselves. Some... a few... are much worse. Much of the time you'll never know which, but it's you that counts, what *you* think of them. Some people can really pull the wool over your eyes, kiddo."

I went to get Della a beer, grabbed one for myself, sat and stared at her for an hour or two. Neither of us talked. Silently, in my own way, I was worshipping her. I wondered who the real Della was, but deep inside I had always known. She was my salvation.

iii

"String," I say, "where are we going? Is it dangerous?" It feels dangerous, the cool air chilling me instead of comforting me this time, the darkness haunting, not hiding. It's as if the dark here is a presence, not just an absence of light.

He turns and leans gently towards me, lowering his head and looking at me through wide eyes. They glimmer, reflecting the memory of the strange light in the cavern behind us. "Not dangerous," he says. "Wonderful!" He walks on, then stops and looks at me again, head to one side, one corner of his mouth raised in a sardonic smile. "But dangerous if you're on your own. Dangerous, without me." He moves on.

For a moment I speculate on what String did before the Ruin, before he took on the mantle of a Lord. But the mere idea of him existing in a normal world seems alien and abstract, and in a way it disturbs me more than the knowledge of his Lordship.

Around an outcrop of rock the darkness recedes, and suddenly we arrive at another cavern. This one is open to the sky. A great split in the rock, millions of years old, has formed what is effectively a deep pothole, its entrance eroded by weathering until the walls have shallowed out into a gully. It reminds me of a great fossilized throat, and String and I are standing in the stomach. The hairs on my neck perk up and goose bumps prickle my arms and shoulders. I have the sense of being an intruder, like walking in on someone having sex or gatecrashing a funeral. But the feeling is more primal. I feel as though have offended a god.

The gully appears empty, and accessible only from the tunnel we have just emerged from. The floor is uneven and raised at one edge like a ramp to the walls. I can see no reason for my unease, but Della always told me that feelings tell more than sight, and I'm terrified. I assume that String's words have made me nervous and skittish, but when I glance at him he appears in the same frantic state. That scares me more than anything: the idea that this man is scared of whatever sleeps here.

"What is it?"

String does not hear me, or chooses not to. "Can you feel the power? Does it grab your skull, twist your spine? Can you sense the majesty of this place? This is the real god, Gabe, this is the genuine Provider. A god you can feel. A god who will help you, cure you." He looks at me, his eyes wide and alive, glimmering with emotion. "You'll be cured. Made better. Just like Jade. Just like all the others outside."

I want to go. Suddenly the last place I want to be is here, in this deep gully that encases me like a prison, or a tomb. But String grabs my arm and guides me to the edge of the hole, the place where the ground is ramped against the wall. I start to tremble as we approach it, and I think I can feel String shaking as well.

He hauls me up the slight incline until we are standing on a small ledge, our heads touching rock where the overhang curves inward.

I look down. There is a large stone slab on the top of the raised area, edges blurred by time. I try to convince myself that its surface is not decorated with crude letters and drawings, but they are there, and they will not be denied. The pictures show mere remnants of what must once have been a magnificent tableau: half a reptilian head; the face of a god in the sun; a trail of bones, skulls crushed under wagon wheels. The words are similarly weathered, and I cannot decipher any of them. But for that, I am pleased. They look so alien — so unlike anything I have ever seen, in life or history — that I can barely imagine how old they are.

"I think it's a tomb," String says. "And whoever is buried here must have been someone… special. This is where the power comes from."

I can feel it, an implied vibration that enters my holed shoes and seems to shiver my bones, fingering its way through my marrow and cooling everything it touches. I want to shout, but something prevents me. It feels like a hand over my mouth, but I can still breathe. I want to run, but I am restrained. Something holds me where I am, though String is standing several steps away.

Then I can go, and I do. I turn, shout incoherently, and run. String tries to hold me, but grabs only my attention.

"Not that way," he hisses. I realize that I had been heading towards the blank, strange wall of the cave. I spin, throw his hand from my arm and sprint into the tunnel. The darkness seems more welcoming than the polluted light of that place.

It takes me several minutes to find my way out. Emerging from the cave is like a rebirth. The daylight is wonderful. I keep running until I am far from the ravine, almost at the moat of broken glass, and there I collapse into the dust and stare up at the sky, eyes closed, while the sun slowly burns my face.

iv

"Did you see it all?" Jade says. There is an unfamiliar weakness in her tone. I open my eyes. She is standing over me and moves forward to block out the sun.

"Christ Jade, is there any more? Anything else you're waiting for me to find out on my own?" I can feel the coolness of tears on my face, soothing the sunburn that stretches my skin across my skull. I'd been crying a lot recently. It was not unusual, lately, not only for me but also for the world in general. If tears could heal we'd all be a damn sight better than we were before the Ruin. But tears could only hurt and haunt, and remind us of our eventual, inevitable weakness.

"You saw the library? And the…." She cannot say it. I feel a sudden burst of anger.

"The what? The library and the what?" Perhaps she thinks I really had not seen it, but I'm sure she can see way past my anger. I'm sure she knows all there is to know about me. I feel transparent, the same way I am with Della. Only with Della, I like the feeling. She comforts, she does not confuse.

"The tomb," she mutters.

I nod, anger draining with my sweat and tears. "Yes, I saw the library, and the tomb. Or whatever it is. I hated it."

"It's not bad, it's —"

"How the fuck do you know what it is? How do you know it's not bad?"

Jade recoils from my outburst and I revel in a momentary glee at the brief panic in her eyes. "String healed me, Gabe. I told you, I showed you." She put her hand to her chest, as if to hold in the goodness that had replaced her Sickness.

I sit up. "With the aid of whatever lies in there?"

Jade nods. "It's something old and powerful. We can't pretend to understand it, just as Christians don't presume to understand God. He frightens them, maybe, but they can't ever hope to explain Him. It's like that with this place. It has something wonderful, and there's nothing wrong with using it. String has found out how to do that. He's doing some *good* in the world. You know as well as I do, there's precious little of that going on anywhere else."

I begin to laugh. I stand up, feeling the fear being cooked away by the sun. Or if not removed altogether, then diluted somewhat. Fear is a strange thing when you're dying — sometimes, it seems so pointless.

"I've come this far." Jade and I walk slowly back to the large tent in the middle of the settlement, a great sweeping structure held up by steel stanchions and sheltered from the outside by two layers of light, soft material. Suddenly something clicks into place. The color of the tent raises an uncomfortable sensation in my guts.

"This is a Lord Ship," I say. "What's left of the ship he crashed in."

"He used it to build the whole settlement," Jade says.

"Always thought the Lords were an evil bunch of bastards, in it all for their own gain." Della's words echo: *The worst thing, kiddo, is that they're going to be gods.*

Jade shrugs. "What you were meant to think, I suppose."

"No," I say. "No, it's something I was told." I feel an incredible sense of disquiet as I realize that my future — my life, my soul, my continued existence and well-being — now relies upon Della being both right and wrong. I hope the Lords were not all as selfish as she made out; and, in whatever strange way it may be possible, I hope that String is a god.

I wonder whether she knew that String was a Lord when she told me of him.

v

String is in the large tent, sitting at a table in the corner. The space beneath the main canopy is divided by swaying curtains of the same material. I touch it, rub it between my fingers, surprised at how light it is. It feels almost oily to the touch, yet I can see through it.

"It's extremely strong," String says. "It's all that survived the crash. Apart from me, of course."

"What about the motors, engines? Weapons?"

String shakes his head. "The mechanics of the Ship burned when the pile melted down. I got away before it went up. The fire didn't touch this lot, thankfully. It was built to endure. As for the weapons, that was a fallacy. The Lord Ships never carried weapons. We were a mobile, self-sufficient government, not an army." He stands, gestures us towards him. Tiarnan is already there, along with several other men and women. There is food on the table, glasses, bottles of wine and, in the center of the table — as if honored for its very existence — a large bottle of Metaxa.

"Please sit down." String waits until Jade and I have taken our places before he sits. He turns to me, his expression slipping into seriousness for a moment.

"Tomorrow morning, I will cure you."

"How?"

"A potion. Simple. Rubbed into your chest, your temples, your stomach, it acts quickly. By tomorrow evening the growths will have hardened and dropped off. They will not recur." String hands me a glass of wine. His blasé statement stuns me with its simplicity. He is talking about my life or death, yet he promises everything with a confidence that makes it difficult not to believe.

I turn to Jade, who is staring ravenously at the food arrayed across the table. "This is how he did you?"

She nods, but does not look at me. I can hardly blame her. There is more food here — in both variety and quantity — than I have seen in months. Lamb, roasted whole; a piglet, apple stuck in its mouth like a swollen tongue; fresh fruit; duckling, sliced and presented with pancakes and sauces; crispy vegetables, steaming as if to gain our attention.

"Why not now?"

String shakes his head. "Tomorrow. The power of the place is at its greatest around dawn. You'll feel it when you wake up. You will be fresher, stronger from the food. Tomorrow, Gabe."

I am too tired to argue, and I have come too far to risk upsetting him now. I wish Della was here with me, ready with an apposite phrase or two, but at the same time I'm glad she is not. At least at a distance I can adore her fully. If she were here, it would be too obvious.

We eat. We drink. The evening passes gloriously slowly, and I surprise myself by enjoying most of it. Dusk falls, but the heat remains, trapped within the tent by the folds of strange material hung out like drying hides. String is a polite host, accommodating and generous with his precious food and drink. I satisfy my hunger ten-fold, feeling guilty when I think of what Della may be eating tonight, but also aware that if she knew she would be selflessly happy for me.

We emerge into the night with the stars and the alcohol flows ever more freely. String makes his excuses and disappears. Couples pair off and begin to make love shamelessly under the heavens. I see the occasional light scar on chests or abdomens, but no signs of the fully-fledged Sickness. It is like a new world. I see a flash across the horizon and Jade points it out. "Shooting star," she says.

Soon, the revelry dies down and is replaced by the soft moaning of lovers, the slow movement of shadows close to the ground. Jade and I walk to the banks of the dried stream and sit amongst the fruit bushes and rows of tomatoes. The smells tempt our taste buds, even though we are still full from the meal. I pluck a tomato and bite in, closing my eyes as the warm juices dribble down my chin. I see small shadows skipping between plants, scratching on the dry ground; a lizard, as long as my foot and with glittering eyes, runs up the slight bank towards us. We sit as still as we can, waiting for it to scamper away. It waits, frozen by starlight, staring at us before turning and walking casually back into the stream of plants.

Jade giggles. It is a sound I have not heard from her, and I like it. She reaches for my shirt but I push her away.

"I'm ugly," I say. "This is a good place. I can't show my ugliness to it." I wonder if the Metaxa or wine was drugged, because I cannot help but feel fine.

"You're not ugly. It's the Sickness that's ugly, the world, the people in it. Not you." She shuffles next to me and begins unbuttoning my shirt. This time I let her. "Tomorrow, all the ugliness will be gone."

"Is there anything else, Jade? Anything you haven't told me? Is this it, is this all?" But she is taking her own clothes off now and she does not answer me. I think I see tears, but it could just be other worlds reflected in her eyes.

vi

I may be dreaming.

The ground feels solid beneath me as I sit up, the sky looks as wide and intimidating as I have ever known it. I see a dart of light streak from east to west, and wonder whether it is a shooting star or another satellite destroying itself in despair.

I hear a sound that is familiar, but out of reach. My head is light, and it feels as though I am spinning around the world. A dream, maybe, or too much wine and Metaxa?

I stand, careful not to wake Jade where she sleeps beside me. She is still naked, and her skin looks grey and dead in the moonlight. I reach out and touch her just to ensure she's still there. She is warm, and my touch imbues her skin with life.

I hear the noise again. Jade stirs, turns, mumbles something. I cannot distinguish most of the words, but I think I hear my name, and an apology.

There is movement from the other side of the streambed. The noise quietens, and as it fades recognition dawns: the crunching, tinkling sounds of the huge boat crossing the moat of glass. Something has come into the camp. I wonder if I should wake someone, tell them, but then realize that whatever is happening is a part of the camp's life — they would surely have guards out there day and night. Instead, I slither down the bank and push my way into the mass of vegetation.

Voices reach me, quiet and muted, issuing orders. Then the sound of wheels on the dusty ground, like a fingernail on sandpaper. I push through the plants, breathing heavily to draw in the smell of growing, living things. Dark shapes dart away from me, one of them scampering across my feet with a panicked patter of claws. I walk into what can only be a spider's web, the soft silk wrapping around my face and neck, and rub frantically to clear it away. After a time I begin to think I am lost, walking in circles between the ranks of plants, but then I reach the opposite bank. I'm surprised at how wide the streambed is. It looked a lot narrower in the daylight.

A voice mutters nearby. I'm sure it is Tiarnan, the guard who brought us in. His tone is quiet but firm, confident but casual, as if he's well used to what he's doing. I crawl slowly up the bank until I can see over the gentle ridge.

The sound of wheels begins again as I catch my first glimpse of the wagon. It is about the size of a car, a flat-bedded trailer moving roughly on four bare wheels. There are three men pushing it. In the darkness, at first, I can barely make out what they are transporting. But as it nears me on its obvious journey into the ravine, sudden realization strikes. It looks like a cargo of clothes, but why three men to push it?

Bodies. Piled high on the cart, limbs protruding here and there, moving with a rhythmic *thump thump* that could so easily be the sound of a head jerking up and down against the wood.

I gasp, duck down, a scream screeching for release. But I contain it. Somehow, I hold in my terror and let it manifest itself only inside; a rush of blood pulses to the growths in my chest and bursts one, and I have the sudden certainty that I am about to die, here, now, within sight of a strange crime and an expanse of lush plants. My breath comes in ragged gasps, as if someone else is controlling my respiration. I try to calm down, but my heart will not listen to me. I want to double up in agony, the pain from my chest sending tendrils of poison into my veins, spreading it slowly but surely throughout my body.

That's the poison from the Sickness, I tell myself, it's leaking into me and soon I'll die. And then maybe they'll add me to the cart and wheel me away, to wherever they're taking the hundreds of other meaningless corpses. I take another look over the bank and see Tiarnan standing down by the glass moat, exposed in starlight. He and three other men are lifting bodies from the moat-boat onto a second cart. As I watch, Tiarnan's partner fumbles and there is a sickening clout as the body hits the ground head first. He bends to pick it up, and I hear something which makes it all seem so much worse, if that is possible — a quiet laugh.

I turn and try to spot the first cart, but it has already been swallowed by the blackness. The grumbling of its wheels sounds like the gurglings of a giant's insides, issuing from the dark throat of the ravine. I wonder where they are taking the bodies. A breeze sighs through the rows of plants at my back.

It's the fertilizer, String had said.

The lake of dead bodies; the massacre I had heard and not seen, the terrible twitching of the dying as flies already began to settle on the fresh blood; the sound of wagons that night, a mile or more from where Jade and I had made love and slept.

I feel sick. Not just nausea brought on by the Sickness, but a sickness of the soul. I double up in pain as more tainted blood floods my system. As utter darkness begins to blank out the moon and stars, and the agony recedes into faintness, the last thing I hear is the interminable rumble of the loaded carts being pushed across the stony ground. Again, and again.

vii

Jade is looking down at me. I experience brief but vivid déjà vu. Is Jade my guardian angel? Her face is a mask of concern. As my eyelids flutter open she looks up, beckons someone over. I think the sky is a deep grey color, but then realize that I am inside one of the tents.

String is there. He looks similarly worried, though his eyes betray something else, a confidence that I find strangely repulsive.

"Jade, I saw…." I begin, but though I remember espying something terrible, I cannot recall exactly what it was.

"Keep still," she says, a quiver in her voice, "just lie still. The Sickness almost had you. String gave you the cure. Rubbed it on your chest, your temples, your throat. He thought you might have been too far gone, so he fed you some of it as well."

"Fed me?"

Jade shrugs apologetically. "A tube, into your stomach. You'll have a sore throat for a while. You were wandering around in the fruit plantation when I found you, mumbling, calling a woman's name. You looked like the walking dead."

Memories begin to force their way into the light. With them

come terrible images, and an awful realization that turns me cold.

"Jade, I saw bodies, hundreds of bodies. They're using them, storing them." I am whispering, but as soon as I begin String appears above me again, his hand lowering towards my face. I cry out, certain that he is going to silence me forever, but Jade is holding me down as String places his hand on my forehead. His skin is cool and clammy.

"He's burning up. It's a fight, now, between the Sickness and the cure. I hope I got him in time, but sometimes it's a matter of will. The cure is just the catalyst."

Faintness clouds my vision, but I bite my lip and try to stay conscious. I have to tell Jade, warn her, make her get away from this place.

"Will you tell him?" I hear her ask. I can imagine her expression, distant and worried, just as she looked when there was more bad stuff for me to know.

"Not yet." String replies. "Later, when he's better. Not now."

"I think he saw something," Jade whispers.

I sense String looking down at me. "I'll have words with Tiarnan. Stay with him, Jade. He's got a fight on his hands." Footsteps recede into the distance. All I can see is the unremitting greyness above me. "If you need me, ask someone to find me. I have some work to do."

Jade bends over me again, softly telling me to be quiet, conserve my strength. And although I have some things to tell her, my body forces me to obey her. I drift once more into welcoming unconsciousness.

viii

I feel different. Lighter. As if a weight, both physical and mental, has been lifted from me.

I sit up. I am still in the tent, but alone. The flap moves softly in the breeze.

Again, I wonder whether I'm dreaming. But the bed beneath me, hard and slightly bowed in the center, feels solid. The air smells good, laden with the scents of cooking. I have a burning thirst and a sore throat. That's where they put the tube in.

"Jade!" I can hear nothing from outside. Inside I feel changed. I suddenly realize what is different.

I lift the rough cloth shirt I am wearing and look at my chest. The growths are crusted black with leaked blood, looking like shrivelled mushrooms sprouting from dead flesh. But I am not dead. It is the Sickness that is no more, stumped in its tracks, driven from within to shows itself as a crispy, rotten mess on the outside. Displaying its true nature.

Tentatively I lift my hand, suddenly desperate to touch myself there but aware of the pain which will inevitably come with the contact.

"Go on," Jade says from the entrance. "It's all right. Touch it. See what happens."

I look up, all wide-eyed and scared. Jade is smiling and the expression suits her. I touch one of the growths with my fingertips, barely brushing it. It feels hard and dry, like an overcooked sausage. There is no pain, no sensation of contact at all. I touch it again and jump as it falls off and tumbles to the ground. Lying in the dust, it looks like nothing.

Beneath the old growth there is a flash of bright pink skin. New skin.

"It'll fade to white," Jade says, moving towards me, tears in her eyes. "What did I tell you? Isn't he something?"

"I feel different," I say.

"You're better. I remember the feeling. You're just not used to being healthy. It's cleaned your blood, driven out all the bad stuff. You're cured, Gabe." She runs her hand across my chest and the growths come off, sprinkling into my lap and onto the floor like a shower of black hailstones. All I feel is a slight resistance, a tugging at my chest. "You're beautiful."

I reach out for her and hold her close, crying, feeling happy and sad and scared all at the same time. "Jade, I saw something terrible."

She pulls away. "The bodies?"

I nod, struck dumb with surprise.

"Gabe...." Jade looks away, avoiding my eyes, and I terrify myself by laughing. It reminds me of the soft laugh of Tiarnan's partner as he dropped the body, but that only makes it harder to stop. I want to hate myself but find I can't.

"Is this really the last thing, Jade?" I ask through tears of mixed emotion. "Is there anything else after this? Whatever it is I'm going to be told, or see, now?"

She looks at me nervously, shaking her head. "This is just about the biggest, Gabe."

We stay silent for a while, me waiting for her to talk, Jade sniffing and wiping tears away from her cheeks. She cannot meet my gaze, her hands will not touch me. We are islands separated by a deep sea of knowledge. I am waiting for her to let me take the plunge.

"Right," she says, standing back and preparing herself. She looks into my eyes. Suddenly, I don't want to hear what she is going to say. Out of everything possible, any words, that is the last thing I want to hear. Because it is something terrible. "Right," she says again, wringing her hands. I swing my legs from the bed in readiness to flee the tent, steal the moat-boat and make my escape before she can say any more. But String is standing in the doorway. I pause, my heart thumping inextricably clean blood around my body, but find myself too scared to enjoy the sensation.

"Shall I tell him, Jade?"

She shakes her head. "It's about time I levelled with him, I think." I sit back down. Jade steps closer until we are almost touching.

"Gabe, the cure that String gave you is distilled in the presence of the tomb, under the mountain, in the realm of the flight of birds, from the brain fluid of the dead." She turns away and looks pleadingly at String.

I feel empty, emotionless, a void. I should feel sick, I suppose, but I've had far too much of that already. I'm shocked, but somehow not as surprised as perhaps I should be. I feel disgust, but secondhand, as if this is all happening to someone else. "Oh," is all I can say.

"All things must be made use of, Gabe," String says, a note of desperation in his voice as if he's trying to persuade himself as well as me. "It's a new world. If humanity wants to go and slaughter itself, then at least I can bring some small measure of good from it."

"Did you kill them?" I ask. It seems the most important question to me, the pivotal factor that will enable me to handle what has happened, or not.

"What?" String seems surprised. He could just be buying time.

"Did you kill them? All the dead people I saw last night. Being taken into the mountain. Did you kill them?"

"No." He looks me in the eye, his gaze unwavering. He smiles grimly, tilts his head to the side. "No. You heard them killed, so Jade tells me. You saw them dying out there, alone, in the heat. We just use the raw material."

"Brain fluid?" I am filled with a grotesque fascination in what has happened to me, abhorrence countered with a perverse fascination. I wonder briefly how he knows of the cure — how he discovered it — but shove it from my mind like an unwanted guilt.

String nods. "Yes. I won't tell you the details."

"Good," Jade murmurs. "Gabe, come here. Come here." She throws her arms around me, hugs me to her. I can feel her tears as they drip onto my shoulders, run down my chest. It feels good.

"Are you leaving?" String says.

"Damn right!" I don't believe I could stay here.

He smiles, and this one touches his eyes. "Good." He turns away.

"String." He glances back, squinting either at the sun or in preparation for whatever else I'm going to say. "Thank you." He nods as he walks away.

Later, Jade and I leave. The moat-boat takes us across the broken glass. I realize that I have never considered what the moat is intended as protection against; now, I do not want to know. I try to avoid standing on the darker patches in the wood, but they are everywhere, and it is almost impossible.

String is nowhere to be seen. Perhaps he is beneath the mountain, beyond the place of books in the cavern that the birds know all about. Brewing.

Tiarnan has had the trike oiled and serviced. This time, on the way back down the mountain, we take it in turns.

Part Five
The Substance of Things
i

"Sometimes, you'll have to put up with bad things to accept some good," Della said. "'There are more things in Heaven and Earth,' and all that. Sometimes, you may not understand how good can come from events so terrible. But there are places we were never meant to see, ideas we were never meant to know. Even if it's a person doing these things, it's with blind faith, not pure understanding. Maybe that's why it's so special."

She was in her garden again, stubbornly wheeling herself between fruit bushes, plucking those that were ripe, cleaning the others of the greasy dust that hung constantly in the atmosphere. I was following on behind her, bagging the fruit and wondering what she was going to do with so much. There were only so many pies she could make.

"I can't see how any good has come of the Ruin. Millions have died. The world's gone to pot." I thought of the marks on my chest, slowly growing and expanding. I had still not told her. "Millions more are going to die."

She looked up at me from her wheelchair. "If you see no good in the Ruin, it's 'cause you're not meant to. Me, I see plenty of good in it."

"What? What good?"

Della sighed. I wanted to hold her, comfort her, protect her. But I knew I never could. "Look at all that," she said, indicating the basket of fruit I carried. "I'll never use all that. A few pies, a tart, a fruit salad. All that's left will turn brown, decay, collapse in on itself. Then I'll spread it on the ground and it'll give new life to the seedlings I plant next year. New from old. Good fruit from bad flesh." She took a bite from a strawberry, cringed and threw it to the ground. "So, in years to come, when all the mess of the Ruin has cleared up or rotted down, the world's going to be a much safer place."

I did not understand what she meant. I still do not understand now. But I like to think she was right.

ii

We arrive back in the town and make straight for the harbor. There is a ship at anchor there, a large transport with paint peeling from its superstructure and no visible emblem or flag of any kind.

"Pirates?" I guess.

"That's all there are nowadays, I suppose." Jade has become quiet, withdrawn, but I am uncertain as to the cause. We made the journey from String's in one go, traveling through the night and keeping a close lookout for roaming gangs of bandits. I'm still not sure whether I believe the cannibal yarn Jade spun when I first arrived here, but I kept my eyes wide open on the way down. Wide, wide open.

I wasn't about to be eaten after receiving a miracle cure.

"I suppose I could find out where it's heading."

"Good idea," she says. "I'll try to get us some food."

There is a subject that we are both skirting around, though I can tell by the air of discomfort that she is as aware of it as I: Where are we going, and are we going together?

iii

"When you've got a tough decision to make, don't beat around the bush. That'll get nothing sorted, and it's prevarication that's partly responsible for the mess the world's in. Remember years ago, all the talk and good intentions? Farting around, talking about disarmament and cleaning up the atmosphere and helping the environment, while all the time the planet's getting ready to self-destruct under our feet."

Della threw another log on the fire, popped the top from a bottle with her teeth and passed it to me, laughing as it foamed over the lip and splashed across her old carpet. It was an Axminster. I wondered what it was like in Axminster now, how many people were living in the carpet factory, whether it was even still there.

"Take that Jade. Now, whatever it is she wants she's already made up her mind, she's that type of woman. So why piss around when time's getting on? Ask her what's up, tell her what you're up to. That'll solve everything."

She scratched at her stump, drawing blood. Not for the first time I wished I could write down everything she said, record it for future use. But somehow, I thought I'd remember it all the same.

"If there's a problem there, with you and Jade, it'll be there whether you confront it now or in a week's time. Pass me another chicken leg."

I passed her the plate. She laughed at my retained sense of etiquette. "Manners maketh fuck-all now, Gabe. Faith maketh man. Just you remember."

iv

I open my eyes, the remnants of a daydream fading away. I wonder how Della could have known about Jade all that time ago. I wonder how she could have known about String. I realize that, in both cases, it was impossible.

Faith maketh man. I certainly have faith. Whether it's fed from somewhere or I make it myself, I possess it. And it possesses me.

I move away from the bench as I see a uniformed man come down the gangplank from the ship. There is a noisy crowd on the mole, trying to get a glimpse of what is being unloaded from the hold. A few men in army uniforms lounge around, cradling some very unconventional firearms. I guess they could wipe out the town within an hour or two with the hardware they're displaying.

I approach the man, hoping the uniform is not a lie. "Could you tell me where this ship has come from? Where it's going?"

He spins sharply, hand touching the gun at his belt, but his expression changes when he sees me. Perhaps he thinks I may have some money because I'm a European. I prepare to run when I have to disappoint him.

"Came from Australia. Goes to Europe. Take you home, eh?" He rubs his fingers together and I back away, nodding.

"Hope so."

Jade is sitting on a wall near a row of looted, burnt shops. She has some fruit, and is surreptitiously nibbling at a chunk of pink meat.

"How did you get that?"

She smiles. "Used my guiles and charm. Made promises I can't keep. Just hope I never see him again."

I frown. "Well, maybe it won't matter."

"What do you mean?" she says, but I think she knows.

"The ship's going to Europe. Are you coming with me?" There, right out with it. No beating around the bush. No prevarication.

"No," she says. I feel myself slumping with sadness. She hands me some meat, but I do not feel hungry. "Have you got someone there?"

I look at her, thinking, trying to decide whether or not I have. "Not as such," I say. "Not really. I don't think so."

"And what does that mean?"

I shrug. "I've got faith in someone, but I don't really think she exists." If you know someone's faith, you know their soul. I feel that Jade has always known my soul, and I think I may love her for that.

"I can't come, Gabe," she says. "It's not too bad here. I know a few people. I'll survive." She nibbled at some fruit, but I could tell that she was less hungry than me. "You could stay?"

"You could come."

We leave it at that.

v

As I board the ship, a roll of Jade's bribe money sweating in my fist, I hear a sound like a swarm of angry bees. I glance up and see the flash of sunlight reflecting from one of the Lord Ships. It is at least two miles out to sea, drifting slowly across the horizon, but it provokes the reaction I expect.

The whole harborside drops to its knees. Soldiers go down too, but they are soon on their feet again, kicking at the worshipping masses, firing their guns indiscriminately into huddled bodies. I search the crowd for Jade, then look for the alley she had pulled me into on that first day. I see the smudge of her face in the shadows, raise my hand and wave. I think she waves back.

The ship remains at anchor long enough for me to see the bodies piling up.

Hell

"May you live in interesting times."

When she was thirteen, religion found Laura. She didn't go looking for it, of that I was sure, but just as an insidious cancer had taken my wife seven years before, so religion stalked my lovely daughter and eventually stole her away. At least, that's what I thought at the time. God is always so easy to blame.

She left in the night without saying goodbye.

The day before, we'd taken a trip to the local park. Laura wanted to find a suitable location for a photo shoot — she had dreams of becoming an actress and was slowly composing a most impressive portfolio — and I had a day owed to me at work, so we agreed to make an afternoon of it. I carried the picnic hamper and Laura nattered every step of the way, her nonstop chat and nervous laughter inherited from the mother she had barely had time to know. The hamper was heavy and the day was hot; we had jam tarts and cheese and cucumber sandwiches and bottles of beer for me and orangeade for Laura. She spoke of her hopes for the future, while my thoughts drifted to the past. I'd often come to the park with Janine, my wife, Laura's mother. I smiled inside, a sort of comfortable melancholy that had all but replaced the raging grief. Then Laura tripped me and stole a bottle of beer from the spilled hamper; I ran after her and tackled her onto the grass, and the afternoon turned into one of those times you never forget, taking on a hue of perfection that cannot be eroded by the tides of time. For those few hours everything was faultless. Bad news was something that happened to unknown people in faraway lands. On the way home Laura hugged me and kissed my sunburned cheek, and she told me she loved me. And I knew that I'd be fine because in her voice I heard Janine. In her smile I saw my wife.

She left in the night without saying goodbye.

There was a note in her room to tell me why she'd gone. She'd scribbled it in a hurry as if afraid the dawn would find her out. It spoke of God and fear and faith and perfection and guilt and envy, and I thought she meant that she felt bad living as she did. But in truth, that note only went to confuse me more.

If only I'd known then that she had not even written it.

I tried to cope, I did my best, but in the end I went the only way I could to survive. I turned to Hell.

It had been a terrible six weeks since Laura had gone. I hadn't heard a word from her, and although the police stressed that they were hunting high and low, they drew a blank. The International Police Force had been notified and her details had gone onto their database... although in a way I hoped I'd never hear from them. If I did, it may mean that her genetic fingerprint had been matched with that of a body pulled from the Volga in Moscow, or her dental records related to what was left of a car crash victim in France; a million possibles snicking and snacking through the organization's computers until *match* was found, *match*, a convergence of information that would mean a lifetime of misery for me instead of a vain, empty hope.

So they searched, and I searched, but all the while hope was slipping through my fingers. Whichever radical cult she'd hooked up with, they would have taken her far away from me. Already I would be little more than a vague memory in her mind, a confusing image of what a father should have been, an unbeliever, a waste. I sent out a plea over the net — there were groups that provided a search service, both electronically and, more expensively, physically — but even they admitted that the chances were slim. Most of the religious groups that had sprung up over the past decade eschewed technology, and it was already likely that Laura was essentially removed from existence.

All she'd have left would be herself, and whatever skewed faith she had found.

More than me, at least.

The route to Hell can only be found by those who need it the most. It is never advertised or discussed openly in public — there are no books about it, no documentaries — but just as the true reality of things is hidden beneath the manufactured patina of everyday life, so most people know about Hell. They know about it and believe in it, but they never honestly feel that they need it.

Things can never get that *bad*, they think. *My life can't drop to* those *depths, surely.*

I went looking without knowing what I was looking for. I'm sure that's how I discovered Hell so easily. I was wandering the streets one evening, listening out for anything that sounded like a religious meeting. There were many gatherings in the city, many religions, all of them right and all of them wrong, as ever. My walk took me along one street, down the next, across open shopping plazas and through a park. There were a lot of people around now that the sun had gone down, and all those I saw appeared to have somewhere to go. I was aimless, and I stuck out like a gorilla with blue hair. My face was slack, my eyes wide and demanding, my mouth moving silently, betraying my encroaching madness. Because I truly believed that's where I was: at the edge of madness. Janine was seven years in her grave, her perfume as fresh in my nostrils as ever. And now Laura was gone, stolen from me by the perverted followers of some god that had never and could never existed, her mind probably taken from her, twice removed from me. My memories of her were beginning to feel unfair. They should have been *her* thoughts, not mine. It seemed so wrong that I should have more recollections of my daughter's life than she, had the brainwashing gone as far as I feared.

I fled the stares and snickers and found myself in an old preserved side street, the cobbles shining with evening dampness. The gutters overflowed with litter, a drunk lay sleeping in a puddle of piss and vomit. I was way off the beaten track. Perhaps I'd been aiming here all along.

Nestled between the rear entrance of a smoke-filled pub and an unknown Chinese restaurant stood a door. It was clean and freshly painted, so out of place. A sign hung above it, looking so perfect, so appropriate, that I knew it was placed there just for me. The flush of warmth and peace mimicked what I would have felt had I found Laura herself, and for a few seconds I was sure, *certain* that everything was not *going* to be all right... it already *was*.

Hell, it read. Calmed if you enter, damned if you don't.

The door opened on frictionless hinges. The ground shifted beneath my feet to carry me into the room, and I felt as if I was flying towards my fate. I did nothing to prevent it. I was not afraid. I'd heard about Hell from drunken friends at the tail end of parties and strangers in airports, and I knew it was the place for me. I needed a dose of misfortune. Things were bad for me, but so much worse for so many other people. I needed to be told this for sure.

I needed to *see*.

The room was certainly not what I'd expected, but I guessed as I entered that it was merely one of many portals into Hell. It was small, certainly not much larger than the average living room, with several chairs lining one wall and a huge holo-image projected against the wall opposite. It did not move, but it didn't need to. It depicted a scene I remembered from my days as a teenager, a time when wars raged and the camps had just been discovered in North Africa. This image was taken from one of them. Dry desert. A few stick figures in the foreground, their skin as yellow as the sand, their eyes as dead. And in the background, like some false forest sprouting from the hot desert wastes, hundreds of stakes holding their dead offerings aloft. Desert wildlife, unused to such a proliferation of free food, had made its home amongst the bodies. Lizards fed on the coagulated blood at the bases of the stakes, while scorpions, beetles and flies feasted on the more recent dead. And the eyes of the wandering stick figures in the foreground... when I'd first seen this image twenty years before, I remembered thinking that they looked like they wanted to die. Now, seeing again, I knew how wrong I'd been. These people wanted so much to have never lived at all.

"Bet you're glad you weren't there."

I spun around and was confronted by the most sensationally attractive woman I had ever seen. I hate to use to term "unnatural beauty" — even then the phrase circled my consciousness like a ghost, too dangerous, too unknown to admit to — but if her beauty were natural, then the world was indeed a wonderful place.

"Er...." I said, glancing at the holo, then back to the woman.

"They were killed like that for their beliefs," she said, face growing serious, her emerald-green eyes darkening as though she were seeing the scene for the first time. "There wasn't enough wood to make full crosses, not enough nails to hold them up, so they sharpened the ends of the poles and set the people on them. Into their anuses to begin with; then as the killings went on the murderers became more experimental. One man was found weeks later with the spike through his lower jaw, protruding from his mouth. They say he died of dehydration and heatstroke, his skin flayed by the sun, eyes removed by wandering carrion." The woman looked at me again as if daring me to challenge what she had said. "Women suffered particularly terrible fates."

I could say nothing.

She smiled gently, and even the lightest touch lit up her whole face. "But that was a long time ago, and it's the here and now you're concerned with, yes?"

I nodded. I felt crazily controlled by this woman, as if she was a teacher and I a young, snotty-nosed pupil. She turned and walked back to the comfortable chair she had been sitting in when I entered. It was a rocking chair, a small table beside it with a cup of steaming tea and a half-read book lying face down.

"I need you," I said. The intention was not sexual and she seemed to know that. My desperation was welling, the idea that I was nearer than I had ever thought possible — always, inside, was the niggling fear that Hell was just a myth, an urban legend — almost bringing me to tears. There was no shame behind my need, simply the knowledge that something had to be done. Right then, I was not prepared to go mad.

She stared up into my eyes. It felt as if she was viewing my soul, bare and helpless before her.

"Oh God, yes," she said. "Yes you do." She smiled again and asked me to take a seat.

I looked around as I crossed to the chairs. There was a tall rubber plant in one corner with pale spots on its leaves and dried roots showing through the powdery soil. There were more important things, I supposed. The gruesome holo of the impalings was the only hint at decoration. The chairs were comfortable-looking but functional, no ostentation here, no grand entrance to Hell. Simply a waiting room, and a woman whose like I would never see again.

I turned around, smiled at her and sat down.

The smile froze for an instant as I felt a stab in my left buttock. The woman's calm expression did not change. She picked up her book, still smiling, and took a sip of tea. The room faded, seeming to dissolve away from me, the woman's gentle smile remaining in my vision like a Cheshire Cat grin, and I imagined her whispering in my ear *I thought it would*. I tried to stand to see what had stung me, but before I could rise from the seat I found myself somewhere else entirely.

There.

A quiet suburban street. Cars parked along the side of the road, gardens well-maintained, privet hedges trimmed. The houses were all freshly painted, roofs newly tiled, lawns lush with grass of a constant length.

I was in a bus or coach, my seat so comfortable that it must have molded to my form. The air in the coach was of a perfect temperature and humidity. On a small table in front of me sat several bottles of water, wine and beer, and three packed meals, red self-heating lights all glowing. The lighting was at an optimum level, and although it seemed that the sun shone brightly outside, the windows filtered the glare. It was perfect.

Glancing down, I saw that I was firmly strapped into my seat.

Be glad you don't live here, a voice whispered, so intimate that it felt as though it originated inside my head.

I looked outside again and nothing was wrong. Kids played along the pavement, parents chatted over fences or washed cars or cut lawns, a family cycled along the street, passing so close to my window that I could see a shaving-cut on the father's face. They seemed not to notice us. It was so silent inside the coach — if there were other passengers, their attention was concentrated on what was happening outside — that a sense of foreboding built rapidly, a feeling that nothing could be right with a scene that looked so perfect. Something bad was coming. It *had* to be. We were, after all, in Hell.

My breathing quickened and I almost went to rap on the window, but then I remembered where I was and why. I'd come because I wanted to see things like this. I needed to know that my life wasn't so bad after all.

There's no such thing as perfect, the voice purred, soft, androgynous, a tickle in my ear.

And then the madman came.

It only took a couple of minutes from beginning to end. Our coach moved silently to one side to allow the high-powered car to roar past, scream into a skid and mount the pavement. A toddler disappeared beneath its front bumper and reemerged as a red streak on the pavement, baseball cap fluttering in the car's slipstream like a wounded butterfly. A bigger kid went flying, parting company with his bike and spinning through the air, blood spiralling as it caught the calm afternoon sun.

I saw a parent open her mouth and heard the scream, and I thought *at least Laura's still alive, somewhere.*

The car struck a garden wall and the driver tumbled out... and then the true terror of what we were about to see became apparent.

He had guns. Slung around his neck, a belt dangled hand grenades like poisoned apples, full of death. A knife gleamed in his belt. His face was grim and spattered with blood, as if this was just another stop in a slew of mayhem, and I saw that he had a good haircut, manicured nails, a fake tan. I wondered what had driven him to this.

The madman stepped in a soft, red, wet mess next to his car. He wiped his foot slowly and carefully on a clump of grass. And then he opened fire.

I ducked, but the coach seemed to be beyond his sight. He swung the guns around, left, right, left again, then dropped one and plucked a grenade from the belt. People tumbled, sagged, screamed, shoved themselves under cars and behind doors with shattered legs, tried to catch their blood. Sounds and colors combined, the bloody red roar of rifle fire, the black explosions of grenades, the glinting screams of agony as windows burst out and glass lacerated, crumpled brick brained, fire rolled and added to itself.

Overhead, storm clouds had gathered from out of nowhere, and lightning forked down beyond the street. High up I saw a passenger plane struck and begin a slow, terrible roll towards earth.

Our coach pulled away quickly, leaving the scene of devastation behind. I should have been shocked, but there was only relief.

Be glad you didn't live there, the voice whispered again. A woman across the aisle smiled softly to herself, and I knew that everyone was being spoken to.

"Where are we?" I shouted. The woman frowned at me as if I was disturbing the climax of a particularly moving opera. "Where *are* we?" But I knew. I think it was just panic.

"Shut up," said a soft voice from the seat in front of me. I could not see the person speaking. The straps did not allow any intermingling.

"But is all that supposed to help?" I said. I turned to the woman, feeling the need for eye contact, but she had averted her gaze. It was dark outside now and there was a definite sense of movement, but the windows gave no reflection. Unless she chose to look at me I may as well have been talking to myself. "Seeing those people shot," I continued, "murdered in cold blood, and that plane falling from the sky, who knows what the passengers were thinking? How can that help, all that pain —"

"It helps because you've never felt it," the man in front said. His voice was still low but it carried, bearing authority and experience and a weariness I had never encountered before. I wondered how long he had been here. The certainty that it was forever sent me cold. "Be glad."

"Glad?" I said, but nobody answered. I already knew what he meant. I tried looking from the window instead, and right then I'd have given anything to be able to see my reflection. It was light inside the coach but the windows were a matte black, offering me no glimpse of how my eyes had changed over the past few minutes. First I had been in the waiting room and now I was here, and whatever had happened in between was lost time. Perhaps I'd been drugged.

"Were you drugged?" I asked the woman across the aisle.

She turned to me and I saw for the first time how striking and wretched she was. I had never thought to find beauty in sorrow, but her hooded eyes and downturned mouth, the sallowness of her brown skin and her lank black hair... I found it all so alluring. Perhaps because I saw a reflection of myself at last.

"My son was drugged," she said.

"He's on here too?" I looked around, straining against my straps to see if there was someone else with this woman's eyes. But however hard I tried I could see no one else, only the grey tuft of hair rising just above the seat before me. It wavered in an unseen breeze.

"No, he's dead," she said. I thought she smiled, but it was a grimace preceding an outpouring of tears. "They took him from school and gave him drugs, fed him them like they were candy, made him an addict and made him dependent. He couldn't move without his fix, couldn't wash or eat or shit. They turned him into their slave. His chains were drugs, his life was theirs, and there was nothing... *nothing* I could do. Nothing *anyone* could do. People say they care until they realize that they're helpless, then they fade away into the background, try to make you forget they were ever there. Maybe it's guilt. I lost a lot of friends after my son was taken from me. Just at the time I needed them they left, because they couldn't help and they couldn't live with not helping."

She wiped at her eyes but the tears had already ceased. Perhaps there weren't that many left. "Then they sent him back to school with a pocketful of drugs and a flick-knife. He was expelled quickly, my Paul, expelled and arrested and beaten and arrested again and released and beaten, beaten by everyone. Helpless. I'd lost touch with him by then... long before then... but I wouldn't have been able to do anything anyway. I was helpless. When they found him... he was half the weight he'd been when I'd last seen him."

"Sorry," I said when she seemed to stop talking and fall into a trance, staring at my feet or somewhere far beyond. "I didn't think — "

"He always wanted to be an architect," she said. "He was nine years old when he died." She saw me properly for the first time then, her eyes seeing instead of looking, perhaps probing to discover whether I was someone she could really talk to. "So young, and yet he knew his future so well. How can they steal that from someone so young? How *could* they?"

I turned back to the window after offering her an awkward smile. I thought of Laura and how, at least, she was still alive. I assumed. I *had* to assume.

"Hell is other people," the grey-haired man murmured.

"And what the fuck is that supposed to mean?" I didn't raise my voice, but I was angry.

"I'm not offering an opinion," he said, "merely quoting."

There was nothing I could say to that, and I felt ridiculously admonished. I glanced across at the woman but she was staring down at her hands, twisting them in her lap. In this strange light it looked as if she was kneading shadows.

I wondered how this could be helping her, and in doing so I realized that it was already making me forget my own problems. Laura was still on my mind — she would *always* be there — but after the woman's horrible story my own problems felt lessened. Probably not exactly what Hell had intended... but one of my fellow passengers had greater problems than me. I often told myself that there were a lot of people worse off, but I'd never actually met them.

"*Oh Jesus!*" said a voice from further along the coach.

And the windows lit up again.

They were moving us through a town that was dying.

I glanced at the woman across the aisle but she was staring from her window as well, seeing all the same things, probably equally shocked.

"I never thought there was anywhere like this left," I whispered. Nobody answered me, and I hoped that it was because they agreed rather than because they thought I was naïve.

There was a man standing at the base of a flight of steps, jabbing continuously at his arm with a needle, arcs of blood spattering the pavement at every attempt, and his mouth dribbling as he shouted *I have no veins, I have no veins.* Whatever was in the syringe initially must have drained away by now, but still he searched, not seeing his own life fluid leaking from him, even when he sliced the needle up and down his wrist and a group of watchers stood back so that the resulting fountain did not stain them. A pack of mangy dogs crossed the street with their tails held high and their noses low to the ground, but I turned away.

"God," I said, glancing over to see what the woman had seen. The back of her head told me nothing.

The coach moved slowly along the street, and the people did not appear to see us. If it was a holo it was beautifully arranged. It picked up every minor facet of reality. A particular sun-glint from a dusty window; steam rising from a dog's piss as it raised its leg against a wall; shadows sitting in the cracks in pavements, hiding from daylight like the men I could see hunkered down in shop doorways, not wishing to be a part of things.

I tried waving but no one saw, or if they did had no wish to respond. I wondered just how programmed and pre-set this was.

The buildings stared out with shattered windows. A naked woman hung from one of them, her flesh grey and bloated with time, rope digging so far into her neck that rolls of skin and flesh had closed around it. She may have been pretty in the past, but now she was a smear on the wall of the building, a fluid stain marking the masonry below her. I really didn't want to know what that meant.

A group of men were gang-raping someone in an alley.

A dead person lay in the gutter, ignored and left for the flies and rats.

A lost child wandered along the pavement, crying, raising its hands but catching nobody's attention.

"Sick," I said, "this is just sick."

But I had never been anywhere like this, hardly even imagined it. Wherever Laura was now was surely better. She wouldn't be seeing these things, wouldn't be subjected to such horror, no matter how much the sect brainwashed her and tried to pull her further and further from any sort of life she knew.

I retched and leaned forward, grabbed a bottle of water and tried to drown my nausea. There must have been some additive in there for such use, because I felt better within a few seconds. I strained in my seat and looked back at the mouth of the alley. There were no signs of what I had seen; at least it was out of sight now. Out of sight, out of mind, someone had once said to me. I'd wanted to hit them, because Janine had been out of sight for three years by then.

"I'm so glad places like this don't exist anymore," the woman across from me said.

I looked over in time to see her misted breath clearing from the window. "So you think it's a recording?" I asked.

She glanced over and smiled. "Sure it is." *How stupid of you*, her voice said, so I did not pursue it.

"Hell," I said. "Hell on screen. So... why not just beam it to our nets?"

The woman did not answer. I heard a shifting in the seat in front of me, but the man said nothing.

Outside, more things were starting to happen in the run-down street. Isolated incidents at first — a man being beaten against a car, a young boy kneeling astride an equally young girl, knife drawn, her hair tangled in his fist — and then something more concerted, more significant. I was not consciously aware of things changing, but between one blink and the next the trouble-strewn street had opened up into a plaza. A church stood at one side, a line of rag-tag market stalls at another, and the blank walls of warehouses completed the square. A road ran through from either side.

Within seconds of the scene imprinting itself on my mind, a battle had begun.

The women carried no weapons. Their clothes were varied, their skins different shades, but each of them had the same dark expression on their face. Whatever they were fighting for, they were confident in their cause. Every point of impact resulted in the same outcome: one dead woman; one policeman splashed with blood, spark-stick drawn and buzzing as it searched for more skin to sear and break. It was a slaughter. And they hadn't even drawn their guns.

I pressed my face to the glass, disgusted and shocked but unable to tear myself away. Had this happened somewhere in the world, some vague point in the history of an Eastern European state that my schooling had failed to touch upon? The women looked like those I'd see in the street at home — any one of them could have been Laura or Janine — and the police... they were up to date.

Totally up to date.

Body-molding armor, shifting and flexing with each movement or muscular tick. A transparent sheen around their head which was a helmet and oxygen mask in one, solidifying micro-seconds before anything impacted upon it, parting and opening as and when necessary for the wearer to breathe or speak or eat. The spark-sticks and the drill guns. Everything I was used to.

"This is now," I said. "This is happening now."

Time is an illusion, came the soft voice from inside my head. *Be glad you're not here at this time.*

"I'm not a woman," I said.

For the first time the voice answered me directly. *But you may have been a policeman.*

I watched a woman fall to the ground and a policeman kneeling beside her, fending off her waving arms and deftly crushing and melting her throat with one glittering lunge of his spark-stick.

I saw how right the voice was. "Who are you?"

Be quiet, it said. *Watch. It's all part of the service.*

"Anyone being talked to in here?" I shouted, and the silence from the others in the coach was my answer.

The battle erupted all around the coach but never touched it. There was murder and death and execution, but the one thing I never saw was the taking of a prisoner. These police, for whatever reason, had been instructed to simply kill. No crowd control for them, no law-enforcing, no friendly chat with someone who may have had a vague idea to break a minor law... these were out on a subdue and destroy mission the likes of which I could never have imagined.

"Is this how it could be?" I asked, and the disembodied voice answered.

Was, could be, will be is not important. You're not here, that is important. You're no part of this. Be thankful.

"I am," I said, and I was. The coach moved on, we passed scenes of terrible pain and cruelty, and I was thankful.

I began to realize how Hell could really work.

The windows went dark. I slumped back in my seat and all hint of external influences passed away. I'd been smelling the fear of that square, hearing the screams and dying sighs, tasting blood on the breeze and the tang of discharging spark-sticks. Now, with nothing more than the slight aroma of my own sweat to keep me company, it seemed all the more shocking.

"That was horrible," I said.

"Yes."

"What's your name?" I asked. The woman turned to look at me.

"I'm not going to tell you. It's personal."

I frowned, went to tell her my name but then thought about what she'd said. We were in Hell after all, and I tended to agree. *Personal.* She didn't want to get personal, and I could understand and empathize. What was happening here was way too internalized to get involved with someone just because they happened to be sitting across the aisle. Even the voice came from inside, as if I was actually hearing it somewhere else and only its meaning was being understood here.

"I'm so sorry about your son," I said, and she averted her eyes and looked at the black window.

I leaned forward and picked up a bottle of water, changed my mind and popped the seal on a beer. The bottleneck widened and a head developed, and I took my first frothy mouthful, sighing at the synthesized real ale taste. I still didn't know how they managed it, but it was perfect.

Closing my eyes, I leaned back in the seat. Laura surprised me and ran across my memory, laughing as a six-year-old and leaping on Janine's back just months before my wife died. I remembered the day vividly. I remembered being depressed and miserable and non-communicative, because both Janine and I knew that she was dying and there was nothing we could do. Fate had done that, to Janine and to me, and I hated it. I hated that Laura would grow up without a mother. And I took out my hate on both of them, because there was nothing and no one else to suffer it.

Reliving the memory, I knew that I should have relished that moment, *every* moment, not lived in a haze of hate. I saw Laura's eyes as she leapt on Janine, Janine's smile as she caught our daughter, and I realized for the first time that my wife was as happy then as she had ever been. Her smile was not for Laura's sake, nor for mine. It was genuine. A true statement of joy. I should have been a part of that, not apart from it.

I opened my eyes and I was crying. I wiped at the tears and took another swig of beer, and it didn't taste as good. That was the trouble with artificiality — it could never maintain a constant. Like memories it was only an approximation of the truth.

"My daughter has been taken away by a religious sect," I said. "I don't know where she is and I may never her back."

"At least she's alive," the woman said.

I thought about this, wondering just how we were supposed to take this journey as a healing exercise when we could still talk. "I'm sure your son still loved you, even at the end. My Laura will have been brainwashed to forget me. Love has no place in the sects... not for anything outside, at least."

The woman didn't respond and I said no more. I finished my beer, each mouthful more rancid, and then I opened one of the meal containers and ate salmon in white wine sauce. It was real salmon. It melted in my mouth and released the sterile taste of mass-produced fish that had never swum in a river, never known rapids. A smaller container held a slab of apple pie and custard, but once opened I could not bring myself to eat.

I suddenly felt bad, being able to eat and drink after what I had

just seen. The scenes outside looked so very real. They smelled
and sounded totally genuine. I'd just seen dozens of people dead
and dying, and I was ready to sit back and drink bad beer and eat
salmon. I looked around guiltily, but the woman across the aisle
was chewing thoughtfully on a mouthful of something, and from
the seat before me I could hear the unmistakable sounds of eating and drinking. I glanced across at the woman again and caught
her wry smile.

"I wonder what's next," someone said from further along the
coach. Their voice was muffled and dull, and I wondered just
how large this vehicle was. I shifted in my seat but the straps held
tight, as if aware of my sudden interest in looking around.

"*Titanic,*" someone answered, their voice even quieter. "I've
always wanted to see the *Titanic* going down."

"Natural disasters make for good viewing," the first voice said.
"Give me a hurricane or earthquake over a war or riot any day."

Be patient and you will see, said the voice in my head, and it must
have spoken to everyone because silence fell once more.

There was a sense of movement as we were transferred from
one scene to the next, but I could not tell how fast we were
traveling. It wasn't like a ship, or a hover train, or an aircraft,
because there were no sounds at all to indicate that we were passing along rails or through air turbulence. The sense came from
inside — an occasional dipping of the stomach or a twinge in
my inner ear. I wondered how far we were traveling and just
how big Hell may be, when the windows brightened once again
and I was faced with the answer.

Hell was huge. If it had boundaries they were scores of miles
apart, at least. It had sky, and land, and dazzling sunlight. And
when it came to pain, suffering and death... it knew *no* boundaries.

Perhaps even now Laura was being lectured in the traditional
Hell, the metaphysical place where wrongdoers suffered and pun-
ishments were meted out, and where Satan presided over his flung-
down domain, plotting vengeance, scheming to reattain his right-
ful place amongst the angels. But however thorough her brainwashing at the hands of the cult, they could never show her this.
If she were here with me now, then she'd believe. Then she'd
know that Hell is of our own making, and we have been manufac-
turing and perpetuating it on our own planet ever since we crawled
from the primeval swamp. The place I traveled through was
simply a bringing together, a distillation of all bad things.

I looked from the window and felt sick.

Be glad you aren't here, the voice purred, and I began to cry.

The coach was moving slowly, painfully slowly, across a wide open plain. In the distance a row of snow-capped mountains pointed at the sky like a giant bottom jaw. The top jaw was a line of dense stratocumulus clouds hanging threateningly across the whole horizon, waiting to close at any moment and bite the scene away. The plain itself, for as far as I could see, writhed and flickered and shifted in and out of focus, and at first I thought my tears were distorting trees and bushes and setting them moving. But I wiped at my eyes again, pressed my face to the window with my breath held... and I saw that the movement was people.

The whole plain, every spare spread of ground, was smothered with humanity. Hunkered under trees, sitting on the sides of small hillocks, hiding beneath tarpaulins or coats pinned to upright sticks, staring up into the sky or scrabbling around in the dust for food, adults drinking from deflated water bags and children hanging onto sagging breasts, bodies coughing blood, eyes leaking blood, mouths gushing blood as people fell to their knees and vomited, some rushing to their aid but trying not to get too close, living-dead wrapping corpses in dirty clothes and men digging long burial pits, the wrappers scratching at sores on their arms, the diggers wiping bloody red from their eyes, birds sweeping down to peck morsels from bodies left out too long after death, and sometimes from those so weakened that they could not wave the birds away, could not save their eyes or testicles or dignity in the few moments they had left in this world before passing painfully into the next....

I gasped out loud and heard similar sounds from around the coach. Even the man in front of me, all but silent and dismissive in his invisibility until now, muttered something under his breath that may have been a prayer.

And then the sounds and smells made it in from outside, and I knew that there was always worse.

Moans, cries, the stench of shit, rot, sighs, screams, muttered desperation, food gone-off, vomit, vomiting, fresh exhortations from a new volunteer helper, the disbelieving mumbles from the thousands who had seen it all before. They knew that nothing and no one could help. I saw a gaggle of nuns threading their way through the hundreds of acres of dead and dying humanity, and I almost laughed at their blind devotion and foolish belief that anything could ever be any different. One of them would stop every now and then, bend down, cross herself and a bundle of rags on the floor before moving on. I wondered how many of them would be alive next week, and how many black and white habits were already hugging corpses in the ground.

We passed by a burial pit. As ever, the diggers did not look our way — we were not there, so there was nothing for them to see — and I had an uninterrupted view of the hundreds of bodies piled at one end. The digging could not keep up with the dying, and even as corpses were wound in old cloth or sacking and flung into the pit, the mountain they had been taken from grew.

This close to so many dead I could see how extreme their affliction was. Something hissed inside the coach and the odor was suddenly beaten back by a sweet perfume, but I still got an idea of how bad this would smell, how awful the stench of rotting family and friends could be. There was so much blood. The bodies had bled out, their fluids leaving through existing holes and new ones alike. Stomachs were split, chests ruptured, noses rotted away, eyes pushed out of their sockets by the explosive pressure of blood seeking release. I'd heard about Ebola Zaire and Marburg, but this looked so much worse, even more violent than those nightmare viruses. A sheet of flies lifted from the corpses as if flicked at one end, swung around to a new patch of opened flesh and settled once more. New life for old, I thought, and I saw maggots squirming in a dead child's mouth.

Two young women tipped a body onto the base of the pile and turned to leave with their stretcher. I thought they were crying, but one of them turned and looked directly at me — *through* me — and I saw the blood leaking from her eyes. Even had I been visible, she could not have seen me.

As we passed by the burial pit I saw an old man rooting among the dead. He was lifting limbs and prising mouths open with a thick stick, knocking out gold teeth, plucking jewelry from swollen fingers, and as we moved on I heard the jingling of his booty as he shifted a big rucksack from one shoulder to the other.

The windows began to fade to black and I turned to the woman across the aisle, but then the voice rang up inside my head one more time. *Sometimes it's impossible to believe just how bad things can get.*

And the windows brightened again.

Something was screaming. It Dopplered in from the distance, and at first I thought it was someone inside the coach shouting at what they saw, rebelling, running along the aisle as they sought escape. But then I realized that the sound came from outside. Some of the people across the plain looked up and I followed their gaze… and thought help was at hand.

The aircraft screamed overhead so fast that I could not identify it, let alone make out its nationality. It left behind a shimmering wake and several cylindrical objects high in the sky, spinning and falling through the turbulent air until they each sprouted a parachute, bursts of compressed gas firing them away from each other, spreading across the plain until the five were slowly closing down like the fingers of a grasping giant's hand.

Medicine, I thought, a cure, parachuted in by some benevolent government who couldn't risk putting their own people in and infecting them as well. The coach moved slowly across the plain and the cylinders floated lazily down, and more and more people stopped what they were doing and looked up. The ill lying on sheets or bare earth shielded their eyes if they could move, and the less-ill stood and stared, pointing, chattering excitedly, some of them even eschewing their fear of contact to hug their neighbors and rejoice that someone, at last, had done something good for them.

Sometimes it's impossible to believe how bad things can get, the voice purred in my head, and I didn't know if it was memory or the words being spoken again.

Either way, I went cold.

"No...." I whispered, and I heard the word echoing up and down the coach as we all saw the first parachute land.

The explosion was at least three miles away, off towards the snowy mountains that looked so picturesque in the distance, but it rapidly blossomed out, an expanding ball of flame rolling along the ground and rising into the air, burning stick-people tumbling before it. The rest of the cylinders landed then, bursting open one by one and allowing their magic to work, igniting the earth and air, and the bodies in between. I saw some people raise their hands in joy when they realized that peace had come for them at last, and others turned to run and were caught by the speeding flames, hair igniting and faces melting away. The burial pits exploded as withheld gases were fired. Makeshift tents were blasted along the ground from place to place as the firestorm set in, and soon bodies accompanied them in the air, sucked helplessly into the ever expanding walls of fire. The nuns were running. Nothing could save them now.

As the fires from the separate explosions met, the windows in the coach faded to black.

I could still feel the heat, hear the screams, smell the stench of everything burning. I was panting. Sweat ran down my sides and a cool breeze issued from some unseen vent, but mere machines could not understand that fear and terror and anger cannot be cooled. It takes more than a breath of fresh air to do that.

I snatched up a bottle of beer and drained it in one go. It tasted foul but the subtle alcohol hit felt good. I kept trying to glance over my shoulder, through the window and back the way we had come, because I wanted to know if there was anything we should be doing for those poor people back there. Diseased, already doomed, then bombed and burned. There was no hope but still I looked back, seeing nothing in the blackened glass, not even offered my own wretched reflection to rage against.

"It's terrible, terrible," a voice said from in front of me, probably several seats down. It fell apart even as the man was talking, tears breaking through and giving a raw edge to his words, cracking his breaths. "It just... it's... those poor...." He wailed then, sending a shiver down my spine, making me want to shout at him to stop, just shut up, because *I couldn't take this now that the windows were dark.* I searched for another bottle of beer, but I had only water left. The woman across the aisle hissed at me.

"What?"

She lobbed me one of her beer bottles. I caught it from the air and smiled at her, a pained, nervous twitch of my lips that did nothing to find its way through what was really there. She did not smile back. "Never did drink," she said. "Just another drug."

I looked away embarrassed. But still I took a small sip and sat back, eyes closed, trying to cut out the crying.

It occurred to me that so far I had only seen the woman, no one else. There could be two more or twenty more people in here, perhaps two hundred more, the seats were so large and well padded that they seemed to all but absorb any noise made by the coach's occupants. There was the man in front of me — I could still see a wisp of his grey hair — but so far as I knew that was it. Voices, yes, but no more people.

For the first time it struck me that this could all be for me.

Perhaps everyone who resorted to Hell had this sort of treatment. Maybe anyone else was an actor, put here to treat me as they'd treated hundreds, maybe thousands before. Show the scenes outside, tell their stories, make me realize that I was *never* worse off than everyone.

I took another swig of beer and the screaming man stopped screaming. There was a thud, like a door slamming shut or a page being turned in a heavy book, and then silence.

The man in front sighed, and I saw a hand raise up and smooth down his wispy hair. It was old, wrinkled, calloused, the hand of a manual worker. I wondered if he worked in the inner-city farms, or the sewers, or the tunnel projects that were meant to link city to city, country to country.

"It doesn't matter anyway," he said.

I caught a whiff of burning bodies, as if a flake of scorched flesh was caught in my nostrils. "Of course it matters!" I said, wanting to shout. "Didn't you see them? Poor bastards, poor...." I trailed off because I realized how inadequate anything I could say would sound.

"It's all put on for us because we're in Hell, and that's how they do things here," the man said. "Ha! I can't even see you, for all I know you're a machine with reaction software, or just one of *them*." I heard him tapping his fingers against the window, as if trying to read dark Braille there. "In fact, I'm sure you are."

"I'm not!" I said. "Maybe *you* are! Maybe everyone on this coach — "

"Not me," he said. "But I don't worry or hold it against you, because what's the capital of Syria?"

"Huh?"

He was silent for a couple of seconds and I saw the woman looking over, interest arching her eyebrows. I suddenly felt unreasonably good, seeing something other than fear, dread or sorrow on her face.

"I suppose I'd have to be quicker than that to catch out reaction software, wouldn't I?"

"Absolutely, Sir," I said in a slow monotone, and the woman snorted.

Something made the coach sway slightly, and I heard a couple of coughs as people tried to ignore the sick movement in their stomachs. I glanced at the window, waiting for it to brighten again and terrified at what I would see, but it remained dark.

I wondered where Laura was right then. It felt strange thinking of her, because it was almost certain that she wasn't thinking of me. At most I was an invader in her memory. In a way I wished that I could forget as well, but she wasn't in pain, wasn't burning or being shot. I sent love to Laura, knowing she wouldn't hear it but doing it for myself. It didn't help, but I pretended it did.

The windows brightened and I thought we were back. Back *where* I wasn't exactly sure — somewhere deep in the Welsh mountains, perhaps — but at least our journey was at an end. The view from the window was wonderful, a mountainous rural paradise, and I sat back and smiled as the coach moved slowly through the scene.

So come on, I thought, show us pollution or global warming or deforestation or disease or death. But the image remained pure, the trees and shrubs and flowers and grasses grew lush and healthy. Things weren't so bad after all. There were a lot of people much more worse off than me. What this meant for them I tried not to consider, because this trip was all about me, and for the woman across the aisle it was purely about her, and so on, and so on....

If thinking that way worked I was not about to argue.

It was only as I noticed the shapes slung between the trees that I realized we still had some way to go. They came into focus, my breath hitched, my heart stuttered. And I knew it wasn't a holo or a movie or an act.

It was more than that. I knew for certain that this, all of this, was far more real than anyone could have guessed.

I knew, because I recognized one of the shapes strung up on the barbed wire.

Laura.

"Laura!" I strained in my seat, fighting against the straps. I needed to press close to the window, closer to Laura, just to make sure it was her. Her hair was tangled in a knot of wire above her, arms flung out and bleeding where they were tied, legs dangling. I recognized the dress she wore... she'd first worn it on her thirteenth birthday. I'd bought it for her. Expensive. And even before the party started she spilled orange juice down it, and she started to cry because her party was spoiled. I'd told her that it was the girl, not the dress that mattered. The girl inside....

"Laura!" I screamed again. The strap was biting into my waist as I reached for the window. The coach was moving along slowly, and other hanging figures were coming into view. Some of them were still but for the movement of birds and other carrion creatures, but most of them still moved where they hung, each movement drawing more blood or further cries or moans.

Laura moved.

I sat still and watched, and just as she passed out of sight behind a thick clump of trees she shifted again, her mouth falling open into a scream I heard from afar.

"That's Laura out there!" I shouted, having no comprehension of how this could be so, simply knowing that it *was*. I could no longer see her but her scream remained. "That's *Laura!*"

"Hey, I'm sure you didn't see — "

"Don't tell me I don't know my own daughter!" I shouted at the woman, and she flinched as if slapped.

I looked back at the window and it was fading to black. The atmosphere had changed. The coach jerked slightly, as if struck from one side, and the windows flared brightly again for a couple of seconds before blacking out. They'd only let us see some of the pain and suffering out there this time, and I was sure I'd glimpsed something even worse happening ahead.

Perhaps they didn't like what I was saying.

"She's still alive," I said, kicking out at the chair in front of me. "Hey! You! My daughter, she's still alive on those trees. I have to get her!"

I saw the man's tuft of grey hair turn as he tried to lift himself to look at me, but we were too securely fastened. "It's a holo, a make-believe. It's not really happening. And if it is your daughter maybe she's an actress, perhaps they paid her to act — "

Perhaps, I thought, but then I remembered the pain I'd seen on her face and the scream I'd heard. Laura was *my daughter*. I'd seen her in pain enough times — scraped knees, toothache, the broken arm when she was nine — to know that she could not have been acting.

I wished that she *had* been taken away by a sect.

I grasped at the strap around my waist and pulled. It did not budge.

"Are you sure it was her?" the woman said.

I nodded without looking up, still tugging at the strap, trying to find where it was buckled. I thought of Janine on her deathbed, how the panic in her eyes had been for the daughter she was leaving behind, not for herself.

I hated myself for not looking after Laura.

There was a sighing noise from somewhere along the coach, and a few in-drawn breaths. Footsteps approached along the aisle. The passengers were silent once more, and I felt a shadow approaching.

"*Positive?*" the woman hissed.

I stopped messing with the strap and looked across at her, just as a dark shape manifested between the two seats in front of us. "It was Laura," I said.

The thing leant down towards me. It looked like a huge beetle, with a hard shiny skin and a head twitching with several small antennae. Somewhere in there, perhaps, was a man or woman, but just then I felt as if I was looking a denizen of Hell right in the face. I'd never seen anything like this before.

The thing clicked and clacked, reaching out one black hand and offering me the open end of a stun-gun.

Kill me, I thought, *they'll kill me for seeing what I've seen...*
...or perhaps they'll just add me to it...
And then it flipped on its back, hands grasping at air as the woman stretched her left leg and kicked its ankle. "I reckon you've got maybe three seconds," she said, crouching back in her seat as if afraid to touch the thing again.

I looked down at where the shape was struggling on the floor. Thoughts rushed at me as I decided what to do first — Are there more of them? Does it have protection software? Is it going to kill me? — and for the half-second it took these to whirl through my head the world stood still. Its armor seemed to impede it, and when it reached out to grab my chair and haul itself up, I kicked out at its hand. The armor was as hard as metal and I gasped as pain dug through my foot.

The thing paused, looked up at me, antennae twitching, perhaps signalling.

I kicked again, using my heel this time, connecting squarely with the dark visor. I heard a crack and but hoped it was artificial. The thing flung one hand up as it rolled back. I reached out and grasped its wrist, twisting, feeling the armor harden under the contours of my hand, the stun-gun slipping from its grip —

I had maybe a second left until the thing shook off its confusion and came for me.

I kicked again, three times, aiming at the visor every time. It was constantly trying to rise, only my kicks keeping it down. *I stop kicking, up it gets*, I thought. So I kicked yet again, and again, glancing at the mean-looking black stun-gun in my hand, trying to figure out how the hell to use it. There was a silver button and what looked like a trigger, again in silver, so I leaned over, forced the barrel end against the thing's cracked visor and pressed both.

The button must have been a voltage booster.

The thing — and I really hoped there wasn't a man or woman in there — only twitched for a second or two before it lay still, smoking.

"What's going on back there?" I heard someone shout, and I welcomed the distraction. Looking down would mean seeing what I had done, and I was afraid that it was a very bad thing. The normal stun-guns carried by law enforcement were designed to do just that: stun. From the stench of hot meat I was afraid that this one had done much more.

"I'm getting off," I said.

"Don't be mad!" It was the man in the chair in front of me, still unseen, thinking he knew best.

"My daughter's out there," I said, "and she's bleeding and dying. Besides, I thought you said it was all false." I paused; he said nothing. "I'm getting out," I said again. Maybe I was trying to talk myself out of it.

"If there's one of those... things in here, there'll be more out there. Lots more."

I felt around with my fingers, trying not to look because I didn't want to see whatever damaged, dead thing lay inside the armor. I'd heard about genetic alterations, gene mutation... I'd heard about it far too much. I didn't want to see it as well. My fingers scraped the smashed visor and I tugged free a loose piece of composite.

"You sound like you've seen — " I began, but then the dead thing moved.

It hissed, expelling a stinking breath right up into my face. And I heard a voice, soft and persuasive, deep inside my head. This was much more personal than the voice that had introduced the horrific scenes. This was not only inside my head but inside *me*, reaching out from places I'd forgotten or tried to forget, sounding like my poor dead Janine and my dying Laura combined... and it was telling me to sit back down.

You don't want to get up.

You don't need *to get up.*

"Don't listen to it," the man in front said, and the injured thing at my feet growled a stinking threat up into my face, stinking and angry.

"How do you know — " I began, but then I stamped back down on its face, feeling my boot heel striking something soft. Inside me, the soft voice grew harsh before fading away.

"What is it?" I hissed, starting to hack at the strap around my waist with the rough-edged plastic. My own blood spotted my trousers.

"Demon," the man said.

I stopped for a second and glanced up, but even his hair was out of sight. "You're just kidding me, right?" I started sawing at the strap instead of hacking, and the heavy threads began to pop apart. The thing at my feet moved, I stamped again, and the man gave me his answer.

"No. And yes, I suppose. And yes, I have been here before."

The woman across the aisle snorted. "And the prize for the most ridiculously confusing answer goes to...."

"I won't tell you my name," he said.

"I don't think she was expecting you to." The threads were

parting faster now, and I guessed I had maybe thirty seconds to go. Then all I had to do was exit the coach, dodge however many more soldiers, droids or demons there were, find Laura where she was strung up between trees, get her down and navigate my way out of Hell.

Easy.

I laughed manically as the strap popped free. Standing up, I saw the coach for what it really was. As wide as the coach on a train but much longer, so long that perspective stole the end from sight. And all the way along, chairs like my own sat at each window, with a narrow aisle in between.

I turned around and the same sight greeted me, except this time there were shocked faces watching me from each chair. I caught a few peoples' stares, even though I tried not to. There was interest, anger and resentment in equal measures, and I realized that those who had no idea what had happened here must be blaming me for their tour being halted.

"How the hell do I get out of here?" I asked, stepping into the aisle and glancing over the chair at the man in front of me.

"Same way the demon got in," the man said. And I wondered how he could talk at all.

I'd once seen the results of a speed-bike crash. The rider had been thrown against a wall and was a broken, shattered mess. Limbs askew. Shape changed. I never thought I'd see the same in someone living.

"Huh?" I uttered stupidly. I could not form words because what I saw stole them from me. He was so badly battered and misshapen that it must have hurt him to live.

"Up there," he said, nodding back over my shoulder.

I turned and looked along the aisle, noticing a dark patch in the ceiling which could only have been a trapdoor. "Do you know the way?" I asked turning back.

His face did something that may have been a smile, and he shook his head. "I've been out there once before," he said, "thinking I could change things, imagining I could help the hopeless. That's how I got this." He didn't point to anything, but he didn't need to. I could not make out where parts of him started and ended. Tears burned in my eyes and throat, but I guessed that he probably wouldn't appreciate them at all.

"So up there is out?" I said. And I thought, out of where? Out of the coach and into the forest and barbed wire and Laura? Or out of Hell? Back into that waiting room perhaps, the stunning woman standing by the wall painting and pointing out intricate details of cruelty and pain I hadn't noticed before.

"If you must go," he said, "yes, up there."

I looked at him and wanted to ask him how I could help. But he'd obviously come here for a reason, whether he'd found his way in by accident or not. I could only guess at what traumas he suffered day in, day out, to warrant a second visit to this awful place. He blinked slowly, one eye only closing halfway because of the knot of scar tissue on his eyelid, and I took it as a message. The strap was to stay around his waist. He wanted it that way. He'd always be confined now, however his condition had come about.

That's how I got this, he'd said, talking of what was outside.

I turned and walked to the trapdoor, and as I looked up through it I could see reflected light coming in from somewhere. Somehow, it smelled like what I had seen outside should look: blood, rot, pain, death, anguish, nothing fresh, all of it corrupted.

Laura.

"I want to help you," the woman called from her seat. I turned and saw her straining at the strap, glancing nervously at the motionless thing lying by my vacated chair. A wisp of smoke curled from its broken visor, but I was sure I could see black movement in the shadow cast by its body.

"Why?"

She looked at me, frowning, trying to speak but unable to find the words.

"Why?" I said again. I wasn't used to people helping me, and I didn't believe it now.

"Laura's still alive," she said. And I nodded, because her son Paul was dead and perhaps, in this, she could shed her helplessness.

"Not if we don't hurry," I said, and that was that, agreed. I found the shard of visor composite and knelt by her side, hacking, pulling, slicing and sawing at the strap until it came apart. She stood shakily, hanging onto my arm as her tired legs tingled their inactivity away.

"I'm Chele," she said.

"Hello Chele. I'm Nolan." I went back to the trapdoor, knotted my hands and motioned her to climb. "What can you tell us?" I asked the mutilated man as Chele heaved herself up through the trap. I heard her banging about above the ceiling, suddenly wondering whether I'd sent her up first on purpose. If there were more of those demon things up there....

"More demons," the man said.

"Don't tell me they're demons; there are no such things as demons!"

"No such thing," the man repeated, and a rattle in his throat may have been a chuckle. "Well… this is a strange place, and strange things happen. Last time I was here, when I was out there in all of it, I saw one of them sprout wings and take flight."

"Cyborgs," I said. "Is that what they are? Constructs? Artificial —"

"They are what they want to be," he said, "and here, most of them want to be demons."

"Hey," Chele called. "Something's moving out there!"

I looked at the blackened window of the coach, as did the mutilated man. "How did you…?" I began.

"There are so many worst nightmares out there, it's not even worth me telling you," he said.

"Why did you come back?"

He looked at me with his tortured eyes. "To remind myself I'm not still here. I really wish you luck."

Laura, a voice said inside, and I was wasting time. It was probably a waste of time to begin with — I'd seen her blood, seen the pain in her expression — but the bastards had stolen her away and hung her up out there…

…and for the first time since seeing her I actually began to wonder why she was here.

If Laura, how many others?

"Hey, you, I'm moving off, are you coming?"

"Yes," I said up into the dark rectangle above me. I jumped up and held onto the hole's edges, glancing around me before I hauled myself up. The expressions on the few faces I could see told me that they thought I was mad. As for the mutilated man, he had no expression… but his eyes spoke volumes.

Goodbye, they said.

I scrambled up through the hole and into the space above the coach, a false-ceilinged area that must have been intended for ventilation and security.

"Hey, you," Chele called from ahead.

"My name's Nolan."

"Well Nolan, there's a door up ahead, and something out there smells." She crawled on her hands and knees and I followed.

"I should have brought that demon thing's weapon," I said, but Chele didn't hear. I paused, looking behind me and then ahead again, terrified that I'd see another one of those things crawling my way.

Chele eased herself around, hung her legs out through a low opening in the wall and dropped out of sight. A second later I heard her strike ground. I edged forward and looked out.

Chele was squatting on her haunches, picking at the lush green grass, sniffing it, running her hands across the bright daisies that grew in profusion between the coach and the trees. Dark things darted in the air around her head and she waved them away. I waited for them to attack her, pierce her skin and puncture her insides, but then a couple landed on her arm and they were only flies.

I dropped to the ground next to Chele, knees buckling and rolling me into the grass. I ended up on my front, breathing in the beautiful aroma of grass and dirt and the wilds, nothing artificial here, nothing made... all natural. I closed my eyes for a second and remembered a time with Janine, lying in the sun and making her a daisy chain.

"Where's the coach gone?" Chele asked quietly, mock-calm.

I knelt and turned back to the coach... and it was not there. There was *something* there, something big and heavy where the coach should be... but perhaps that was my memory playing tricks, because all I could actually see were rolling meadows, clumps of trees, a valley leading down, down, a river following its route to see where it went.

I turned and looked at the trees I'd seen from the coach window.

Then back again at where the coach should be.

"It's gone," I said.

Chele almost laughed, but the sound didn't sound quite right so she stopped. It was too much like madness. "If this is Hell I'm going to start being a naughty girl," she said. And I knew that something awful was going to happen.

It was the way the birds sang, fast and energetic, as if they were keen to finish and leave.

It was the way the river flowed away from us.

It was in the blue skies darkening with clouds, how the trees behind me seemed to be a mirror image of those in front, right down to snapped branches and bloodstained trunks.

The threat was there, palpable, hidden from view, but smelled and sensed the more I looked at our surroundings. "Laura," I said. I started to run back along the line of trees.

"Nolan!" Chele called. "I don't know if I can run!"

Right then I didn't care. I'd known this woman for an hour, she'd put herself in unknown danger to come out here and help me, but I didn't care. My only concern was Laura, and whether she was still alive.

As I ran and heard Chele's pounding footsteps behind me, I began to glimpse shadows shifting within the treeline to my right. I looked head-on, but I could only see them from the corner of my eye. They moved all wrong, these shadows, shifted position when branches were still, darted from trunk to trunk, evaded my stare but still gave themselves away. If they were demons and they chose to come at us now, we were finished. Pure luck had given me the upper hand with the thing in the coach, luck and Chele's help, and I hadn't even had the presence of mind to grab its stun-gun when I came outside. *Last time, I saw one of them sprout wings and take flight*, the mutilated man had said.

I'd smelled burning meat when I thrust the stunner through the broken visor, and the thing had been twitching in pain, and there was no way at all I could have done that to a droid, they were just too strong.

Demon….

More movement in the trees, and this time when I looked the shadows made no effort to hide themselves. They were human-shaped, loping along, steadying themselves against trunks, easily keeping pace with us as we ran in the open. Some were deformed, with hunched shoulders and huge heads. I glanced back at Chele; she had seen as well, and she put on a spurt of speed and caught up with me.

"We have nothing," she said, and I started looking around for a heavy stick or a fist-sized rock with which to defend ourselves.

Up ahead, between two trees, what looked like a giant spider web spanned the space between the trunks, black lines against the clear blue sky. I slowed and saw that it was comprised of long, drooping lengths of barbed wire. At its center, where dozens of wires crossed, chunks of something clung to the barbs. I didn't want to look, I knew I *shouldn't* look, but Chele's horrified gasp drew my eyes down to ground level. A body lay beneath the web, torn and distorted where its weight had ripped it from the constraining wires, flesh weakened by rot, bones parted by death. It provided a feeding ground for small animals now, and I tried not to look too closely. I did not recognize any species.

"That's not Laura," I said, but for a few seconds I did wonder. Perhaps in this strange place, ten minutes on the coach had been ten hours out here. I looked again, saw that the shape wore the remains of a boiler suit, not a dress. We ran on.

And the figures came out from beneath the trees.

One second the landscape was bare, and we could have been hiking through the unspoilt uplands of Switzerland or the foothills of the Himalayas. The next, thirty people had stepped out to watch us go by. And they were out of nightmares.

The hunched shadows I had seen resolved themselves into wretched shapes bent double, the huge heads great rolls of barbed wire. They were ape-like in their attitude, some naked, dirty, covered in sores, and where the wire pressed to their shoulders it had settled into the flesh, finding the hard bone easier to rest on. They looked at the ground, never seeing more than four steps in front of them. Perhaps that was from choice.

The others, those standing upright, were bedecked in all manner of military paraphernalia. I saw an old Nazi uniform, all leather and belts; a white outfit from some Arctic warfare unit; a braided jacket from the Napoleonic Wars; dirty green camouflage from the more recent European conflicts. Sandy desert garb, drab olives, a bulky NBC suit... more I did not recognize. And looking into the faces of those wearing the uniforms, I knew that there was nothing at all regular about these men and women. There was a desperation about them all, a glint of defiance in their eyes, as if all the deserters from history had gathered together to avoid, or perhaps accept their punishment.

A few carried weapons, some of which I recognized, others I did not. The glinting gold shell, clasped in the fist of one of the women and feeding green tendrils into the veins on her wrist... I had no idea what that was or what it was designed to do. All I could be sure of was that it was bad. The woman's face told me that, and the scarring around the moist socket where her right eye should have been.

"Who the fuck are you?" one of the men said. He stepped forward until he was standing nose to nose with me. I could smell the sweet rottenness of his breath, stale sweat, and something worse wafting from a dirty bandage on his right shoulder. He carried a serrated knife clotted with dried blood.

"I'm looking for my daughter." I glanced over his shoulder and past the milling people, trying to see beyond their threat to the trees where I thought Laura hung. They were only a couple of hundred yards away. I could run there in a minute, be holding my dear, dear daughter to my chest within a minute more, nursing, comforting, hoping that I was not too late and would need comforting myself....

"I said, who the fuck are you? Not, what the fuck are you doing? If I want to know what you're doing for I'll ask, what the fuck are you looking for? Get it?"

"Fucking right," I said, wincing inwardly but unable to avoid the sarcasm. "And as for who I am, my name's Nolan. Not that it's any business of yours."

The man stepped back, his eyes went wide and he brought the knife up in what looked like an expert defensive attitude.

If he goes for me now, I thought, that's it; no hazy knife defences learnt in karate when I was sixteen are going to save me.

"What are you... where are you from?" He looked at Chele as well, and the others suddenly seemed more interested. Even those hunkered pretences at humanity seemed to raise their heads.

I saw something in this madman's eyes — not fear as such, but caution and… hope? I told him what I was sure he wanted to hear. "We're visitors here," I said, "and I've just seen my daughter back there between those trees. Strung up." The man had a pair of wire cutters hanging from his belt. His hands were slashed and scabbed and scarred, as if his favorite hobby was crushing glass bottles by hand. "You did it, didn't you?"

"You're from outside?" His eyes went wider and the knife dropped down.

"Yes. Listen, you've got to help me — "

"How did you get in here? Why didn't the demons stop you? Where are they, are they following, are they coming?"

"I got past one, jumped the coach, that's all. Chele here offered to help me. I saw my daughter. And if you don't stand out of my way…." I cast my eyes across the gathered throng. My threat was so weak, it didn't even warrant finishing. I'd never felt so scared, so downright terrified, not even when I'd seen Janine lying there in her deathbed. Then I had known what was happening, and I'd almost come to terms with the fact that there was no chance for her, just a long, slow end. Now I had no idea what state Laura was really in, whether she was alive, whether she'd recognize me or even *want* me….

I'd never felt so damn scared.

"Come on!" the man said, reaching out for me. I drew back and he snorted, shook his head. He had long wild hair, black teeth and boils on his face, but his eyes were bright and intelligent. "Come on," he said, "we'll help you!"

He turned to his followers — if that's what they were — and shouted: "Drop the wire! These are from outside!"

"They all are!" an unseen someone shouted.

"Yes, but these shouldn't be here. They're *alien*."

I pushed past him, sick, angry, desperate to find Laura. Chele came on behind me. The people followed her, I could hear them mumbling and chattering excitedly, but I forged ahead. Nobody seemed willing to stop us.

I broke into a run.

And then I saw Laura.

And the skies darkened, fat drops of rain like spatters of blood hit my skin, a fast, violent wind smashed through from behind the trees, the branches shook, the barbed wire web swayed back and forth, and I heard my daughter's cries as the wire tore her more. Her dress was wet with blood, which at least showed that she was still bleeding. Dead people don't bleed.

"Oh Jesus!" I gasped, because my pale-skinned daughter was a red-faced demon, her eyes wide and her mouth foaming. "Oh sweet Jesus, just why…?"

"Hey," Chele said, hugging me quickly, tightly, before rushing to the foot of the nearest tree. She was a big woman; I noticed that for the first time as she began to climb. Her clothes were baggy and black, designed to hide her size, and she moved up and along the branches with a grace I could scarcely believe.

The rain was even heavier now, and dark clouds boiled the sky. Through the copse of trees I could see mountain slopes being assaulted by the weather, and creeping down the mountainside like the shaky legs of an old, angry god, two tornadoes twisted their way towards us. Black Teeth and his people were gathered behind me, muttering amongst themselves in a language I hoped I would never know.

"Daddy," Laura said weakly. I smiled and went to answer, but then I felt myself slipping down and out, the rain turned warm on my face as my tears mixed, and someone caught me under my arms as I slipped to the ground.

She's alive, I thought, alive and she knows me, she sees me, and she's not ignoring me or telling me to leave her alone, let her live her own life, not like I'd been expecting, not like people had been telling me, because she'd run away with a religious sect and who… who had even told me that in the first place?

"Laura!" I called out, but it was Chele I heard in response, her voice cutting through the tempest.

"Grab hold," she said, and I heard a sharp snick as wire was cut. I thought I had my eyes open but I could not see anything, and I may have been mistaken. Someone was holding me against them, their hand on my forehead. "Hold her weight, hold it! Ease her down. That's right… that's right… gentle now, she's a baby…."

Gentle now, she's only a baby, aren't you just a big baby? I'd used to say that to Laura when she was five, it would annoy and delight her in equal measures as I swung her around in my arms, called her my little baby and set her down on the grass, watching as she staggered with dizziness. She'd giggle as she fell over…

…Laura cried out, and I sensed the source of her voice lowering until it was at my level.

"Laura!" I called, trying to stand, to see.

There was the sound of an explosion from higher up the hillside and the sky was suddenly filled with grit, splinters and leaves. I opened my eyes in time to see the sky falling in.

"We have to leave here!" Black Teeth shouted into my ear.

"I want my daughter!" I shook off restraining hands and went to the trees. Chele was already back on the ground, trying to snip wire with a pair of cutters she'd liberated from someone. Laura was bleeding and crying and writhing. She wanted to stand and walk, I could see that, but pain held her tight.

Another explosive sound and this time the ground shook, the skies turning from dark to black as the tornadoes plucked trees and earth and rocks and mixed them into a barrage of natural shrapnel. I ducked down and knelt beside Laura, pulling a strand of wire carefully away from her wrist. The rain sluiced the wounds on her body, washing the blood into the earth. I put one hand under the back of her neck and lifted slowly. I looked into her eyes, promising that I was here for her.

"Daddy," she said, "you came to rescue me." I could barely hear her but I read the words in her eyes.

"Yes honey."

"I hurt."

I nodded. "I'll look after you now, honey, don't worry."

"Now!" Black Teeth shouted, and I noticed that most of the people he'd been with had vanished.

Chele appeared on Laura's other side and held her up, draping my daughter's arm gently across her shoulders. "Where to?" she shouted.

Black Teeth said something but he was already turning away, his words lost to the storm.

We followed, lifting Laura because she could not move her legs, and each cry made me want to stop and hold her to me. At the same time I was enraged, ready to take revenge for what had been done to her. I kept my eyes on the madman's back. The wire cutters had vanished from his belt, but that meant nothing.

He hadn't denied putting Laura up there in the first place.

The storm pushed us on and the tornadoes shook the earth, sucking it up and raining debris down around us. A shattered tree trunk speared into the earth twenty yards to my left. It groaned and fractured, and jagged splinters fired out like the spines of a tarantula. I felt a sting in my leg but kept on moving. I tried to haul in a breath but the air was moving too fast, being sucked away, and I remembered hearing about people whose lungs had imploded during tornadoes.

Laura had her head down. Her hair was blowing about her head like some mad Medusa, but her teeth were gritted, and I knew that she was holding onto consciousness to help Chele and me as much as she could.

Black Teeth was standing by a huge mound of boulders just ahead, gesticulating and shouting as if challenging the weather to a fight.

He turned and stepped behind the rocks, and we followed.

There was a cave. The entrance was small and sheltered, lit by burning torches tied onto the walls, but it soon widened into a sizeable hollow beneath the ground. It was filled with people. Behind us, the roar and savagery of the tornadoes and the accompanying storm. Ahead, a cave swarming with those who had sacrificed Laura to the barbed wire. Where my best chances lay I had not had time to consider, but the storm was death for sure. My knee was bleeding where the shard of tree had slashed through my trousers, but I welcomed the cool dribble of blood into my shoe. It made me feel alive. And it meant that Laura was not bleeding alone.

"Where the hell are we?" Chele whispered.

Laura moaned and suddenly became heavier. "She's fainted," I said, hoping that was all. We carried her farther into the cave, her feet dragging on the floor, and no one moved their legs to let us pass. They put her up there, I thought, remembering my first staggering sight of Laura bleeding and twisting on the wire, hung up to cure like a slab of ham. I wondered why the hell they may have lured us down here.

We found a slightly raised area of the cave, free of people, dry and dusty and flat enough so that Laura did not roll when we put her down. I was tired and terrified, panting with fear and exertion. Chele seemed the same. Her eyes were shifting constantly, looking here, there, somewhere else, never fixing on one place or person for more than a few seconds. It was a form of shock I had seen in my own bathroom mirror the night Janine had finally passed away.

"Chele," I said. She looked at me, and I smiled to hold her gaze. "Thank you. I couldn't have done it without you. I'd still be out there in the storm." As if to emphasize how bad that would be the noise increased for several endless seconds, the vibrations knocking grit from the cave's ceiling and raising a sheen of dust in the air. There was no panic or screaming, only a disturbing look of resignation on most of the faces I could see, as if they couldn't care less if the tornadoes plucked them from their hiding places.

I'd seen that look before as well. The faces of concentration camp survivors from World War Two.

It became hard to breathe for a few seconds as air was sucked from the cave, and then the chaos ended as soon as it had begun.

Outside, silence. There was no light coming from the tunnel entrance, but no noise either, no sounds of destruction. Could a tornado die out that quickly, I wondered? Could it possibly all end so soon?

"Hey, Nolan," Chele said. "I did it for me as much as you." She kept her voice low because there wasn't much chat in the cave. Most of those who had come in before us were already camping down for the night. A kid was crying somewhere, someone else was whimpering quietly into the subdued light cast by the burning lanterns. And I was sure I could hear the covert sounds of sex.

"Thank you anyway," I said. "You didn't have to leave that coach. I know what happened to you, I'm sorry... and up until ten minutes ago I could have related to it. But look... look at her... look at my baby...." I burst into tears. They'd been threatening for a while, I knew that, but terror and adrenaline had kept them at bay. Now, as safe as I thought we could possibly be, I found it easy to cry. When I felt Chele's arms close around my chest and back I cried more, because she must have cried so much herself. In a way I felt embarrassed, shedding so much grief over my child when she was still alive. But Chele would know how I felt. I was so sure of that that I didn't even look up. She would know.

Perhaps by touching and holding me, she could gain some vicarious sense of joy and relief.

"Let's help your little girl," she said, releasing me suddenly and squatting next to Laura. I joined her there and touched my daughter's cheek, feeling the stickiness of blood and the coolness of dried tears. Her eyes fluttered open and looked up at me, and even though she didn't smile I knew that she recognized me. As she slipped back into unconsciousness I hoped she felt safe.

"She's lost a lot of blood," I said, trying to see the shading of her lips and skin in the poor cave light. "And her arms...." I peeled back the sleeves of her dress and winced as they stuck in places, either tangled with dried blood or driven down into the wounds by the tight wire. There were puncture wounds all along her arms from the barbs, and longer, deeper cuts where the wire had been wound and pulled taut by her own weight.

It must have hurt so much. I was crying again, but this time there was rage mixed in with the relief, and while I spat on my handkerchief and did my best to clean some of the wounds I was listening out for the voice of Black Teeth.

"I'll ask if there's any — "

"I'll go," I said. "If you don't mind sitting with her? She's asleep now, and I need to talk to these people."

"I don't mind," Chele said, but she looked at me strangely.

"I'll only talk," I said. "And I'll get what we need for Laura."

Chele nodded.

I leant over Laura and gave her a kiss on the forehead. She whimpered slightly in her sleep. I hated to imagine what she was dreaming.

Standing, turning around, I took my first proper look around the cave. It was big enough to comfortably house the thirty-or-so people accompanying Black Teeth. They huddled in groups or alone, sitting beneath burning torches set in the walls. Some of them seemed to be eating, others sleeping, and one couple were screwing in a darkened corner, unconcerned at being seen or heard. They were mostly dressed in old uniforms bordering on rags, many of them carrying wounds and deformities whose causes I could only guess at. Some wore glasses, a few glittered with jewelry. The pathetic creatures I'd seen carrying the rolls of barbed wire were gathered together at one side of the cave, already sleeping. Any pity I should have felt was wiped clean at the thought of Laura sleeping uneasily behind me. Whatever quirk of fate had made them the workhorses of this sick band, I could not feel sorry. They could shake their heads, say "No," and I'd never feel sorry.

"How is she?" Black Teeth asked. He was standing a few yards away, nearer the cave entrance. A woman was washing his face with a dirty rag. Her movements were soft and tender, but her face was hard.

"Do you care?" I asked.

He blinked a few times as the cloth passed across his eyes, smearing dust and dirt over his eyelids. "No," he said. "I've seen too much to care. But I'm trying to be polite."

"She needs painkillers, bandages. The worst wounds need stitching. We want clean water to wash her, food and drink, and a way out of here. She needs a doctor."

"He was a doctor, once," he said, nodding towards one of the malformed wire carriers snoring at the other side of the cave.

I glanced over and then back at him. The woman dampened the cloth on the cave wall, wrung it out and returned to her cleaning duties. Black Teeth barely seemed to register her ministrations.

"Clean water?" I said. "Food?"

"Food!" the madman shouted, and he was greeted by a few angry murmurs. "He wants some of our food!"

"Can't you smell it?" a voice called from the shadows.

"You're welcome, alien," someone else said.

"Barb him!"

"I've just seen some of your people eating," I said. "You *must* have food."

Black Teeth shoved the woman away, and she retreated to the rear of the cave. "We're left food each day, so long as we string up enough fodder. Some days eight is enough. Some days, eighteen. We never know, we're never told, so we always do as many as we can. When we come back here, there's food or there isn't. Mostly there is. We work hard."

"You worked hard on my daughter." I couldn't contain the rage. This bastard was trying to *explain* himself to me.

"She was fodder." He motioned me to follow, turned and walked to the mouth of the cave. He glanced back over his shoulder when he sensed that I had not moved. "We should talk," he said.

I was shaking with a combination of anger and hopelessness. I could never attack him and win, even if I could find violence within me. It all felt so pointless.

I looked back at Laura. Chele was holding her head in her lap, cleaning blood from her face. If talking to this man would help my daughter... so be it.

I followed him to the narrow cave entrance, feeling eyes on my back like gun sights.

"Look," he said. I didn't realize we were outside until he spoke, but as I looked around... so much had changed.

The storm had not only abated, all evidence of its existence had vanished. The sky was swimming in stars, not a cloud in sight, and from somewhere behind us the moon shed its borrowed light across the landscape. The grasses, shrubs and other undergrowth had vanished, torn up and deposited in piles already rotting and drying out. The trees were ghostly skeletons of wood, denuded of leaves.

"It's changed so much." I said.

Black Teeth sighed and nodded. "We've barbed in many settings."

"But why do it at all?"

"If we don't, we'll be taken away and fed in elsewhere, used as fodder in another nightmare. What choice is that? What would *you* do?"

"I'd rather die."

He laughed, but it was bitter and sad. "Yes, well, maybe... but here, there's more than dying. Never forget where you are. Alien." He looked at me, staring, trying to see past or through me. Yet again I couldn't help but notice the intelligence in his eyes and I wondered what he'd been before he found himself here. Somehow I didn't want to know.

"The food," I said. "The water."

He shook his head. "There *was* food and water left for us today — we had a fruitful day — but it's been turned bad because we helped you."

I shook my head. "That's crazy. What sort of control could they have to actually *make* food turn bad?"

"They?" he said. "Capital 'T'? So, who are They? The government? The military? The evil Galactic Empire? The Bliderbergs? God himself?" he looked up to the sky, his eyes moving jerkily as if counting the stars. "You know what I was before? An anthropologist. I lectured on ancient civilizations, specializing in social and political aspects, how the organizations in an old civilization can affect us as well, even if there are no direct links whatsoever. Harmful, eh? Dangerous? 'They' must have thought so. Because they stole me away and — "

"My daughter never did anything that could have been a threat to anyone."

"No. No. Maybe not. Well, that's my 'threat' theory blown out of the water. Not that I ever really believed it anyway." He smiled and I knew that he was playing with me now, perhaps enjoying my discomfort and pain and confusion because he'd passed up the chance to barb me.

"I don't know," I said. "Maybe... well, someone controls all this."

"Really? What if it *is* God? Where's the limit to His control?"

"Don't be stupid. God is dead, didn't someone once say? Besides... if I ever did believe, that's been wiped out since Laura was taken away from me."

"*Si Dieu n'existait pas, il faudrait l'inventer.*"

I raised an eyebrow, partly in surprise, mostly because I hated being condescended to. I wasn't about to ask him what it meant, but he told me anyway.

" 'If God did not exist, it would be necessary to invent Him.' Voltaire."

"Great," I said. "My life is now full. And you? You believe in God? Living here, like this — "

"What else is there for me to believe in? The goodness of Man? Give me a *fucking* break." He'd suddenly gone from relatively quiet to loud and angry. I thought he was going to strike out.

"You have medicines, though? Bandages?"

"Same provisos as the food and drink. Today... probably not. Let's face it, you brought the storm and rotted our food. I hardly think there will be plasters and sterile gauze for you."

"I hope you die," I said. It surprised and shocked me, and it was a stupid thing to say. He could kill me here and now. He was mad, after all.

Black Teeth didn't even register the comment. He looked out over the landscape, perhaps scouting for trees to use for tomorrow's work.

"I need to get away from here," I said quietly, turning to go. "I need to help Laura."

"The reason I spared you," he said, "was because I thought you'd know the way out. You're an alien, you should never be in here. For me you were... hope. That's all." He turned to me, and the sudden change in his expression was startling. In the starlight he looked like a little boy who had lost his ball over a neighbor's fence, and now he was asking for it back. Innocence hid the blemishes on his skin and the murder and madness in his eyes.

I shook my head and his expression changed again.

"So what?" I said. "Are you going to barb us now? Now you know I can't help you?"

"I should. We should. They look up to me because I've been here longer than any of them. They'll call for it. You should go."

"You're helping me again? Why?"

"I've never got to talk to any of the people we barbed before. Never known them as anything other than fodder."

"Not even my daughter?"

He looked at me, his eyes dead and resigned to worse than death, and suddenly I wanted to leave as soon as possible, run, run aimlessly from these terrible, pathetic people.

"She was asking for you all the time I strung her up," he said.

I turned and left him instantly, not allowing myself time for thought or reflection. It was the only thing I could do.

"Through the cave," he called after me. "A tunnel. Don't come back out this way, otherwise you're our fodder again. Go elsewhere. At least then it won't be me who has to kill you."

I didn't acknowledge him. I didn't want to see into the eyes of the man who had seen my daughter begging for me, and done nothing to help.

Inside the cave, eyes were upon me. I looked into the face of the woman who'd been washing Black Teeth, and there I saw envy. Someone else, a young boy with an old man's face, seemed ready to kill me. A woman touched my ankle as I walked by and looked up, and I wondered whether she wanted me to kill her. The copulating couple at the rear of the cave were still going at it, noisier now, and their cries and grunts added a surreal background to my walk to Laura and Chele.

I knelt down beside my daughter and touched her face. She was still unconscious.

"We need to leave," I said.

Chele shook her head. "She's unconscious, not asleep. We shouldn't move her far."

"I'll carry her."

"Nolan, she's not a little girl anymore, and — "

"Believe me," I said, looking into Chele's eyes to add emphasis, "we need leave right now." I held her gaze for a few seconds and nodded.

She looked around the cave, her eyes glittering fearfully in the weak torch light. "Which way?"

"Through the cave. Down there to the back, there's a tunnel."

"What makes you so sure?" Chele looked where I had indicated, and I knew what she was thinking. There was very little light back there, and the only people who'd apparently ventured that far were the fucking couple. And what *did* make me so sure? Did Black Teeth really want to help me, I wondered? That ex-academic whose living now comprised of hunting down people like cattle, winding them in barbed wire and crucifying them between trees?

Threat was as prevalent in the cave as the sounds of sex and the smell of rot. Out there, through the cave mouth, I knew that there was very little left.

"We have no choice," I said. And I hated that. "Come on, help me lift Laura."

We picked her up and hoisted her onto my shoulders, so that I was carrying her in a fireman's lift. There was movement around the cave. The people were fidgeting as they realized we were preparing to leave.

"It's pitch black back there," Chele whispered.

I started across the uneven floor, moving away from the oases of light and towards the humping lovers. I heard Chele behind me, and I wondered whether she'd follow me over a cliff and into a pool of molten rock.

Laura was heavy, but the weight was almost comforting. It bore down to let me know that I was helping my daughter at last. She wasn't as limp as I'd expected — her arms lay tight down my side, and her legs were all knotted muscle — and I suspected that she was waking up. In a way I wanted her to remain unconscious for a little while longer, at least until we were away from these people.

They were standing now, some of them mumbling, others just watching. I only recognized a few words; food, water, bastards, barbed, stupid. They had no hope, no future, no life, and we were responsible for them not having anything decent to eat or drink tonight.

The rutting couple were louder than ever, and now I could see them, pale like landed fish. Beyond them was the black maw of the tunnel. The poor light threw their rampant shadows behind them, huge and monstrous, as if they were some mythical horror guarding an underground tomb.

I passed by the final group of people gathered under the last blazing torch.

One of the copulating couple began to scream, the other grunted, both voices androgynous.

I lowered an arm from around Laura, walked calmly between two people and lifted the torch from its rudimentary wall mounting.

"Take this." I handed it back to Chele, making eye contact with first one, then the other person I passed by, challenging them to confront me. If they did, there was nothing I could do to protect myself. The only defence I had was my bluff and bluster. So I stared, trying not to let my fear show through.

Another scream from the couple. They'd been rutting for at least fifteen minutes, and the climax seemed a long time coming. There was nothing titillating in the sound, only sickening, because it was more a cry of pain than anything else. Maybe it always had been.

Chele led the way towards the tunnel, and as we passed the screwing couple they let out their final, screamed exhortations. And the torch revealed them for what they were.

The woman sat astride the man, blood and sweat running down her back, buttocks spread provocatively as she glared at us over her shoulder. Her body must have been very fine once, but now the curves were slashed and the swells were torn, knobbled with scar tissue. The man writhed beneath her, a high keening issuing from his throat. I had a frank view of where they were joined, his penis still locked inside her. And I saw why they had both been screaming.

The woman held onto a long strand of barbed wire. Its end was twisted several times around the man's scrotum, and she'd pulled it tight.

"Want some, alien?" she asked.

Their blood was mingling down there.

I turned away, the acidic tang of bile rising in my throat. Chele had hurried on and I followed the jumping light, glad that Laura was still unconscious. Laughter followed us down into the tunnel, slick as puke, just as sick. *Have fun*, I thought I heard someone say. It could have been Black Teeth bidding us farewell.

I wondered just where he'd directed us. Wherever, it couldn't be as bad as where we had just escaped from.

And I thought of the riots and the shootings and the disease-stricken valley being napalmed....

"Why is this happening?" I said, suddenly feeling tears looming once again. Things had been happening so quickly that I'd barely had a chance to think. It seemed like days since I'd escaped the coach, but it was probably no more than an hour or two. Chele kept on walking, offering me no answer. It was a hopeless question.

"Dad," Laura moaned, "you're hurting me."

"Honey, we've just got to go on a little longer. How do you feel?"

"Everything hurts."

I was already flagging beneath her weight, but I managed to stretch and give her a kiss on the chin. "A little longer. Chele, we need to move a long way quickly."

"You think they might come after us?"

I thought of what Black Teeth had said, about how outsiders were fodder and that barbing them was all they knew. Perhaps he'd fancied some sport, for once. The thrill of the chase. Maybe, for him and his people, revenge would taste sweeter if they had to work for it.

"It's crossed my mind," I said. "Any signs of this tunnel leading anywhere?" I had my head down with the weight of Laura slung over my neck, so I couldn't see much more than my feet and Chele's shadow, thrown back by the torch.

"Hang on." She stopped and we stood there for a few seconds, silent and still. "No sign of a breeze," she said. "Can't hear anything. If they're following, they're very quiet about it."

"Let me down, Dad."

"Honey.... " But she was heavier than ever, and in a minute or two I would not be able to manage any more. I hadn't kept in shape, especially since Janine had died. I'd let myself go.

I set her down gently and she hissed, leaning back into me.

"Laura?"

"Pins and needles," she said, and she giggled. "Bloody pins and needles!"

Laughter was the last thing I'd expected. Screaming, maybe, but laughter... and maybe that's why it felt so good when I joined in.

Chele simply stared at us, unable to see a funny side. "They'll hear us back in the cave," she said. "They'll think we're laughing at them."

"We are!" I said, laughing out loud. "Did you see that couple? That barbed wire? What else can we do but laugh!"

Laura shook her legs, her giggles mixing with groans of discomfort as her circulation returned. Some of her wounds glinted once more as fresh blood started to flow. Her pains became real again, her laughter stuttered and she remembered that she had a lot more to worry about than pins and needles.

"Daddy, don't let them do it to me again," she said. "Please, please don't — "

"I never will," I said, wanting to hold her and hug her and love her here in the dark, in a cave in a place that was an idea of Hell. But Chele was glaring at me and I knew we had to leave. "Can you walk, honey?"

Laura nodded. "I think so. I hurt everywhere, so at least it's pretty even."

"Do you feel weak?"

She nodded. "I think I need a sugar rush. Don't suppose you have any chocolate?" She looked at Chele then, almost as if seeing her for the first time. "Thank you so much," she said. I felt a hot rush of pride for my young, insightful daughter. She didn't know Chele and could have no idea of how she had come to be here with me. But still, she knew a friend when she saw one.

"It's my honor," Chele said. "Your dad… he let me help him, and now I'm helping you. And you're both helping me. More than you can know."

"Chele was on the same coach — " I started, but then Chele cut in.

"Later, Nolan. Please, I want out of here and I really, really think we should leave. Laura? You agree?"

"Dad?" Her voice was a plea in itself. I nodded, Chele headed off and I walked behind Laura, ready to catch her should she stumble or faint.

The tunnel turned and erred downward, so steep in places that we had to brace ourselves against the walls to prevent our feet slipping out from beneath us. We were going deeper and that wasn't good, but the air was also changing — its smells, its tastes, its textures were different from the cave and the place we had left.

Lost underground forever, I thought. Now there's an interesting idea of Hell. I started looking out for the creamy reflection of skeletons.

And then I looked around, wondering where the coach could be and whether I was looking into some spectator's eyes at that very moment.

"All those people…." I said.

"What?" Chele did not turn around, and Laura seemed content just to listen.

"All those people in that valley. The disease. The bombs. All stolen away from the real world, all fodder?"

Chele did not answer, but the light jumped along the walls as if startled, and I guessed that she'd shrugged her shoulders.

The numbers staggered me. And I wondered how many people went missing every year around the globe, how many are never found. What chance that a relative will see them on a journey through Hell?

What was the likelihood that I would find Laura whilst trying to come to terms with losing her?

I thought about Black Teeth's comments, wondering whether I'd created my own god or simply found the real One at last.

There was a loud crack behind us, like two rocks being smacked together. We stopped, wide-eyed and fearful, as a sound bathed us in echoes. It was a sigh or a roar, a whisper or a shout, all concepts of distance and time making it difficult to discern.

Another crack, followed by two more in quick succession.

"They're gunshots," Chele said. And as if in answer the cracks turned into one long string of explosions, and the whisper or roar emerged as very definite, very desperate screams.

"They're being slaughtered," I said, thinking of the pathetic people we'd left behind, dancing in the cave as bullets found them.

"I can't be sorry," Laura whispered. "I can't be sorry at all." And her voice, quiet though it was, cut through the destruction.

We stood there for a minute, avoiding each other's eyes and listening to the murder. I heard screams and shouts between the gunfire and towards the end, as the volume seemed to decrease, moaning and pleading and crying between the intermittent shots. Chele moved the torch so that its liquid light shifted back along the tunnel the way we had come. I looked at her, caught the flames reflected in her eyes, and we both knew what the other was thinking.

Laura said it. "Maybe they'll come for us now. The demons… maybe they'll come."

"Let's go," Chele said, turning away and heading back into the tunnel. She did not wait for a response, evidently not expecting one, and I realized that she was taking over. Before, leaving the coach and challenging the group of people head-on, my hurt and desperation for Laura had driven me. Now that I had Laura back perhaps Chele thought that I was losing focus, my attentions divided two separate ways: internally, to what I should be doing for Laura; and externally, trying to get us out of this. Whatever *this* may be, exactly.

"What are they?" I asked Laura, whispering because I was still listening out for the sounds of pursuit.

"Dad," she said, and fell silent without turning to look at me.

"Honey? What?"

She glanced over her shoulder, and it hit me hard how much she had grown up.

I remembered the time when I thought that I'd grown from a child into an adult. It was when I fought back against the bully at school, a fat, ugly prick of a kid, who seemed to relish taking out all his own inadequacies on other people. He had terrible acne, so he beat up little kids. He had big ears and a long, hawkish nose, so he beat up little kids. He was fat as a cow, so he beat up little kids. Many times one of those little kids was me, because I was small and weak and insecure, and fighting back had just never even crossed my mind.

Until the bully slapped me around the head in front of a girl I was *desperate* to impress.

My reaction was instant and unconscious, fuelled as much by raging hormones as a need to protect myself. One kick to the balls and a flurry of little fists to the fat bastard's nose, and he never picked on me again. He hit on other kids more than ever... I'd beaten him up, so he beat on other kids... but never me. And people looked at me slightly differently after that. Not only because I'd fought back, but because I'd stood up for myself in the face of superior odds. And that, as any kid knows, is what you're supposed to do when you're an adult.

Kids have a lot to learn.

"I really don't want to talk about it right now, Dad," Laura said, and I wondered whether she'd ever look back and realize exactly when she'd grown up, and what she would she see in that memory. Faces beneath the trees, metal barbs sinking through her skin, demons storming in from blackened skies, forcing themselves down to her, onto her...?

It didn't bear thinking about, but I knew that I'd have to ask her soon.

"Stop!" Chele said suddenly, and like three drunken Stooges we walked into each other in the dark. The light from the torch blazed across the jagged tunnel walls, revealing an intricate map of dust-strewn spider webs. No spiders, just their ancient webs. Somehow that was worse.

"What!" I hissed. I was jumpy enough without Chele pulling a stunt like this, and for the briefest moment I was actually pissed at her. Then I remembered what she had done and I felt ashamed at my blaze of anger.

"What's that noise?" she said. She was holding the torch in both hands, away from her body so that the light from the flames did not dazzle her. "It sounds like... something moving down the tunnel. Lots of somethings. Scraping the walls."

Laura hugged herself to me and I could smell her, stale blood and bad breath and fear. I kissed her on the temple. I was determined not to picture what was coming along the tunnels at us, but the more I tried the worse the images were; demons merging with the dark, black body-suits, their antennae twitching at the dank air like mandibles, legs and arms stretching out to fend themselves from walls and floor and ceiling, scampering along and feeling more at home when their hands clawed through the thick spider webs —

"Water," Laura said. "It's water, and it's coming from *that* way."

She pointed past Chele in our direction of travel.

"Underground river," I said. "That may not be such good news."

Chele looked at me and her expression was a mystery. I thought she wanted me to say or do something, but I couldn't figure out what. I shrugged and raised my eyebrows instead, and she was about to speak when we heard more noises in the cave tunnel. And this time they *were* coming from behind us.

Clicking, like the chatter of a thousand electrical switches, or a field full of crickets in intense discussion. The echoes added to the effect. It sounded wholly alien and threatening, and I could not believe that whatever was making that noise would be good for us. The fact that it was approaching at a staggering rate did not bode well.

"That's how they talk!" Laura said, and her eyes were so wide and terrified that I felt my knees weaken with fear.

I held her, both of us sharing in the comfort. Chele moved and I thought she was coming into the embrace as well. I would have welcomed it. But she changed her position slightly, cocked her head, looking first up the tunnel and then down.

"We go down, we hit the water," she said. "We go back… we have to face whatever's making that noise."

Again I thought of man-sized spiders, or spider-sized people, scampering through tunnels with automatic weapons held to bear.

"The water," Laura said. She broke away from me and staggered down the tunnel past Chele.

"I'll go first," Chele said, trying to slip past Laura without harming her with the flaming torch.

"Hurry!" Laura said. "Hurry, Dad!"

I glanced behind me but couldn't see much. The tunnel had narrowed down considerably and my bulk blocked most of the light, casting my shadow far back along the floor. I wondered whether I would be able to tell when the first of the demons came out of its own shadow into mine.

The clicking increased in volume and intensity, as if they could smell us.

As we turned a sharp corner, the sound of water changed quickly from a whisper to a roar. It drowned out the noises of excited pursuit. That wasn't necessarily a good thing. Each passing second I expected a hard hand to settle around my neck, or a slew of bullets to blast out my heart and lungs onto the damp cave floor.

"Dad!" Laura screamed, and her voice was fading away fast.

And then the light went out.

I realized why as I too started to fall, tumbling in the pitch blackness, falling into another world entirely.

A world where Hell was wet.

The room was a pool of mud. I had time to make that out before I plunged straight in, and also in that split second I caught sight of two shapes struggling on the surface, twisting and writhing themselves deeper even as they tried to escape, sweeping the muck in swirling patterns with their hands, kicking it into slow-motion ripples, bubbles popping from their mouths and noses, slower bubbles rising to the surface from their clothes and popping ponderously, releasing the stench of underground, and the smell filled the air above it as the mud filled the room below, an almost visible miasma that stung my lungs as I inhaled before I plunged in.

I managed to hold my head up, keeping my eyes and ears and mouth free of the viscous mess, but the rest of my body felt twisted all ways with the suction hauling me down. I kicked for something solid to stand on but there was nothing. The mud oozed around my legs and body, cold and wet and sickeningly intimate. I looked to where I thought was up but I saw a window, smashed and allowing more mud to flow into the room. I glanced to my side and there was the ceiling.

I listened for the clicking of the pursuing demons, but such clean sounds would have been so out of place here. They were gone. *Where* they had gone I had no idea. Where *we* had arrived at was equally bemusing, but thinking about it would be of no help. Survival was my main concern.

That, and Laura.

I'd rescued her from one hell and taken her into another, and now there she was rolling in the mud, thrashing herself lower and lower, sinking, sinking....

"Laura!" I yelled, and it must have been a mumble to her mud-cloaked ears.

"Dad!" A bubble formed at her mouth and burst her plea into the air.

"Keep still! Don't struggle, you'll go deeper!" Saying that, I trusted my arms and tried to swim to Laura. She was closer to the wall than me, the parts of her that did show above the surface quickly being swamped by the tons of mud gushing through the broken window. And in thrashing my arms and kicking my legs, the mud's hold on me was tightening. I slipped deeper, feeling the cold kiss of filth on my chin and earlobes.

What sort of God...? I thought, remembering my recent conversation with Black Teeth so far away. What sort of God would rescue my daughter from such a fate, only to drown her in mud and shit?

One angry at my disbelief, perhaps? I tried to say sorry but it came out like hate.

"Don't move, dammit!" Chele shouted, her voice clotted and wet. I managed to turn my head slightly, looking from the corner of my eye, and there she was. She'd made it to the corner of the room and she must have found a piece of heavy furniture to stand on, because it looked as if she was balancing on the surface of the mud itself. She was a wet black sculpture, her clothes so heavy that her sleeves had doubled in length and the hem of her heavy sweater was kissing her knees. I was shocked to see her small breasts bared and lathered in mud. I was even more surprised at my reaction — embarrassment at first, but then a definite stirring, an unbelievable hardening as my daughter struggled her last and we all faced a slow, dreadful death.

"Chele…" I said. More than anything it was a plea.

She was looking around desperately, first at me, then Laura — who by now was little more than a hump shifting below the surface of the mud — and then around her, repeating the process, looking for something to do… and I realized with sad resignation that she was frantic with helplessness. She was not in control at all. She had no idea of how to save us.

I started trying to swim to Laura. The mud was amazingly heavy, and it took what felt like minutes for me to sweep handfuls of it behind me, try to step forward, kicking through the rising mess like a moonwalker in slow motion.

"Keep still!" Chele said.

"She'll be dead," I said, not turning my head, keeping all my attention on the few signs I could see of my daughter. Muck still gushed through the window but it seemed to be slowing now, finding its own level. Outside the room — whether we were in a house, a hotel, whatever — there was the steady roar of millions of tons of mud flowing past solid buildings. A thousand years of erosion in minutes. Even as I moved I heard the rumble of what could only have been a structure collapsing.

"Nolan —"

"Unless you've thought of any way out," I said, "there's nothing else to do." I started to cry, the tears washing clean streaks down my face. A glob of mud spilled into my mouth and it tasted of nothing I'd ever tasted in my life before.

"Here!" Chele shouted. "Catch this!"

Something heavy slapped the side of my face. I flinched away, images of what gruesome fish could live in something like this crowding in. What would they look like? What would they *eat*?

"Grab it!" Chele screamed. Another crash came from somewhere far away, as if to emphasize her urgency.

I turned my head slowly and lifted a hand clear. I was too heavy to move and the muscles in my shoulder and back screamed at me to stop. But if my body had already given up the ghost, my mind had not. *Could* not, not while Laura may still be there, still alive, holding her breath as her world turned black and the mud probed at her nose and mouth with its cool, grainy fingers.

I grabbed the sleeve of Chele's sweater and turned my hand so that it was twisted around my wrist. "Do you think you can — ?" I asked.

"Shut up and let me try." She sat on whatever piece of furniture she'd found and began to pull. She was a black and brown statue, her arms and shoulders flexing slowly, so slowly as she heaved back on her sweater. She was topless now, but I was glad that I no longer found that exciting. If I had... it would have been sick. *I* would have been sick. We'd probably all die in here, whether Chele thought she could pull me in or not.

I moved my legs slowly, trying to climb up so that my body lay across the surface. The less of me in the mud, the easier it would be for Chele to pull me out. I looked across at the window. It had ceased flowing in now, but outside I could see and hear a great river of muck flowing past our building. Things scraped against the walls, dragged along. Vehicles, perhaps. Uprooted trees. Bodies.

"Come on!" Chele hissed. I was moving, but so slowly....

Laura was still there. She'd stopped struggling, and at first I thought she was dead, floating there just below the surface and presenting little more than a hump in the mud. But then she moved; a hand broke through, fingers splayed, twisting slowly, slowly as they opened a shallow pocket in the surface. Shallow, but deep enough to meet her nose and let her grab in a breath.

"She's there!" I said, and I was ready to go to her, swim through the filth and hold her up and clear her nose and mouth so that she could breathe again, clean her up like a newborn baby, give her another chance of life.

"Look at me, concentrate on *me*," Chele said, and I knew that she was right. I would not serve Laura by dying.

Chele pulled, I pushed and in a couple of minutes she was able to reach over and grab one of my hands in both of hers. She strained again, and I could see where some of the mud was being diluted and washed from her body by sweat. It was drying as well, fading to a lighter color as her own heat bled the moisture from it, cracking as soon as it dried where her muscles worked to pull me to her.

I felt something solid beneath my knee, and with a huge burst of effort I lifted a foot, let Chele give one more pull and then I was up there with her.

I felt drained. Totally, completely exhausted, like a battery flickering on the last dregs of its power. Not long until I ran out. And I couldn't allow that yet.

"The demons," Chele said, but it was a question that I did not have the strength to answer. I looked up at the solid ceiling through which I assumed we'd fallen, and there was still no sign of any pursuit.

"Laura." I saw Laura's hands still circling, still moving around each other to maintain a dip in the thick mud, at the bottom of which I could just see her nose. Perhaps she was standing on tiptoes, just high enough to be able to breathe... if she could keep the mud at a slightly lower level. If it became more fluid, or if another surge came through the window now, she'd be finished.

"They can't let this happen," I said, "not after what we've been through to save her. They can't."

"'They' are probably trying their damndest to get you out of here or kill you," Chele said. She had her arms crossed over her chest. Her sweater was rolled into a sodden ball, resting by her feet.

"We'll need that again," I said, picking it up. "Is that all right?"

She lowered her arms. Dried mud came away from her chest with a crackle. She looked as if she had leprosy, but I felt that interest again, the unconscious stirring at the sight of her nudity. "Not as if I need it," she said, but she was joking. She even smiled.

I nodded my thanks. "You're lighter than me. You lay out straight and throw this to Laura. Once she's got it, I'll haul you in." Chele nodded. I looked away.

She threw the sweater out before her and then splashed herself down across the thick mud. I knelt on the furniture — bookcase, dresser, whatever — and kept hold of her ankles. It took three more throws until the sweater landed across Laura's twirling fingers, and I realized that we were cutting off her meager air supply.

I could only hope that she realized what was happening... and hung on.

She did. I pulled, finding a reserve of strength I would never have believed in before, desperation tightening my muscles, excitement kicking in when I saw Laura emerge head-first from the mud like a child birthed from the earth. She was gasping and coughing up great clots of muck, her eyes still squeezed shut, and I only wanted to bring her to me so that I could hold her and help her. I hauled, pulled, strained until I could reach down and grasp Chele under the arms and lift her up with me. As she came so did Laura, and then the three of us were hunkered down on the furniture, the mud sloshing around our ankles but we were out, free, *alive*.

"I must…" Laura gasped, fingering mud from her ears and nose. I wiped it from her eyes, "I must… have done something really bad… in a previous life."

I could only cry. Chele touched my shoulder and left her hand there long enough for it to matter.

We were still there, wherever there was. And they were probably still after us, whoever they were. And the only thing I wanted to do was to move, get out and away from this building and see what awaited us outside.

I held Laura for ten minutes, cleaning mud from her face, finding her again. Chele wrung out the sweater as much as she could and slipped it back over her head and arms. She stood and leaned against the wall as Laura and I loved each other and wished that none of this had ever happened.

"What do we do now?" Laura asked at last, ending the silence we adults had not been able to break.

As if lured by Laura's voice there was a loud thumping, crackling sound outside, clear above the roar and grind of the moving mud.

"Oh no," I said. They were here. They'd followed us, found us and now they were coming, and what fate could we expect from those demons? No slow death, of that at least I was sure. They'd hold us down and shoot us. After some of what I'd seen today, that may almost be a blessing.

"Wait," Chele said, bending down so that she could see through the window and across the surface of the mud-river. "It's not the same sound."

"Then what — "

"Gunfire," Laura said. "That's gunfire, yes, but it's pad-rifles. I heard them a couple of days ago when…." She trailed off. It must have been bad if she didn't even want to tell her father about it. It wasn't the usual crack of gunfire, more like a whiplash ending with a heavy thud. I'd heard about pad-rifles. They weren't nice things. They fired super-heated composite which spread out in the air to something the size of a fist. By the time it struck its target it was solid again. Being shot with a pad-rifle was like being hit by a medicine ball at fifteen hundred miles per hour.

More reports, closer this time, and then we heard the familiar crackle of machine gun fire joining in.

"There's a battle going on out there," Chele said, looking around our room as if contemplating staying.

The mud river seemed to be flowing faster, and even though inside the room was relatively calm, the sounds of scraping and rumbling from outside was becoming more violent. Another gunfire exchange, another heavy grumble of a building collapsing into the muck, and that made up my mind.

"We can't stay here," I said. "This place isn't designed for that."

"What do you mean, 'this place'? You don't even know where or when we are."

"We're in Hell," I said. "We're in a place designed to make observers feel happy with their lot. Bad things are *meant* to happen here, people are meant to see, and sitting tight will only draw it to us." I looked around, suddenly having a clear and dreadful sense of being spied upon.

"Are they watching now?" Laura asked.

"I don't think bad enough stuff is happening to us yet." I smiled grimly at my daughter and felt so powerless when I saw the fear in her eyes.

"I just want to go home," she said. "I want Mum back." I hadn't heard that from her in a long time.

"Then let's go," Chele said, standing and edging her way to the window. "I think whatever we're standing on goes as far as the window."

"Then what?"

She shrugged. "Through. Outside. You and I are aliens here, Nolan. We get to the action, maybe we'll have an idea of how to find our way out."

We left the room through the shattered window, moving from the sunken furniture and balancing on the sill, before stepping across to the head of a wall protruding above the mud river. And once outside, we were able to turn around and see where we'd come into this particular Hell.

"Where are the caves?" Chele said. "Where are the tunnels? Why didn't they follow us through?"

Looking up at the two-storey house, I could only shake my head and wonder. The dislocation... the sense of wrongness... it was terrifying.

It was a normal dwelling, detached, quite large. The windows were smashed, the guttering shattered, the slates cracked and crazed. Its masonry was peppered with bullet holes and a couple of larger impact craters. These could only be from a pad-rifle. There was something splashed high on the wall next to an upstairs window. It may have been blood.

In both directions along the street more houses stood drowning in the river of muck. It stank of shit and rot, as if all the drains in the world were venting here. It was black and thick, steaming in places, twisting with deceptive currents. Every now and then a car came floating by. Some of them trailed engine parts behind them like loose guts. These came to rest further down the street against the side of a church, like wayward souls seeking entrance and acceptance. The mud river deposited them there and then turned a corner, probably picking up more vehicles and carrying them further away… or perhaps simply disappearing altogether.

It had to stop somewhere.

I looked back at the house we'd emerged from and wondered what was behind it. I had the crazy idea that there would be timber posts propping up the façade, perhaps a litter-strewn studio lot, a maintenance yard for Hell where the demons dressed and undressed each night, smoked cigarettes, talked about who they'd killed that day and whether they were revisiting Mud tomorrow, or perhaps they'd be on coach duty, did you hear about Dave the Demon who some visitor killed before going alien in Barbed Wire, and wasn't he in for some fun when he was found…?

"Nolan," Chele said, "we have to decide what to do."

"What?"

"Look." She pointed quickly towards the center of the flow where the mud ran fastest, glancing at Laura to see if she'd noticed.

"I've seen worse than that," my daughter said, and when I finally saw what they were talking about my heart sank. She shouldn't be growing up this quickly, experiencing these things, having her teens slaughtered by trauma and pain and a realization that anyone she saw, *everyone*, was capable of these things.

Three bodies had been tied together and they now flowed by in a tangled mess. It looked like a man, a woman and a child, and I guessed that the man had done the tying in an effort to keep them together in the flood. If that were the case he'd dragged his family to their deaths, because his skull had been shattered by a bullet. His wife and child seemed untouched, but they did not move. The mud had made them its home.

We watched them drift off towards the church and I wondered where in the world they'd come from.

"Good sense says we go that way," Chele said, pointing downstream after the bodies. "But logic says we go that way, where the action is. That's where we'll find our way out." She pointed upstream, and the three of us looked along the flooded street towards a large open area at the end. It may have been a park once, but many of the trees had been torn down or submerged. From this distance I could see shapes protruding above the flow of mud, but I could not make out what they were. Buildings? Hills in the landscaped park? Beyond the park I could see nothing, because a heavy, mucky-looking mist engulfed the view.

From that direction came the continuing sounds of conflict.

"Do we really want to just walk into that?" I said quietly, reaching out to touch Laura's shoulder.

Chele was looking around, probing the mud gently with her feet on either side of the wall. "We have to. Remember, we're not meant to be here at all. We broke in to find your daughter."

I felt a stab of guilt at that, the fact that Chele was only here because of me, but she'd come of her own accord. And her voice held no hint of blame.

Does she feel nearer to her son now? I thought. My daughter's a stranger to her, but does rescuing her make Chele's dead son seem that much closer?

"Those demons, those caves."

"Another scene," Chele said. "We saw several ourselves before we left the coach, remember? We just slipped from one to the next. Accidentally or on purpose it doesn't matter."

"But if the demons are integral to this place… the law-keepers… surely they'd have just followed us through?"

Chele strode along the wall several paces and stood with her hands on her hips. She seemed to have found something that pleased her. "I don't pretend to know any more about this place than you," she said, and I felt almost annoyed at her ignorance. "Now come look at this."

Laura and I followed to where Chele was standing and looked down. There, moored against the outside edge of the garden boundary wall, bobbing on the gloopy current, sat a shallow dinghy complete with paddles.

"How long has this place *been* like this?" I said. Long enough to have boats… a *long* time.

"It's just a scene, Dad," Laura said then. "Make believe made real." She rubbed her wrists and winced as the muddied scabs broke. Blood showed through and dripped into the mud river creeping past the wall. A part of her would forever be in Hell, now. A part of all of us, because we had all taken cuts and lost blood. It would merge with the mud, and perhaps tomorrow it would be a part of something even more terrible.

There was a prolonged bout of gunfire from upriver and a roar as another building collapsed, unseen.

"Let's not think about it," I said, thinking all the same. Machine guns, pad-rifles; it was a war up there. And here we were preparing to paddle right into it. "Let's just go."

Chele knelt at the front of the dinghy, with Laura in the middle and me at the back. It sank so that its rim was almost at the level of the mud, and I feared that any surge or wave would swamp us, the weight dragging us instantly down to whatever lay below. I knew that we wouldn't be the first or last bodies added to this rancid river.

Just as we were about to set out the thudding shock of a pad-rifle sounded from somewhere nearby. The rounds roared along the street, and I saw the flowering explosions of brick and mortar as they struck a house on the opposite side. Great clots of masonry strafed the mud, its splashes remaining visible for a few seconds as they were carried away on the current. Windows burst in, a third of the roofing slates were smashed into the air like a flock of startled birds, the front door and surround exploded into the guts of the house, holes the size of our boat appeared across its façade. We ducked down as low as we could get, frightened but fascinated, and watched in awe as the house slumped down into the mud like a tired old man. The pad-rifle continued firing for a few seconds more. It pounded the debris into dust and then fell silent, until the only sound was the crunch of the mud river sucking the house remains down into itself. Soon, the only sign that a building had existed there at all was the central staircase, exposed to the elements like the bare backbone of some long-rotted beast.

"That was from nearby," I whispered.

"Stray rounds," Chele said.

"No way, that was sustained. Someone targeted that house. This one might be next."

"If we move they may see — "

"If we don't," I said, "they'll find us when they come looking."

"Maybe we can be on their side," Laura said quietly. I was almost relieved at the naïveté of her statement. There was some child left inside her after all.

"Row," I said, untying the rotten rope and pushing us away from the wall. Chele picked up an oar and sank it into the mud.

It was like rowing through porridge. Although the mud flowed like a river and kept its own level like water, when I tried to pull on the oar it felt like concrete. I could see the muscles standing out on Chele's neck as she heaved. Laura sat in front of me, stroking the terrible wounds on her arms with muddy fingertips. I thought about infections and gangrene and pollution, and as if conjured by my musings a rat the size of a small cat ran along the top of the wall we had just vacated. It stared at me with a hunger than could never have been manufactured. This may just be a scene, as Chele had said, but its components were real enough.

We tried keeping to the relative shelter of the buildings and garden walls, rowing against the flow, gaining inch by inch. At one point my paddle snagged on something and I nearly lost it. Reaching down into the mud my hand closed around something soft and yielding, and pulling it away from the paddle realized that whatever it was wore clothes. I did not look down lest I saw it.

But I did catch sight of things in the gardens to my left. I thought they were shrubs and trees at first, branches stripped of leaves and left bare and pale in the grey light. Then I realized that they were limbs. Dozens of bodies were drifted together against one wall, half submerged arms and legs and heads protruding above the mud as if stretching forever for dry brickwork. Faces with mouths and eyes filled with muck. Torsos with horrific wounds. Slicks of blood around them, dark and shiny like oil on water.

I turned away and kept paddling.

The gunfire continued, more sporadic now. Perhaps the numbers on both sides were so reduced by the fighting that there weren't that many left to shoot.

I hoped that was the case.

"Push harder!" I said, heaving back, feeling my biceps burning, my back straining with the effort. I'd been close to collapse since we saved ourselves from the quagmire. Whatever kept me going now, it would surely not last for much longer. If we let up the current would grab us and drag us out into the faster-flowing central spread of the flooded roadway. And from there… who knew.

Either that or we'd be three more bodies washed against a wall.

Laura dipped her hands in on either side of the dinghy and started to pull as well. She flicked mud up at me — it stank stale and dead, as if filth itself could rot — but I didn't mind. She was helping. And perhaps having something to do would divert her attention from whatever she was still dwelling upon.

I knew her so well. I was here, we were moving, but she still felt far from saved.

Things floated by. At one point a slick of fresh blood enveloped the boat, and the fleshy objects squelching against the wood were stark against the dark brown mess. Many other things, too; a real mix and match of a life, as if someone's history was being systematically destroyed somewhere up ahead. A perverse, reverse evolution. There was a shoe, laces still tied but empty; a notebook, pages sprawled like a dead bird, one side used, the other waiting for thoughts that would never come; an unopened tin of dried rice; a sock; a dinner plate, still stained with the grease of its last supper. Spectacles, a boxed pen set, half of a door, a flap of leather from a torn jacket....

It went on.

And then we reached the end of the street where the mud opened up into a lake of filth, and at last we could see what the humps protruding from its mess were.

Bandstands. Three of them, the one in the center so tall that its whole platform was above the flood-line. It reminded me of small-town America, hot dogs, Fourth of July parades and brass bands. The other two were smaller, submerged beneath the mud with only their roofs and supports touching daylight. And on each bandstand, people with guns.

Fighting over nothing but mud, filth and shit.

Dying there, flipping into the air, spinning, tumbling into the muck and being carried slowly towards us by the current, past us eventually, back along the street.

More corpses to meet the wall.

The central bandstand seemed to be under siege from the other two, and it was here that the pad-rifle fire had originated. Strangely, its impact on the wooden structures was minimal, and at first I thought it was because they were so open that most rounds missed. But then I saw someone stand against the railings of the central bandstand, prop a pad-rifle on the rail before him and loose off three rounds at the structure to our left. The first two struck a woman hunkered down on its roof, shattering her like a broken mannequin and flinging her pieces far out over the mud. The third round hit the edge of the roof... but only a few shards of wood sprung out.

"It's all selective," I said. "All this destruction is selective."

"They're pad-rifles," Chele said. "You can't pick and choose — "

"You saw what happened to that house. How do you think those two bandstands are still there?"

"Bad shots," Laura said. The gunfire erupted once again, figures dropped and splashed into the mud, some screaming, guts blown out, limbs askew.

The buildings still stood, bearing the designer scars of battle.

"Have they seen us?" Laura asked. We were bobbing against the gable wall of a house bordering the park, pressed there by the current and exposed to anyone who happened to glance our way.

"I think," I said, "that their own little scene simply doesn't include us." I was comfortable with this idea, if a little confused, and it seemed to fit right into what we were seeing.

"It'll have to stop soon," Chele said. "They'll all be dead."

There was a sound like the buzzing of distant insects beneath the gunfire. And as the three powerboats roared into the park — two emerging from the distant haze of mist, one coming straight up the street behind us — and a line of bullets coughed out brick dust by our heads, I realized how wrong I was.

We *were* involved. Hell, I realized, can never be selective. It's there for the benefit of everyone.

The boat slicing through the mud behind us slowed down, and a man on the bow loosed a burst of suppressing fire at the bandstand on the left. The noise was shockingly loud. Another hail of bullets came our way, kicking up great gouts of mud and releasing its stench into the air. Bullets buzzed by our ears, ricochets singing behind us, and I was sure I could feel the breeze of their passing, smell their rich metallic tint as they exploded against the wall and the boats' hulls.

The driver of the powerboat fell back, his face swallowed by a fresh red hole.

"Oh God," Laura said, turning her head away, and I could see that she'd been splashed when the bullet had struck him. She caught my eye and, inexplicably, tried to smile. It came as a grimace, teeth bared, eyes wide, and for a second — for the first time in my life — I was frightened by my daughter. What madness could she have inherited from this place?

"Into the boat!" the man on the bow shouted. They drew up next to us and he fired again. Tracer rounds tore across the mud lake and strafed the bandstand. Two people dropped, one of them sliding into the mud, and one of the boats from the mist immediately pulled up and disgorged several more fighters onto the tattered wooden structure. They picked up scattered weapons and immediately opened fire on the central bandstand and our boats.

"Quickly!" the man shouted, ducking down as the gunfire increased.

"No," I said. We shouldn't go with them, should never take sides, because once we did that we were truly embedded in this scene, part of the play and bound into whatever climax awaited these pointless people. The man looked at me, wide-eyed and disbelieving. His machine gun drifted in our direction. Its smoking barrel looked hungry.

Something stung my elbow. I looked down and saw a rosette of blood opening on my muddied sleeve, and my arm went numb. A bullet had kissed me. Laura guided me to the edge of the dinghy, stepping over into the powerboat and taking me with her. Blood ran down inside my sleeve, warm and shocking, and it dripped from my fingers as a dark brown paste. It was carrying dried mud with it. I wondered what bacteriological horrors were seeping hungrily into my wound even now.

In the back of the powerboat sat half a dozen people. They all looked tired, underfed, sick, but their eyes gleamed with excitement. Some of them glanced at us, but most had their eyes on the body of the dead driver where he was leaking across the timber boards.

They all carried weapons. I saw at least three pad-rifles.

"Chele!" I said, turning to hold out my hand. She was hunched down in the dinghy, hands over her head, trying to present as small a target as possible. The wall of the house was all but disintegrating under the hail of lead, and a fine powder drifted in the air and stuck to our wet clothes. Chele stood slowly, glancing over at me. She was readying herself to jump. She looked like a ghost.

"We can't stay here," one of the people said, leaping to the wheel and leaning on the throttle. The boat started to pull away. I reached out for Chele and she jumped.

"Laura!" I said, but she was already there. Between us we hauled Chele in, trying to keep low as the bullets sang around us like angry bees. The boat was humping fast across the mud lake now, each impact feeling as if we were striking concrete.

I reached for one of the pad-rifles strapped to the engine mounting. I expected them to jump at me, fight me for it, maybe even shoot me... but if we were going to get out of this I had to do something.

The sound was almost unbearable, the stink of mud richer and more nauseating than ever, and I could taste blood in the air. Perhaps that was the red mist I saw.

I pulled Chele and Laura close to me, hugging the pad-rifle to my left side. Its heavy plastic was strangely warm, its wide barrel and gas-ports wicked-looking, black eyes promising so many horrors yet to be seen.

"It's a reinforcement boat," I said. "Nobody can last long on those bandstands, not when they're so exposed. Everyone on this boat will be dead soon, including us, if we don't get out of here."

"How do we do that?"

"I have this." I nodded at the pad-rifle. Laura refused even to look at it.

"But — " Chele began. But she did not have a chance to finish.

Sometimes, when everything's as bad as you think it can get, it gets worse. Misfortune upon terror upon horror... all crowd in to drown their victims, ensure a completed job.

The boat was just approaching the central bandstand when someone shouted out: "Demons!"

I looked up and saw several black shapes circling slowly down from the grey sky, wide webbed wings drifting them skillfully towards our boat.

"Now we're finished!" a woman shouted out, and I swear there was joy in her fear.

"They're here for them!" The voice came from the bandstand. Someone was leaning out, pointing at us, and I knew without looking that it was the madman from the barbing world. Black Teeth.

He'd been spared for some other fate.

As the demons swirled down, their wings now cracking at the air, the fighters in the boat turning to look at the three of us, bullets zinging past from both directions as we came under concerted fire from the sunken bandstands... I knew that it was time to fight.

"Chele — "

She spun around and hit the gunwale hard, the impact audible even above the gunfire. Laura cried out. Someone laughed. I dropped to my knees beside Chele and flipped her onto her back, hearing the impact of bullets on bodies behind me. There were several thumps as corpses hit the deck, but Laura was beside me, pressing her hand to the terrible wound in Chele's face, holding in the blood, wiping away what was left of her eye where the bullet had blown it out, crying, crying for this stranger who'd helped me save her from her cruel crucifixion. And someone was still laughing.

I glanced around and saw Black Teeth leaning out over the mud, ignorant of the bullets biting at his clothes and hair, or perhaps simply not caring. He was pointing at us, his hysterical eyes wide open. I looked at his hands and imagined them wrapping barbed wire around Laura's wrists, touching her as he did it, his eyes glinting as his fingers strayed, and before I really knew what I was doing I'd brought the pad-rifle to bear.

As if badly scripted, the gunfire paused to add gravity to the moment.

I held the weapon waist-high. I'd seen these things working, so I knew I didn't need to aim.

Black Teeth stopped laughing for a second and stared at me in disbelief. Then he smiled again, showing the rot in his mouth. Shook his head. He knew I'd never do it.

I pulled the trigger. The balustrade misted into fragments and the madman splashed back in a wash of red. His laugh seemed to hang in the air for a few seconds like a cartoon speech bubble, or perhaps it was the rifle report ringing in my ears.

At least I knew what fate he had been spared for.

The thought that the demons had known what would happen — had perhaps engineered it — was too dreadful to contemplate, although it all made perfect sense. They were the scriptwriters and we were the actors, although our lines and actions were subconscious, not learnt.

"Daddy!" Laura shouted, and a black shape knocked me from my feet.

I kept hold of the pad-rifle as I went sprawling, holding out one hand to break my fall, feeling it slip in something leaking from one of the corpses. The shape closed in on me again and thumped my back twice. I realized it had landed. I could feel long claws curling into me, clenching, finding purchase so that it could finish the job… whatever job that was.

Were the demons here to kill us, or let us go? I had no idea. But I had no time to waste thinking about it.

Chele was dead, most likely.

Laura might be next.

I heaved myself up as hard and fast as I could, hoping to catch the demon unawares. It worked, partially, and the thing slipped from my back, clutching out chunks of my flesh as it did so. I screamed and it screamed back, its voice like that of a giant tree frog, a bass rattle that set my hairs on end. I had to bring the rifle to bear — *had* to — but at the same time I wondered why nobody in the boat was firing at the thing. I shook my shoulders, pushed sideways as if to turn on my back. Claws raked my skin. Something tapped at the back of my neck, and I felt the warm dribble of blood around my ears and scalp.

The gunfire had started again, and the air smelled of hot metal and death.

Laura leapt into view, landing right by my face and launching herself at the demon. It grumbled at her and waved its wings. One of them caught her under the chin and sent her falling back over Chele's prone body, but she had set it off balance and allowed me to scramble away from the clenching claws. I stood, spun around and aimed the pad-rifle.

For a second, silence fell across the whole scene once again. Gunfire stopped. Shouting ceased. Even the flow of the mud seemed to lessen, the steady roar of debris pushing past buildings dulled. The demon sat frozen against the edge of the cockpit, its black armor wet with my blood, antennae flipping at the air. Its visor was black and held no reflection.

Briefly wondering if I was about to do something awful and unforgivable, I pulled the trigger.

The pad struck the demon in the chest and blew straight through, punching a hole the size of a dinner plate. It took out the side of the powerboat as well. There was a huge splash in the mud twenty yards away and the air turned red, blood misting on the steady breeze and settling on the faces of those watching. Clots of flesh fell from the demon and pattered lightly around its feet. It looked down at its chest. For a second I thought it was going to come at me again, uninjured, hardly even inconvenienced —

blood, it bled, it was just like us

— and then it toppled back over the smashed gunwale and disappeared into the mud.

"Holy shit," someone said. I heard awe in the voice. "They bleed. They *bleed*."

Our boat listed as tons of mud surged through the rupture in its side. The gunfire opened up again, and for a few seconds bullets whistled past our heads from every direction.

They're shooting at me, I thought, *I've destroyed some illusion, ruined something fundamental to their existence here, and they're trying to kill me.*

But then I realized that the weapons were aimed elsewhere. A demon danced on the bow of the boat as bullets struck it, before falling back and landing by my feet.

There were several other demons circling the scene above our heads, and a couple of them opened fire with their own weapons. Air flash-fried as the tasers struck downwards. One burst hit the bandstand we were moored against and danced across its timbers like St. Elmo's fire. A woman jerked and spat as the charge entered her and seemed to light her from the inside, exploding from her eyes, ears, mouth. The demons cackled and croaked and fired some more, some of their shots finding targets. But they were no match for the firepower arrayed against them. Fighters on the boat and all three bandstands had opened up against the demons, and within thirty seconds all but one had been brought down. Most of them hit the mud screeching, clicking for help, bleeding, wings trailing and tattered. And on each impact, a cheer went up from their intended prey.

The one remaining demon, wings pushing frantically, tail trailing like a streamer behind it, rose out of range of our weapons and stayed there, circling on warm currents. It was so high up that we could barely see it. A few bursts of gunfire still cracked out, but all aimed skyward. Down at our level calm had descended, as if none of the people could remember what they had been fighting for.

I wondered what was to come next.

"Dad," Laura said, "she's still alive!"

One side of the boat was submerged now, and its passengers were scrambling across to the bandstand, those already there helping them up. I looked at Chele. Her face was a ruin, both eyes shattered by the bullet, her nose exploded outward... and Laura was right! There, where her nose had been, bubbles appeared in the blood and ruined flesh. They enlarged, withdrew, grew again and popped. Her mouth was open and her tongue was moving like a wounded fish in its red-water cave.

"Jesus." For a crazy second I was going to leave her in the boat. Grab Laura, get up onto the bandstand, take the pad-rifle with me and try to get us out of here, out of Hell, back to that place we called normal but which I thought would never be normal again. She was awfully wounded and even if she did survive, what would the future hold for her? A lifetime of operations, plastic surgery, engineered flesh replacing her own, artificial eyes giving her a sterile view of her world... and perhaps, eventually, a trip back here. To show her that things weren't so bad after all.

I laughed out loud.

Laura frowned, and several people turned to look at me, some of them only halfway to escaping from the sinking boat. "What?" I said, smiling. Laughter must be something none of them heard very often. I smirked at Laura and she actually smiled back, even though she had no idea of the source of my mirth. Then I looked down at Chele and my good humor vanished.

She was my responsibility now. I knew that, and I hated it, and I hated myself for hating it.

"Help me with her," I said. Laura grabbed her feet and I lifted her under the arms, holding the pad-rifle pressed between my arm and side. As we shuffled her towards the high side of the tilted boat her head tipped back. She coughed and cackled deep in her throat. She would choke on her own blood if we didn't get her upright soon.

"Help us!" I said, and hands reached out.

We managed to haul the unconscious Chele up the sloping deck, over the gunwale and onto the bandstand. The boat drifted away seconds later, caught by the current now that no one was holding onto it anymore, and as it spun lazily towards the street we'd come up a few minutes before it tipped over. Mud gurgled in and sucked it down, down to whatever the depths held. Soon there was only a whirling pattern on the mud where the boat had been.

Seconds later even that vanished.

I stood on something wet and red and disgusting, wondering which piece of Black Teeth was beneath my feet. His heart, empty of pity? His mashed eyes, and all the terrors they had seen? Perhaps it was his hands, his fingers that had wrapped the wire around Laura's wrists.

I ground my feet and smiled. I'd never, ever killed anyone before. The closest I'd come was thinking about killing myself.

"She's still breathing, I think," Laura said, kneeling next to Chele's prone body. I looked, so helpless.

"What now?" someone asked. "What now, now that we've killed the demons? Are we free? Can we go?"

"Don't be so stupid," someone else answered.

"How long has this been happening?" I said, looking out over the mud and hefting the pad-rifle.

"What do you mean?"

"*How long?*"

"Forever."

"Minutes...."

The answers were all wrong, though all the speakers obviously felt them to be right. I could sense no confusion there, no doubt.

And then I saw something that was nearer to home than anything I'd seen since escaping the coach with Chele: a disturbance in the mud, halfway between the bandstand and the ruined houses. At first I thought it was the mud river passing over a ditch or culvert, but I noticed that the hollow in the surface was moving, passing across the lake like the concave shadow of a cloud. It was a wave caused by something unseen, an outside influence in here.

And it was so close to home because I knew exactly what it was.

"There!" I said, pointing.

"What? Where? What?" They all spoke, and the tone of their voices all said the same thing.

"How can you accept all this so easily?" I asked, disgusted. The people looked at me, a couple of them frowning as if they'd forgotten something vital. I brought up the pad-rifle and glanced at Laura. She knew what was about to happen and ducked down, covering Chele's wounded face with her own body. I felt so proud.

Still nobody answered my question, so I opened fire at nothing.

The third shot opened a window to reality.

There was a face revealed there, cringing away from the rupture as glass exploded around them. The woman looked out and the shock was rich and honest. The blood made it so, because she must have never expected to end that day bleeding. And it was as if she saw this scene as it really was for the first time. Before, behind the protective glass of the coach, it was played out for her; a holo clip, a flash of history or a keyhole onto the future. Now it was different. Now she could see and smell and sense the truth of things.

The rest of the coach was still invisible, but the wound in its side located it. I could imagine where it was, if not actually see it, so I swivelled a few degrees and fired again, blasting out a panel and revealing the fluid workings of its engine. I turned again — I saw the woman's fear as, for a split second, she stared into the pad-rifle's barrel — and fired twice more, smashing holes in the rear of the coach. They were sharp-edged rents in its skin, like shrapnel wounds bleeding reality. More faces stared out. One of them screamed; I could hear him, hear the pain and shock as he tried to dig shattered glass from his throat. I knew that no one could help him because they were all strapped in. Hell... it was a very personal thing.

The last thing I could feel was regret or pity.

"We can get out," I said, turning to Laura where she knelt beside Chele. "We can get on this thing and get out of here." I looked around at the others, their gazes switching between me and the strange, stark holes in the false façade of their lives. "You're an entertainment, you know that don't you?" Even as I said it I knew it was untrue — they, and we, were far more than that — but my loyalty was clearly defined: my daughter. That was it, the be all and end all, the reason I'd come here in the first place. The fact that my visit had given me the opportunity to rescue her and actually bring her back to me... that was a stroke of luck and fortune I could not consider. Right then, getting out was my prime concern.

The idea that I could be destroying this for everyone didn't cross my mind.

The woman in the coach stared at me, unable to move, awaiting her fate with sad, staring eyes. I turned away but still felt her gaze, accusing, confused.

"You *do* know," I said again, and the people on the bandstand stirred as if an invisible breeze had raised their heckles. "You all remember what you were — "

"Of course we do!" a woman said. "And we know where we are, and why we're here and... we're not as stupid as you think. But...."

"But what?" I prompted.

"But the demons," one of the men said. He was looking over my shoulder as he spoke, and I knew that that we were still a long, long way from the end of things.

I looked back at the coach. It was motionless and the sharp-edged rents I'd blown into reality danced with dark shapes. Struggling people joined them at first, but then they were totally blotted out as the shapes took control. New faces stared out... faces with antennae and visors reflecting nothing of our fear and confusion. And then the demons came out. Not only through the holes I had created with the pad-rifle, but also through new gaps in the background scene of houses and mud and mist. Trapdoors opened in the coach's roof, shedding demons like confetti to the sky. They spiralled upwards, ten of them, fifteen, twenty, and others flowed into the mud, burrowing just below the surface, aiming for the bandstand and casting strong wakes behind them.

People started screaming. They'd brought down a few demons, yes, but the initial flush of success was smothered by the sight of dozens more vectoring in on us. Back came the fear. Back came the supernatural awe that these things inspired.

I aimed the pad-rifle at the swimming shapes and fired into the mud. It exploded upward and outward as if a depth charge had blown, scattered wet filth to the breeze, raining down around us brown and black, and red where I'd hit one of the damned things. More came in, lines of bubbles the only evidence of their route now that they'd gone deeper.

"Open fire!" I shouted, looking around at the terrified people. Their guns aimed tentatively at the skies, the mud, and some of them fired a few rounds.

In their eyes, their stance, I saw only hopelessness.

The sky darkened as a dozen demons swept in. I shouted at Laura to drag Chele to the center of the bandstand floor — I wondered whether any tunes had ever been played here, any brass victory marches or string pleas for peace — and I fired again. The gun thumped in my hands as it expelled a shot; until now it had been recoilless. The round hit a flying shape and turned black into a rain of red, but when I fired again there was a loud hiss of gas, a broken thunk from inside the rifle, and it died in my hands.

I spun the weapon around to use as a club. But I didn't need it.

The demons didn't come for me or Laura. Not even for mortally wounded Chele. It was as if we were invisible observers, and the slaughter was a show put on especially for us.

The clicking of their communications was a low, seismic tickle through my spine, standing my hair on end, sending pains through my teeth. Everything went hazy and dim, as if my sight was picking up atmospheric interference.

Mud-covered demons emerged and squelched up onto the bandstand. Others landed from the sky. They walked with the same gait, struck with the same deadly precision.

Not one of the people fired again before they died.

The demons lashed out with lengthened limbs, claws slashing through clothing and flesh, the air turning red, bodies spinning away as insides leaked out, other demons catching them and crushing their heads, paralyzing with stun-guns, gutting with elongated claws protruding from where their elbows or knees should be, pushing them from one to another like cats playing with a mouse, slashing or stabbing, moving on, plucking out an eye, emptying a gun into a chest, moving on again. The bandstand floor was awash with human stuff.

It ran over the edges and flowed away with the flood, spreading like a bruise on its surface, heavy bits sinking, lighter pieces — scalps and eyeballs and flayed skin — floating towards their final resting place.

There were screams and gasps and the air stank of blood and shit. I felt the greasiness of the slaughter coat my skin, tasted death.

It lasted for thirty seconds.

Everyone was dead but us. Most of the demons turned to leave, but two came our way. They were clicking and clacking quietly, a casual chat during a walk in the park. Their dark body-armor — grown or worn, I still couldn't tell — was slick with blood. I despaired at the hopelessness of it all, the unfairness, and I selfishly turned away from Laura. No man should see his daughter die.

I looked out over the sea of mud and waited for the end.

"Dad!" Laura hissed. Her voice was so imploring I had to look.

The demons had nudged her to one side and were standing over Chele, kicking her with their clawed feet. When she did not respond or move one of them slung her easily over its shoulder. Blood dribbled from her wounds and added its own signature to her carrier's armor.

I stepped towards them. There was nothing I could do, but it was an automatic reaction.

They stopped dead-still and the crackling of their communication increased in tempo and volume. It went for a gentle hush to a chaos of static, a white noise in which anything could have been said. The unencumbered demon brought up its stun-gun and aimed it at my face. Laura gasped. I looked at Chele's back, trying to make out whether or not she was breathing, but I couldn't tell.

The thing holding Chele dropped over the side of the bandstand and into the mud, skidding across the surface. It disappeared into the mists just as the second demon suddenly took flight, climbing until it was little more that a speck against the brightening sky.

"They left us," Laura said. "We're still alive. They left us alone. Why would they do that, Dad?"

I looked across at where the coach stood still and holed, and shook my head.

"I'm cold." She was shivering. She may have been shivering for twenty minutes but I hadn't noticed. I went to her and held her, careful not to touch the weeping wounds on her wrists as fresh tears fell onto my arms. They darkened the mud dried there.

"We should go," I said, understanding none of this.

"Where have they taken her?"

"I don't know."

"Was she dead? Dad, do you think — "

"I don't know, honey. Let's go."

"Where?" Laura looked around, so frightened and vulnerable that I never wanted to let her go again.

"There." I pointed at the coach. Its outline was becoming visible now, a haze around the holes like heat-haze on a blazing summer afternoon. "That's the way out. Wherever we are, if there's a door-way that's it."

We walked around the bandstand, avoiding the bodies and body parts, looking over the edge into the flowing mud. On the opposite side to where we'd landed we found a tatty old boat, barely capable of floating under its own weight. There was an oar there, though, and it pulled at its rope like an eager puppy.

Things were calming. I looked around, trying to make out exactly what was changing, but I was trying to see something that wasn't there rather than something that was. Perhaps the mud was a shade lighter, moving a touch slower. Or maybe the light had faded slightly, and all the wrongness was simply less visible now. The houses were still there, but the street we had paddled up was indistinct, an accidental break between buildings instead of an intentional roadway. The smells were diluted too: blood yes, but old and stale; shit and mud, faded and dry; the tang of the memory gunfire.

Slowly, now that the events were over and things had changed, the scene was shutting down.

"Into the boat." I helped Laura over the handrail and held her hands as she lowered herself down. I followed, careful to spread my weight squarely, but the dinghy was surprisingly buoyant and steady. As I untied the mooring rope and pushed us out into the current, I found that we were being carried straight towards the prone coach. I didn't even need to paddle.

The nearer we approached, the clearer the coach emerged, until by the time we nudged its side I couldn't believe it had ever been invisible. Its surface was matte black and smooth to the touch, all curves and arcs without a sharp angle in sight. We'd arrived directly beneath one of the windows shattered by my pad-rifle fire, and I stood in the dinghy and hoisted myself up to look inside.

The smells should have warned me, but by then I was exhausted and turned off to everything.

I could see the occupants of two seats through the smashed window. They were both blackened husks, still smoking from boiled eye sockets and violent red rents in their skins. Clothes were burnt off or melted into their flowing flesh. The one farthest from me seemed to be slipping slowly to the floor, scorched flesh allowing the body to pass fluidly beneath the restraining belt.

Something dripped.

And then I heard the frightened voices from further along the coach.

"Come on." I warned Laura about the sight that awaited her and boosted her through the smashed window. She took her time getting in, trying to avoid the sharp glass teeth that sought her soft skin. She had enough wounds already. I followed her quickly, taking some cuts but not caring.

"Who are you?"

"I want mummy, I want mummy…."

"What's happened?"

"Please don't kill us."

There were several more dead people, fried in their seats by the demons, but the living outnumbered them. After what I'd seen and been through I could hardly look at them without thinking, *Cattle. Sheep.* The demons had only killed those with a direct line of sight through the blown out windows. Presumably the survivors had seen nothing of the battle that followed my pad-rifle attack on the coach.

"We're just hitching a ride," I said, looking at the few pale, scared faces in view. "Don't mind us."

"Dad, we're moving." Laura was looking through the smashed window and when I bent down I could see the bandstands moving quickly out of sight. The scene darkened and vanished. Somebody screamed. There was a sudden, intense acceleration that flung me down into the aisle and Laura onto the carbonized lap of a seat's former occupant. A screaming sound erupted through the ragged holes as the coach traveled its strange route.

I clung onto a metal seat support leg as we picked up speed, feeling myself shoved along the floor, forces conspiring to drive me along the coach to break my bones against its rear bulkhead. I could just make out Laura's hand where it clasped the chair's hand rest. I wanted to reach up and lock fingers, reassure her — she was still in the lap of the burnt corpse, and it was probably still hot — but I couldn't move. I lay there and let events carry me along, my cheek pressed flat to the floor, part of my view through the shattered window and into nothing outside.

We were being guided, herded, coerced, steered and pulled along, I was certain of that now. Every event, every movement since I'd broken out of the coach to rescue Laura from crucifixion, had been preordained. Attacked when required, left alone or allowed to escape when it best served their intentions and plans… whoever They were. Knowing did not stop it happening, could not prevent the eventual outcome, whatever that may be. I may as well fight against life itself, or rage against God.

So I lay there, waiting... and very soon the screams began once more.

The darkness ended and daylight came again. The cries increased, and I heard Laura's voice amongst them. I pulled myself up, slowly, fighting the forces still crushing me to the floor, tucking my toes against seat supports so that I was not torn away and flung down the length of the coach... and I saw why there was screaming.

I almost lost my footing, but I'd come this far. Instinct for survival kept me where I was, even though every sense inside, every civilized part urged me to let go.

This was Hell as it must have seemed in the past, created in the image most expected. Rivers of fire flowed across the landscape, erupting in brief bursts of bright white flame as sufferers were thrown in by gangs of blackened humanoids. The gang would turn around and lumber back to a roughly-tied cage, extract another screaming victim and repeat the process, again and again. There were deep, smooth trails between the cages and the burning river, worn away by the shuffling monsters over decades or centuries. Nearer, as if arrayed along the route of the coach for our benefit, thousands of people hung crucified on the rigid skeletons of previous victims. Some of the dying people smoldered and burned.

We passed a valley where thousands of naked people tried to dodge showers of molten rock falling from some invisible height. They went down when they were struck and were trampled or burned. Hundreds more damned were thrust into the valley through doors hidden in its depths, like gladiators pushed into the arena to face certain death. I could hear their screams, smell their scorched flesh, sense their agony in my bones. The air was filled with a whole concerto of pain, suffering and death. Even the screams of the passengers could do nothing to hide that.

I saw more. Even though we were a distance away, and the people were really only pale shapes leaping and running and dying against the dark volcanic rocks, I could still somehow make out terrible details: the spectacles worn by one of the men, their bridge pasted with white tape, lenses smashing into his eyes as clumps of rock struck his face; a woman shielding her baby from the onslaught of lava, her back burned bare and roiling with blisters, yet still she didn't yield; and a child, walking slowly and calmly through the chaos, her face turned my way, eyes filled with something I could not identify in this nightmare place.

There's always a survivor, someone said into my ear, and I glanced to my side. It must have been the wind.

The scene faded quickly, letting the impenetrable blackness return beyond the window. The coach was still accelerating, but if I let go I'd be torn from Laura forever. She looked at me. Her eyes were wide and terrified, her face bloodied and lined with pain and fear, but she smiled.

I smiled back, and for a moment there was nothing wrong.

And then sunlight burst into the coach. There was a valley outside, a mosaic of odd-shaped fields coating the slopes, a long lazy river snaking down to where the hills faded away in the distance. There was a crowd of people in the foreground. They provided a further splash of color to the lush green grasses, their summer clothes and tanned flesh merging to form a giant painter's palette across the valley floor.

They were all looking up.

As the coach moved by, the perspective was all wrong. We were still accelerating, I could feel my insides distorting and my eyes twisting in their sockets, but we still had time to see the giant airship fall in a graceful, leisurely fireball from the sky. The people did not run. They stood there and looked up as if not believing this could happen, even though they could see the flames scorching the sky and the burning people falling like foolish descendants of Icarus.

The front end of the huge ship plowed into the crowd, flames spreading like ripples on a sun-bleached pond. I thought I saw the girl again, wandering unconcerned through a meadow —

The window flipped back to black.

"Daddy," Laura said, but then we were blinded with light, the sun shining off fields of ice and snow, huge wooden houses and hotels like boils on the mountainside, the faint black lines of ski lifts heading towards the summits, tiny black dots zigging and zagging down towards an evening's rest and chat and drinking. And then the cloud of white behind then, following slowly at first but gathering momentum, sweeping the skiers down at two hundred miles per hour and crushing them into red splashes, crashing through buildings, burying everything, *everything*, and walking across the snows in the foreground without a care in the world was the little girl, and —

There's always a survivor, someone said —

The scene changed instantly from one of light to dark, the sea at night. A huge swell moved mountains of water, and there were dozens of little boats out there, each of them crowded with thirty or forty men. In the distance oil burned on the water's surface, but none of the men looked that way. They were staring at something else, a black shiny-skinned monster gliding through the swell, and then it coughed out fire and one of the boats exploded into splinters of wood and bone. Men screamed, gargled as they drowned, and the cannon fired again, wrecking another boat. There were men on the deck with machine guns, laughing as they shot the survivors in the water, one of them aiming for hands and shoulders so that the victim would be unable to swim, drowning slowly. The gun fired again, again, and each time a boat came apart, spilling men whole and in pieces into the sea for the bullets or the cold or the sharks to finish off.

The girl bobbed gently in the foreground, watching us. Her dress had spread out around her and she looked like a huge jellyfish. Bullets splashed and I wanted to shout a warning, but somehow I knew it wasn't required.

There's always a survivor, the voice said again, and another nightmare scene manifested, and another, and another. Soon they were racing by like the frames of a film, indistinguishable singly but making up a moving image of pain, suffering and death as I had never before imagined possible, and —

There's always a survivor.

Chele dropped down from a hatch in the ceiling. I could barely hold on; Laura was pressed back into the stinking, crackling remains of the corpse in the seat, but Chele seemed unconcerned at the acceleration. Her eyes had gone, and out of their sockets protruded thin, weak antennae. Her face was darkened around the eyes and nose where heavy bruises were forming, and along her hairline knobs were pushing through the skin, looking for all the world like horns forcing their way from her skull. One of them split the skin as she approached and she tilted her head as the antennae came through, perhaps picking up on some distant demonic discussion.

She reached for Laura.

I tried to lean forward but the motion of the coach pushed me back, pressed my loose skin and flesh against my bones until I thought that I'd be ripped away from my skeleton.

"Dad!" Laura hissed as Chele's hand closed around the back of her neck. "Dad, thanks for coming for me. I love you Dad... thanks...."

I didn't come for you, it was for me, I thought, but I wasn't about to say it even if I could.

Chele's hands were blackened, the solid armor of the demons, and her nails had grown long and taken on a metallic tint.

The coach accelerated some more and from the window I could see the hazy image of the little girl.

...always a survivor....

My vision darkened and senses receded. I saw Chele open her

mouth to laugh as her other hand swung around, sharpened nails aiming for Laura's exposed throat, and then I could see nothing.

I heard laughter. Chele's cruel laughter punctuated by the clicks and clacks of her throat hardening and closing in, allowing her no more say in the matter of her fate than, in truth, any of us have.

When I awoke there was a dog licking my face.

I was lying in a gutter. A few people must have passed me by because there was money scattered by my feet. I sat up slowly, looked down at myself, checked for broken bones, finding an ache or cut on every square inch of skin I touched. I could hardly blame them for not stopping to help, because I should be dead. Little did they know I'd just been through Hell.

I recognized the street. I was lying on cobbles, I could smell Chinese food and as I sat there rubbing my head, the mutt still trying to lick my hand, two drunks burst from a door behind me and staggered along the pavement. They threw some slurred abuse my way but they were too pissed to do anything other than talk.

Laura.

Perhaps I'd been in there, in the pub with those men. Maybe I'd drunk myself into oblivion after oblivion, coming back again and again for weeks on end. The barman would know not only my name and life story, but my direct banker's number as well. Perhaps by now he even owned my house.

I looked for the door between the pub and restaurant, but there was only a bare spread of wall.

Laura.

I was covered with dried mud and blood, some of it my daughter's. I could smell her on me. I could remember her, how she'd thanked me what seemed like minutes ago and how I'd kept my selfish truth silent from her in those last few moments before… before….

I stood and ran home, ignoring the pain and stares, the comments and shouts, trying not to see the scared looks on kids' faces as I breezed by. And with every step I took I expected a meteor to come blasting down out of the sky, a gunman to turn a corner with fifty pounds of explosive strapped to his chest and a belt-fed machine gun spitting death, a wall of water to come washing along the street, thirty feet deep and carrying the city's story with it, sweeping up history and washing it clean.

I looked for disaster and death, but I saw only typical, mundane life. I wanted to stop people in the street and tell them just how fucking lucky they were, why didn't they smile, why didn't they *live*.

But right now wasn't the time.

Now, I had to get home.

And Laura was there. Huddled on the doorstep like a shame-faced kid come home after her first night away. She was in a worse state than me, and when I saw her I burst into tears. She looked up, smiling and crying at the same time, and our tears weren't of sadness or despair or fear. They were because never, ever have two people been so happy to see each other alive.

I knew what we were, and I whispered it into Laura's ear as the world went on around us.

"We're survivors," I said, "because there's always a survivor."

I believed that. *They* let us survive.

I should tell people what I know and what I've seen, but somehow it feels secret and forbidden. And every time I work my way to doing so I see Laura sitting in the sunlight or browsing through a book or cooking us a meal, and I dread changing anything. It's all so perfect now; it's drawn us together, and it really feels as though we're doing Janine — my wife, Laura's mother — proud.

Besides, sometimes I see demons in the dark.

So I live with the guilt and bad memories, and the certainty that every time I go to a concert or sports match with Laura I can cast my eyes across the crowds, and know that amongst them there are people who will suffer a horrendous fate. Normal people who will find Hell, not because they need it, but because Hell needs *them*. For fodder.

I feel terrible. I hate myself for saying nothing.

But I live with it.

There are worse things in life, after all.

The First Law

1. THE DEVIL'S CHAPLAIN

On their fifth day adrift at sea, they saw an island.

At first, there were only teasing hints of land: a twisted clump of palm fronds; darting specks in the sky which may have been birds; a greenish tinge to the underside of the soft clouds in the north, just above the horizon. They should have felt impelled to paddle towards it, but five days of sun, thirst and heat had drained them of hope. They lay slumped in the boat, their skin red and blistered, tongues swollen, lips split and black with dried blood.

Their ship had been torpedoed and sunk five days earlier. So far as they knew, they were the only survivors. They had begun to feel cursed, not blessed.

"I think there's an island there," Butch said, "unless the clouds are green with envy." He was small, normally chipper, and one side of his face was badly bruised from the sinking. He knelt at the front of the lifeboat and stared out across the sea, a grotesque figurehead.

Roddy closed his eyes against the blazing sun, but still it found its way through. It was as though his eyelids were turning transparent through lack of sustenance. The lifeboat had been capsized when they found it, and any supplies previously stored on board had been swallowed by the sea. On the third day it had rained, and they had managed to trap enough water in cupped hands and bundled clothes for a few mouthfuls each. Since then, they had gone thirsty. Roddy felt life seeping from his body with every drop of sweat.

Ernie was the only officer with them, but thankfully he had refused to pull rank. He seemed to acknowledge, as they all did, that their position levelled anything so fleeting as grade. They had all been thrown together by the disaster of war, into the same class; that of survivor. So he prayed out loud instead, and at first his praying had helped, until Roddy had commented on how prayers had not aided the other three hundred of the ship's crew. Since then Ernie had been sitting at the stern, spouting occasional brief outbursts of worship as if to goad the others into violence.

It was not that Roddy had no sense of religion. It simply felt redundant out here, in the middle of the ocean. Today, he thought, God was indifferent.

"Definitely an island," Butch said. "Look. Leaves, or something. Covered in bird shit, too."

Roddy managed to raise his head and upper body until he was sitting up. Joints creaked in protest; he moaned in sympathy. His stomach felt huge and heavy and swollen. Ironic, seeing as he had not eaten for days. The sun beat at his forehead like a white-hot sledgehammer, trying to mold him all out of shape. He followed the direction Butch was indicating and saw an island of dead things floating by. But among the brown leaves, several huge egg shapes clung on with wispy tenacity.

"Coconuts," he said.

"Must be migrating," Butch commented.

Norris, apparently asleep until now, raised his hairy head. "Do they migrate?"

"Stupid bastard," Butch muttered, but it was to himself more than Norris. Survival may have thrown them together, but it could not change the way they all thought of the cook. He was unliked and unlikeable. He had been on three ships which had been sunk in the past year, and if anyone attracted the badge of Jonah, it was Norris. He took any such suggestion to heart and fought the man who made it, which only drove the gossip underground and made it harsher.

"Shut your mouth, Norris," Ernie said. "Of all the people God would choose to put on our boat of survivors — "

"I put myself here, mate," Butch cut in.

"Of all the people," Ernie continued, unabated, "we get you."

Norris sat up and winced. "What do you mean by that, you trumped up shit?" His lips were bleeding. Skin had sloughed from his burnt forehead, and now hung down over his eyes. Roddy wondered vaguely whether it helped to keep the sun at bay, and almost put his hand up to his own forehead to see whether he was in the same state.

"He means," said Max, "that you're a Jonah. A curse, a bad omen. You're the Ancient Mariner, and you wear our lives around your scrawny neck."

"Ancient! You're the ancient one, you old bastard. Look at you, big and bald...."

Norris trailed off when he saw that nobody was paying him any attention. Max did not bother to fill him in on the significance of what he had said. Butch was banging on the gunwale with the palm of his hand, trying to attract their attention. Max stood in the center of the boat, and Roddy marvelled once again at his resilience. He was over six feet tall, big without being fat, bald as a baby and about as mild-mannered. The wrong man for a war, Roddy had always maintained. Max was intelligent, educated and sensitive, and Roddy had seen him cry more than once. He was also one of the bravest men Roddy knew. But his was a bravery gained by confronting his fears and grabbing them by the throat, not the blind boldness of rushing a machine-gun emplacement without a second thought. That bordered more on foolishness in Roddy's book. Max was brave because he would never let his fears defeat him.

"Now I see it," Max said.

Butch stood as well, but became annoyed when he could not see the island.

"Sit down, shorty," Max growled. "I'm lookout for the next couple of hours."

"All heart, you are." Butch sat but remained staring forward, as if willing the island into view.

By now it was obvious that the tides, winds and fate were carrying them towards the land hidden below the horizon. The ceiling of clouds reflected dull green, giving them a tantalizing glimpse of what the island might contain. Hours passed. The sea lifted, tilted and dipped them closer. Ernie sat at the stern and said thanks to God. Hope had begun to bleed into their thoughts, reviving them, aggravating their hunger and thirst with possible assuagement on the island. Ernie prayed, and they all heard and wanted to believe him. Maybe God had been watching them, guiding them on their way with a wave of his hand, steering them towards the island, and salvation.

As darkness began to fall and the land slowly emerged out of the sea, Roddy felt an emptiness inside. It was as though he were looking at a nothing, a physical manifestation of the void in his beliefs. He tried to thank God, but found his thoughts as cold and as empty as the island before him appeared.

He looked around at his companions. None of them seemed inclined to paddle to reach land any quicker. It was as if they were all enjoying these final, brief moments cast aimlessly adrift.

The sounds from the island hurt their senses.

After five days at sea, with little more than the soporific waves and their own voices to listen to, the cacophony of the breaking waters was almost unbearable. Half a mile out from the island the sea smashed into a barely visible reef, turning white and violent. Their boat nudged its way through a toothless gap, as though guided in by a helping hand, and Ernie sat with his eyes closed and his mouth working, prayers tumbling forth like bodies from a sinking ship. Spray from the disturbed sea swept across the boat and soaked them. Roddy could not help opening his mouth and tasting the water; salt stung his dried and split lips, and the bitter tang of the sea drained once more into his throat.

"Thank God," Norris said, and Ernie agreed.

"Can't wait to meet the native women," Butch called dryly.

"Thought you had a missus at home," Max said.

"At home, yes." Butch nodded, and Roddy could not help but laugh at his semi-serious expression. His laughter was short-lived. It was not the place for it, and they all felt that; silence reigned once more. Merriment did not sit right with the roar of the surf behind them.

When the boat nudged onto the beach, Roddy felt a sick lurch in his guts. Everything was suddenly real, solid; and he noticed the pattern of grain in the wood of the boat for the first time. He saw how some of the oar mountings had begun to rust and dribble a red stain onto the timber. He could feel the tightness of his shoes, the abrasiveness of their insides as though they were already full of sand. He was even aware of his own body, in more detail than at any time during the past five days. His bruised left elbow, where he had struck it jumping from the burning and sinking ship. The splinters in his hands and forearms, from his struggle to turn the capsized lifeboat upright. His memories held weight, too. He thought of Joan, his girlfriend back home, and realized that she had barely entered his mind since the sinking. Now, with the possibility of survival clear again, images of Joan were flashing back. Her willing smile, bottle-green eyes, generous nature. A hard, bitter kiss on the day he had left her to go to war. For a while he had thought that she was blaming him, but he knew now that her anger was directed elsewhere, at an unfairness impossible to personify. Her bitterness had stayed with him, transferred in the kiss.

The island was reminding him of who he was.

Butch climbed from the boat and fell drunkenly to his knees on the wet sand. Max followed, then Norris, who staggered further along the beach. He was staring beneath the palm trees skirting the sands.

"Come on," Roddy said to Ernie. The officer remained at the

stern of the boat, unresponsive, rocking with the gentle movements of the lagoon. "Ernie!"

Ernie's eyes blinked to life. Moisture replaced their dark sheen. "God brought us here," he said, but it sounded more like a challenge than a statement.

"Yes, sir, He did," Roddy said, though he doubted any truth in his words. He would like to think it was the case, but his faith said no. His faith, drummed into him by his parents and peers, hanging in a void in his heart where truth ached to penetrate. "God brought us here."

"But why?" Ernie stood and walked unsteadily along the boat, pausing at the grounded bow. He looked down at the sand, staring at the smudged footprints of the others already on the beach. Then he glanced back at Roddy, and his voice was distorted. "Why?"

"Why what?" Roddy asked, but the officer was climbing from the boat, stepping gingerly as if afraid that he would sink at any moment.

Roddy followed. He felt a moment of disorientation, so used was he to the constant movement of the boat. His stomach lurched as it tried to maintain the motion, then settled again. The sand was warm, even through his shoes.

Norris had wandered along the beach, the others waited in the shadow of palm trees. Leaves hung from the high branches, pointing down at the men like the wings of great sleeping bats.

Roddy fell to his knees with the others, wondering why he did not feel at all liberated. "At least it seems pretty verdant," he said. "Where there are palms, there's water, and birds, and animals. Fruit too. Food and water. Safety."

Butch frowned. He was staring out to sea, apparently coveting the terrible five days just gone by. His face was bleeding again but he seemed not to notice. Flies began to buzz him, thinking him already dead.

"Butch?" Roddy said. He did not like seeing the little man so quiet. It was unnatural, disconcerting in the extreme. "Butch? What say we go and find the native women?"

"Doubt there are any," Butch said. His gaze never faltered; he wanted to avoid looking back at the island for as long as possible. "This place feels dead."

Roddy shivered, aggravating his sunburn. It was a strange statement, especially from Butch, but it seemed so right. Roddy tried to shake the words but they were spoken now, and they held power. "Max?" he said, searching for something. Comfort, perhaps.

Max looked at him long and hard. Roddy had known him for a long time and he had never seen a look like this. He knew that Max was vaguely superstitious, but he had never actually seen him afraid of something he could not see. Max's superstition was like the trace of his own religion, in that it was inbred rather than self-propagated, handed down through generations instead of defined and created through personal experience. Even though Max was a thinker, some things were planted too deep to think around.

"We make our own Hell," Max said.

"What the fuck is that supposed to mean?" Butch exploded, digging his hands into the sand.

Max shrugged. "It just seemed to sound right. This place feels all wrong. We'll have to be careful."

"How can a place be wrong?" Roddy asked. Max was frightening him, badly.

"It's God's place," Butch said, imploring Ernie to back him up. "Isn't it, sir? God's own place, and He's saved us from dying on the sea." His hands had closed tight, and sand flowed between his fingers like sacrificial blood.

"I'm sure God doesn't know a thing about this place," Ernie said. He turned and looked past the palm trees, to the rich wall of foliage hiding any view further inland.

"Bollocks!" Roddy said. Hiding his fear. Becoming angry so that he could not dwell on what he was really feeling, the jaws of doubt even now gnawing at his bones. "Crap. Get your act together, you lot. We've got to find water, food and shelter. Norris!" He stood and called along the beach to where the cook was rooting around by a fallen tree.

"There's something blowing bubbles in the sand," Norris shouted back.

"Come here, we've got to start getting ourselves together," Roddy said, but then he felt his knees beginning to betray him, and he fell onto his rump in the sand. He slumped slowly onto his back, a hand catching his head and easing it down. Nausea overtook him, then a swimming fatigue that worked to swallow him whole. As his eyelids took on a terrible weight he tried to see the first stars, dreading that he would not recognize any of the constellations. But the palm trees hid them from view, and darkness blanked his mind.

He was not really unconscious. Everything moved away for a while; noises coming from an echoing distance, sensations of heat and pain niggling like bad memories. Voices mumbled dimly, words unknown. He felt the cool kiss of water on his lips, sudden and sweet, and he opened his mouth and glugged greedily.

"Steady," Max said. "Not too much." He was kneeling above him, twisting his shirt so that drops fell into Roddy's mouth.

"Fresh?" Roddy asked.

Max nodded. "There's a stream further along the beach." His face was grim and he said no more, but Roddy felt too tired to pursue it.

The five of them sat where they had landed for an hour, taking turns to walk to the stream and soak their shirts in fresh water. Max had made a half-hearted search for a smashed coconut to use as a cup, but found none. There was little talk, but their attitude spoke volumes. Ernie had stopped praying.

When Roddy's turn came to fetch the water he relished the time alone. He realized that he had experienced no privacy for five whole days, even performing his toilet in front of the other men. The sea roared at the reef to his left, the silent shadowy island was a massive weight to his right, threatening at any moment to bear down and crush him into the sand. He tried not to look into the jungle, averting his gaze from darkness as he had as a child, struggling to convince himself that what he could not see would not exist. Even the silence seemed wrong. Where were the animals? Away from the attention of his fellow survivors, the feeling of being watched was almost overwhelming.

When he reached the stream he eased himself to his knees and leant over the running waters. In the vague light of the clear night sky, he was a shadow. The water spilled and splashed past rocks holding out against time.

The banks were scattered with things carried down from further inland, and he tried to see what they were in the moonlight. A huge feather, tattered by whatever had torn it from its owner. A dead thing with many legs, as big as his hand and hairier. Something long and slinky, with oily scales glimmering in the silvery light and a pasty smudge where a chunk had been taken from the body.

All bad things, Roddy thought. All dead. But was dead necessarily bad?

He soaked the shirts, stood and made his way back to his companions. They were silent, as before, but there was a tension between them which was almost visible. If he could see it, Roddy thought, it would be black and dead as the things in the stream. He wondered whether his brief absence had allowed him to register it more certainly, like leaving a room and then noticing its smell upon reentering.

"At least there are animals," he said. "Something we can eat." Nobody answered. Max looked at him, but in the dark Roddy could not read his expression. He was glad.

They each took another drink, but the water tasted different now. Roddy thought of the dead things as he drank and it was all he could do to keep it down. It no longer smelt fresh, but rancid. It soothed his dried throat, however, and for tonight at least he did not care what harm it may do him.

They agreed to spend the night on the beach. They all lay out in the open, in case something fell on them from the palm trees. Their breathing slowed and deepened until a sudden grinding, rasping sound jerked them all from the verge of sleep.

"What the hell?" Butch called.

"His demons are come!" Ernie yelled.

"All mutations," Max said.

Roddy sat up and saw their lifeboat being sucked back out to sea. Whatever minimal currents there were had now turned, and the boat was drifting further and further away from the beach. In the moonlight, it was a nonchalant sea monster.

Shorn of their dreams, the men sat silently and watched.

"We could swim out and get it," Norris suggested. "It's our only hope."

"Go on then," said Butch. "Just tell us how to cook what's left of you when you wash up on the beach."

"Could be anything in there," Max said. "Sharks. Jellyfish. Octopus."

"Creating your own hell?" Roddy asked, but regretted it at once. He was scaring himself as much as the others. Max stared at him darkly, as if trying to share a secret or steal one back.

So they all sat and watched the boat bob closer to one of the gaps in the reef. Roddy felt helpless and exposed. He recalled a time in his childhood when his mother had seen him away on a bus for a school trip. He had not wanted to go on his own, he so wanted her to come, but control was snatched from him totally the instant he boarded the bus. His mother waved and he wanted to wave back, but his arm seemed not to work. He could only cry as the bus pulled off, taking him further away from comfort and safety, hauling him towards whatever imagined doom those in charge deemed suitable for him. He had sensed the vicarious running of his life even then — his mother, the teachers, the bus driver with his mass of hair yellowed by cigarettes — and he had felt it again throughout his time in the navy. Sent here, ordered there, guided not by the hand of fate, but by the sadistic whims of war.

Never had the feeling of impotency been so strong as when he watched their boat drift away.

He felt an incredible emptiness inside as the boat was dashed to shadowy shards on the reef. Their last tenuous link with the outside world had been broken. Or cut.

There was nothing they could do. The darkness seemed to inhibit conversation, so they soon slept again. As he finally drifted off, Roddy realized that he had not slept properly for over five days. The haunted silence of the island gave them the sensory peace they needed to sleep, if not rest.

Crazy ideas juggled around in the nether regions of sleep. Like maybe the island wanted them gone for a while, so that it could do whatever it had to do. All mutations, Max had muttered. Even mutants had need of food.

Sleep was wet and waterlogged with dreams. Twisted images of violent waters corrupted with oil and refuse and blood, grumbling torpedoes slamming in to finish the job, limbs floating past fins, cries drowned out half-called, hope sinking away beneath them, pulling them down, sucking them into the dark. Roddy thrashed in the sand, working it into skin split by five days of sun, choking on it as he dreamt of teeth shattered by the pressures of deep water.

A voice came from the void, clear and high above the tormented sounds of hot metal warping and snapping. Its words were hidden but its meaning clear, the panic evident in its troubled tone. Thoughts, ideas and sentences flowed together into a collage of desperation. God was mentioned, prayed for and then discarded, with an outpouring of tears greater than the troubled world should ever allow.

Roddy surfaced from sleep like a submarine heading for the light. He saw a twitching shape along the beach. Ernie, jerking in his sleep as jumbled catechisms fell from his mouth to be muffled forever in the ageless sand. Pleas to God and denials of Him in the same sentence. Faith in salvation and a piteous, hopeless resignation. It was horrible to hear because there was no sense, and Roddy thought he should go and wake Ernie, drag him from whatever depths of nightmare he had sunken to.

But he was afraid. Scared that once he reached him, Ernie would already be awake.

There were other noises around them in the dark, a background mumble and chitter from the island that had not been there when they first arrived. Secret things were happening. The whole place had been waiting for them to sleep before coming back to life.

Roddy glanced towards the jungle and saw a shape under the trees, a shadow within deeper shadows. It was a woman, naked and flayed by disease, and she was holding out her hands, her mouth open in a silent scream. Joan, he thought, but it was not her. The tortured woman wanted to tell them something, but she could make no sound. As the palm fronds moved in the sea breeze so her arms wavered, drifting in time to the shadows. Her jaw worked in synchronicity with the sea, and sighing waves mimicked the voice she could not utter.

Then a cloud covered the moon and the image vanished into leaves and shadow.

Ernie muttered on. The sea stroked the land. More clouds passed overhead and clotted the moonlight, and as total darkness fell Roddy closed his eyes to hide from it all.

"Get away! Get it away! Oh God, help him!"

"Kick it! Use a rock or something, kill it!"

Roddy was woken from monotone dreams to a bloody red nightmare. Max and Butch were standing next to him, looking along the beach, stepping back and forth and shouting. He leapt to his feet and cringed as his wounds and burns reminded him of their existence.

Then all pain went. Feeling fled, replaced by a numbness of mind rather than body.

Ernie was lying in wet sand, but it was not wet from the sea. It was dark and cloggy, lumpy and glistening. A layer of flies flickered across its surface like a black sheet caught in a breeze; lifting, landing, lifting again. Ernie twitched redly in the morning sun. Something was eating him.

"Uh!" Roddy could not talk. He could hardly move, and he stood there as his legs cramped beneath him, oblivious to the pain, hardly conscious of his spasming muscles.

The thing was huge and grey, its head darting in to snap delicate mouthfuls of flesh from Ernie's throat and face. Its body was almost as long as Ernie, where he lay in a smear of his own blood. It glanced at them as it did so, expressing no fear or trepidation. Its eyes were lifeless black pearls in the thick probe of its head. It wore a shell, scraped and scarred, patterned with smears of its breakfast's blood. The beach stank of aged dead things.

A series of thumps came from behind. Roddy spun around in terror. Norris dashed past him with a length of wood held high, rusted iron fitting still visible on one edge. He hit the creature and fell back as the vibration jarred his arms.

"Come on!" Max shouted, running forward to help. He grabbed the length of splintered wood from the stunned Norris and smashed it down on the shell, careful not to strike the giant tortoise's head in case he drove it deeper into Ernie's face. It had no apparent effect. He turned the board over so that the iron fitting faced down, and brought it arcing over his head once more. It left a bright splash of scarred shell, urging Max into greater effort.

Butch had found a rounded stone the size of his hand and he threw it at the tortoise, retrieved it when it rebounded, threw it again.

The tortoise snapped another mouthful of raw flesh from Ernie's face. Roddy thought it might have been his nose.

He looked around for something to use as a weapon, but could see nothing. His heart was thumping in his chest, his tongue sandy and swollen and raw. He needed a piss.

Ernie was dead.

He stumbled next to Max and kicked sand at the creature's head, spraying it across Ernie's open face in the process.

"Careful!" Norris shouted at him.

Roddy almost laughed. "He's dead," he said, still kicking, dodging away when Max brought the board down on the shell once more. The wood splintered and cracked, the heavy end dropping next to the tortoise's front legs.

The thing turned and left. They were all surprised at its speed as it hauled its weight up the beach and disappeared into the foliage beneath the trees.

"Bastard!" Butch shouted after it. Roddy had an unsettling feeling that it had left because it was full, not as a result of their ineffective attack. The way it had looked at them, as though they were little more than the trees it rubbed against as it retreated back inland, turned Roddy cold.

"Oh Jesus, where the hell have we ended up?" Butch gasped, stumbling backwards until he tripped over his own feet and fell onto his back. Humor was his defence mechanism, but sometimes even that could not work. Sometimes, things were beyond a joke. Butch's hands were bleeding.

"Big tortoise," Norris remarked. "Make a hell of an ashtray."

"Shut up," Butch said, "just shut up, you bloody jinx. It's your fault we're here anyway, if you hadn't — "

"What?" Norris demanded.

Butch did not reply. He turned and stared out to sea, shaking, his grubby shirt pasted to his body with sweat. He licked blood from his hands and spat it at the sand. The movement was animal, Roddy thought.

"Take a look," Max said, nodding at Ernie's ruined body.

Roddy shook his head, started to walk away. He had seen enough. He was not yet twenty-five, and he had seen a thousand dead men. Max grabbed his arm, and Roddy wondered once again what he had meant last night, what were all mutations.

"Roddy, take a look," Max said again. His bald head was blistered and crazed from the sun. His confidence was still there in his voice, camouflaged beneath dull shock.

Ernie was a mess. Where his blood had not been disturbed, it still speckled the sand with spray patterns. He tried to avoid looking at the face because there was little left to see. He noticed a pulped book lying at the dead man's side, and wondered how the hell Ernie had kept his Bible through everything that had happened.

He saw the officer's left hand. Wounded and cut, the blood already dried and caked into a black mess. He looked at the right hand, bent and lifted the cool arm, just to make sure that what he was seeing was not imagination.

"Cut his wrists," Roddy said.

"What?" Norris asked. Butch looked up.

Max turned and walked a few steps before sitting down, facing away.

"He slit his wrists," Roddy said. "In the night. Must have done it awhile ago; the blood's already clotted." He spotted something glinting on the blood-soaked sand by Ernie's hip. He knew how useful a knife would be, but he could not bring himself to pick it up.

"God-fearing fool decides to off himself instead of facing up to what God had given him," Norris muttered. "We could live here for years, and he tops himself as soon as we're out of the sea."

"I heard him, I think," Roddy continued, trying to ignore Norris's dismissive tone of voice. "I woke up in the night. Half woke, anyway. He was mumbling, moaning. It wasn't very nice."

"What was he saying?" Butch asked. He was staring wide-eyed at the corpse now, as if he could accept death dished out by a victim's own hand above that caused by something unknown. In a way, Roddy admitted to himself, it wasn't so bad. It displayed a weakness in Ernie, not a strength in this unknown place.

"I didn't listen for long. I can't remember. I was tired. I was dreaming. I went back to sleep." Did I? Roddy thought quickly. Straight back to sleep? He glanced at where he had seen the shape beneath the trees, but there was nothing there.

Nobody said anything. Even Norris turned away and walked off towards the stream.

Roddy sat next to Max where he was making vague shapes in the sand.

"I think we should go inland," Max said sullenly. "See if there's any sign of life here. Any inhabitants."

"I don't think there will be," Roddy said, and Max did not argue. They both knew what he meant. This was the most inhuman place either of them had ever seen.

"Still, I think we should move. Don't you? Don't you think we should move?"

Roddy nodded. "We've no supplies, no cover, no weapons. No radio. No hope, unless we find something we can use."

"Weapons against what? Use for what?" Max looked up at him, and Roddy felt his heart sink. He'd always regarded Max as educated, wise in the ways of the world, if not academically. Now he just looked confused and lost. And maybe scared.

But Roddy did not want to see that, so he turned away and blanked it from his mind.

"What did you mean about mutations?"

"Sorry?"

"Yesterday, just before the boat went. You said 'all mutations,' or words to that effect."

Max shrugged, then smiled. The expression was so unexpected that Roddy found himself smiling along with him, though he didn't know why. "It's a thing Darwin said. When we landed here it reminded me of what the Galapagos are supposed to be like."

"Isolated," Roddy said.

Max nodded. "When he and his colleague came up with the theory of evolution, they said it all depended on variation in a species, caused by mutation. So, by definition, we're all descended from mutants. And the stronger ones among us...."

"All mutations," Roddy finished. Max nodded and Roddy shook his head. "Max, you have a way of losing me and scaring me at the same time."

Max shrugged. "It's not relevant. Just the idle ways my mind chooses to occupy itself, I suppose. My warped sense of the interesting." He stood. "Maybe we should bury Ernie. Before this place eats him."

The four of them buried Ernie on the beach, his bible on his chest. Max pocketed the knife after wiping it in the sand. Butch was silent and intense, trying to catch their eyes to take comfort in contact, but hardly succeeding. Norris was quiet and distant. Max and Roddy worked side by side, and Roddy took immense comfort in the smells and sounds around him. Human smells, human sounds.

By the time they had finished the sun was rising, hauling up the temperature. After they drank from the stream, trying their best to ignore the dead things washed up on its banks, Max suggested they go inland. Butch agreed willingly, and Norris said that it was as good an idea as any.

It was strange leaving the beach. Just under the trees there was a line of rotting seaweed stretching along the sands, drawn there by the last storm. It marked the demarcation line between sea and land, a barrier between two utterly different worlds. Roddy did not want to cross it. He looked around at his bedraggled, hungry companions, and saw that the feeling was mutual.

"What's wrong?" he said, but with awkward questions came hard answers.

"You tell me," Max replied.

Nothing more was said. Each buried in his own thoughts, the four men moved away from the beach and into the island.

2. INTO THE TREES

Roddy had expected a long, harrowing journey through dense jungle. Snakes dipping down from trees to kiss his shoulders. Spiders in his hair.

They were all equally surprised when, within five minutes, they emerged from the cover of trees onto a wide, undulating plain. The four men paused to rest and take in the view, their bodies weaker from their ordeal than they had at first thought. Hearts thumped, blood pumped through muscles jaded by five days of inactivity, hunger and thirst. The sun continued its attack, relentless and indifferent. Burnt skin peeled and revealed raw pinkness below to the heartless rays.

Roddy knelt on the ground and ran his hand through the rich grass. It looked almost like a meadow or hillside back home in Wales, but there were no daisies here, no dandelions. The grass felt sharper than it should, angry to the touch. It bent stiffly and sprang back with a rustle, shaking itself at his audacity.

"Anyone for cricket?" Butch asked, but he received no reply, not even a rebuke. Instead, they walked out into the grassland.

Ernie was dead. So were the rest of their crew, but Ernie had been a survivor. He had been one of them, if only for five days. That length of time had set them apart from the rest of the ship's compliment, and losing Ernie was like losing the ship all over again. Their hopes, however vague and troubled they were, seemed to have sunk with him. The men were silent. They walked immersed in their own worlds. Ernie was with all of them, in all their thoughts; either lifelike and spouting prayers, or dead and bleeding into the sand.

For Roddy, Ernie was still the gibbering shadow in the night, talking himself into a hopeless death while a shape moved under the trees, trying to shout out and encourage him. Or perhaps to tell them something through the silent dark.

Roddy had not mentioned his hallucination. He put it down to hunger, but subconsciously there was something else there. Something with a pleading mouth and flayed, torn skin.

None of them had been able to say a prayer over Ernie's grave. Roddy hated that. He felt as if they had let Ernie and themselves down. God must not be too happy with them today.

Four sets of feet whispered through the grass, kicking up angry puffs of insects. From the position of the sun Roddy could tell that they were moving north, towards the highest point they could see from here. He reckoned the mountain — hill, really — to be a thousand feet high, its gentle lower slopes wooded, the higher parts splashed with clumps of color like an artist's well-used palette. It was smooth-topped, well worn by time, speckled with outcroppings of a dark, sharp rock. It dominated their view in one direction, hiding whatever lay beyond. In the other direction, west and southwest, the grassland drifted away towards a hilly, heavily wooded area. Steam rose from this jungle, drifting straight up into the air until it was caught by an invisible breeze and condensed into wispy clouds. A few birds swung to and fro high above the island, rarely flapping their wings. They circled higher, swooped down, circled again. Roddy felt observed.

"This is a horrible place," Norris mumbled.

"Why so?" asked Max. His voice was a drone. It sounded as though he needed to hear other voices, without caring what they said. Even if it was Norris doing the talking.

"Don't know," Norris shrugged, apparently disappointing him. They walked in silence for a while, then Norris spoke out once more. "Just feels horrible. Like a hillside before rain. Loaded."

"Loaded with your bad luck," Butch muttered, but for once Norris did not retort.

"Where are we going?" Roddy asked. He looked back the way they had come and saw a series of wavy lines marking their progress. It could have been scattered dew, but the grass was dry.

"What, you want a plan?" Butch said, almost smiling.

"To the top of the hill," Norris said, nodding north. "If it's a small island we'll see all of it from up there. If we're lucky enough to have landed somewhere more substantial — "

"What, like the moon?" Butch quipped.

" — then we'll be able to see where to head for," Norris finished. He ignored Butch, much as an adult disregards a permanently annoying child. Maybe that was why Norris was not really liked. He had no humor.

"Let's stop and rest," Max said. "Have a think about it." They sat in the grass, only fifteen minutes after setting out from the beach. Norris remained slightly apart. Butch picked a blade and slipped it into his mouth, but spat it out with a disgusted grimace.

"I'm so hungry," Max said, verbalizing all their thoughts.

Roddy closed his eyes and leant back, supporting himself on outstretched arms. He was aching all over. His flesh felt weak and weighed down by hunger. "We must eat, Max," he said. "Let's leave finding out where we are for later. For now, we've got to eat. And drink."

"Wonder where that tortoise went," Butch said. All four men quickly stood.

They headed across the meadow to where they thought the stream would be, hiding itself beneath the lush covering of trees it had encouraged. Where there was water there would be food, fruits and berries at the very least.

Roddy felt the silence turn from intimidating to threatening, as though they had passed an invisible boundary. He thought of what Norris had said, the calm before the storm, and looked up into the sky. But the unfaltering blue depressed him, holding no promise of shade from the sun or fresh water to catch in their cupped hands. The thought of the stream made him go weak, because he had seen the dead things in it. And he had drunk the water.

If the island would kill its own, then what of the invaders?

The thought came from nowhere, but it chipped away at his mind as they walked towards the trees. Ernie was already dead, victim of his own knife. But even that was simplification; the blade had not killed him, it had merely been a tool. Something deeper and darker had been Ernie's undoing. He had been a fair and reasonable officer, but the minute he set foot on the island he had changed. Praising God to high Heaven, but still missing Him, still sensing His absence. Mumbling prayers in the night as if they would bring him closer to God. Or bring God back to him.

God is everywhere, Roddy's parents had impressed upon him. He had believed them because they were his parents, he always did as he was told, and he knew that his elders were wiser than mere children. As he passed through his teens he took on board his own views, and the duty-bound faith he had been given as a child had slowly dwindled, leaving a black hole in his heart where belief should sit. God had, effectively, vanished.

Roddy was often terrified of what He would think if He really did exist. God is everywhere, his parents had said.

Not for Ernie. Not last night. Last night God had not been here, and Ernie had been abandoned. He was no longer on God's Earth, and Roddy could only hope that he had found his Heaven. Or maybe he was nothing more than a mutilated corpse rotting in the sand.

As the grasses gave way to bushes and trees, and the sound of running water drew them on, the men perked up. Butch came out with a shallow quip; Max snorted; Norris remained mercifully silent. Roddy felt shadows close about him, but they did not bring the cool relief he had been craving. The sun no longer struck his cracked skin, but the heat was just as intense, and pain still bit in from all sides.

"More like a forest than a jungle," Max observed. He was right, though the trees were higher and more closely spaced than in forests back home, their roots visible as if trying to escape the soil. Silence pervaded the scene, a pregnant peace. All four men could feel eyes upon them, and they glanced up into the canopy of leaves and hanging vines every time one leaf whispered to another.

The forest floor was covered with a low, rich green crawling plant, its questing tendrils wrapped around trunks in an endless attempt to climb to the heights. Hints of movement caught Roddy's eye, but every time he turned to see what was causing it only stillness stared back. The light was good, even under the trees, but dormant night vision was teasing him.

"I can hear the stream," Butch said, head cocked. "This way. Christ, I'm thirsty enough to drink the Thames."

"Stupid enough, too," Norris muttered.

They headed towards the distant chatter of the stream. Roddy jumped as something tapped against his ankle. He cursed and staggered several steps to one side, until a tree stopped him.

"What?" Max asked.

Roddy shrugged. "Something in the undergrowth. Don't you see?"

"Probably — " Butch began. But he did not finish.

The ground around them burst apart. Shrill cries accompanied the movement as the low lying undergrowth parted and shuddered. Shapes scratched at their knees and thighs, then fell back to the ground, scurrying away under and across the foliage. None of the shapes were ever still enough to focus upon, so Roddy could only make out a disjointed montage of what they had startled into action. He saw curved blades catching the sun, domed heads jerking up and down as the creatures moved. Feathers floated in the eddying air. Red splotches marked the underside of beaks, like identical spots of wet blood.

He backed against the tree and tried to force himself up towards the branches, but then he shook his head and laughed to quell his racing heart. "Birds," he said. "Don't panic."

The others had reacted in their own instinctive ways. Max was kicking out left and right, Butch jumping up and down on the spot, Norris scrabbling around on his hand and knees, trying to regain his lost footing. As Roddy's words registered and the small, gawky birds jumped and fluttered away from the men, the panic eased.

"Scared the living shit out of me!" Butch shouted, laughing with nervousness and relief. Max closed his eyes and shook his head. He looked around, catching Roddy's eye and smirking. Norris stood and brushed at his filthy clothes. He stretched his neck in unconscious mimicry of the fleeing birds. He did not speak, and when he caught Roddy's eye he turned away in embarrassment. His knees and elbows were dirty and damp from his frantic squirming on the ground. His face was red from the same. Roddy almost felt sorry for him.

"At least we know we're not alone," Butch said, "though I didn't think much of yours, Max."

"Scared the hell out of me," Max said. He was rubbing beaded sweat from his head, flicking it at the ground. "I didn't realize I was so on edge."

Roddy thought he was lying. He thought Max was more than aware of the tension squeezing the four men. An anxiousness built up from outside, as well as within, and threatening to snap at any moment. Perhaps the birds startling them had been a good thing, a release valve for the growing pressures of their unforeseen situation.

"Never seen birds like that before," Butch said. "Like fat chickens."

"Quails," Max said. "At least, I think so. Flightless."

"Why the fuck be a bird and not be able to fly?" Butch asked. His fringe, greasy and lank, annoyed his eyes, so that he had to keep blinking. "Like a fish that can't swim." He glanced at Norris, obviously about to come out with some cutting witticism.

Max barged in before Butch could get himself into trouble. "No need to fly, because there are no predators here."

Butch frowned, causing his eyes more aggravation. "That tortoise was a shit of a predator, if you ask me. It was eating Ernie."

"A scavenger," Max explained. He slapped his neck to dislodge a tickling fly, forgetting his sunburn. "Bollocks!"

Flightless birds, Roddy thought. Mutations. The fittest surviving, a mutation in their species eventually eschewing flight. It all added to the strangeness of the place. "More mutants." Max nodded at him.

"Dinner, all the same," Norris said. For a few brief seconds, the others had not been paying him any attention. Now they all turned to look, just in time to see him fall back to his hands and knees. He scrabbled in the shallow undergrowth, leaves and dirt spinning around him. For a moment Roddy thought he'd lost it, and a terribly bitter thought passed through his mind. He wondered whether the others would have any qualms about leaving a madman behind, if it came to that. He hated the thought, despised himself for thinking it, but an idea could not be un-made.

Then Norris stood again, cursing some more, and kicked out at a fleeing bird. Luck, or fate, or something more sinister intervened. Norris's boot connected squarely with the creature's rear end and launched it on its maiden flight. Straight into a tree.

They all heard the subtle sigh of tiny bones breaking.

"Yeah!" Norris shouted. "Got you! Yeah!" He raised bloody fists above his head.

But the creature was not quite dead. It squirmed at the base of the tree, fluttering useless wings in an attempt to reverse millennia of evolution and regain its flight, lift off and take itself away from its inevitable end. Nature held its secret tightly to its chest, however, and Norris's heavy boot finished the bird's struggles. Roddy was sure he saw a hint of something dark in Norris's eyes as he ground his foot down.

"I'm not eating that," Butch said. "Roddy said it's a mutant.

Could catch anything."

Max opened his mouth to explain, but thought better of it. Instead he headed off between the trees, aiming for the sound of running water. In the distance, calls and rustles marked the route of the fleeing birds. They had still not stopped, as though pursued by something inescapable.

"I mean it," Butch said.

Norris did not know what to do. Roddy stepped past him, frowning, looking down at the dead thing spilling its insides onto the damp forest floor.

"Roddy?" Norris said, and it was the first time Roddy had ever heard the man use his first name. It sounded bitter coming from the cook's mouth.

They left the bird. Norris stepped away hesitantly, perhaps waiting for the others to turn around and change their minds. But Roddy eventually heard footsteps following them, and the dead bird remained where it had fallen.

Bleeding. Steaming. Taking to the air at last.

Roddy caught up with Max and matched his pace. Butch and Norris followed on, muttering profanities at each other.

"More mutants," Roddy said. They walked in silence for a few moments, but Roddy could not bite his tongue. "What's wrong, Max? What's bugging you, mate? I hate seeing you like this."

Max did not answer for so long that Roddy thought he hadn't heard. He was about to cover the tracks of his last statement with something banal, but then Max turned to him, and his eyes were dark, and even the sun glinting through the trees did not imbue them with any real hope.

"The whole world's populated with mutants," he said. "That's the real philosophy behind Darwin. Everyone is different, so simultaneous faith is a foolishness. Ernie was a fool, but he was a real believer, and he had devout faith. And he loved his faith, and it all came to nothing for him. It fooled him in the end. Drove him to do what he did."

"He was a fool because he believed so much in God?"

"No," Max said. "No. He was a fool because he let his belief rule him. His faith stagnated, didn't allow for progress, something new. It's an arrogance, I suppose, but this place has nothing in common with what he believed in. When we came here, he thought he'd been abandoned. So he used his knife on himself, and gave in without a fight." He rubbed his neck, wincing as the dead skin flaked and opened up bleeding wounds. "That's what's wrong. If faith can't save you, what can?"

"I have faith," Roddy said, but Max looked at him, and Roddy felt foolish.

"Faith in what?"

Roddy did not answer. His words echoed back at him, like the best lies always do. They walked together in silence and Roddy realized that, even after all this time, there was something he still had no inkling of. "You've been a sailor all your life," he said to Max. "You've been around. Shit, you're older than my uncle. What do you think? What's your faith?"

Max shook his head, but not in denial. He simply could not answer. It was as though the question of his own beliefs had never raised its head. Until here. Until now. A question with no answer, because a man like Max never revealed himself fully to anyone. He was as much a mystery as the complexities he mused upon. Wasted in war, Roddy had always thought. A man like Max should be creating, not destroying.

They came to a more overgrown portion of the forest. With moisture collecting and dripping from palms, and flashes of color hinting at the secret assignations of birds high in the trees, it looked more like a tropical jungle. They paused for a while, catching splashes of water on their tongues, listening to the steadily increasing murmur of life around them. Roddy tried to tell himself that it was because the sun was rising higher; the island was coming to life. But he could not help but identify a hidden amusement in the alien banter, a titter here, a low, throaty chuckle there. The animals, now that they had taken the opportunity to examine and test these newcomers, knew the limit of their threat and were laughing at it.

"This way?" Max suggested, pointing along a gentle dip in the land. Nobody had an opinion, so they headed in the direction he had indicated. The sound of the stream was becoming louder, so it seemed that they were moving in the right direction.

They had to pick their way through low thorn bushes, the thorns positively carnivorous in the subdued light. They looked around for something substantial to eat. There was nothing. The heat was wafting at them now, as if blown out from some invisible orifice in the island, seeking them through the trees. Their filthy clothes were soon pasted to their bodies, aggravating their already cracked and sore skin.

Each way they turned, they were presented with more difficult obstacles to overcome. They decided to climb the steep bank of the dip and encountered a slope of sharp, cruelly exposed stone.

It resembled slate but glittered with buried quartz, showing off the richness of nature on the island. Keen edges kissed lines of blood into unprotected skin.

Roddy was certain that they were the first people ever to land here. They must be. The place felt so untainted, so elemental, so pristine. If someone had been here before them, there would be signs of it in nature; but what existed here was a pureness of environment, with no sign of outside influence whatsoever. Roddy had always had a respectful fear of the sea, but that was different. Man's natural state was not floating in a metal coffin, putting himself at the mercy of the waters. Here, on the island, he felt even more out of place. These four puny survivors of a terrible war were succumbing to the dominant party.

What about the shape under the trees? he thought, but dismissed it immediately. Shadows. Just shadows. Anything else was simply too terrifying to consider.

They made it up the sharp bank and found themselves elevated, overlooking the stream where it gurgled merrily in a small canyon. The sides were steep, but not unclimbable, and it was only about twenty feet to the bottom.

As he watched Max beginning his descent, Roddy started shaking. Something squirmed in his stomach, scraping at his insides with claws so sharp that he wondered whether he'd swallowed something else along with the water from the jungle leaves. Every step they took, their route was becoming more difficult. Plants sprang out of nowhere, rocks sharpened themselves on their fear, trees melded trunks to form almost impenetrable barriers. Everything conspired to make their progress more hazardous.

Yet he felt guided, by an insistent and heavy hand.

He knelt down gently, head swimming, and then he knew that he had been brought here to die on this small cliff. He would fall and smash his skull on the rocks below, and while Max tried to scoop his brains back into his head Roddy would look up at the sky, and see a moon he did not recognize slowly appearing against the blue, a ghost emerging from the mist, mocking him as his world went dark.

"Roddy!" Max called. The others were already scrambling down the slope, and before his panic could take hold Roddy slipped and slid down to the gully floor. He did not fall, he did not die, but neither did he feel elated. He sensed the land laughing at him, amusing itself with the mild deceit it had planted in his mind. The stream was the sound of that laughter.

It was gently flowing, cool and fresh, and at its deepest it came up to their chests. It twisted and turned in its little valley, disappearing downstream around a rocky corner curtained by overhanging plants. The men stripped and bathed. There were no dead things here. Perhaps the remains on the beach had been drowned further downstream, to deter any visitors from venturing inland. But here, the air was clear of the taint of decomposition, and the sun still found its way through the leaves and branches to speckle their damaged skin.

The water was fresh. Butch tasted it, then gulped it down. Even Norris smiled and refrained from passing some derisory comment.

"Water, water, everywhere," Max said. Roddy smiled, because he knew what Max meant, and Norris grinned in confused acknowledgement of his eventual acceptance. They all drank and swam, and washed away dried blood and caked dirt.

When they had finished, they climbed from the gentle waters to lie out on the bank and let the sun dry them. Butch remained in the stream. He bobbed in the current, floating a few feet, standing, doing it again.

The surge came from nowhere. Without even a sigh to announce its appearance, as if air and water conspired to fool the men's senses. Butch turned and stared upstream at the rolling, tumbling, refuse-laden wave of water plowing towards him. It frothed, like a rabid sea monster angry at the irony of its affliction.

Roddy stood, absurdly conscious of his nakedness. He opened his mouth but nothing came out. He felt a draining flush of hopelessness, the same feeling he had experienced watching his ship split and sink. No hope, he had thought to himself then, no hope at all for anyone left inside.

Now he thought the same. Except he whispered it as well, like a prayer to the dying. "No hope."

Just before the water lifted Butch from the streambed, he glanced at Roddy, and suddenly his eyes were very calm, his expression one of equanimity rather than fear. It was a split second, the blink of an eye, because then the wave swallowed him in a flurry of limbs. His head broke surface several times, but he could only utter bubbles. The men watched helplessly as Butch was tumbled away from them, mixed in with the wood and weed and dead things also carried along by the surge.

Roddy started running along the bank. Stones snapped at his bare feet. Breath caught in his throat, possessed of sharp edges. But Butch was firmly in the water's grasp, and it held him close and low, attempting to drown him even before he struck the wall of the gully further downstream. Roddy tried to shout, but his voice was lost in the angry white-water roar. He sensed the others following him. Their company made it all seem more futile.

He could have made it, Roddy thought. He could have swum to shore. It was impossible, of course. But it seemed that for Butch, even the intention to survive had been absent.

In the waters, jumping from the foam, speckled red for brief instants, Roddy was sure he saw tiny snapping things. It may have been the boiling water itself, spinning Butch in its violent grasp. Or it could have been something in the water with Butch, but surviving there, belonging there, revelling in the violence.

Butch was swept under the overhanging trees and plants, just before the stream twisted out of sight. For the instant before he was pummelled into protruding rocks Roddy saw him, eyes closed, mouth wide open. His bruised face had been struck by something, and he was drowning in blood as well as water.

The wave struck the rocks, scouring its contents across the blackening surface, then surged away downstream. It left behind its load, floating in the suddenly calm waters: a tree branch, stripped of bark; a bird of paradise, bobbing like a drowned rainbow; and Butch, still spread on the rocks, his snapped left arm wedged into a crack and holding him there.

His head lolled. He looked like he was falling asleep, and at any moment Roddy expected him to look up and his bashful grin to appear. His head fell lower, however, until his chin rested on his chest. And then they could see the damage to the back of his head, and Roddy knew that he would never be smiling again.

They had to cross the stream to reach him. Roddy could not bring himself to enter the water, even though it was back to its normal self, as if the bore had never been. He wanted to mention the snapping things he had seen, but he felt foolish; there were no apparent bites on Butch's body, only cuts and scrapes. He watched nervously as Max and Norris waded across, arms held wide for balance.

Max paused in front of Butch, his attention focused on whatever was beyond the rocky outcrop around which the stream disappeared. He was still for a long time. Roddy was on the verge of splashing out to him, shaking him awake and shouting at him, when he turned.

"No sign of the wave downstream," Max said casually. He looked briefly back upstream, indicating to Roddy the wet, scoured banks where the freak surge had made its mark. Norris seemed not to hear, nor understand the implication. He was staring at

Butch, disgust stretching his face out of shape.

Roddy was glad he had not gone in. This was not a normal stream, not like the ones in the forests and valleys back home. It was a wrong stream, one which could conjure a wave from nowhere and then suck it back into itself, without having to spread it further along its length. It was flowing at its normal gentle rate once more, carrying away the detritus left behind. The colorful dead bird spun slowly as it headed for the beach.

Roddy thought the wave must be waiting somewhere. Tucked on the streambed, pressure building, ready to appear again when the time was right. Like now, while Max and Norris were trying to free Butch's trapped arm without touching the bone protruding through the skin.

But perhaps that would be too easy.

"Get him out," Roddy said, "get him out, now, get him out." He rocked from side to side, wincing at the pain from his gashed feet but enjoying the sensation at the same time. It told him he was still alive, his brain was connected. He looked down at his pathetic body. His ribs corrugated his skin and his feet bled onto the rocks. His blood was a black splash on the ground. It seeped between stones and was sucked in quickly, the land as desperate for sustenance as they were.

The two men eventually backed across the stream with Butch trailing between them. Norris seemed frantic to keep Butch's head up out of the water, as if a dead man could drown. They reached the bank and Roddy helped them haul the body out. They lay Butch down on the wet rocks. His head was leaking.

Roddy had seen worse sights than this when the ship sank, but now it was different. Just as Ernie's death had hit them badly, the sight of Butch lying cooling in this cruel place felt like a punch to the chest. He had been a survivor, one of only a few left from the ship's crew. He had been valuable. A *friend*.

"Just where the hell did that wave come from?" Norris asked. "What caused it? There aren't any clouds, no rain. The stream's back to its normal level. I didn't feel…." He prattled on, but Roddy soon cut out his voice. He was becoming aware of the expression on Max's face.

The big man looked defeated. His arms hung by his sides, shoulders slumped, water dripping from his ears and nose to splash into rosettes on the rocks around him. Pinkish sweat, colored with his own blood, dribbled down his forehead and around his ears. The burns and scabs on his head were open to the elements. His eyes were shaded from the sun. They looked dead.

"Max?" Roddy said, and Norris shut up. "Max."

Max turned and looked at them, and Roddy saw that some of the drops were tears. The big man was crying. They were silent, unforced, trickling salt-water into his wounds. "He was only a kid," Max said. "How old was he? How old was Butch?"

Roddy shrugged. "Nineteen?"

Max nodded. "Just a kid."

"Where did that wave come from?" Norris said again, now that the silence held their attention.

Max looked back down at Butch, shaking his head slowly, hands fisted. "Something very wrong," he said.

"The wave, though," Norris whined.

"Something very wrong with this place." Max turned and went back to where they had dumped their clothes. He hauled on his trousers and shirt, wincing as aches and pains lit up his body. He said no more.

Roddy remembered an occasion several years ago, when he had been more scared than at any time in his life. One of his friends had borrowed his father's motorbike and offered to take Roddy for a ride. Once committed, there was no backing out. At each jerky change of gear, Roddy was sure he was going to be flung off backwards, smashing his head like a coconut on the road. The bike tilted this way and that as his friend negotiated blind corners, hardly slowing down. He had the blind confidence of the young.

It was not the speed that terrified Roddy, or even the thought of being spilled onto the road. It was the lack of control. The fact that his life was, for those few minutes, totally in the hands of someone else. He'd felt like pissing himself when he'd considered that they were not even particularly close friends. What a way to die.

The fear he felt now was more intense, more all encompassing. It made his terror at the youthful lark pale into insignificance. Now, he feared not only for his body — a body already ravaged by war and hunger and thirst — but also his mind. He was being stalked through the dark avenues of his thoughts, and he had yet to see the pursuer. All the while, the island sat smugly around them. How could logic and self-awareness continue to exist untouched in such a place? A place that seemed happy to kill them, and determined to do so.

Not for the first time, Roddy wished that he had more faith in God. He had seen what belief had done to Ernie, but perhaps his faith had been too blind, too passive. It was ironic that a war which had seemed to bring many people closer to their faith, by forcing them into challenges of mind and spirit, had driven him further away. While people dying on beach-heads prayed to God, Roddy could not understand how God could do that to them in the first place. If He did exist then He was cruel indeed.

They buried Butch away from the stream, so that any future floods would not wash away the soil covering him and expose his body to the elements. None of the men spoke because they could all feel danger watching them, sitting up in the high branches or raising beady eyes from the stream. It watched them where they toiled, and laughed, and counted off another victory on skeletal fingers.

3. NAMING THE NAMELESS

They headed inland. None of them felt like walking, but they were even less inclined to stay near Butch's grave. The chuckling stream threatened to drive them mad.

They remained within the jungle. It seemed to stretch on forever, as if the grasslands had never existed, and the flora and fauna of the place began to reveal more of itself to them. Much of it was strange. Max seemed to find solace in trying to identify birds and plants, but his comfort was short lived. For every species he knew, there were a dozen he did not. A snake curled its way up a tree trunk, bright yellow, long and very thin. Max went to name it, but then several scrabbling legs came into view around the trunk, propelling the creature's rear end, and Max turned away. Roddy recalled the story of the Garden of Eden; how the snake had been cast to the ground, legless, to slither forever on its belly, eating dust. This creature did not belong to that family. This thing, in this place, did not subscribe to the ancient commandment.

They saw another snake, with gills flaring along its flanks and green slime decorating its scales. Max stared at it, frowning, trying to dredge an impossible name from his memory. Impossible, because the creature had no name. "Slime snake," Max said, and named it.

"You should name it after us, if you must," Norris commented.

"Who'll ever know?" The finality in Max's voice turned Roddy cold, but the big man would not be drawn. He was too keen to continue with what he called his naming of parts, as if the entire island were one massive machine and the slithering, flying and scampering things were the well-oiled components.

In a place where the trees thinned out, they saw several giant tortoises picking regally at low foliage. They skirted around the clearing, and Roddy checked the shells to see whether there was any recent damage. Norris was all for attacking the creatures, but to Roddy it seemed pointless, and Max said something which persuaded them that they were best left alone. "Why annoy them more?"

The reptiles raised lazy heads as the men passed, watching them with hooded black eyes. One of them may have had bits of Ernie still digesting in its gut, but to the men they all looked the same. Roddy mused that the same probably went both ways; the idea chilled him to the core, and he did not dwell upon it.

The more Roddy saw, the more he came to acknowledge the alienness of the island. Max's strange naming process only helped to exaggerate the feeling. And he also came to see how they had all taken so much for granted, and how their ignorant assumptions had led them into strangeness. They had been washed up on an unknown shore after five days at sea, putting the perceived peculiarity of the place down to the fact that they were somewhere none of them had ever been before. The sense of disquiet had been borne out by Ernie's sudden suicide. But even that had not alerted them as it should have.

Now, with Butch being snatched away so soon after Ernie's death, Roddy felt like he was waking up. Surfacing from a nightmare into something more disturbing.

They had all maintained a blind faith in the rightness of things, and now they had been led astray. Just as Ernie's faith had fooled him, so they were being deceived by their ignorance.

"Two-headed spider," Max called out, pointing up into a tree. Roddy gasped and stepped back when he saw the huge, hairy shape hanging there, as big as his head, legs jerking as whatever they grasped struggled its final death throes. There were indeed two fist-sized protuberances at its front end, though whether they were heads or other organs for more obscure purposes, Roddy could not decide.

"Lizard-bird," Max said.

"Greater-mandibled mantis."

"Three-ended worm."

"Tree sucker."

"Yellow bat."

His naming continued. The men took a chance with a bush of yellow berries, hunger overcoming a caution which Roddy was coming to consider more and more useless. To protect against the unknown, he thought, was impossible. They were at the island's mercy. And, in a way, this made him more relaxed. He had never before felt resigned to an unseeable fate, not even when the ship was going down; then, he knew he could swim. Here, he was slowly drowning in strangeness, and there was nothing he could do. He knew nothing.

Until he saw the woman. She was naked, her body seemingly tattooed with nightmares, muscles hanging in sepia bunches. She was standing beneath a tree to his left, waving imploringly at the three men. The sun came through the canopy and speckled her with yellow pustules.

"Black lizard," Max called. Norris was with him, further ahead.

The woman held out both hands, her mouth open but silent. Roddy could see that she was shouting. A shadow moved across her body and she seemed to change position. She did not move, but flowed, as she had the night before. She lived within the shadows, and their shifting dictated her own motion.

"Large-headed quail. Big bastard."

Roddy tried to shout. He opened his mouth, but in sympathy with the ghostly form beneath the trees he could say nothing. The woman began to shake her head, waving more frantically. Her body crumpled with helplessness as shadows shifted across the sunbeams breaking through the trees and blotted her from sight.

"Triple-horned toad."

Roddy could not move. He was sure the shadows had possessed teeth. They had been voracious.

He began to shake and the pressure of the island pressed in from all sides. The ground crushed against his feet, driving them upwards to meet his head where it was being forced down by the hot, damp air. Bushes seemed to march in from all around, the trees stepping close behind, closing in, threatening to crawl into him and make him a fleshy part of them. Rooting and rutting in a vegetative parody of rape.

He thought he cried out, but the only reply was Max naming, and Norris mumbling something unheard.

The world tipped up and Roddy was tumbling, striking his head and limbs, thorns penetrating skin as he fought with the ground. Sight left him, and sound, and then all his other senses fused into one all-encompassing awareness — that they were intruders, alien cells in a pure body, and that slowly, carefully, they were being hunted and expunged.

Then even thought fled, and blessed darkness took its place.

When he came to, the sun had moved across the sky. The ground was hot beneath him. Norris and Max were sitting back to back on a fallen tree, chewing on something, looking around between each mouthful like nervous birds.

Roddy lifted himself onto his elbows and tried to shake the remaining dizziness from his head. He felt weak and thirsty, and his stomach rumbled at the tang of freshly picked fruit.

"The sleeper awakes," Norris said, somewhat bitterly. Max turned and glanced at Roddy, then continued his observation of the jungle.

Roddy did not recognize his surroundings, but that meant nothing. It did not *appear* to be the place where he had collapsed, but viewed from a different perspective, after however long had passed, he could easily have been wrong. Off to his right may have been where he had watched the woman and the shadows. His skin weeped and smarted with a multitude of thorn pricks, and thorny plants sat smugly all around. Looking up between the treetops he could see darting shapes leaping from branch to branch, sometimes flapping colorful wings, occasionally reaching out with simian grips. Myriad bird calls played the jazz of nature.

He was more lost than he had ever been.

"Max?" he said, but it came out like a death rattle. He coughed, sat up fully and leant forward. The ground between his legs was crawling, shifting, fuzzing in and out of view. He shook his head again, then realized that he was sitting on an active ants' nest. He shrieked, stood uneasily and stumbled to the fallen tree.

Norris glanced nervously at him, then back at their surroundings. Max looked around casually, but Roddy could tell from the way he was sitting — hunched, tense, puffed up like a toad facing a snake — that he was concentrating fully on the jungle. Between the two sat a selection of fruits, of all colors imaginable and a few barely guessed at. Some were wounded and dripping, others whole and succulent.

"Are those safe?" he asked, then realized that he no longer cared.

"Not dead yet," Norris said, but Roddy was already crunching into what looked like a cross between and apple and a kiwi fruit. It tasted sour and bland, but the crunchy flesh felt good between his teeth. With each bite, his soft gums left a smear of blood on the open fruit.

"I feel dreadful," he mumbled.

"You've been out for two hours," Max said, not looking around. "You were feverish at first, then jerking and shouting. Couldn't wake you up. Couldn't tell what you were saying, either, but it sounded important. To you, anyway. Had to pull a load of thorns out of your face — those damn things work their way in like fishhooks. Then you calmed down, after about half an hour, and you've been quiet ever since." There was little emotion in his voice. Hardly any feeling. He sounded devoid of the old Max Roddy knew, his voice a fading echo of the big man.

"Two hours?" Roddy received no answer. The two men watched the trees, munching half-heartedly on insipid fruit. Roddy followed their gaze, saw only jungle, trees and more jungle. There was an occasional sign of movement as a creature, named or unnamed, skirted the three men. The steady jewel-drip of water from high in the trees made its eventual way to the ground. Nothing else. No moving shadows.

"There was something before I passed out," Roddy said, frowning, taking another bite of fruit. "Shadows, or something."

"What exactly?" Max asked suddenly. He turned, fixing Roddy with his stare. His voice was Max again, but Roddy suddenly preferred the monotone of moments before. He wondered what had happened while he was out.

"Well, a woman," Roddy said quietly.

Norris snorted. "Cabin fever." He laughed, but it was a bitter sound.

Max stared at him for so long that Roddy became uncomfortable. "What? Am I green? What?"

Max looked back into the jungle. Whatever he expected to see remained elusive; his shoulders slumped and he shook his head. "While you were out, Norris went to look for food. He was back within five minutes with that lot, but he thought he'd been followed."

"Stalked," Norris hissed. "I told you, I was stalked. Like a bird hunted by a fucking cat."

"Followed by what?" Roddy asked. His stomach throbbed, and he felt like puking. His balls tingled, and his chest had tightened to the point of hurting. He realized suddenly how human perception was sometimes so blinkered, so ruled by the present. Until now, they had not actually been threatened by anything dangerous. The island was crawling with weird life, but the only real way they had been interfered with was by the tortoise. And even that had been scavenging meat already dead. Now, if what Norris and Max were saying bore truth, there was something else with them. Following them.

"I don't know what," Norris said. "I didn't actually see it." He threw the remains of a piece of fruit at the ground.

There was silence. Max did not say anything. Roddy waited

for Norris to continue, but he was quiet.

"So?" Roddy said. "What? You heard something following you?"

"No, I didn't. I felt it. I sensed it. I didn't see or hear anything." Norris spoke with a hint of challenge in his voice, as though fully expecting Roddy to mock his claim. But Roddy only nodded, and Norris went back to scanning the jungle.

"Maybe it was your woman," Max said, but Norris snorted again. "We'll have to be careful."

The three men sat and ate, gaining sustenance and fluids from the fruit, not worrying about what it would do to their stomachs.

"How do you feel?" Max asked after a while, and Roddy nodded. He felt terrible, but he was conscious.

"Must be weak," he said. "From the sea. Maybe the berries were bad. Or the stream water." He felt terrible, true, but also rested. Grateful, in a way, that he had been removed from things, if only for a while.

Roddy watched the trees. He was not looking for the woman because he was certain he had never seen her. If he *had*, it was too awful to dwell upon. If he *had* seen her, she was walking dead.

There was movement everywhere, and soon he felt tired. "What are we really looking for?" he asked. "I mean… the whole place is alive. It's crawling."

"We'd better get a move on," Max said.

"Where to?" Norris stood and spilled fruit onto the ground, most of it merging instantly from sight as if camouflaged or consumed. "Just where are we going, anyway? We've hardly been here twelve hours, and there's only three of us left. It's hopeless. It's hopeless."

As Norris turned away to hide bitter tears, Roddy recalled his own reaction only hours before, when the surge of water had plucked Butch from the world. Hopeless, he had known, and he had not rushed to help. Perhaps if he had still held hope in his heart then, he would have been able to grab Butch, hold on, drag him from the water's grasp. With hope, he may not have had to die. But Roddy could also recall Butch's last glance, and wondered whether he would have welcomed rescue at all.

"Nothing's hopeless," he said, but the words hung light and inconsequential in the air. A shadow of birds fluttered across the sun.

"No," Max said, "Norris has a point. We're walking nowhere. In one place, we can make shelter and gather food. Moving, we're vulnerable. To exhaustion, or to whatever else may be around."

Shadows in the trees, Roddy thought. Stalking. Perhaps even guiding.

"I'd like to get out of this place first, though," Max continued, looking nervously at the permanent twilight beneath the green canopy.

"How about the mountain?" Roddy suggested. "It was our first aim, before we decided to come in here."

"Why *did* we decide to come in here?" Norris asked. Max did not answer, and Roddy felt afraid to, because he thought maybe they had been steered. Lured by the promise of water or food, but lured all the same. Guided by their own misguided hope, misled by the faith they had in providence. Lied to, eventually, by the belief they grew up with that, however strange something was, it was God's plan that it should be so.

"I suppose it's part way," Max said.

"Part way where?" Norris was shaking his head, denying the fact that they had control. Or maybe he was dizzy, thought Roddy. Queasy from the fruit. Had the woman in the shadows eaten of it, before her skin was flayed and her muscles clenched in a death-cramp? Or had he seen her because he had eaten the yellow berries?

"Well," Max said, rubbing sweat from his scalp, "from the mountain we can survey the land. Look for help and... well, keep a look out. And it's out of this place, and that's just where I want to be."

"Amen to that," Roddy said. He felt an odd twinge at his choice of words.

"Survival of the fittest," Max said, scooping up some fruit and shoving it into his pockets.

Norris grumbled, "I don't feel very fit."

"A walk will do you good then." Butch should be saying this, Roddy thought. He should be the one having a go at Norris. But Butch was dead.

"This way," Max pointed. Roddy trusted him. Norris merely followed on behind.

After an hour of walking up a slow incline the trees ended abruptly, and they faced up the gentle slope towards the top of the mountain. And on the slope, catching the high sun and reflecting nothing, like a hole in the world, sat the tomb.

Roddy was eighteen the first time he had seen Stonehenge. After the initial shock it had preyed on his mind, its sheer immensity belittling his own existence. He had never been able to come to terms with the time and effort spent on its construction. History sat huddled within and around the stone circle, and in a way it was truly timeless, an immortal artifact of mankind's short life. But it was also a folly, massive and utterly impressive, but a work of affected minds nonetheless.

His shock now was infinitely greater.

The three men stood speechless, looking up at the rock. It sprouted from the ground half a mile away, rising fifty feet into the sky. It was a featureless black obsidian, reflecting little, revealing no discernible surface irregularities. It appeared to be roughly circular in shape, rising to a blunt point. Around its girth grasses and a kind of curving, pleasingly aesthetic bramble formed a natural skirt, bed in dust and soil blown against its base by aeons of sea breezes. It was a marker of some kind, obviously, and the only thing the ancients usually found worthy of such a grandiose statement was the corpse of a king, or a sleeping god.

It was not the appearance of the monument that sent the men into a stunned, contemplative silence. It was impressive, but no more so than a warship cutting the sea with the sinking sun throwing it into bloody silhouette. The reaction came from the undeniable solidness of this thing, the suddenness of its existence before them. Realization that this place was or had been inhabited, by whatever strange people had built it, sent cracks of doubt through the fragmented image the men had built up in their own minds.

Roddy despised the island, and he hated this thing. He could see the beauty in it, the history and dedication contained within its strange geometry. But the idea of meeting the people who had carved or constructed it, the race who could exist here on the island in peace and apparent prosperity, filled him with a dread he had never thought possible. It made him feel sick.

"Oh my God," Norris gasped at last.

"I think not," Max said.

"It's huge," Roddy said. "Massive. I mean, how? It must weigh five hundred tons. It's huge. Massive." He was aware that he was repeating himself, but the words felt right. Huge. Massive.

After spending several minutes standing and staring, the men urged themselves onward. From the jungle behind them erupted a raucous explosion of bird calls, and as Roddy turned a cloud of gaily colored birds lifted and headed back towards the sea. He wondered whether something had startled them. He thought of the vision he had experienced before his collapse, the woman's shredded skin and bare muscles, the way she had motioned, the wide eyes and frustrated, silent scream.

He hoped they had left all that behind, rid themselves of worry by leaving the jungle. But he berated himself for entertaining such foolishness. The whole island lay beneath them, even though the jungle no longer surrounded them. They still breathed the air above the island, still saw fleeting glimpses of the place's fauna. Much remained hidden, Roddy knew, but whatever haunted them would surely drag itself out of the trees, like an echo of themselves.

It took them a few silent minutes to reach the rock. Max hurried on ahead. Norris walked at Roddy's side, glancing continuously over his shoulder.

"More unusual than it seems," Max said as they arrived. He leant against the stone, dwarfed by its size. His hand was flat and his fingers splayed across its smooth surface, and Roddy expected them to sink in at any moment, subsumed into the sick fleshy reality of whatever it was they were seeing. But nothing happened. Max ran his hand across the rock, palm pressed flat. "Much stranger." His skin made a soft whispering sound as it passed over the surface, audible above the background noise of the island. He took it away, blowing into his open palm and watching the subtle layer of dust cloud into the air.

"How so?" Norris asked. He approached the stone nervously.

Roddy stood back, unable to move nearer, experiencing a peculiarly linear vertigo as he looked up towards the top of the landmark. It felt like he and the stone were growing, expanding into the pointless surroundings, while everything else shrank back to reveal the skeleton of the world underneath. He expected at any time to strike his head on the ground, but his fall seemed to last forever.

"It's so smooth!" Norris gasped, drawing Roddy's attention back to eye level. "Like glass." He swept his hand across the surface, mimicking Max's earlier movements as he blew dust from his fingertips. "This dust is gritty. Sand. Finer, though."

"Most dust is human skin," Max said. Roddy wondered why the hell he chose to come out with his facts at the most inopportune of moments. Encouraged by Max's comment, he could not help but imagine the rock as a giant altar to some malign deity, sucking to itself the flayed skin of its victims. They petrified and disintegrated, sticking to their god, merging into one, clothing it with themselves in eternal, unavoidable worship.

"Yeah, thanks Max," Norris said. Roddy and Max glanced at

each other, eyebrows raised, at the cook's use of the familiar. "That's just the sort of useless fucking comment we fucking need right now. Butch would have come up with something like that, if he hadn't drowned himself."

"What do you mean, drowned himself?" Roddy shouted angrily. His voice sounded muted here, as if tempered or swallowed by the huge rock.

Norris did not respond. He kept his hands spread on the rock, leaning there, eventually resting his forehead between them. "Come on. You saw his face."

"Ernie killed himself," Roddy said, "Butch was killed. A world of difference, let me tell you. There's no way — "

"Sorry, sorry, sorry," Norris sighed. He sounded muffled.

"Sorry I said anything," Max said. "Can't help saying what I think."

"The sort of junk that flows into your head, you should just shut up all the time," Norris said. "Just leave us to it. Just let us get on with things." He stared back down the hill at the jungle, an expectant look in his eyes.

The three men fell silent, each for different reasons, each mulling over their own confused thoughts.

Roddy approached the rock but could not touch it. It seemed distasteful, like a huge living thing, standing there inviting and expecting their attentions. Max walked around its girth, taking a minute to describe a full circuit. Then he did it again, left hand in constant contact with the rock, left foot kicking at the plants growing around its base. Once or twice before he passed out of sight he paused, knelt closer to the ground to examine something in detail. Roddy was curious, but too on edge to ask him what he was looking at. In many ways, he didn't want to know. To some extent, for the first time ever, he agreed with Norris. Max just had the habit of saying the wrong thing.

Or the right thing. And maybe that's why it was so frightening.

"I don't think it's manmade," Max said as he completed his second circuit.

"How do you know?" Roddy was intrigued, even though his heart told him to leave here as quickly as possible. The rock seemed to focus all his bad thoughts, nurturing them and giving them life. For the past few minutes he had been thinking about Norris's words: *You saw his face.* Butch, standing in the stream, staring at the wall of water bearing down on him. There had been no time. No hope. Had there?

"Too smooth, for a start," Max said. "It's been here for a long time — far too long for it to be manmade. It's been scoured smooth by the wind, formed into this peculiar shape by... I don't know. The way the wind blows down from the mountain. Or up from the sea."

"But it's so regular."

Max shrugged. He looked almost embarrassed. "I know. But I'm certain it's natural. There's more. Take a look." He walked some way around the rock, and Roddy followed. They left Norris sitting with his back against its black surface, nervously watching their progress. He kept glancing at the jungle they had just left, Roddy noticed. Waiting for something else to leave it, following them.

Max knelt and pulled back the skirt of grasses and bramble, wincing as thorns pricked at his already bloodied hands. "It dips into the ground," he said. "Curves down. Like it's not planted here, but was always here."

"How long's always?"

Max did not answer. Instead, he stood and glanced over Roddy's shoulder at Norris. From where they stood, Norris was mostly hidden. Only his feet and legs were visible, but there was always the chance that he could still hear. So Max's voice was low.

"There's something else," he said. "Follow me." As he walked, he talked. "I can't find any tool marks anywhere. Even on what I'm going to show you. It's just a freak of nature, I reckon."

"Like this island," Roddy said.

"This island's no freak," Max replied eventually. "In fact, I think it's pretty pure."

"Pure?"

"Pure nature." Again, Max had come out with something that sent a cold twinge into Roddy's bones, nudged his imagination into overdrive. You're a good friend, Max, he thought, but I wish you weren't here. Sometimes, ignorance may be better.

"Here," Max said. He pointed.

There was something marring the smooth surface of the rock. At first it looked damaged, struck by a tumbling boulder from above, perhaps, or fragmented by frost over the centuries. But on closer inspection, Roddy saw that this was far from the truth. This small scar on the huge expanse of rock had a purpose to it. A design. Several rows of designs, in fact, running left to right or right to left, each of them strange in the extreme. Roddy reached out and felt the ridged reality of them. He withdrew his hand quickly, because they seemed to move under his touch, communicating their corrupted message through contact as well as sight.

There was no sense to be made from them: some were shaped like bastardized letters from an unknowable language; others seemed to have sprouted from the rock, dictated by whatever was inside. They were knotted diagrams, random weatherings. Archaic language, or representations of things too alien to even try to comprehend.

Here, as elsewhere, there was no hint of tools having been used. No scratches, chips or runnels in the rock. If these markings were hand carved, then it was indeed a work of art, though an art as dark and disturbing as any Roddy had ever imagined. If they were naturally formed... in a way, that was worse. It would be an evocation of Nature's darkest side.

"What the hell is this?" he said. "They're horrible."

"My thoughts exactly," Max whispered. "I really think we should go."

"Are you scared, Max?" Roddy asked. He thought he knew the answer and, if he was right, he did not want to hear it verbalized. Not by Max.

"I've been scared ever since we got here," Max said. "From the moment I stepped onto the beach, I've wanted to leave. And if the boat hadn't been smashed up, I'm certain I'd have gone by now."

"You'd be dead."

Max shrugged. "Tell that to Ernie or Butch."

"You think Butch let himself drown?"

Max frowned, chewed his lip, fighting with contradictory thoughts. He scratched his bald head, peeling scabs to reveal fresh ones beneath. If there was pain he seemed not to notice. "I think he had more of a chance than we like to let ourselves believe," he said, finally. Then, as though reading Roddy's mind: "It wasn't hopeless."

A sense of futility grabbed at Roddy, dragging any hidden hopes he may have had out into the open and butchering them. The black rock stood before him, soaking up his fears, reflecting only the weirdness the scarred area imparted. He turned to Max for comfort, but the big man looked as frightened as he felt. More so, if anything. To see a face usually so full of intelligence and good humor reduced to this — wan, pale, bloodied and empty of hope — was soul-shattering.

"If Ernie was here he'd pray to God," Roddy said, and Max nodded.

"I reckon that's why he's not with us."

They left the markings to fulfil whatever purpose they had been created for. Norris asked what they had found, and Max told him that the rock was naturally formed, not artificial as they had first thought. The cook seemed disappointed by this, and Roddy was tempted to show him the markings. To show him that if the rock was not natural, then whatever had made it was way removed from the human Norris may have hoped for.

They headed on up the mountain. The further they moved away from the rock, the more Roddy felt watched. And the more he thought about the processes which must have conspired to carve the rock out of the land, the more feeble and insignificant he became. If it had been formed by nature, then it was never intended for the likes of man. It was a secret thing nature had done, for its own inconceivable purposes. Now it had been seen, touched, mused upon. Roddy wondered just what must become of those who viewed something never meant to be seen, touched something intended only to be kissed by the wind, scoured by dust.

He looked at his fingertips, where grime from the rock markings clung to his sweat. He had left something of himself on the rock, both physically and mentally. Most dust is human skin, he thought. In decades and centuries to come, he wondered how much of the dust coating the monstrous monolith would consist of Butch, or Ernie. Or any of them. And where would their souls be residing? In the hands of God, becalmed and soothed by the promise of salvation and goodness in the life everafter? Or in the rock? Buried in blackness. Trapped forever within sight of life. Teased and tortured by purely human needs.

The island seemed to be changing, becoming even further removed from the outside world. It was as though by discovering this place they had driven it further into itself, allowing greater disassociation with the world at large. A world of people and machines and war, where pride-scars marred every real achievement and genocide was considered fair sport.

Roddy looked up towards the head of the mountain, then back at the receding rock and the jungles beyond. Further down, across the slowly waving heads of trees and through spiralling flocks of birds, the sea stretched out, past the reef and on towards civilization. A timeless power, pounding itself to pieces on the sharp shores of the island.

They needed food, water, rest and shelter. They craved all the basics, even while immersed in the extraordinary. There was a sense now, between the three men, that they had to reach the top of the mountain, to see whether there was anything else on the other side. To see, simply, whether there was any hope at all. But hope too needs feeding. It fled once and for all before they even got there.

4. NOT QUITE ALONE

The three survivors, hardly talking in an effort to conserve their meager energy, worked their way up the steep incline. The pinnacle of the mountain still lay above and ahead, perhaps only three hundred feet higher. The slopes here were pierced by dark holes, small in diameter but disappearing into invisible depths. Max threw stones into the first few and listened to the rattle and echo of their descent. He soon stopped, because they could not hear them striking bottom. He said they were volcanic, but to Roddy they looked more like throats.

The landscape had changed drastically from the grasslands around the black rock. Instead of bushes and undergrowth, rocks of strangely twisted formations grew from the ground, with a low, loamy grass coating the intervening spaces. Its blades looked sharp. The rocks were shattered into points, shining with oily colors, changing texture and shade depending upon which angle they were viewed from. Heathers sprouted intermittently, strange, sick-looking plants which gave off a stale stench.

It was late afternoon and the sun was dipping towards the horizon behind the men. They were following their own shadows. Roddy found it agreeable. That way, he would be able to tell when something rushed him from behind.

Norris walked on ahead. He had begun mumbling to himself, his words bitter without managing to make any sense. He glanced around continuously, staring past Roddy and Max as though they weren't there, gaze fixed on the pointed black rock receding below and behind them. His eyes were wide, but drained of their constant state of defiance, a defence mechanism against those who mocked or feared the cook as a Jonah. Without that familiar expression, he was even more disturbing. And disturbed.

They came to a ravine and stopped for a rest. Max wandered off along the gash in the land, towards where he said he could hear water cascading into the dark depths. He suggested they should have a drink. Roddy agreed, but at the same time he was simply too exhausted to go looking for one. Far better to curl up here, lick the dew from the ground in the morning. Norris simply failed to answer.

The sun was low down to the sea, bleeding across the horizon and throwing the ravine into shadow. Roddy sat on a rock shaped vaguely like a pig, facing away from the sunset, watching the dividing line between light and dark creep slowly up the ravine wall. Joan had loved to watch sunsets arrayed across the South Wales mountains, he remembered; but at the same time, he realized that her face escaped him. He had kissed her so much, but when he tried to recall her features, there was nothing there. No voice, no smell, no image of the woman he thought he loved. It scared him, but it was also a comfort. He could not wish Joan here with him; bad enough that he was here alone.

The pending darkness tapped into new realms of disquiet. Roddy supposed that this was where the beach stream originated, and he imagined the slit in the earth to be inhabited by spiders as big as his head, snakes ready to eat each other to survive. There must be nooks and crannies down there, home to bats, scorpions, insects. There could even be people, strange half-blind albinos who had never even seen the sea and who had only a vague, mythological sense of the world outside the canyon. Next to him, another rock hunched low in the attitude of a fat-bellied sow. Roddy wondered whether they were wild boar, caught in some ancient volcanic action. Or perhaps they had once been the more adventurous dwellers of the pit, petrified by their sudden exposure to sunlight.

Norris remained standing behind him, still staring back the way they had come. His long shadow gave him all the attributes of a clumsy scarecrow.

When he laughed, that impression vanished. Only a human could laugh like that. Roddy could not remember hearing such a sound for a long time, certainly since before their ship was sunk six days previously. But here it was twisted into something grim and foreboding, caught by the ravine and distorted into an echoing snigger. Here, it was a laugh mad with something.

Norris was pointing back down the slope towards the jungle, giggling and sobbing. He backed up, slipped on flat ground and slid slowly over the edge. He cried out as darkness tugged at his legs.

"Max! Max!" Roddy leapt to his feet and collapsed with leg cramps. As his muscles knotted and writhed he crawled to the drop. His hands left blood smeared across sharpened stones. He was becoming one big wound.

Norris was pawing at a slowly moving slope of scree. Lying at about thirty degrees, his feet hung over a sheer drop into impenetrable darkness. No hope, Roddy thought, but he was determined not believe that, not even here, after everything that had happened. Best for him if he goes, crossed his mind, and the idea felt horribly true. Norris suddenly quietened and grinned up at him, and Roddy realized with a sickening certainty that he thought so, too.

The pit was becoming darker by the minute. The sun was not halting its descent simply to watch the unfolding of this pitiful human tragedy. Roddy reached out his hand, lying as near to the drop as he dared, terrified that he too would be dragged over the edge. "Grab my hand!" he shouted, his voice echoing back seconds later. "Grab it, Norris!"

Norris was swimming in scree. For each handful he grabbed, two slipped past him and spun out over nothing. Their fall into the ravine, a collection of minor collisions with the sides, echoed as a sibilant whisper from the dark. The dark, now approaching from all sides as the sun steamed into the sea.

"Norris!" Roddy shouted, suddenly terrified, petrified that they were all being sucked down, finally, into the island. Butch and Ernie were already there, held below its misleading surface; now, it wanted the rest of them.

Roddy edged himself forward. Only a few more inches, but enough to grasp onto one of Norris's flailing hands. The cook's reaction was not what Roddy had expected; he was silent and still for the briefest instant, then he began to shout. The more Roddy pulled, the more Norris squirmed and wriggled, in an apparent effort to dislodge his would-be rescuer's grip.

The pit yawned wide, dark and silent.

Just as he began to slide, Roddy felt a weight land on his legs. Mumbled words accompanied the impact, spat from a red raw throat, rich in blood and confusion. The sound was horrible, the words worse, because they were utterly without hope. Max was sat astride his knees, hands curling into his belt and hauling back with all his might. It was not enough. "He's still slipping!" Roddy said. "Norris, you're still slipping!" Max uttered something between a laugh and a sob. Roddy could not see him, of which he was glad.

"It's so cold," Norris shouted, eyes flickering up into his head to show only the whites, as if there was much more to see in there. "So cold, so helpless, so hopeless. Where's the point now? Where's the purpose?"

"Pull me up, Max!" Roddy shouted, but the big man was working to his own agenda. He was hauling on Roddy's belt, sobbing, and even in the riot of movement Roddy could feel him shaking. With terror, anguish or elation, he could not tell.

"Oh God," Max began to whisper, his voice curiously louder than before, words carrying the weight of a lifetime. "Oh God, help us, oh God, help us… for fuck's sake, help us!"

Roddy felt his fingers beginning to stiffen and burn with pain. When he was a boy he had always wondered why people hanging onto a precipice in films let go. He thought them foolish; to know that to let go was death and still to do so. Certainly their fingers may begin to hurt, the cramps and pain may become almost unbearable. But when it was a matter of will — when they knew that they could either put up with the pain and live, or relinquish their hold and die — there should really have been no choice.

His grip was slipping. He closed his eyes and gritted his teeth, willing his muscles to hold, cursing them as they ignored his call. Behind him, Max was shaking even more, and his muttered prayers were increasing in volume. He was begging God for mercy, or maybe shouting at him, apportioning blame as he asked forgiveness. But from all Roddy had learnt, he knew that God would never be shamed into anything.

Norris was still shouting, words veering in and out of focus, coherent one second, meaningless gibberish the next. His right hand, until now pawing at loose rock to save himself from the pit, began to push, instantly increasing the pressure on Roddy's grip. He's letting go, Roddy thought. Letting go, in every way he can. What pain is he going through?

"Pull, Max! I can't hold him — "

Everything happened at once. Everything bad. In those few seconds any semblance of control fled into the twilight, and panic found its place and made itself forever comfortable.

First, Max screamed. The sound was terrifying. Roddy's scalp tingled and tightened, and a shiver grabbed hold of his limbs and would not let go. He sensed Max standing up behind him, letting go of his belt in the process. The big man ran, still screaming, across the broken stones and weirdly twisted heathers of the hillside. Roddy turned his head for a moment, watched as Max ran from light to dark. He passed from day to night with the look of someone who could never return.

Then Roddy began to slip forward across the sharp stones. He was fast approaching what he perceived to be the point of no return.

He saw the ghost. The woman did not appear, as though she had never been there, but made herself apparent. She was floating in the darkness near the center of the ravine, slightly lower down than Roddy and the still struggling Norris. She was naked of clothes and flesh, bones glimmering in the failing light, hair sprouting wildly from her patchwork scalp. Her hands were held out, palms up. Her mouth hung open in a forlorn scream, but she uttered no sound. Her eyes were the brightest points in the dark pit, but they gleamed with madness, not intellect.

Norris brought up his right hand, clawed frantically at Roddy's fingers, then slipped free. He raised his hands gleefully, mouth wide open and emitting a high, keening laugh as he slid slowly back on the moving scree. With a shout, he disappeared over the edge. His call continued for a long time, and Roddy could not properly discern the point at which it turned into an echo of its former self. Even the echoes had echoes.

From the pit, a smell rose up. Something dead, something unwelcome. A warning, or a gasp, or the glory in a death.

"Where are you now?" Roddy asked hopelessly, expecting no answer.

The world began to spin. His guts churned and he vomited, stomach acids burning into the raw flesh of his fingers where Norris had peeled away streaks of skin.

My skin, Roddy thought, down there now, under a dead man's nails. I wonder if he's hit bottom yet.

The woman was still there, but fading, pleading with him to reach out and touch her. But somehow he knew it was a deceit, she only wanted him to tumble over the edge after Norris, so he pushed himself back until he was cutting his knees and elbows on solid, flat rock. The woman disappeared, hands held out in a warding off gesture.

He began to shake. The sky was dark, as though the episode had lasted for hours instead of minutes. His limbs jerked and his head began to pound the rock, his nerves pirouetting him into unconsciousness.

He was trying desperately to identify a constellation in the night sky. In some vague way he thought God may send him a sign of comfort, something familiar to hang onto. But as he frothed at the mouth and passed out, everything was alien. Even the stars showed no sign of friendship. They stared down as he battered himself to pieces on the island.

When he came to it was dark. The sun had truly set.

Moisture had settled on him, like tiny glimmering insects mistaking him for the ground. His limbs ached, his mouth was dry, tongue swollen. His neck felt ready to snap if he moved, but slowly he raised himself up onto one elbow. His back, cut and crispy with dried blood, ripped free of the spiky rocks beneath him. Hauling himself from a bed of knife blades would have felt much the same.

It was nighttime, but he could still see, courtesy of a full yellow moon. It hung above the sea, its light shimmering from the surface of the water. Wisps of cloud passed across its face. Stars speckled the rest of the sky. Moonlight played around the edges of the pit, giving it the appearance of a pouting wound, pale and bloodless.

Roddy felt cold, but it was merely one more discomfort to add to the list. His bones ached, his arms were bruised and heavy, his legs sang with pins and needles. When he moved, everything hurt. Muscles cried out against the aggravation.

A moderate breeze was drifting across the island, carrying the tang of brine and seaweed, and other less readily identified smells. Decay, perhaps; death and putrescence. But subtle, like perfume for a murderer. The weather played games with his senses, while his own body sought to confuse him more. He was weak, so weak. His stomach rumbled angrily, calling for food. His gullet felt parched and rough, and the thought of water sent his throat into dry convulsions. Then he noticed that the dew decorating his body was thicker than water. He smeared his hand across his torn shirt and bare neck, and it came away sticky with blood. He must have been rolling around, striking himself on the ground, opening himself up so that his jaded blood seeped down between the rocks. Yet again, the island had drawn its fill.

Norris. His shout when he fell had been part scream, part laugh. Roddy had not even been conscious to bear witness the ceasing of the echoes. And Max had gone too, shouting incoherently, raging and raving into the night even before Norris had fallen. Had he seen the woman? Did the sight of her tortured body, floating in the darkness and gesticulating uselessly, finally drive him to distraction? He'd been shouting for God when he went, and Roddy was not sure whether he even believed in God. But faith was a fickle thing, and Roddy had often seen a sudden resurgence of belief when situations arose to encouraged it. Times when simple logic explained nothing.

He felt so weak. In the dark the ground beneath him was even stronger than before, full of power, vibrating with the life it seemed so hell bent on stealing. Perhaps it had begun sucking their energy from the moment they left the boat, finishing with some before others. Now, maybe Roddy was the only one left. Max had gone, and try as he might Roddy could not bring himself to believe in his survival. There were too many holes up here, too many sharp edges to fall victim to.

The sense of being unutterably alone — not just here, but in the whole world — fell upon him. He cried out with the hopelessness of it all, tried to picture people dying across the globe at that moment in the name of freedom and justice, but their plight did not touch him. Instead he mourned his own torpid, deserted soul, pleading for something to fill it, opening his heart up to enlightenment as he had inadvertently offered his flesh to the island. He waited for the light, yearned the warmth or whisper that would tell him God had found him. Had, in fact, never been away. He recalled his mother's voice as she explained why he should say his prayers every night before bed. "God always knows you're here, but it's best to keep in touch, just in case," she would say. As a lad, he had often wondered what the "just in case" could entail. A slightly muddled God, perhaps, with a memory faded and fuddled with immense age? Now, he knew the case in "just in case." He knew it, but however much he tried he just could not bring himself to believe that he had doomed himself simply by not believing. The God he was aware of from other people was not like that. He forgave, He loved everyone. He was everywhere, all the time, guiding fate. Steering torpedoes into engine rooms. Urging the cold glint of steel along wrist veins. Blowing sudden surges into streams, smashing heads open and laying pagan brains out to view.

But there was nothing other than the island, and the strange, inbred mutated things living here. Survival of the fittest, Max had said. Perhaps God had been here and found himself severely wanting. Here, something else reigned supreme.

Roddy raged and cursed. He shouted at the dark to keep it, and the things it contained, at bay. His wounds were one big agony, but individual pains made themselves known every time he moved. His agnosticism felt obvious to him now, but he knew also that he would have humbly and willingly admitted his mistake if comfort and peace would come to him from the dark.

But the dark gave up nothing. No comforting hand, no whisper of belonging. No animals either. No pig-faced monstrosities crawling from the pit to join their petrified cousins. Nothing.

Roddy suffered his pain and inevitable loss alone.

The night came to life. Sounds came from all around, some of them blatant, the more frightening ones secretive and covert. For long minutes Roddy sat still, certain that his fear would give him away, as something breathed heavily nearby. He could not move. Like the rocks around him, he thought that stillness would fool whatever was there. Then he slowly came to recognize a pattern in the breathing, and realized that he was hearing the sea a mile or two away as it broke onto the reef.

Something sent a shower of stones into the ravine. Claws snickered on rock as whatever it was scrabbled to safety. It trotted away from him, whining and growling.

There was a sound which could have been a shout in the distance, or a groan from nearby. Either way, he did not want to sit here and take any more. He was shaking with fear, recalling childhood days exploring woodland hollows and old deserted mills, the feeling of terror slowly taking hold until rational thought gave way to shouting and headlong flight. He could not afford to do that here, he knew, but still he felt the panic taking a firm grip. The same childhood fears reared their heads again. Things in the dark with him, things he could not see, reaching out to touch.

Roddy stood and began walking parallel to the ravine. He headed in the same direction Max had taken, half hoping through all his despised certainty that he would find him sitting on a rock, smiling sheepishly and running his hand across his bald head. Max would come out with some dry witticism, all the while taking charge of the situation and deciding what to do next. Now that there were only two of them, he would say, they had a better chance. Food, water, shelter for two is much easier to find than for four, or five. And for two who were friends, things were that much easier. So Norris was dead, he would say. So what? So who's going to mourn the death of a Jonah? He would smile as he spoke, but somehow Roddy could not fit the words into his friend's mouth.

Roddy stopped and looked around, vaguely shocked by his train of thought. From the ravine to his left, a sigh rose from darkness into silvery light. He wondered whether it was Norris finally striking bottom. It seemed all too possible. The landscape appeared even more alien at night, throwing up flashes of light here and there where luminous creatures darted or crawled, shadows darkening as animals passed by. The mountain seemed much higher than it had before, and suddenly Roddy knew that he had to make it to the top. From there, as Max had said, he would see everything. Whether he really wanted to do so was a moot point. For now it was a purpose.

The dark felt heavy, the presence of something thick and gelatinous instead of the absence of light. His going was hard, pushing through the night, hands heavy on the ends of his arms, feet blocks of rock dangling from his ankles. He was weak, hungry and empty. His mind felt drained, picked over by whatever they had offended by landing here and then discarded, thrown back into his skull like the mess of organs after an autopsy.

The ravine opened up next to him. Dark and deep and cool, inviting, urging him to enter, forget the hardships of aching muscles and swollen tongue. Another sulphuric sigh, volcanic or organic, neither seemed too difficult to believe.

He thought of Butch and Ernie resting in the ground, where grubs made use of them and the cool earth kissed their skin. He imagined the comfort of lying down, shedding all fears and concerns.

He kept walking.

Each sound moved him closer to the edge. Every screech or growl or cry of feeding animals sapped him some more. His shoulders hung lower, his eyelids dipped shut. Pain merged, physical discomfort and mental anguish metamorphosing into something far more affecting; an agony of the soul, blazing white but invisible in the night. Burning in a vacuum, because Roddy was as drained of faith as any human being had ever been. The worst thing was not his spiritual emptiness; it was the fact that none of it was through his own choice. He felt mentally raped, but his rage at this was tempered by what he had seen over the past couple of years. The men and women he had watched die. The ships, burning fiercely as flesh melted and merged into their lower decks. The bobbing bodies of drowned men, eyes picked out by fortuitous fish. Blazing seas of oil. Lands scoured by war, until the virgin rock of the Earth showed through in supplication.

This island had changed him. Now, it intended to destroy him. Roddy was unable to avoid such intent.

Somehow, he survived the night.

There was nothing on top of the mountain. Roddy was not sure exactly what he had been expecting, but the mountaintop was bare, swept free of soil and plants by whatever winds blew at this altitude.

Day dawned surprisingly; light was something he had not expected to see ever again. Shocked into alertness, Roddy looked down at himself. Blood had dried and patterned his shirt with dark streaks, and his skin was still assaulted by the cruel sun. He looked worse than he ever had. His hands were slashed to scabby ribbons, his knees and stomach cut and ripped by the falls he had so obviously suffered on his climb during the night. Below him, further down the mountainside, the great slash of the ravine headed down towards the sea miles in the distance. The jungle was there, too, a sprawling green border between the mountain and the beach. It looked so alive and lush from up here. So friendly.

Roddy began to cry. If the ravine had been close by he would have gladly stepped into it, revelling in the cool rush of air as he let the island imbibe him. It seemed that the island was holding its breath, and had been doing so from the moment they had landed, yearning for the time when it would once more be free of their taint. Finishing himself now would do that. The view from here was wonderful, the island was raw and beautiful, but it was a vision never intended for the enjoyment of Man. He was stealing it merely by looking. Even from here, he could see shadows moving beneath the trees at the edge of the jungle, like tigers pacing their cage.

He wiped tears from his face with the backs of his hands. He wanted to feel a sense of rebellion against the terrible power of the island, but the emotions necessary to do so were hidden from him. Bitterness manifested itself as desperation; anger brought new tears; defiance ricocheted and struck him as dread. It was hopeless. Perhaps, he mused, it always had been. Maybe they should have listened to Ernie and stayed on the boat. Behind him, Ernie, Butch and Norris were already blending into the memory of the landscape.

Roddy stood and turned his back on the way he had come. He walked across the plateau of the mountain-top, and if there had been a hole he would have slipped into it. A steady breeze blew, cooling him where he still bled. He looked at the bruise on his elbow, the result of his leap from the stricken ship. Now it was surrounded by other wounds, all of them combining to wear him down, drop him down, ease him eventually earthward.

He remembered another mountain walk. Years ago in the valleys of Monmouthshire, following in the footsteps of a man called Machen. His parents had pointed out invisible landmarks and left Roddy to feel the majesty of the place privately. He had been eleven then, just beginning to find his own mind. Looking back now, he thought maybe that was the last time he ever truly, wholeheartedly believed in God. Since then, he had seen cruelties and sadism beyond nightmare. Bravery too, and compassion. But bad weighed heavier on his soul.

As the mountain began to slope down towards the opposite side of the island, Roddy saw the cove. It was at least a mile away, still enveloped in the shadow of the mountain. But the cove and surrounding area were different to the rest of the landscape, marked somehow. Tainted.

In the center of the bay, obviously foundered, sat a sailing ship. Even from this distance Roddy could see that it was wrecked.

There was a moment of shock at the realization that others had been here before them, but it was short-lived. It was obvious from what he could see that no one was alive down there. The area around the cove was dead, a blank spot on a painting where the colors of life were absent, and sea birds were using the wreck as a roost.

Like an animal seeking food, Roddy had suddenly been given a blind purpose. If one group of people would land, so could others. Rescue did not cross his mind, because he knew he was already lost. But if he did nothing else before the island finished him, he had to leave a message for any future visitors.

A warning.

5. HELL HATH NO LIMITS

Once, Roddy had been part of a cleaning out crew on a bombed ship. The effect of an explosion in an enclosed space was dreadful, and he thought he would never really get over the terrible things he saw in that tangled mess. In a way, the worst sights were those bodies still recognizable as such. The rest — the mess on the floors, the splashes across shattered bulkheads — could have been anything.

This was worse.

What Roddy saw scattered around the small cove sent him into deep shock. The more he saw, the worse he felt, and the more he was duty-bound to see. It was as if beholding the sights gave them weight, making them real and significant. He wandered from scene to scene, an observer in the most gruesome and perverted museum ever conceived.

The sea sighed onto the beach, most of its awesome power already tempered by the reef surrounding the island. The air was heavy with moisture, even though the sun had yet to touch this part of the world today. The sand was hot and sharp where it found its way into his shoes, and if there were any creatures viewing his discovery with him, they were silent. The island was still holding its breath.

They were mostly skeletons. In places hair and skin prevailed, but the flesh had long since shrivelled to nothing or been eaten by scavengers. Teeth hung black and worn from gaping jaws. Orchids grew through a ribcage like twisted, rooted insides. A skull was clamped halfway up a thin tree, face plate split open by the growth of the palm through a void where life had once held memory and faith. A skeleton lay wrapped around the boles of two trees, hips split asunder by one, spine snapped and bent outwards by the other. The jaws hung open, full of a nettle-like plant, as if the trees still gave it pain. Two bodies lay in each other's arms, half buried in sand blown by decades of sea breeze. One skull was shattered, the other merely dented and cracked. One bony hand held a pistol. A plant grew from its barrel, pluming smoke frozen forever in time.

Roddy stumbled from one tableau to the next, keening uncontrollably, searching frantically for something on which to blame this atrocity, but finding only evidence of these people's good intentions. A box, lid only slightly askew, contained the faded and pulped pages from dozens of books and manuscripts. Looking closer, Roddy could make out the embossed crosses on their covers.

Rusted knives lay loose between chewed ribs.

A frayed rope hung a corpse from a tree, and a small colorful bird alighted on its bony shoulder. Perhaps it thought the body still held some hidden sustenance, but more likely it was simply gloating.

Roddy stared out at the ship, unable to look at the bodies any more, unwilling to think upon what they must have gone through as they set foot on the island. It was little more than a rotten wreck, masts long since fallen, sails and ropes torn away by the ageless tides. It was stuck firm and most of the timber boarding had been stripped from its ribs. The ship, like those who had sailed in her, lay with innards naked and exposed to the elements. The whole scene was like some sadistic, ongoing sacrifice, laid out as an eternal display for the benefit of whatever had called for it.

Roddy had never imagined such pointless devastation or despair. The agony of the moment hung in the air as if the travelers had killed themselves only yesterday, rather than decades ago. His presence here felt intrusive. But he was no longer alone.

On the air, he smelled fresh blood and bad flesh.

He saw the body along the beach, but it was not until he stumbled nearer that he recognized Max. The big man was still grasping the rusted, blunted blade he must have plucked from the bony grip of one long since dead. He had hacked at his stomach, sawn the blade back and forth, ripping flesh and skin asunder. His head was thrown back, his mouth open in an endless groan of agony, his bald head caked in sand still damp from sweat. The beach around him was black with his own leaked blood.

"Oh Max," Roddy cried. He felt abandoned and deserted; up until this moment he had still harbored a hope that Max would reappear, however unlikely it had seemed. Now, his wish had been granted. Max was back with him. Roddy wondered which of the strange noises in the night had been Max's agonized scream.

As if a plan had at last been played out, the jungle burst back into life. Birds cackled and laughed, other things cawed and clucked in amusement. Even the sea was louder for a time. A breeze swept through the trees and set the branches swaying, palms stroking each other with secret whispers. Something lumbered through the undergrowth inland, snapping twigs and stomping bushes. It never revealed itself and the sound of its movement faded slowly away. For the first time since they had landed here, the island sounded as it should.

Roddy felt dismissed.

He reached for the knife. Max's hands still held a dreadful trace of warmth. Roddy grimaced as he parted the dead man's fingers, intending to prise the knife from where it was embedded between muscles and organs and flesh, use it to part his own skin and finally allow his insides the freedom they so yearned. The rusty handle was sticky with his dead friend's blood.

Max groaned.

Roddy gasped and fell back, feeling nothing but abhorrence for the living dead thing before him. He tried to propel himself backwards, away from Max, but succeeded only in pushing showers of sand into the man's open stomach.

Max groaned again. It sounded as if a cricket were lodged in his throat. His head moved. A muscle spasmed on his forearm, hand closing tighter around the knife. The movement did not disturb the flies feasting at his open wound.

Roddy was going to scream. He felt it welling inside, clearing his head of whatever rational thought had survived these last couple of days, driving controlled emotions out and allowing blind, instinctive panic to take control. He silently prayed to God for help, as though religion were instinctive.

Then Roddy felt himself passing into unconsciousness; his limbs beat at the sand, head spinning. A black shape stood beneath the trees, the naked woman, her arms held out with hands up, the blackness her clotted blood.

All else faded.

When Roddy came to, Max was truly dead. Several small lizards were clustered around the wound in his gut, darting red heads in and out. They glanced at Roddy between each mouthful. He felt too defeated to chase them away.

Somehow, he struggled to his feet. He found it hard to focus. He had been lying in the sun now that it peered over the mountain, and his forehead was stiff and throbbing. The heat was pumping into his head, boiling his thoughts. The black shape from beneath the trees had gone, changed into something different, something solid. Only another skeleton. This one had been tied to the trunk of a dead tree and the rope still held the bleached remains in place. Weed from the last stormy sea had tangled itself around the skeleton's feet. It still had the remnants of long hair, ancient home to crawling things. Roddy thought it had no arms, so he stumbled closer to see.

It did have arms. Even now, as if caused by some drastic trauma to the bone joints just before death had arrived, the hands remained upright on the fleshless wrists. It was a classic warding off gesture, aiming out to sea. He recalled the flayed flesh, the torn muscles. One finger still wore a ring, and Roddy thought it might be a treasure.

He had found his woman, his haunter, the shadow which had revealed itself to him from the dark over the past two days, driving him into unconsciousness. Rescuing him, however briefly, from his surroundings.

She had been trying to warn him, he realized. Trying to warn others. And then memory flooded back, and Roddy realized what he had brought himself down here to do.

The sea sang invitingly, urging him to enter and fill his lungs. Max lay stretched out on the sand, the knife in his guts coveting more warmth to settle into. Ropes swung free and easy from tree branches, complete but for a swinging corpse. Everything implied death. But Roddy had come this far, and though he was not brave, he *was* defiant.

The island could wait another hour for his faithless soul.

There were rusty tools, bleached driftwood, even planks from the shattered ship. The work kept his mind his own, excluding for a while all the intimations of death, all the invitations to do himself the final mischief.

The cross was fine. He thought it would hold.

He tied old rope around each wooden arm and ended it in slip-loops. He stood a thick branch against the upright to stand on and kick away when the time came. The island was silent once more; grudging respect, he liked to think, but he could still sense the satisfied mockery behind the temporary peace. He did not even bury Max; there was little point. The island would have him, wherever his final resting place. He had already bled his life into the ground. Now, he was little more than rotting flesh.

When Roddy had tightened the loops around his wrists, he prepared to kick away the branch. He thought of offering a prayer up to God, but if He was there, then He would surely not hear anything spoken from this place. Roddy thought that the bastardized symbolism of his own death was prayer enough.

He kicked the branch away and gasped as the rope tightened and pinched his skin. He had heard somewhere that suffocation killed most crucifixion victims. He stared out across the cove, past the ship, hoping that anyone approaching from that way would see what he had left to them and take heed.

Behind Roddy, in the trees and on the mountainside, from the ravine beyond the mountain, sounds of merriment filled the air as birds took flight, lizards and small mammals gambolled through the undergrowth. But he felt removed from the island, as if he were already dead, and the noise barely touched him.

As he hung there, he had time to really think about what he had done.

The Origin of Truth

They were stuck in a traffic queue. There was nowhere they could go. They couldn't help but see the melting man.

Doug wanted to turn around, cover his daughter's eyes and hide the sight from her innocent mind. But she had seen stuff just as bad over the last couple of days, and she would probably see a lot worse in the future. He could no longer shield her from the truth. In a normal world, it was only right that his concern translated into action, but the world today was so different from last week. Normal was a word that had lost its meaning.

Besides, she was fascinated.

There were nine television screens in the shop window, and all of them showed the same picture: the man sitting propped outside a baker's, a split bag by his side, crusty rolls and ice slices scattered across the hot pavement. His legs had disappeared from the knees down. He was watching the process, his face stretched in surprise—eyebrows raised, jaw lowered, brow furrowed—as his limbs turned to gas. The view was being captured by a telescopic lens mounted in a helicopter. The picture was hazy and shaky.

The ultimate in victim TV, thought Doug. Somewhere in the north of France this man was dying. And here, now, in London, they were watching him.

"Nobody touch the windows," Doug said, even though he had locked them using his own master control. "And keep the cylinder open." There were three compressed air cylinders on the back seat next to Gemma. One had already run out, the second had been opened for several minutes.

"What about when they run out, Dad?" Gemma said sensibly. Damn her, she was so sensible. "What then? Will the air come in from outside?"

"It already is," Lucy-Anne muttered from the passenger seat.

Doug glared at his wife but she did not turn, did not register his attention.

"It won't, honey," he said instead. "The pressure inside will keep it out."

"But what if those things can *crawl*."

There was no answer to that, so Doug did not attempt one. Instead he glanced at the man on the screens, saw that his stomach was already possessed of a sick, fluid motion. He leaned on the horn. "Get a bloody move on." He wanted Gemma to see as little of this as possible.

"If they were here, honey, we'd know it by now." Lucy-Anne sighed. "They'd have started on the car."

"Don't talk like that!" Doug said.

"It's true!"

"Yes," he replied weakly, "but not... in front of Gemma."

"Why is nobody helping him?" his daughter asked without conviction. She was only ten, but she had learned a lot over the past few days. Like sometimes you just can't help people. If they can't help themselves... and against this, no one could... then it's best to leave them and forget about them, pretend that they never were.

In minutes, this man they were watching from afar would no longer exist, and hours later the same thing would be happening right where they were.

As the traffic moved off Doug heard his daughter turn up the air release valve on the second cylinder. He took one last glance at the TV screens and saw why.

The picture was flickering and spinning as the nanos started work on the helicopter.

Half an hour later they edged out of the city, along with what seemed like a million other people. Doug was unsure as to why the countryside seemed to offer any better protection from what was soon to come. It was survival instinct, he supposed, an urge to flee that was perhaps a racial hangover from all the wars and ethnic conflicts there had been down through the centuries. As children his grandparents had been evacuated to families they did not know to live lives they could not understand, and now he was subjecting his wife and daughter to the same. Leaving what they knew for what they did not. Except in this case, there was no escaping the reason for their flight. No running from what could — and would — be everywhere. May as well try to leave gravity behind.

But he had to do something. There was no argument. There was always a chance.

He kept in the fast lane of the motorway doing little more than twenty miles per hour. His right ankle was aching where he had it tensed on the gas pedal, yearning to press it down and lay out more miles between them and the city. Other cars tried to dart in and out as and when spaces became available, and there were more than a few fender benders. Normally motorists would stop and help. Now they simply slowed down, joined forces temporarily to shove the bumped cars aside with their own, and went on their way.

It was a scorching summer day. Everyone had their windows up. Doug caught the eye of a few drivers and there was always mistrust there, an animal fear of the unknown — even unknown people — in these times of peril. It made him realize how little it had all really changed, how far humanity had not come, even though it liked to think itself way and above the rest of nature. There were those scientists who had claimed to be a few years away from the Theory of Everything. Now those self-same egotistical bastards were clouds of gas radiating outward from the hub of humankind's doom.

Where that center was, few people knew any more. Those who did were dead, mixing themselves with the scientists who had killed them, the laboratories they had been working in, the clothes there were wearing, the test tubes and the microscopes and the particle accelerators and the cultures and the notebooks full of folly....

"Dad, I want a pee," Gemma whined.

"Oh honey, you'll have to hold it for a while," Lucy-Anne said.

Doug glanced across at his wife. He'd been ignoring her. He saw her afresh for the briefest instant and realized how much he loved her. He held back a startled sob.

"But Mum — "

"Your mum's right, Gemma. Hold on tight and you can go soon."

"When?"

"Soon."

"But — "

"Gemma," Doug said, his voice low, "did you see the man on the TV?"

"Yes," she said quietly. "He was all... going."

"He had a nasty... it was a bug, Gemma. It's in the air where he was, and it's spreading. We don't want to catch it, and if we stop — "

"And I don't want you to catch it!" she spurted out, bursting into tears and gasping great hitched sobs into the car. "I don't want you and Mummy to catch it!"

Doug felt his temper rising and hated himself for it. She was terrified; she'd seen people dying on TV, *dying* for Christ's sake. At her age the worst he'd ever seen was a squashed cat by the side of the road. He'd put flowers there, tied to a lamp post. The cat had gone the next day. His child's mind had seen death as a temporary state.

Lucy-Anne had turned fully in her seat and was hugging Gemma, soothing her with gentle Mum-words that Doug could not hear. He reached out and patted his wife's behind, giving her a quick squeeze: *all going to be all right*, he tried to impart. He knew she'd know he was lying, but comfort was important. Civilization was important. Without routine and hope, civilization would crumble.

He remembered the pictures from Rome, beamed in seconds before the cameras were swamped and stripped and dismantled to their component atoms by the nanos: a great cloud looming in the distance; a soup of all things organic, metallic, plastic, historic; rock and water and air. The nanos took it all, dismantled everything and spurted it across the land like reality's white noise.

Oh my God, Lucy-Anne had gasped, squeezing his hand, spilling a tear of red wine from her glass. *Surely they can do something about it?*

They?

Well, the scientists. The.... But she had trailed off as the view jumped further north, showing the whole horizon as an indistinct blur, the land and air merged. Armageddon moved with the wind, the nanos flowing with the air and crawling through the ground itself, so it was said.

"Doug, she really needs to pee."

He looked in the rearview mirror and saw Gemma rocking in his wife's grip. A horn tooted, tires squealed, he glanced forward and slammed on his brakes just as he heard the doom-laden crunch of metal and glass impacting. The accident was several cars in front of them in the slow lane, a Mondeo twisted under the tailgate of a big wagon. The wagon was still moving. Even as a terrible flame licked from beneath the Mondeo's bonnet, and as the driver struggled to open a door distorted shut, the wagon was still moving. It's driver knew that to stop was to die, eventually.

"Oh Jesus," Lucy-Anne whispered, and Doug put his foot down

on the gas. At least something had changed — rubberneckers
had altered their priorities, and they now wanted to leave the
scene as soon as possible. Maybe it was the danger from fire, but
more likely it was the heat of guilt.

"You can go on the floor in the back," Doug said. "You hear
me, honey?"

"I *can't* pee on the floor," Gemma said in disgust. "It's horrible!"

"Do as Daddy says if you're really desperate. If not hold on,
and you can go when we stop."

"When do we stop?" Doug asked, and wished he hadn't. He
saw Lucy-Anne staring at him but he kept facing forward.

"I don't know. What's the plan? Do we have one, other than
leaving our home like… like rats from…?"

"Hey, come on, it was you as much as me! When they reported
the first case in Paris — "

"I'm sorry Doug," she said quickly, and she squeezed his leg.
He liked that, he always had. A touch could speak volumes.

In the back, Gemma worked her way down between the seats.
Soon the acrid smell of urine filled the car.

Doug wanted to close his eyes, cry refreshing tears. There was
a hot knot in his stomach: fear for his family; love for his daughter; a hopeless embarrassment at what she had been forced to do.

"Urine is sometimes used to treat the effects of jellyfish stings,"
Gemma said suddenly, "especially in the tropics. Sometimes they
can't get normal medicines quickly enough, so they pee on the
victims."

He glanced over his shoulder at his daughter, crushed between
the seats, knickers around her knees. What a strange thing to
say….

She stared back at him wide-eyed.

He looked at Lucy-Anne, who appeared not to have heard, then
decided to say nothing. There had been something in Gemma's
young eyes—an uncomfortable sense of loss in a day full of terror—and he did not want to scare her any more.

An hour later they left the motorway. Doug turned north, and
Lucy-Anne did not object. Her silent acquiescence depressed him
more than he could have imagined.

Within half an hour of leaving the M4 the traffic had thinned
out considerably. People could leave the city, but it was not so
easy for most of them to relinquish the motorways, as if the main
roads could lead them somewhere safer.

It was almost midday.

Doug turned on the radio and scanned the channels. Mindless pop, classical tunes linked end to end without a presenter, a conversation on football which he recognized as being about a match played a year ago. A semblance of normality, but underpinned with the terrible hidden truth: that things had gone bad, and may never be good again. He slipped a tape into the player and REM started to piss him off.

Lucy-Anne twiddled her thumbs and only occasionally looked through the windscreen. Doug touched her leg now and then to reassure her, and also to comfort himself. He wished she would do the same back, but he had always been the more tactile one, the one who needed a touch as well as a smile to make him feel good. He glanced at her every now and then, wanting to do more but knowing that there was nothing he *could* do. She knew as well as he that they were not escaping, but merely prolonging the inevitable.

He thought about death, and tried to divert his mind elsewhere. "You okay, honey?"

Gemma whispered that yes, she was okay, but she did not look up.

"So where are we going?" Lucy-Anne said to her hands.

Doug did not answer for a while. A recent signpost had pointed north to Birmingham and Coventry, but their direction so far had been dictated by chance as much as design. "North," he said, because away from France was the best idea.

Lucy-Anne looked up. "Scotland," she whispered.

"Well, we could try, but it depends on fuel and — "

"No, we *must* go to Scotland! Uncle Peter lives near Inverness; we can go there, he'll have us, he'll look after us." She was looking at him now, and her face had come alight. He hated the false hope he saw there.

"Who's Uncle Peter?" Gemma said from the back seat.

Doug snorted. "Precisely."

"Doug, he's not a bad sort."

"You haven't seen him in over ten years. Hell, I think the last time was our bloody wedding!"

"He's a bit eccentric, that's all."

"Does that mean he does odd things?" Gemma asked. "Only, I don't mind that. I quite like people who do odd things."

"We'll go to see him, then," Lucy-Anne said. "Won't we, Dad?"

Doug nodded slowly, already beaten. They would go to see him, sure they would, but what then? That's what was truly bothering him: what then? He had no answer, and seeking it would make him give in, curl into a ball and die.

"Edgar Allan Poe's dying words were *Lord help my soul*," Gemma muttered under her breath.

"What?" Doug asked.

"Huh?"

"What did you say, honey?" Some cars passed the other way, one of them flashing its lights, but he ignored them. As far as he knew Gemma had never read any Poe, let alone read *about* the man.

"Nothing, Dad."

"She's tired and scared, Doug," Lucy-Anne said quietly, so that the sound of the engine would cover her words. "Let's just aim north and leave it at that. When we get there…." She trailed off without substituting the word *when* with *if*.

Doug mentally did it for her.

Another car passed with flashing lights, its driver waving frantically as he sped by.

"Now what?" Doug slowed the car and eased it around a bend in the A-road. When he saw what faced them his foot slipped from the accelerator, and the car drifted onto the grass verge and came to a halt. He forgot to use the brakes. For a while, he forgot even to breathe.

Lucy-Anne was a good mother. She twisted in her seat and motioned Gemma to her, holding her yet again and shielding the girl's eyes with the back of her seat.

"Get us out of here," she said. "Doug, get us out of here, Doug, wake up…."

As the men looked up and saw him staring at them, Doug shoved the car into reverse. He slammed his foot on the gas and glanced in the rearview mirror. If there was another car coming they would meet, crash and burn. At least he hoped they would burn; he did not want to be left alive for these men to be able to get to him, and to Lucy-Anne and Gemma, and do to them what they were doing to the family on the road ahead.

It was the dog that shocked Doug more than anything. Why the dog?

The engine screamed as the car slewed across the road. He glanced back at the scene receding in front of them and saw that the men had gone back to their business. It did not matter. He did not let up on the gas until he had clumsily steered back around the bend and spun into a farm gate to turn around. He smelled an acidic burning, the car crunched against a stone wall, Gemma finally struggled from Lucy-Anne's grip and screamed.

Doug felt like screaming as well. Yesterday, normality, tainted with disquiet over what was apparently happening in the Mediterranean, and a subdued fear that it may come closer.

Today, this.

He shook his head and flicked tears across the dashboard. "We'll try another road."

Lucy-Anne did not answer. She was still trying to hug Gemma, protect her, hide her away from whatever had gone wrong with the world today. If only it were so easy.

That afternoon there was a government announcement over the radio. The Prime Minister gave "grave news" about the southern suburbs of London — they were gone — but he assured people that everything was being done that could be done to find a solution to this crisis. Doug wondered just how far away the bastard actually was. The Arctic Circle, perhaps?

Gemma laughed childishly and said: "Tibia, fibula, tarsus, metatarsals, phalanges."

Early that evening they saw the first signs for Edinburgh. The radio had said no more.

Uncle Peter was more than eccentric, he was plain insane... and he wanted people to recognize his insanity. His whole estate was floodlit against the night, revealing all of what he had done. Some of it, Doug thought, should have stayed well hidden.

As they cruised along his long, winding driveway, the first signs of this madness presented themselves. Every tree bordering the road had had its lower branches lopped off, the wounds daubed with black tar to seal them, the dead timber disposed of out of sight. Nailed to the naked trunks were animal corpses, a species for each tree: a squirrel on a sycamore, a sparrow on an elm, a deer on an oak. It was as if Uncle Peter were a game hunter, but he had run out of room for trophies inside his house.

And the house... this was fairly unusual as well.

"Holy shit," Doug muttered under his breath as they rounded the final bend in the drive. It was a huge old monolith, stonework sills crumbling with age, windows distorted out of shape by the deadly subsidence plaguing the property and promising to drag it, eventually, back into the stony ground. From plinth to eaves the house looked quite normal, if dishevelled.

Above that, the gargoyles took over.

They were all huge, fashioned from plastic and fiberglass instead of stone, and more gruesome because of that. Garish colors and unsettling designs shouted across at them as they coasted to a halt. Bloody teeth, split throats, dragon-eyes, saber-toothed monstrosities that would surely be more than able to fulfil their duties... if, indeed, these things had the same employ as their more traditional greystone cousins. Stark artificial light gave them an added sense of the grotesque. They looked like a kid's book made real.

"Mad as a hatter," Doug said. "Uncle Peter has gone AWOL I think, Lucy."

"He always was a bit offbeat," she whispered, aghast.

"Wow," was all Gemma could say. "Wow."

The car stank. All three of them had urinated — Doug had refused to stop, even when Lucy-Anne had begged him and cried and cursed as she tried to miss her seat as she pissed — and they had not opened the windows for eleven hours. The fuel gauge had been kissing red for fifty miles, and for the last twenty Doug had been silently blessing Volkswagen's caution. The food they had managed to bring with them had gone bad in the heat, a pint of milk had spilled, the oxygen cylinders had run out hundreds of miles back... the engine was making a sickly grinding noise... basically, they were on their last legs.

The car rattled and sighed as he turned off the ignition. He was certain it would never start again, not without a great deal of pampering and cajoling. He was equally certain that he would never need to do either.

They sat staring at the house. Doug was expecting mad Uncle Peter to come running out at any moment, a shotgun in one hand and a bottle of Scotch in the other, pumping a hail of lead at the car as he toasted his own questionable health. But the door remained closed, all was calm. Several crows flitted to and fro across the roof, confused by the light, avoiding the gargoyles wherever they could.

"Crows," Gemma said. "Family Corvidae. For instance, Corvus corax, Corvus corcone, Corvus frugilegus, Corvus splendens and the magpie, Pica pica. Chiefly insectivorous, in winter it will become omnivorous. Earthworms and grubs. And seeds. It eats... it eats grubs and seeds...." She drifted off, leaning between the front seats, staring through the windscreen at the frolicking birds on the roof of the house.

"Where...?" Doug said. "Honey? Where did you learn stuff like that? They teach you that at school?"

Gemma turned to him, glaring blankly. Her mouth hung slightly open and a string of drool was threatening to spill out. "Huh?"

"Honey, what's wrong?" *Not now*, he thought. *Don't let her be ill now, not with so little time left....*

"Dad, I'm so thirsty," she said. Her voice was weak, diluted. Not as strong as it had been moments before. Not as definite.

"Gemma, how do you know all that about crows — ?"

"Leave her, Doug," Lucy-Anne said. "Let's just get her in, can we? For God's sake? We need a rest."

Doug nodded, smoothed Gemma's hair behind her ears, tried to stretch his legs. He could hear the concern in Lucy-Anne's voice, and the doubt, and the fact that she was as unsettled as he. Gemma had never been very good at school... had never taken much of an interest in anything... had been on the verge of being sent to a special school for slow learners.

Corvus corax, Corvus corcone, Corvus frugilegus... Christ, where the hell did she get that from?

"Ahhhh," a voice boomed, and Doug's door was snatched open. He jerked back, gasping in relief at the fresh air gushing in, wondering at the same instant what he was inhaling, whether the nanos were here already, inside him now, starting work on his lungs so that the next breath he drew and let out would mist red in front of him.

"Uncle Peter?" Lucy-Anne said.

"Thought I might see some of my folk over the next day or two," the voice said. Then a man leaned down next to the car to give the voice a face. A wild face indeed, with unruly tufts of hair and cheeks veined with evidence of years of alcohol abuse. His eyes though, they were different. Mad, but intelligent with it.

"Sorry to say," Uncle Peter said, "there's nothing I can do for any of us. But still. It will be nice to have company when the time comes."

Doug, his wife and daughter heaved themselves from the car, all of them patiently helped by Lucy-Anne's Uncle Peter. He held them when their legs bowed, their muscles cramped; and he wiped tears from Gemma's face when she cried. When Lucy-Anne went to him he hugged her close and closed his eyes. Doug felt a brief but intense moment of jealousy, unreasonable yet unavoidable, and he gathered Gemma into his arms as if to ward off his uncertainty.

"Amazing house," he said, staring up at the grotesque decoration three stories up.

"Made them myself," Peter said. "I must be a fucking fruitcake!"

Laughing, they left the mad night behind and went inside.

"London went hours ago," Peter said. "So it said on the TV."
He was peeling potatoes while Doug diced some vegetables. Lucy-
Anne and Gemma were washing and changing in one of the up-
stairs bedrooms. None of them felt like sleeping. "Haven't been
there in a decade. Now all I want to do is to go to Trafalgar
Square and feed the pigeons."

"My father lives in London," Doug said. He took his time with
each carrot he slit, relishing the hard, crunchy sound. It was a
solid sound. Firm. Not too far south of here, solid and firm
were words that no longer held meaning.

"Well," said Peter, but he did not continue.

They worked in silence for a while, Doug thinking around the
subject of death, Peter perhaps doing the same. Everything Doug
did now was tainted with the promise of their own demise: this
food would not be fully digested when the time came; he may
never sleep again, it was a waste of time... so no more dreams.
Gemma would not grow up to go to university, marry, bear her
own children....

"It's just so unfair!" he shouted, throwing the knife at the flag-
stone floor. He regretted it instantly, felt a cool hand of shame
tickle at his scalp. He had not seen this man for ten years, and
here he was trying his best to destroy his kitchen.

And there's another irony, *he thought*. In days... hours... this
kitchen won't be here.

Peter glance at him but said nothing. He continued peeling
potatoes.

Doug wondered whether the old nutcase was as far gone as he
led to believe. "Why all the lights? And the animals on the trees?
And the gargoyles?"

Peter shook his hands dry and transferred the vegetables into a
huge pan of boiling water. "In reverse order: the gargoyles to
keep people away from the house; the animals on the trees to
keep trespassers from my land; the lights so that people can see
what I've done. It took a long time. Why have it all hidden half
the time?"

Doug smiled at the simple logic of it. "But why keep people
from the house?"

The old man shrugged. "Don't like people, mostly."

There was a clatter of feet from the hallway and Gemma and
Lucy-Anne hurried in. They both had wet hair, loose-fitting clothes
that Peter had found in some mysteriously well-appointed ward-

robe, and rosy complexions that made Doug's heart ache.

"Your turn," Peter said.

"Huh?"

"Shower. Change. Forgive my bluntness, but you smell."

"Daddy smells, Daddy smells!"

He relented, and after giving his wife and daughter a kiss — a hard hug for Gemma, a long, lingering kiss for Lucy-Anne — he made his way up the curving staircase to their bedrooms.

There were towels on the bed, a basket of fruit on the dressing table, a bottle of red wine uncorked and breathing beside the bed, two glasses, and a door between theirs and Gemma's bedrooms. *Thought I might see some of my folk over the next day or two*, the mad old fool had said. And though he had claimed to hate people, Doug could see that this was what Peter had wanted more than anything else.

After a hearty meal of steak, fried potatoes, vegetables and great, thick chunks of garlic butter-soaked bread, the four of them made their way into Peter's living room and sat down with a drink. Gemma went to sleep almost immediately, nestled against Peter's arm, and the three adults — though tired — sat talking until the sun set fire to the day outside.

There was a strange atmosphere between them, a feeling that they had known each other forever and that there was not a chasm of ten years between this and their last meeting. Lucy-Anne and Peter seemed especially comfortable, finding it unnecessary to resort to reliving old times or talking about absent — or dead — family members to get by. Instead their talk was of Gemma, what she had done in her short life to date, what she wanted to do. Her prospects.

And for a while, Doug was happy to let this go. He half-closed his eyes, enjoying the sense of the brandy sweeping through his veins and setting his stiff muscles afire, listening to Peter and Lucy-Anne's tempered voices. He found solace in their tone if not their words. He soon tried to tune out what they were saying — because none of it held true meaning any more — and enjoy instead the peace their voices conveyed, the sheer pleasantness of this unreal scene of family conviviality.

But then Gemma stirred and began to mutter in her sleep.

"Never done that before...." Lucy-Anne said idly. And she said no more.

None of them did. There was nothing to do but listen to what the little girl was saying.

"First birds were in the Jurassic period, two hundred and thirteen million years ago," she mumbled into Peter's side.

The old man stared down at her wide-eyed, but he did not move. Moving may have disturbed her.

"First mammals and dinosaurs in the Triassic two hundred and forty-eight million years ago, but the dinosaurs reached their peak in the Cretaceous, one hundred and forty-four million years back. First land plants in Silurian times, four hundred and thirty-eight million years ago." She struggled slightly then, frowning, as if searching for something hidden behind whatever she had been saying. "First humans. Couple of million years ago. Pleistocene epoch."

She sat up and opened her eyes. "Blink of an eye."

"Gemma?" Doug whispered, but then she began to cry.

"Bright girl you've got here, folks."

"Gemma? Honey?"

Gemma's face crumpled as sleep left her behind. Tears formed in her eyes, her nose wrinkled. "Dad," she said. "Mum...." Then the tears came in earnest and Doug darted across the room, lifted his daughter from Peter's side, hugged her close to him.

"Gemma, what's wrong babe?" Lucy-Anne said. Her voice betrayed none of Doug's concern or confusion. Hadn't she heard what Gemma was saying? Hadn't it registered?

"Got a headache," she sniffled into Doug's shoulder. "And I need to pee."

"Here." Lucy-Anne took Gemma and carried her from the room, and seconds later the two men heard her footsteps on the bare timber risers.

Doug was breathing heavily. Something about the last minute had scared him badly, some facet of Gemma's sleep-talking sat all wrong with what was happening, what they were going through.

"Well, I bought her a dinosaur book," he said. "All kids like dinosaurs, but I'm sure... well, that was pretty detailed."

"Like I said, bright girl."

"We're all going to die, aren't we?" Doug said. "You, me, Lucy-Anne... Gemma."

"Of course," Peter nodded. "Nothing we can do about it. But we have some time, don't know how much but there's some. How about we make it the best we can?" He smiled and poured Doug another drink. "Here. Been saving this for a special day."

"End of the world?"

The old man surprised him by laughing out loud. "The end of the world. Hell yes, why not? Might as well enjoy it before those damn little robots get their grubby mitts on it."

The two men drank to that.

"Sun's coming up," Doug said after a couple of minutes. "Today will be the day, I reckon."

"We'll go for a walk," Peter said suddenly. "I have a large estate, you know. A herd of deer, a lake, and a walk up into the mountains that you'd kill for. It'll be wondrous. I'll do a lunch for us. I bake my own bread; you'll faint with delight when you taste it, it's simply heavenly. And I'll even take a few bottles of wine I've been—"

"Saving for a suitable occasion?"

Peter nodded. "Absolutely. A suitable occasion. You'll see, we'll have a fine day. We'll watch the sunset from the mountains. And if it's not the sunset we get to see... well, we'll watch the other from up there. I imagine from what I've heard about it, it will be quite a sight."

"Reality being unmade before our eyes. All matter unstitched. Quite a sight, yes."

"Ah, yes." Peter sat back in his huge chair and steepled his fingers, peering between the arches.

Doug wondered what he saw. "You're enjoying this."

"I suppose I am. Not the circumstances, mind. Just... well, having you here."

"I thought you didn't like people."

Peter looked surprised for a moment, then lowered his eyes slightly. It was the only time Doug ever saw a hint of humility or shame in the old man. "Well, generally maybe... but it's different. You're my folk. And as I said, I knew some of my folk would turn up here sooner or later."

He raised his glass, and the new sunlight streaming through the windows set the liquid aflame.

Before they left the house Peter found Doug in the downstairs bathroom, trying to contact someone on his mobile phone. They'd already tried the TV that morning... a blank screen and an endless repetition of *God Save The Queen*.

"Selling your shares?" The old man smiled.

Doug could only stare at him for a few seconds, trying to see whatever was behind the joke. "Well actually, I have a couple of friends living in Newcastle. I thought I'd... try them. See if they're still there."

"Any reply?"

"No. No, none. Line must be down, or maybe they're working

on it. Or something."

Peter stared back, chewing his bottom lip for a few seconds, obviously turning something over in his mind before he said it. Then he put his hands on Doug's shoulders and drew him close, so close that their noses were almost touching. When he spoke, Doug smelled Brandy and tobacco. It was a sweet smell, lively, not at all unpleasant. It inspired a surprising nostalgia for his long-dead grandfather.

"Doug," the old man said, "let it go. We'll likely be dead before sunset, all of us, and there's absolutely nothing you, me or anyone can do about it. And the crazy thing is... it doesn't matter."

"How do you figure that?" Doug said, anger rising like the sun in his chest. "Why doesn't it matter that my wife and my daughter are about to die?"

"*Everyone* is going to die. *Everything* is being ruined. Within a day or two, there will be nothing left of the surface of this planet, just a sea of mindless, voracious mini-robots. Nothing animal, mineral, metal. And when there's nothing left for them to destroy, I guess they start to take each other apart, reconstruct, take apart again. Everything will be pointless, forgotten, and the only physical thing left of humanity will be a few space probes wandering the stars and a century's worth of radio and TV transmissions winging their way into deep space. Nobody to grieve, nobody to remember, nobody to miss us. It will be like we've never even existed. Nothing... will... matter."

He squeezed Doug's shoulders as if trying to knead the truth into his unwilling muscles.

Doug stepped to the window, pulled the net curtain aside and stared out at the rising sun. It seemed bigger than usual, redder, and as he glanced away he retained its image on his retinas. Looking at the hillsides, the forests and the sloping moorland leading up into the mountains, the sun's red afterimage touched them all.

It was a beautiful sunrise, maybe because it was one of the first that Doug had ever truly taken note of. It could be that dust in the air further south — dust, or those things — was catching the sunlight and spreading it across the sky, breaking up its colors and splashing an artist's palette of light over the lowlands. But if this were the case, then it was a gift from the end of the world. There was no way he could refuse it.

He thought about what Peter had said. He didn't agree with him — he thought that everything mattered now more than ever, because love was still here even when hope was not — and then he turned back to the old man.

"Well we can't let it beat us, I suppose."

Peter nodded.

Doug smiled back, pleased at the compromise he had made.

They circled around the back of the house and headed toward the forest smothering the lower hills. Peter carried a rucksack bulging with fresh bread and choice cuts from his fridge. Lucy-Anne shouldered another bag which clinked as she walked.

Doug carried Gemma. He sang softly, enjoying the look of contentment and happiness on her face, loving the way the corners of her mouth turned up whenever he spoke, as he had always loved it. There was nothing more wonderful in the world than seeing his daughter smile when she saw him. It told him that he was doing all the right things.

"All right sweetie?" he asked quietly.

She planted a kiss on his cheek, leaned back and smiled at him. "Yes thanks, Daddy. You can let me down now, I'd like to walk."

"It's a long way."

She shrugged, looked up into the blue sky. "I don't care. It's a nice day for a walk. It's good for you, anyway."

He stopped and lowered Gemma to the ground. She hurried away and his vision blurred, the tears came, but he fought them back. If she saw him crying, her final day would be an unhappy one. He could never do that to her, no matter what Peter said, however sure he was that nothing mattered anymore. He could never hurt his baby.

Soon they were in the woods. Peter pointed out dozens of species of flower and heather to Gemma, who nodded attentively and smelled the blooms and prickled her fingers on the heathers, laughing. Lucy-Anne fell into step with Doug and held his hand, saying nothing. Their touch was communication enough, every slight squeeze of fingers or palm sending message of love, companionship and comfort back and forth. It made him happy.

Squirrels leapt from branch to branch, flashes of wondrous red. Birds sang from high in the trees, and occasionally fluttered around below the cover, snatching morsels from the ground or simply singing their unknowable songs.

Twenty minutes after leaving the house Doug shuffled the mobile phone from his pocket and dropped it as he walked. He did not worry about littering. And he felt no parting pangs.

Newcastle was only two hundred miles away.

"There used to be gold in these here hills," Peter called out from where he had walked on ahead. "Even did a bit of prospecting myself. Swilled sediment around in a pan for weeks on end, anyway."

"Did you find anything?" Lucy-Anne asked.

"Not a sliver, a filing or a nugget. But it was a nice few weeks, I'd take lunch with me and a good book, spend the whole day out in the wild and get back just before it was dark enough to get lost." He had stopped, and stood staring through the last of the trees at the hillside looming above them, hands on his hips, shoulders rising and falling as he struggled for breath.

He was an old man, Doug kept having to remind himself. They were walking too fast, rushing to get from here to there, wherever here and there were, because of what would take them soon. "We should slow down," he said. "There's no hurry."

Lucy-Anne glanced at him and smiled, her eyes glittering with tears she would never cry.

"Strange how some metals are so valuable," Peter continued, in a world of his own. "Strange how we're so ignorant, we think we can classify the importance of all the things that go to make the world. Rock, now. Rock. *That* should be the most valuable. Holds it all together, after all."

"I thought gravity did that," Doug mumbled.

"Lithium is the lightest metal there is," Gemma said. She had been skipping along in front of them, pausing occasionally to bend down and stare at a flower or a rock of some crawling thing. Now she became still, and as she looked up into the sky — there was nothing there to see, nothing but blue — she continued. Her voice was the voice Doug had always known, but her words, her tone, her knowledge was pure mystery.

"It floats on water, has a specific gravity of nought-point-five-seven. Relative atomic mass six-point-nine-four-one. It's used in batteries, and its compounds can be employed to treat manic depression. It was named in eighteen-eighteen by Jons Berzelius." She sat down heavily and leaned forward, her head resting between her knees, talking at the ground. "But of course, it was his student Arfwedson who actually discovered it."

Then she was sick.

"What the hell was that?" Doug called. "Eh? Peter? What was that?" He ran to his little girl as he shouted, barely wondering why he expected the old man to know what Gemma was talking about.

Lucy-Anne reached her first and scooped her up, ignoring the spatter of sick that fell across her front. "Honey?" she said. "You okay? You feel okay?"

"Headache," Gemma said weakly, her face buried in her mother's neck.

Doug reached them and stood behind Lucy-Anne, smoothing damp hair from Gemma's pale face. She was sweating; drips of it ran down and pooled darkly on Lucy-Anne's shirt, and she stank of vomit.

Yesterday dinosaurs, today lithium, Doug thought. Hell, I know nothing about lithium. Is this what they teach kids in primary school nowadays?

Peter strolled back to them, concern creasing his brow. "What was that she said?" he asked.

"Does it matter? She's ill." Lucy-Anne was angry, Doug could tell that the moment she spoke, but she did not wish to reveal it to her old uncle.

Peter, however, was wise behind that crazy beard. "Sorry Lucy-Anne. Thoughtless of me. It's just... well, you've a very bright girl there."

"Research into nanotechnology began in the early '80s," Gemma mumbled. "And there were lots of scientists convinced — "

"Gemma," Doug said, confused and afraid and upset. It was not his daughter saying these things, not the Gemma he knew, the little girl who loved the Teletubbies and Winnie the Pooh and riding her tricycle and helping him dig the garden, so long as he moved all the worms out of the way because they were icky.

This was not her.

"Wait, leave her, listen," Peter said.

" — that it would be the new engineering. The Japanese created the first robots small enough to travel through veins, shredding fatty deposits or cancerous cells. The AT&T Bell laboratories in New Jersey constructed gears smaller in diameter than a human hair, and an electric motor a tenth of a millimeter across was built... and then it went top secret, and the various bodies involved started turning the positive research to more warlike ends." There was a pause, just long enough to mark a change of tone. "As always, Man is distinguished only by his foolishness, and nothing good can come of him."

"Gemma, please honey...." Lucy-Anne said, and there was such a note of helplessness in her voice that it froze them all, for just a second or two.

Then Gemma whined, cried for a few seconds more and fell asleep.

They could not wake her.

Doug and Lucy-Anne refused to leave her side, so Peter hurried away and soaked his shirt in a nearby stream. He squeezed it over Gemma's face as Doug held her in his arms. The water splashed on her skin, ran across her closed eyelids — they were twitching as her eyes rolled behind them — and they even forced some of it between her lips.

But Gemma would not wake up.

"We have to go back," Lucy-Anne said. "Get her to bed, make her warm." Her voice cracked as she spoke, and Doug could see the truth of their situation in her eyes even as her mouth tried to deny it.

"You know there's no point, honey," he said carefully. "By the time we get back to the house it'll be lunchtime, and I doubt we'll set out again before... the end of the day. And..." He looked up at Peter where he stood a little distance away, giving the family the space he assumed they needed. "Well, Gemma will be as comfortable up in the hills as she will in some bed hidden away indoors."

Lucy-Anne's mouth pursed tightly as she held back tears. "I wanted her to be awake when we died," she said quietly. "Is that selfish of me?"

Doug felt his face burning and his nose tingling as tears came. He had been thinking the same thing. "We'll be together," he said, "whether she's awake or asleep."

"What was she saying?" Peter asked quietly. "About the nanos? She was talking about the nanos, wasn't she? Have there been programs on television, documentaries, news items? Never watch it myself, but it seems to me that was all pretty technical for a pretty little girl like Gemma."

"It wasn't her talking," Doug said, and he hugged her tight to his chest. She was warm and twitching slightly in his arms. Her eyelids flexed as her eyes rolled. He looked up at Peter. "Can we go now?"

Peter frowned and wanted to say more, Doug could see that. But the old man nodded and smiled, and waved them onward. "You carry her for now," he said to Doug. "I'll take her from you when you get tired."

"And then I'll have her," Lucy-Anne said. She stayed close to Doug, reaching out every few steps to stroke her daughter's hair or touch her husband's face.

The going was more difficult, the hillside becoming steeper as they emerged from the forest, but the views did much to alleviate the pain Doug was already feeling in his back and legs. His daughter might only be small, but asleep like this she was a dead weight. Dead people are heavier, he seemed to remember reading somewhere, and the thought chilled him. But then he almost smiled. When they died, they would weigh nothing at all.

"Lovely view of the house and gardens from about here," Peter said, letting them pause and look back down the way they had come.

Doug lowered his daughter to the ground. She groaned slightly, mumbled something, but he didn't try too hard to hear what it was. He was afraid it would be something he did not wish to know.

Peter was right. The forest coated the hillside way down into the valley, and at its edge sat his house, its grounds and the winding driveway leading down to the road. Thankfully the animals and gargoyles were well hidden from this distance, so the scene took on a sense of magnificence and innocence, untainted by an old man's paranoid foibles. It was also possible too to see just how isolated this place was. Roads crisscrossed the countryside here and there, but the patchwork of fields which Doug was used to in the more farm-oriented lands to the south was all but absent here. The land was retained entirely by nature.

"I'll take a turn now," Peter said, stooping to scoop Gemma into his arms.

"Peter, come on, you're not the young man you used to be." Doug reached out and tried to take Gemma from his arms, but the old man's expression was one of such hurt that he stepped back and raised his hands in supplication. "Just don't overdo it, " Doug said. "I can't see me and Lucy-Anne carrying the both of you."

They continued uphill, Doug and Lucy-Anne walking either side of Peter so that they could constantly touch their daughter, hold her hand, chatter away in an attempt to wake her up.

"How much further?" Lucy-Anne asked after another few minutes.

"We've no destination," Peter said. "Tell me when you're happy to stop, and we'll stop."

She nodded. "I want to walk forever. If another footstep will give us another second, I want to keep walking."

Doug knew what she meant, but he was also aware that she was not serious. They could fight for another few seconds, or they could sit and talk and eat a final meal, drink a last glass of wine.

He would never make love to his wife again; never feel her sigh on his cheek as she came; never have a play-fight with her while Gemma attacked them both with her array of teddy bears; never eat a TV dinner; never swim from a sun-drenched beach out to a yacht; never appreciate a good painting, a thrilling book, an evocative piece of music... he would never hear music again....

Doug lived for music.

"Here," he said. "We stop here. We'll live what we can here, there's no point going any higher or any further." He gave Lucy-Anne a hug and kissed her neck.

Peter eased Gemma to the ground, stood and flexed his back, groaning and cursing. "Bright girl, maybe, but she's a heavy one too."

As if on cue, Gemma woke up and began to talk once more.

She told them about viroids, nucleic acid strands with no protein coating, and how they cause stunting in plants. She divulged the basics of chaos theory, especially relating to weather patterns and spread of infectious disease. Then after a pause she was back onto nanotechnology, and how the silicone-based technology had transmuted into a biology-based technology over the past few years. And how self-replicating nano-machines had been created, manmade viruses which had one major advantage over their natural counterparts: they could function perfectly well on their own. They consumed organic and inorganic materials alike, breaking them down, rearranging their constituent parts, creating more of themselves. They did not need a host to replicate.

And they were unstoppable.

Peter opened a bottle of wine and poured three glasses, but only he drank. Doug and Lucy-Anne tried to quieten their daughter, but Gemma only waved them away, told them she was fine and then continued her bizarre monologue.

And the strangest thing was, her eyes were sparkling as she spoke, her hands formed shapes in the air as she illustrated her thoughts and ideas, and she smiled as she revealed another complex truth. It *was* her talking, Doug realized. It *was* Gemma saying these weird, wondrous things; his daughter, his little girl. It was not long before all three adults knew for sure what Doug had suspected all day: that Gemma had not known any of this before now.

She was learning and imparting at the same time.

"Gemma," Doug tried again, "how do you know all this? Who's telling you? Gemma, you're making Mummy and Daddy sad."

She stopped. Instantaneously, half-way through a series of equations that had lost the adults the moment she had begun reciting them. She looked at Doug, and behind her enthusiastic face he saw his tired, scared daughter. "I don't want to make you sad, Daddy. I really don't. But some things have to be said."

She looked away again, facing south, as if challenging their approaching doom with examples of what humanity had achieved and learned in its too-brief time on the planet. The fact that the doom was a fruit of humanity's misdirected labors did not matter any more than the cause of wind or the sound of clouds mattered. "There's nobody else to say them," she whispered. And then she started again.

The association of reflex points on the feet and remote organic functions....

Fractionation, and how liquid air can be divided into its component parts at minus one hundred and ninety-six degrees centigrade....

Brownian movement, and from there Einstein, and from there the unified field theory, and then superstrings and the theory of everything....

"Make her stop!" Lucy-Anne shouted, standing up and walking away. Her glass spilled red wine into the earth. "Please, Doug," she said, without turning around, "just bring our daughter back for a while."

Doug remembered a time a couple of years before when Gemma went through a short stage of waking in the night, screaming. It was only a week or so, but the sound of her scream was terrifying, and after the first night neither of them slept at all until it ended as suddenly as it had begun. And when they asked her what was wrong she could only say *The moon, Daddy, the moon was in my room and it was* cringing *at me.* He had never really understood what she was afraid of, not then, because the moon was a familiar thing, and the man in the moon was something she loved.

Now, he thought he could see what had disturbed her during those few frantic nights. The man in the moon was something she had known from her storybooks, but that same man *cringing* at her was something new entirely, something threatening and unpleasant and secret, a bastardization of what she had once known.

And that was why Doug felt like he did now. With death approaching, his daughter scared him because she was acting as she never had before. She was still Gemma, but she was a *strange* Gemma.

He would not have time to come to terms with this new strangeness. He would have to live with it, and die with it.

"She's trying to tell us something," Peter said.

"Huh?" Doug could not look away from his daughter. If he did, something might happen.

"Gemma is trying to tell us something. She's imparting information… ideas, theories, histories… she's throwing a jigsaw at us and asking us to complete it." He was becoming more animated now, standing up, pacing as he drank and thought. His expression was wide and frank, not narrow and sardonic as usual.

Doug shook his head. "Peter, she's terrified. She's seen people dying on TV in the last couple of days, she saw… she saw a bunch of men raping women in the road. I don't think Lucy-Anne covered her eyes quickly enough…." He trailed off. Lucy-Anne was coming back, wringing her hands, sitting next to Gemma and trying to soothe her out of whatever hyperactive trance she was in.

Peter glugged another glassful of wine and gave himself a refill. "It's like she's reliving the life of humanity in the face of its end. Flashing our collective memories in front of us before we drown."

"She's just rehashing stuff she's heard."

"You know that's wrong, Doug. Don't you?" Peter held out his hand as if offering some invisible truth. "It may be incredible, but what's more incredible than the here and now?"

Doug looked away from Gemma and felt something lift from his shoulders, some strange weight of responsibility, as if the old man's words had convinced him that none of this was his fault. He closed his eyes and breathed in deeply, smelling the wine Lucy-Anne had spilled.

"So what is she trying to say?" He thought to humor Peter, but as he spoke he realized he was curious. And, perhaps, there was a spark of truth in the old man's mad words.

Peter shrugged, but he was twitchy now, more animated than before. "I don't know. That there's hope, perhaps? A way to stop all this?"

Doug barked a short, bitter laugh. "And we'll be able to do it, will we?"

Peter frowned, then shook his head. He stared down the valley to the south where somewhere over the horizon past, present and future was being nulled. "Of course not. But it would be one bitter irony, wouldn't it?"

That made them go quiet, all except for Gemma. *One bitter irony*, Doug thought. *Oh yes indeed.*

He looked at Gemma, listened to what she was saying and tried so hard not to find sense in any of it.

It did not work. He found sense. They all did.

Gemma fell back into an uneasy trance, but she never stopped talking. Even as she slouched down into Lucy-Anne's arms and her head drooped to one side, the endless monologue continued, spewed out like good breath fleeing bad flesh. A few birds landed in a nearby tree and twittered and cocked their heads, perhaps listening, perhaps not. And what would they hear, Doug thought? Unknowable banter, or unbearable truths? Because wherever Gemma was recalling all this from... or reciting it... it was beginning to hurt.

She knew what was happening, that was what became apparent soon after she lost consciousness again. Most of what she had been saying over the last hour or so — the superstring theories, freezing air, viroids — all formed some small part of a larger plan that was coalescing, slowly, in the air around her. If the hillsides could echo all her words at once, perhaps it would form something that he and Peter and Lucy-Anne could understand, but as it was there was truly nothing they could do. They all heard the desperate intent in Gemma's voice... a painful thing to hear in a girl so young, so innocent... but none of them could move upon it.

They felt more powerless than they ever had before.

"There must be something," Peter said to no one in particular, opening a second bottle of wine and seeking truth and solace in the grape. "There just must be something we can do."

"Dare we hope?" Lucy-Anne said. "Really, Doug? Dare we hope?"

He hated himself for thinking her foolish, and he hated all of them for being so ineffectual. He hated, most of all, the pointless information they were being subjected to. Why them, here and now? Why not someone who could do something with it?

"Because there's no one else left," he said quietly.

"Hmm?" Peter raised an eyebrow past another glass of wine

"I said there's no one else left," Doug said. "Gemma's telling us all there is to know because there's no one else to tell. What did you say, Peter? We're living all humanity's knowledge in one go, like a drowning man?"

Peter kicked at the loamy ground as he replied. "Well, I only meant it... you know, metaphorically. There must be someone else, someone who can do something with this...."

"No, you meant it. You did. You believed it when you said it."

"How does this help us?" Lucy-Anne said, staring down at Gemma where she twitched and mumbled in her lap. "How does this give us hope?"

Doug stood and walked to his wife and child, sitting behind them so that he could hug them both close to him. "It doesn't."

In the distance, way down the valley, a heavy mist seemed to be forming out of the daylight.

"It doesn't help us, honey. We're beyond help. We've given evolution a helping hand and nudged ourselves away."

Lucy-Anne shook her head, twisting from beneath his arm so that she could look at him. "No, Doug. Peter? He's wrong isn't he?"

Peter came to them as well, but he did not reach out to touch them. He sat calmly to one side, content at last. "Maybe the truth is, knowledge can never be its own undoing. We're not being teased, we're being taught, right up to the last. Our questing mind goes on, even when nothing matters anymore. That's good enough." He smiled, drank another glass of wine. "Ahh. A fine year. Whatever year it was, a fine year."

The mist had moved quickly up the valley, and now Doug could see that it was actually dark and thick, like a brown soup churning through the air, consuming everything it touched. Nearer, as close to them as Peter's house, birds dropped from the sky, flowers shed petals, leaves fell from trees as the nanos commenced their senseless, programmed task of deconstruction. And every leaf that fell, every bird that was taken apart, soon gave up its component parts to make more of them.

Gemma woke again and sat upright, turning to look at her parents and her great-uncle. "It would have been so easy," she said sadly. "The answers were all there, if we'd only had the will to help ourselves."

"Come here," Doug said, and she hunched herself into his hug, wrapping her arms around her mother's waist at the same time.

Light began to fade and a strange hissing sound drowned out the birds and the breeze, like a trillion grains of sand dancing in the air.

Doug's sight faded, his skin itched, his insides turned warm. He went to tell his family he loved them, but he could no longer speak. His muscles still worked, though, for the moment, and so he hugged them. They hugged him back.

At least they would all be together in the end.

Mannequin Man and the Plastic Bitch

She was a dream. He had imagined her once, he was sure, and as she lowered herself and began grinding her hips Tom had that sense of déjà vu again. He licked at her vulva and stroked her arse and she pushed down... and he thought that in the dream she would be dancing, not fucking. Or maybe it was that elusive dance of love.

He had paid for his troubles to be taken away, soothed and suckled and swallowed by this plastic bitch. Within a few minutes they'd been bearing down heavier than ever before, because he'd experienced that which he'd never believed in, thought existed only in songs and poems and his own warped mind... love at first sight.

Stupid, naïve, and utterly impossible. She probably had a dozen men every day telling her they loved her, and maybe once or twice in her life she'd actually believed. But none of them really *did* love her, or ever could. Love a whore? Love a plastic bitch?

Stupid.

"Love you," Tom said, but his words were stolen by her pussy pressing into his mouth. He told her with his tongue instead, a gentle touch as if he were eating the dish of his life. She let slip a small squeal of pleasure.

None of them had ever done that with him before.

He paused, she stopped sucking him, and they lay there for a few seconds looking at each others' sex and wondering what was happening.

And then they started again... but it was different. There was a tenderness that hadn't been there before. Tom lost his sense of desperation — he didn't *have* to come, not just yet — and she started taking her time. It became a pleasure, instead of simply a transaction.

"Love you," he said again, careful this time to pull away so that she couldn't help but hear.

There was no reaction. Tom gazed at her goose-pimpled buttocks, the sweet crack pouting at him from between them, and suddenly he wanted to shrug her off, turn her around and kiss her.

But kissing was never allowed. Too many viruses were targeted orally.

"I love you," he said again, trying to force her off. In his naïveté he thought that showing her she didn't *have* to suck him would set him apart in her mind. But when he flipped her over her stare was as hard as before, her mouth firmly set. Her eyes, though… there was a depth there that had been absent when he'd first entered the room.

She sat beside him on the bed, staring.

"What's happening?" Tom said, because something was. The whore shook her head, but there was doubt in the way she hesitated, doubt or confusion.

She — Honey, she'd told him her name was Honey — reached out and grabbed his dick, squeezing and kneading it like a cow's teat. He couldn't lose his hard-on, much as he believed this to be so much more than sex, and when she lowered her head and started sucking he sat back and closed his eyes.

Wondering what was going on.

Thinking of the women, genuine or artificial, he'd thought he could love.

Realizing here and now that this was, in reality, the one and only time.

He came, and when the pleasure had passed and he looked down he thought he'd sprayed across her face. But then he saw that the moisture on her cheeks was tears.

She smiled and wiped her mouth. There was no hate in her eyes.

That, at least, was a start.

"What do you like?" Tom asked.

"I'm not allowed to like anything."

He smiled. "Yes… but what *do* you like?"

She looked at him so long and hard that he thought she'd malfunctioned. But then she let the ghost of a smile touch her features. "You're talking as if we're on a date."

"We are, aren't we?"

"How much did Hot Chocolate Bob charge you for this?"

He thought of the slimy, drugged-up pimp he'd negotiated with on the street. "Two hundred." Realizing he'd forgotten to do it, he plucked a credit card from his pocket and offered it to Honey.

She nodded her head slightly and glanced over his shoulder at the wall clock. "Then for another seventeen minutes yeah, we're on a date."

"So…?"

She took the card, tapped in the amount and scanned it. She should have shown him first so that he knew he wasn't being swindled, but he trusted her. Stupid of him, blind, but he trusted her.

"Isn't it a bit late to ask me?" Honey said. "You get your kicks out of knowing what you missed?"

"Sorry?" He frowned, genuinely puzzled.

Honey smiled again as she handed back his card. "I like it from behind so I don't have to see the customer's face. I like it up the arse. It gives my snatch a break. I like it fast, that way I don't have to pretend — "

"You weren't pretending just then."

She shrugged. "Sometimes it feels okay."

"Don't believe you. *Sometimes*? How often?"

Honey didn't answer. The silence hung heavy and awkward until Tom spoke again.

"Anyway, I didn't mean sex. I meant *everything*. What do you like? Whether it's permitted by your pimp or not, you must have your likes and dislikes. You must have enough life for that, at least?"

Honey looked down at her feet, stretching her toes. She was still naked, but it didn't seem to bother her in the slightest. Then she looked up at Tom through her golden fringe. The image was so shy and lonely that he wanted to take her in his arms, buy her, get her the hell out of here forever.

Trouble was, there were no places to go.

"I like dancing," she said. "There's a club three floors down in the basement, and sometimes if I'm having a slow night I'll dance to the music."

"On your own?"

"Of course on my own. The music's torn apart by the time it gets up here, gutted by the floors and rooms between us, but I still get the beat. Sometimes I can even identify the songs." She looked away from him, out the window. It was still daytime but heavy smog made it twilight. The sodium street lamps fell like moonlight on her face. "I like the slow ones."

"I can't dance," Tom said, full of regret, wanting so much to be able to hold her for his remaining twelve minutes, pirouette around the room, jive into true love.

"I'll teach you," Honey said, and then she frowned, stood, walked to the dressing table and lit a cigarette. Confused. Perhaps not knowing what she'd said, nor understanding why.

"What else?" he asked, rescuing her. He looked at her naked back, buttocks and legs, imagining that he knew the geography of her already, was able to go there and touch her exactly how she liked to be touched, and where, and for how long.

"Finger puppets." She blew smoke and smiled. "I love finger puppets. The more intricate the better. There's a Chinese guy down the street. Lunchtimes he brings out this wooden box, sits behind it and puts on a puppet show. He doesn't try to hide or pretend it's not him doing it, but it doesn't matter, because his fingers have such sweet movement. He dances and fights them across that box, and for a few minutes it's another world, more imagined than any netcast or movie. He touches you, that guy." She paused for a while, turned to look at him. "Or rather, the finger puppets touch you. He just moves them. For a while they have a life of their own."

Tom was caught up in her eyes. She looked happy, and he was glad that he'd brought it on by asking questions.

She spoiled the moment by glancing at the clock again, but he persisted.

"Anything else?"

"I like being held. That's all. Just held. After some of the things that have been done to me...." She trailed off, running her fingers along a white scar across her belly. Tom had thought it was a poorly done repair job when he'd seen it earlier, but now it was something worse. Far worse.

"Have you ever been in love?"

"I'm a whore. An artificial, a plastic bitch. I'm incapable."

"I'll bet you're incapable of *enjoying* anything, either. Like finger puppets and dancing and being held."

Honey lit another cigarette.

"Can I hold you?" he said.

She sat on the bed next to him, crossing her legs demurely, folding her arms and hiding her breasts. It gave her such a sense of innocence that a lump came to Tom's throat.

"Only... I can't dance. And I left my puppets at home."

Honey looked at the clock. "You can hold me for six minutes."

"Longer," Tom said, shuffling over and wrapping Honey in his arms. It was awkward at first — strange, after what they had been doing, that a simple touch could feel so clumsy — but after a minute it got better. The tension in Honey's muscles drained away, her head dipped onto Tom's shoulder, she dropped her cigarette and sighed heavily. "Longer," he said again.

"Three more minutes."

"Honey…." He hated that she was still clock-watching. He knew that all this wasn't just a part of the act, another twenty dollars-worth, because he could feel the heat of her skin and the coolness of tears on his chest. Something had happened, removing the sex from this moment and replaced it with something far, far more.

Tom knew that Honey had not been designed for that.

"I want to stay like this forever," she said, and it was like a punch to Tom's chest. "Forever. But you saw Hot Chocolate Bob. You… don't know what he's like. You just can't imagine." She lifted her head to look at him. "If we're five minutes over he'll be up here. He'll kick you out, or worse, and as for me…."

"What? What?" Tom didn't want to know what the pimp would do, but he thought that knowing would take some of her hurt and bleed it into him.

"Us plastics are quite hardy," Honey said. "We can take a lot of beating."

"Part of the design," Tom said bitterly.

"Part of the design. Warriors and whores. Need to take abuse."

"Come with me!" he gushed, realizing how foolish this sounded. An hour ago he'd paid some pimp for a fuck with a random whore, and now he was asking her to run away with him, *be* with him. Foolish, but it felt *so right*.

"Don't be stupid," Honey said.

Tom felt defeated, lost. And stupid. "I'm sorry." He'd come in this artificial whore's mouth, and he thought that gave him the right to tell her he loved her. *Stupid*.

But he *did*.

"Do you mean it?" Honey said, after a long pause.

"What?"

"What you said earlier. Do you mean it? I've heard it a million times before, but I've never had cause to believe."

"Come with me and give me a chance to show you."

She was silent again, staring at him, and Tom felt as though he was being appraised inside and out. Could she see inside? he wondered. Could she penetrate to the deepest parts of him, the secret centers where even he did not hold reign?

"I'd risk everything," she said. Tom wasn't sure whether it was a statement of fact or intent.

"Then come— "

"I can't, not now. Kiss me."

Tom leaned forward and kissed Honey, and she tasted of her name. Smoke and cheap food and himself, she tasted of that too, but it was all sweet. He held her head and pulled her to him, kissing her, his eyes closed, the skin of his palms and fingers tingling where he touched her skin.

She pulled away at last. Her eyes were wide and moist, her breathing fast. She glanced at the clock. "Time's up."

Tom sighed heavily, wondering what to say. He was running out of time and needed a plan, but his brain didn't function. He shook his head angrily, furious at himself, unsure of where the fury came from.

And then Honey saved him.

"Tomorrow," she said. "Lunchtime. I'll stay here instead of going down the street for food. There's a back door, down an alley next to Hell's Bookstore on Ashley Street. You know it?"

"I'll find it."

"Come here then. And take me away."

"You're sure, you believe me, you're sure?" Tom gushed, stumbling over own thoughts.

There were footsteps on the landing outside the door, and the handle rattled.

"Go!" Honey said. And in an instant she was a ragged, hard whore once more, a plastic bitch built for sex and sucking and little more, sitting back with her legs splayed and another cigarette in her hand. Tom despised the transformation, and he suddenly wondered whether she'd been kidding him all along. The doubt was reinforced when he tried to discern hope in her eyes: there was nothing there. Only a vagueness, a vacancy, waiting to be pumped full of the desires and fantasies of her next client.

" 'The *fuck*?" a voice said from behind him. "*Time's up, shithead.*"

Tom turned around, and Hot Chocolate Bob stood in the doorway.

"I was just leaving."

"Best you do. Got a lawyer outside, real slimy type, top dog, criminal defence, ready to stick it in Honey's ass. Like that, don't you Honey?" He grinned as he spoke, and the paleness of his skin was countered by his black, rotten teeth. He was bald, no eyebrows or facial hair, and his eyes were networks of broken veins. Tom wondered which drugs he did. Probably all of them.

"You know I do, Hot Chocolate Bob." Her voice was low and

sultry. It dripped sex.

Tom didn't want to turn around and see Honey like this. He looked at the pimp instead and felt his rage building, percolating through the layers of apathy he'd drawn around himself over the years and filling him with energy.

"Out. Now." The pimp wasn't joking. Tom could see the bulge of a piece on his belt and his eyes glittered like loose diamonds, the sign of a military-level optical chop. If he'd had his eyes done he'd likely had other stuff as well, and Tom had no desire to mix it with him right now.

Later, maybe.

But not now.

"'Bye sweetie," Honey called mockingly as he passed the pimp at the door. "Your juice tasted good, Honey wants more, come back soon."

He needed to turn around and see her one more time. Just in case he was wrong. Just in case she'd lied. But the pimp had pushed past him into the room, and the two of them were muttering together like lovers, and there were wet sounds that Tom didn't wish to know.

"... like it like that...." Honey said.

Tom hurried away from the room, passed a dozen more just like it, and walked quickly outside to find escape.

The sun was setting by the time he approached his street, and the night people were out. It was as if the dusk dictated style: the roads heading into town filled, and the people almost all wore black. A dark tide of humanity flowed into the city, accompanied by the clinking of chains, the buzzing of zips, the musical tinkling of jewelry, visible or otherwise. Some of the people had been professionally chopped — eight feet tall, three arms, four breasts, one guy with a huge dick swinging unhindered between his feet — but most had chosen merely to adapt themselves. Tattoos and piercings were the least of it. Amputations, scoops of flesh removed, dyed skins, divided penises, all manner of mutilation was at home in these crowds. Nothing was a surprise.

It made Tom wonder just where these people would go next.

He'd seen it all before, but it never ceased to fascinate him. That people should act like this — tear themselves apart, wound for pleasure or pleasure through pain — confused him. But sometimes, just sometimes, he wondered whether being artificial simply meant that he could never understand.

They were heading for the clubs. There were dozens in the city, most legal, a few not. They buzzed every night and bled every day, bled money to the law and literal blood from their cellars and other hidden "rooms." Tom had visited them a few times in his wanderings and he'd seen some things… some awful things. The nearest he came to these clubs now was the occasional visit to a brothel, and always, *always*, a brothel where the whores were artificials. After what he'd seen once or twice in club cellars he had no wish to know more of what people could and would do to themselves. And to each other.

Now, walking against the flow, his vision darkened by the sunset and the stares of those passing by, Tom felt doubt stabbing at him.

It was cruel, this doubt, because it was selective in what it recalled. He knew that Honey was beautiful, but try as he might he could not see her face. He could imagine her breasts, her thighs, her flat stomach and moist pussy, but her face eluded him. And her voice, that was gone too, swallowed along with the setting sun. *Like it like that.* He could remember the words but not the voice that had spoken them. He grabbed at his head, trying to save the memories. Hands over his ears to stop any more of her voice from escaping. Over his eyes, to hold her image in.

He walked into someone and felt the sharp sting of metal spikes picking at his clothes. The person shoved by before he had a chance to look properly, for which he was glad.

"Almost home," he said to himself.

"Home is for pussies," a voice mocked from the crowd, but Tom had no idea which of them had spoken.

He turned into his street, breathing a sigh of relief when the flow of black-clad people reduced to a trickle. He passed a final couple of leathered-up teenagers outside his house. The boy had a pierced tongue, the girl was bare breasted and frowning with the weight of chains connecting her nipples to her eyelids. They both smiled at Tom and nodded a polite greeting, the girl's breasts jiggling with the gesture. He knew their parents. He wondered if their parents knew them.

"Honey," he said as he palmed his doorlock. The flat was small and compact, big enough to live in but not too large to become unmanageable. "Honey, won't you tell me the truth?" Doubt again, buzzing at him like ghostly bees, flitting past his ears and eyes and mouth as he tried to remember her voice, her face, her taste. It felt as if she was a dream, fading away as the day wore on.

Would she be there for him? If he smuggled himself into that rank building tomorrow at lunchtime, would she be waiting with her bags packed, ready to run off with him and risk the wrath of that bastard Hot Chocolate Bob?

Tom doubted it. True, his existence felt different today. It was fresher, brighter; Honey had brought something in that had been missing or sought for so long. Not only love, but a sense of importance in himself. A sense of living, not just existing. The sun had seemed warmer and closer upon leaving the brothel, even through the smog. The streets were cleaner, the smiles more real, the adverts flashing across billboards less cynical and more concerned.

Yes, things felt so different.

But good things never happened to Tom. That's not the way his life was built, it wasn't how his hat had been put on. Bad things clung to him like shit to shoes.

Would she be there? He doubted it. But the very last thing he would do was not go, just to find out.

He listened to the sounds of the night, trying to perceive just how they were different tonight from the night before. There were sirens and shouts, drunken youths singing in the streets, buzzed artificials screaming as the bad charges slowly but surely cauterized their insides. At one point Tom heard gunshots from somewhere deep in the city.

By three in the morning he admitted defeat and left his bed. He logged onto the net and sat back, closing his eyes as he tried to find somewhere to go, a place that would be safe for Honey and him. It was a fantasy, of course, and he knew it. Dream tropical islands awash with happy-ever-after were not for her kind.

Not for him, either.

Later, as the sun smudged the smog in the east and turned it pink, Tom connected to the net point, closed his eyes and accessed his recharge site. He input the correct code, sat back and felt tiredness recede as his power cells gulped their fill.

Tom always watched the sunrise. However tired or run-down he was, he'd see the sun climb out of the industrialized eastern suburbs of the city and heave itself skyward on pollutant legs. It never failed to cheer him, however depressed he felt, and this morning it worked more than ever.

Because he was in love. *Love.* That elusive, haunting myth. The place he'd never thought he would be.

Love.

The Baker had finally done it, even if it had taken fifteen years to have effect. If only he were alive to see it now. Tom smiled and closed his eyes for a moment, remembering his old friend. And then he thought of Honey and opened his eyes again.

The morning washed last night's doubts away. Tom made himself some toast and sausages, drank a pint of orange juice, visited the toilet four times before the sun had cleared the chimneys and sprung free into the sky above the city. The smog was always dissipated in the morning. It was as if industry paid worship to the sun for the first hour of the day, and then when the main shifts began, worship turned to profit. The sun never seemed to mind. It came and went, came and went. It was the reservoirs and food chains and fields that were protesting, and strenuously. Tom was fortunate enough to be able to afford lab-grown food, but there were many who were not.

Honey, for one. What diseases could she have? What malfunctions waiting to happen, tumors biding their time, rots working away at her joints and flesh?

"I love her," Tom said, shaking his head to dispel the negative thoughts. And he said it again, because he liked the sound and feel of the word in his mouth.

The Baker had given him the virus of love fifteen years before. A clumsily written input program, Tom had actually felt it take root inside his head, spreading electron-tentacles, feeling its way into his artificial cortex and brain-stem... and then vanishing as it sought to establish itself fully. He'd never thought it would have taken so long. The Baker — Tom had never even known his real name, great friends though they were — would have been a happy man today.

He spent the next hour sitting at his window and looking out over the city. He hadn't found anywhere to flee to, but he was sure that they'd find a good place, a safe place. He had no idea of what to do if Hot Chocolate Bob confronted them in their escape, but he was confident that they could slip away unseen. The thought that Honey would have changed her mind — or, worse, had been playing with him all along — came once, and once only. He killed it. He chased it down into the pits of his mind, drowning it in other, more established forms of hopelessness and fear.

Totally unprepared, lightened by a love he had never been designed to feel, Tom set out just before noon to rescue the plastic bitch that had stolen his heart.

The change in the streets was as breathtaking as ever. Last night they had been flooded with people in black, a tide of leather and metal and mutilation with one single, enveloping thought: pleasure. It was as if that flow of people was a solitary organism, pushing through between buildings and parks and walls, penetrating the city to plant its thoughts and intentions, leaving the pale residue of hopelessness behind as dawn drove it away.

By morning, the streets belonged to the workers. People thronged the pavements and cars coughed their way along roads. Thousands flocked east towards the factories — those who could not afford monorail or tube tickets — with many more filtering into office buildings or sweatshops built in deep, cavernous basements. Steam hissed from manholes and there was the intermittent *thud* of accumulated gases burning off in the sewers. Something flew by just over Tom's head, and he saw the trailing heatstick of a policeman. The platform dipped and bobbed before accelerating away and disappearing down a side street, aiming to ruin someone's day.

Tom tried to keep himself to himself, which wasn't difficult. He was an artificial, and with so many people opting for body chopping he was camouflaged by normality. And he was dressed in the uniform of a factory worker, even though he did not work: the Baker had seen to it that he had enough money to want for nothing. So he blended in, becoming one of a crowd. A crowd that shed curiosity like water from oil.

It was not a long walk to the area of the city where Honey worked. Shops and offices gave way to boarded-up buildings and plain-fronted stores, many of them selling counterfeit produce and dealing drugs, or worse. Tom knew of several places down here where an artificial could buy a black market charge, and he began to see a few of them around. The worst of the buzzed people could barely walk, let alone see and talk. They screamed; there was always screaming. Illegal charges were like fake foodstuffs: they'd feel and taste the same, but eventually they tortured the body and polluted the mind, leading to a slow death.

The gangs were here as well. Some were all human, like the Draggers, renowned for tying perceived enemies to their cars with sharpened chains and driving at speed through the city. In turn there were the artificials' gangs, who rarely named themselves because identity was something they shunned. Rebellion was their cause, their drug, and most of them chose to get buzzed even if they *could* afford legitimate charges. The Draggers fought for money and turf and women and drugs. The artificials rebelled against creation. Such differences ensured that they rarely fought each other.

The gangs that *did* fight each other were the mixed ones. But daylight was their enemy, the night's exertions drained their energies, and for now Tom felt safe.

Three human Draggers hung around by a gambling emporium. They looked tired and drawn, pale from whatever they had taken the previous night, and they didn't even look as Tom passed by. He caught a whiff of drugs bleeding from their pores. Blessed with the gift of love and loving, how could these people demean themselves so?

But love and loving... that was something *he* had now! He looked up out of the concrete canyon and grinned at the hazy sun.

A burst of laughter brought him back.

The buildings fell back to reveal a small, shaded park, so boxed in by façades that only a weak, pale green grass grew. Hidden from the sun most of the time, the park was home to escaped pets and carrion birds. Tom had been here before but only once, and only at night. The sights he had seen had chased him away, the gutted dogs and bloated crows too fat to fly, too big and mean to tackle. Here was evolution aggravated and progress tainted.

Now, during the day, it was home to people having fun. They danced and jigged and laughed, and Tom tried to shrink into himself and move away quietly until he saw what the people were watching.

Here was the finger puppet man.

He sat crosslegged on the ground beside the stump of a long-dead tree. Before him was a wooden box, about the size and shape of a coffin. Along the length of the coffin, back and forth, up and down, danced the most fluid and lifelike puppets Tom had ever seen. They captivated him from that instant, drawing him into the crowd, pulling him through to the front, between hard shoulders and muttered curses from those he shoved aside. His view was better here, and all the more amazing for that.

The Chinaman sitting behind the box was impassive, expressionless. The only sign that he was even awake was the subtle twitching of his cheeks as his eyes shifted left and right to follow his finger performers. It looked for all the world as if the puppets were controlling the man, not the other way around.

Tom looked closely at their carved wooden faces, and he was sure he saw smiles directed at him.

A clock struck one o'clock somewhere unseen, and he realized suddenly that he had somewhere else to be.

He walked around the shaded park twice before he saw the sign for Ashley Street. It was a lane rather than a street, and an alley more than a lane, home to a few squat fast food shops, a couple of porn palaces and a chop shop that stank of blood and desperation. A couple of its regular clients hung around outside, bad advertising if ever Tom had seen it: the woman had no nose or eyelids, but bled profusely out of open veins above her eye sockets; the man displayed his mutilated genitalia, balls the size of footballs and a dick like a joint of uncooked pork.

"Need something doing?" the man asked.

"Leave him, he's a fake," the woman said, dismissing Tom with a bloody glare.

"Doesn't look like one."

Tom walked by, feeling their pained eyes on his back. They were wondering what he had, he knew. Secretly craving a look beneath his skin and flesh. Well... they'd be surprised. In a way he too was chopped. The Baker had seen to that.

He passed Hell's Bookshop and found the alley Honey had mentioned. Its walls were so close together that Tom's arms brushed them as he made his way along, stepping over a vagrant who may have been dead. Before him — the shadow at the end of the alley, a great wall of black concrete pointing at the pink sun — stood the whorehouse.

Tom was amazed to find the back door open. It wasn't as if such a salubrious establishment needed a rear entrance for shady patrons.

As he opened the door and a flush of smells came out at him — the tang of sex, old greasy cooking, smoke, drugs, the sparkle of ozone from an illegal charger somewhere — he realized that he had not yet seen Hot Chocolate Bob.

Not out on the street, working his patch.

Not down in the dead park watching the incredible puppeteer.

Which meant, very likely, that he was inside.

Tom closed the door behind him, but he made sure he knew where the handle was.

He thought he could remember where to find Honey's room. It was on the third floor, facing out onto the street. He hurried along the dark corridor, stepping on things that cracked or snapped and, in one case, squealed. He tried not to look down because he didn't want to see, didn't want anything to mar this moment, this occasion when he would do the most valiant thing of his life: rescue his love from the purgatory she had been created for, and which she endured still. Why she endured it he did not know. It was something he might ask her... one day.

He reached the stairs and quickly moved up towards the third floor. At each landing he sensed doors opening around him; just a crack, wide enough for the inhabitants to see out. A couple of times he heard a relieved sigh when they saw him walk past.

There were many sounds permeating the air, turning the dank stairwell into an echo-chamber for the whole building. A blasting television here; a whining drill there; the screams of a child from far along one refuse-strewn corridor; the grunting of sex; a soft mumble somewhere else; as if someone was trying to talk themselves out of this hellhole. And smells as well, even worse than those that had hit him upon opening the door. Shit, piss, cabbage, saliva, rotten food, death, spunk, cordite, smoke, drugs... very little good, hardly any sweet. Neither belonged here.

Honey was both, and her time in this place was now numbered in minutes.

Tom had found her door. He ran up the last flight of steps and stood before it, surprised at how nervous he felt, how terrified that she'd only mock him when he opened the door. She'd be sitting there with her legs open and her hand held out, ready to scan his card and take her ten measly percent.

"No," he said, shaking his head. "No. No. She's better than that. She meant it. No."

Someone pushed him from behind. He spun around to look into the wizened face of an old man, tall and angular where he had been chopped in an attempt to avert aging. "Yes," the old man said. "Yes. Don't torture yourself son, do it. She's sweeeettttttt!" His voice rose into a bird-like cackle. Tom leaned back against the door as the old man stumbled away along the corridor, laughing to himself and shrilling "Sweeetttt, sweeettttt!"

The door opened behind him and Tom stumbled into the room.

"Tom! *You came!*" And there was so much relief and joy in Honey's voice that Tom knew, beyond the shadow of a doubt, that the love was not his and his alone.

Here was hope. Here was trust. Here was the rest of his life.

Honey had caught him in her arms and he twisted around to kiss her.

"No time for that!" Honey said, kicking the door shut. "I thought you'd be here half an hour ago. Hot Chocolate Bob will be back anytime, he knew I wasn't going out, he'll be here to have me. We have to go. We have to go now!"

"Come on then!" Tom said. Honey had a rucksack over her shoulder, and today she wore no make-up. He didn't know how he could ever have forgotten her face. He saw her for what she really was and loved her more. Years of abuse with her face pressed into pillows and against walls had given her skin a pale sheen, but he had enough money to sort that out. He'd give her new skin. He'd give her anything.

"You're going to have to do something for me, Tom," Honey said. "It's the only way we'll get out." She swung the backpack his way and quickly stripped.

Tom went cold.

"You want me to — "

"If anyone sees me out of this room with you — *anyone* — they'll tell Bob. He'll be on us in seconds, and... I've seen him kill before, Tom. He wouldn't hesitate today."

"But it's so dangerous."

"I know. Tom... let me down. Turn me off, let me down and get me out of here."

Tom knew that this was a drastic step. Reinvigorating Honey would take hours, and he'd heard that half of the plastic artificials this was done to never came back. They weren't designed for this. It was like killing a human in the hope that they could be resuscitated.

She put her fingers into a fold beneath her left breast. Tom saw the muscles on her wrist tense. "I'll do it myself if you don't. But I want you to do it."

Honey removed her hand. Tom reached out and slipped his fingers inside the fleshy slit, felt her Christ valve — so named for its artificial powers of death and resurrection — and twisted it sharply to the right.

Honey gasped and slumped into Tom's arms. "I won't watch," he said. He closed his eyes and felt her wrinkling lips pass across his mouth, heard a hissing exhalation of love as her weight lessened. Folds of flesh hung over his arms, a warm rush ran down his legs as she voided herself, steam rose around him and stung his nostrils as he breathed in sharply....

And it was over so quickly.

He tried not to see Honey's flattened, lifeless face as he rolled her up and stuffed her and her clothes into the rucksack.

At every step, every landing, every corner in the staircase, he expected the pimp to be waiting for him. He would have no defence, no way to fight off such a person. Run or die, that was all. No bluffing, no pleading, no fighting... just running.

The stairwell didn't seem so dark on the way down, nor so pungent. Maybe it was because the sun had edged around and found a break in the smog, bathing the stairs in heat and light through a rooflight. Or perhaps it was simply because here he was, escaping this pit for the last time with the woman he loved over his shoulder.

The Baker had told him a few things he should look out for, but he had never explained exactly what love was, what it would do, how it could change the way Tom thought. He guessed that the old bastard could never have explained anyway, genius though he was, and so he had simply neglected to try.

Tom wished the old man could see him now.

At the bottom of the stairwell he headed along the narrow corridor towards the rear of the building. The door was still ajar — he could just see the slice of light in the gloom — and he had made it. He was there, he was out, and a flush of relief relaxed his muscles as he opened the door and stood facing Hot Chocolate Bob.

The pimp glared at him in comical surprise. He must have seen the guilt in Tom's face, the backpack over his shoulder and the fear in his eyes. "What the fuck?" said the pimp, slipping a silver gun from his belt at the same time and lifting it up towards Tom's face.

Tom used his head. Flipped forward as hard as he could, his artificial muscles writhing and knotting as he pumped them with adrenaline, Tom's forehead connected squarely with the pimp's nose. The sound was sickening. The pain and shock must have been dreadful, because the man didn't even scream as he sank to his knees and slipped down the slimy wall.

"Leave us alone," Tom said. "We're in love." He vaulted Hot Chocolate Bob's splayed legs, kicked the gun down the alley ahead of him and sprinted for Ashley Street. It only took a few seconds, but they were filled with so many thoughts that it felt like hours.

Most of them centered around whether the pimp carried more than one gun.

As he burst out in the street and angled left, Tom felt a foolish sense of elation. He may be away now, yes, but he'd made an enemy, a deadly enemy. From this moment on the city was no longer safe, could never be called home again... but the sun shone down on his adventure, laughter still came from the dead park at the end of the street, Honey's weight hugged his shoulder as if she had an arm draped there and he could smell her on him, *smell* her.

He wondered whether this place would become famous, just as Pudding Lane had in London. That's where the Baker had taken his name from. He'd said that he would be responsible for initiating a new Great Fire, but this one would be a conflagration of love.

Tom ran through the park, noticing that the Chinaman was still entertaining. There were fewer people watching him now but he seemed not to notice, so intent was he upon his little play. The finger puppets bobbed and weaved and stared. Tom wished he had time to stop, but danger loomed large and dark behind him, an almost palpable force that drove him on into the city.

He stopped running after a mile because he was drawing attention. Glancing around constantly, he was certain that he was not being followed. Enraged and bloodied, pride dented, Hot Chocolate Bob would certainly not be silent in his pursuit.

The midday lull was almost over and now the streets were buzzing again. Cars vied for space and ground against each other, coughing out exhaust fumes at pedestrians. Street performers were counting their lunchtime takings, many of them looking sad and despondent as they pocketed a few measly coins. Nobody looked at Tom. Nobody could know what he had in his rucksack.

He felt like a murderer. Honey may well be dead in there, a coiled, folded mess, a smashed egg with no hope of reconstruction. Each time he caught someone's eye he looked away guiltily, blushing with the obviousness of what he had done. Surely they could see it on his face? Surely they could discern the shape of her bulging the ruck-sack, smell her scent as Tom took her towards salvation or death?

But the streets stank of rot and smog and fast food. And anyone who did look at Tom seemed to look away just as quickly as he.

It had always been a city full of secrets.

The sense of threat behind him drove him on. He would have to go back to his flat for a while — Honey's state now made things much more complicated — but he didn't want to stay there for long. Hot Chocolate Bob could know anyone, and it would be easy to snatch Tom's image from the street cameras outside the whorehouse, download a privileged search program from the net — police maybe, or military, depending on who he knew — and trace Tom.

He'd have ten minutes to collect some things, and that was it. He'd be leaving. Fleeing the city if he could, perhaps making it into the mountains where, rumor had it, there were still regions of wilderness to get lost in for those with the courage or need.

He'd been here all his life, and yet he had no regrets at all about leaving. There were no ties here anymore.

Passing by a shop Tom glanced in the window and saw himself reflected back. He didn't recognize the face for a moment and he spun around to see who was behind him. But then he walked on, knowing that he was already changing. Love, fear and desperation had left their mark on his face.

He reached his flat a few minutes later. He remained at the end of the street for a while, trying to spot whether there was anyone waiting for him. All seemed normal. His backpack weighed him down. And the longer he delayed, the less chance there would be of Honey coming back as fit and functional as she had been just an hour before. So Tom strode down the street, palmed the doorlock and went inside.

The place was just as he had left it. It no longer felt like home, because he had slaughtered safety and comfort in the couple of hours he'd been away. But its familiarity was comforting. Tom realized that he was absolutely exhausted. He could do with a charge right now. He looked longingly at the connection port and he even accessed the net briefly, before shaking his head and breaking the link. What right had he to sit and recharge while Honey lay crumpled and twisted in the rucksack like that? Besides which, Hot Chocolate Bob and his cronies may be here at any minute.

No, he had to leave now. If it weren't for his foolish lack of planning he wouldn't have been forced to return here at all, but he needed credit, clothes and something to help him get out of the city. An official pass would have been good, but failing that, there was always money.

He placed the rucksack gently on his bed — how he'd love to be holding Honey there right now, explaining his love and feeling her explanations in return — but it would be crazy to try to revive her here. Memory would have to sustain him for now. In the meantime, he needed a safe place and the time to bring her back.

A safe place....

Perhaps he'd known all along where he would go. He hadn't been there since the old man had died almost fifteen years before, but he sincerely hoped that the Baker's labs were still functional and equipped. Waiting for the right person to come and use them again.

Safety. If anywhere in this hope-forsaken city was safe, it would be the place where the Baker had lived, thought, composed, created and died.

The place where, for Tom, love had been born.

It was crazy what time could do to memory, even that of an artificial. It was as if the years could twist streets, the passing of seconds alter perceptions, smells and memories, take the truth and turn it into distorted ideas of what was and had been.

Either that, or he'd consciously tried to forget.

He'd found the estate easily enough. Twenty acres of industrial and business units, half of them flooded by the swollen river and stinking effluent, was not difficult to locate, even in the city. But once there, distance and direction became skewed echoes of what he remembered. He took the third turning right, the second left and found the unit... but it made net casters, and there were several chopped Draggers hanging around outside, eyes red with menace and blood.

Tom backtracked and started again, trying to make out where he had gone wrong. Wading through a foot of shitty water was not the highlight of his day, but knowing that the Baker's hidden lab was beyond made it almost possible to ignore the stink and the things bumping against his legs. The sun sank in the west. It bled through the polluted atmosphere and cast pink reflections and violet shadows across the buildings, making them almost beautiful. Tom laughed out loud when he found the unit, then frowned when he realized that it was the wrong one again.

His fear grew with every passing minute. The sense that he was being watched — created by his own internal terrors, surely, not by any external presence — grew and grew, twisting him around every few seconds to search for the watcher. He saw a tramp and a few gang members, individual buzzed artificials wandering around awaiting death, a pack of dogs looking for the dead.

Eventually, desperate and exhausted and fearful that the dark would steal his last hope of finding the place that night, Tom sank down against a wall and felt tears brewing. The rucksack weighed heavily on his shoulders and in his heart.

And then the Baker found *him*.

Something inside his head clicked on. He'd never felt it before, had never even been aware of this part of his consciousness, but its sudden appearance opened up whole new vistas of knowledge for him. There was a brief surge of power that made his vision dim and his balance waver, but then he knew so much more than before that he almost cried out in fear, shock and relief. He stood, shucked the rucksack higher on his shoulders and walked around two corners to the Baker's old unit.

It was deserted. The windows were smashed, the door graffiti-strewn and smeared a shiny silver where someone had tried to crowbar it open, the walls crumbled and lined black with flood tide marks. And Tom smiled, because he knew that no one would have ever been able to find the Baker's place.

No one but him.

Here was safety and refuge. Here, in the twist of a handle and the muttering of a special word, was a place where his love had been born and where, ironically, he could save it. Tom unslung the rucksack and slipped two fingers under the flap, feeling the silk of Honey's hair and the oily coolness of her deflated skin.

"I'll save you now," he said.

He reached out, twisted the door handle and muttered, "Pudding Lane."

The ground parted and carried him six feet under.

The inner door opened and Tom walked through. The laboratory was just as he remembered. It looked more like the room of a Dark Ages alchemist, with arcane machinery arrayed around the walls, sheafs of yellowed paper piled high and haphazard on the huge oaken desk at the far end, dusty skylights letting in a faded, filtered light from somewhere outside. The whole end wall was taken up with a huge pinboard and there were drawings, sketches, formulae, potions, textbook extracts and personal memos pinned there by the hundred, a collage of idea and potential that stunned Tom now as much as it had fifteen years before.

The place even smelled the same — spilled chemicals, old experiments, stale thought. It was as if the Baker were still here, ruminating in the comfortable back room instead of being dead. Tom shook his head. An artificial's thoughts were supposed to be his own, but memory was powerful. Here was the Baker bashing a clay pot with a hammer, determined to get at whatever was inside before it was spoiled. He looked up and swore at Tom... and then he was relaxing in an easy-chair, recounting tales of his earlier years as Honorary Professor of Sentience at the university... and then here, pouring a sticky, clear gunge over the back of a dead frog and screaming in delight as its legs spasmed. Memories everywhere. It had been the most amazing time of Tom's life.

"You're as good as human," the Baker had told him, "and better than most."

Among the mess of apparatus were pieces of equipment that Tom recognized from many of the Baker's experiments. He didn't necessarily understand them — not back then, and still not now — but they provided him with a strange sense of peace. To know that the Baker had been busy in this world was a comforting thought. And to know for sure that his influence was still felt —

through Tom, and probably elsewhere as well — went so far as to give hope.

There was a noise at the edge of the room, a rattle of cogs and the lazy squeal of something long-dormant coming to life. Tom stepped back and prepared to utter the exit phrase. He wouldn't put it past the old scientist to have left some sort of guard in this place, a booby trap to bring the roof down should anyone enter after his death. After all, as he'd once told Tom, there were things in here best forgotten. But then Tom felt himself being spied upon; scanned, a horribly invasive sensation that raised his hackles and drew his balls up into his body. A sheen of light passed over him from head to foot and it seemed to reach inside as well, lighting his internal makeup and delving into his head. He felt a brief flush of abandonment as the scan ended — for a moment he'd sensed the Baker's attention upon him — but then the discordant rattle and hum of machinery took on an orchestrated rhythm. Some lights flickered on, a coffin-shaped upright cabinet to his left began to shiver slightly as something inside turned over, and several of the Baker's gophers darted out from beneath the workbench along the wall.

Tom smiled in sheer delight as the little robotic transports hurried about the floor. The scientist had made these things one day when the effort of walking back and forth across the laboratory, searching through cupboards and sifting files had become too tiresome. His casual genius was apparent in their perfection. He could speak his requirements and the next gopher in line would search the lab until it found exactly what the Baker was after. They were remarkable, but their uses were too simple, too convenient for the Baker to be over-excited by them. His efforts had always been directed more left of center.

No instructions were spoken now, yet still these little wheeled creations busied themselves with some secretive business. And as Tom watched for a couple of minutes the pattern became obvious — everything they searched for and found was taken to the cabinet. They'd disappear beneath the desk beside the cabinet and come out again empty-clawed. There were clicks and clunks and soft sighs from in there. The sounds of construction, and creation.

But Tom felt safe. The Baker, though long dead, would never do anything to bring him harm. Tom had been the nearest thing he'd ever had to a child.

"Baker," Tom said. "It worked. It worked just like you said it would!" He slipped the rucksack from his shoulder and placed it on a workbench, realizing as he undid the clasps just how pathetic it all looked. The Baker had sent him into the world to find love, and here he was returning to the old man's labs for the first time with a deflated whore over his shoulder and a mad pimp on his tail. "I know it looks a bit strange," Tom said, carefully opening the drawstring and taking Honey out. She was so light, so *reduced*. "But you should see her, Baker. Really, wait until you see her when she's whole again. She's beautiful. And her mind... she really has a mind, it's true! Her own mind, her own thoughts, her own sense of herself. She likes finger puppets and dancing and being held." He frowned. "She'll have to teach me to dance."

The cabinet rattled and hissed at the edge of the room, gophers flitting on their unknown missions. One of them jumped onto the bench next to Tom and grabbed a lightning-quick snip of his hair. Tom jerked back and watched it return to the shivering machine, his lock held high in its claws.

He looked down at Honey, a wrinkled mask of herself. He would resurrect her now, and for a while they'd be safe. For a while. But he wanted them to live, to go out together, think together, be together forever. He'd already resigned himself to having to leave the city.

Never once did he let failure enter his mind.

Honey would live again. Nothing else was possible.

He left her on the bench as he went to find what he needed.

Ironically for a scientist, the Baker had been something of a Luddite. His science was his own, so personal and unique to him that in Tom's eyes it had seemed almost magical. He'd not even had a net point in the laboratory, and even fifteen years ago that must have inconvenienced him so much. Tom only hoped that the scientist's illicit charging unit still functioned after so long. Of all the illegal units he had seen and heard of this was the only one that didn't eventually kill its user. The others — sold on street corners and in darkened corners of clubs — worked for a time, but they fused and cauterized their users' insides, driving them insane, psychotic or both. The irony was that it was a buzz the artificials could not give up... hence the buzzed wandering the streets, artificial equivalents of the human drug addicts. They even looked the same. But the black bags beneath a buzzed's eyes were caused by burnt blood.

He'd need a lead to connect himself to Honey for the proxy resurrection, and one to plug her into the charging unit. The Baker had kept all his connectors in an old cupboard at the rear of the room, and they were still there now. Tom pulled out a great knot of leads, cables and wires, a tangled web home to many real spiders. He wondered whether they'd become more entangled with time, because at first glance he had no idea how he'd ever be able to part them. But they seemed twisted by design, and in a matter of minutes he'd extracted the two cables he required. He replaced the rest and closed the cupboard door. Strange how neatness was so comforting.

Tom carefully lifted Honey and carried her into the back room, the comfortable place where he and the Baker had used to sit for hours on end talking, discussing, philosophizing. The Baker had never been subtle. He'd told Tom that philosophizing with what was essentially a robot had been one of the greatest pleasures of his life. Tom smiled now as he thought of some of those conversations, pleased that he'd have a few hours to recollect them in full. He felt in need of some of the Baker's wisdom.

He took one armchair and placed Honey in the other. The charging unit was built into Honey's chair. The Baker had done that so that Tom could sit and recharge whilst still conversing. Hungry as he had been to experiment and create, it was the gleaning of knowledge that had been the old man's greatest love. And he'd told Tom that their relationship was unique in all of history — the more they talked and argued and discussed, the more they knew. It was as if their words reacted in some weird psychochemical way, causing truth itself to leak into this room and find a home in their minds.

Tom plugged Honey into the charger and set it to start bleeding power in an hour's time. Then he connected himself to Honey with the proxy cable, sat back and closed his eyes.

He accessed the net. It took several seconds to find the correct resurrection sites, and he grouped them divisionally so that they could be manipulated in order of importance. He only hoped that Honey had suffered no hidden alterations at the hands of Hot Chocolate Bob. If she had… something other than Honey may result from this.

And if that happened, Tom would destroy her and then himself.

He looked around the room, still swimming in wonderful, safe memories. There were worse places to die.

Honey twitched once as the flow of information began. Then she began to undulate slowly, steaming, a bubbling sound coming from within her pale folds. An eyeball oozed from one socket, rolled across her face and then was hauled back in by a tightening of the optic nerve.

Tom did not want to see. So he half-stood, shifted his armchair and sat back down, staring into the laboratory as he acted as a conduit for Honey's resurrection.

He reckoned on six hours.

By that time, perhaps the gophers would have finished the pre-programmed task they were executing.

The cabinet rattled and beeped, Honey stank and bubbled, and Tom decided to close his eyes and let memories of the Baker give comfort.

Tom never truly slept. He could turn down and shut off many of his normal functions — and for him that was akin to sleep — but his dreams were sunken thoughts, consciousness on a reduced level, and here randomness crept in.

Dreams were memories as well, and sometimes memories of dreams. That's why Tom spent six hours thinking of Honey.

Because he was certain he had dreamed of her before.

There were no defined memories in his mind, nothing definitely *her*, but the whole sense of her was there. It was something he had lived with for a long, long time, a presence in his mind living in shadows, existing in places not yet seen or known or understood. Every thought he had about her now — the way she moved her head, spoke, smiled or frowned — was familiar to Tom. Even the way she'd acted when he had first seen her yesterday, the sex, the smell of her as they'd rutted on the bed... all known.

Hidden, but known.

He wondered briefly if the Baker had been aware of her, but that was crazy. Tom would have known. And the Baker would never have been so cruel as to give him love, only for him to experience it with a sister.

No... plain crazy.

He surfaced from these sunken thoughts from time to time and found everything to be the same. The light had dimmed somewhat and Tom realized that it was night outside, but the gophers were still busying themselves, and Honey still sighed and bubbled behind him.

Maybe the familiarity was a product of the virus the Baker had programmed and injected into Tom mere days before dying. "I'm giving you love," he'd said, "and one day I pray you may find it."

For those long years it had always been inside him. And when he had set eyes on Honey, she was everything that love was meant to be.

"Tom?"

Tom drifted back to the surface of his mind. Someone was calling him. Perhaps it was the Baker, because the sounds had stopped from the laboratory, and something was ready.

"Tom... don't say you've gone, not after all this."

He stood from the chair and spun around, and there was Honey. She was curled into the chair, knees drawn up and feet tucked under her behind, as if hunkered down for an evening with a book and a bottle of wine. But she still looked... wrong. Her skin was tinged blue, her eyes dry and harsh-looking, her hair lank and greasy. She could not move, and her flesh lay in folds around her midriff, pooled on the armchair about her thighs. Her eyelids looked thick and heavy. Her breasts sagged down to her waist, nipples pointing earthward.

"You're alive!" Tom said. She smiled weakly and he moved to her side, reaching out to touch her forehead. It was slick and too cool.

"I feel unfinished," Honey said.

Tom made sure the lead still joined them to the buzz unit, closing his eyes to ensure that the net connection was still there. Then he sat on the arm of the chair and put one arm around her shoulders, drawing her to him like a doll, kissing the top of her head even though it dismayed him to do so. "But you're awake now," he said, "and I'll stay here with you until you're ready."

"Where are we?" she asked weakly, and he told her.

"Stay quiet and get some rest," Tom said, "you've got a way to go yet."

"Fuck quiet!" Her voice was low, but full of life. "We've got a lot of getting-to-know-each-other to do, you and I. Tell me about you. Tell me... tell me what it's going to be like for us, and where we're going to go. Tell me how happy we'll be when we get there."

So Tom sat there, holding Honey's shadow as her resurrection was completed, and he told her the things she wanted to hear. Curiously enough, they were all the things he wanted too.

They left at midnight. Honey held onto Tom's arm as she walked across the laboratory, looking down at her feet, concentrating hard on each and every step. The lights were stuttering now, as if losing their will when they realized that their guests were leaving, and Tom was terrified that they'd fail before he and Honey reached the door. He'd find his way out, he knew that... but right now he wouldn't welcome the dark.

The gophers had been inactive for hours. The cabinet was quiet too, but it was a loaded silence, like a pause between breaths or the stillness after a scream. Tom kept glancing at the cabinet as they approached, and again as they passed by, wondering what was in there and whether, by the Baker's weird machinations, it was meant for him. The scanning he'd felt upon entering may have kick-started some long dormant program in the laboratory's terminal, a gift or message for him. A final testimony to the Baker's genius.

They walked on, and Tom felt the cabinet standing behind him watching them go. It was the center of the room, the heaviest point, a black hole drawing everything to it, including his thoughts. Good sense was sucked in too.

At the exit door, Tom paused and Honey rested against the wall. "I've got one thing to do before we go," he said.

"You're destroying the place, aren't you," she said.

He frowned at her. "No."

"Oh...." She did not elaborate, and Tom did not push her. Not now. Later he may ask her what she thought the Baker really meant to him. But for now, he had scant minutes to snoop around. Perhaps, deep down, he didn't want to leave this place of safety and nostalgia so soon.

The cabinet had the dimensions of an upright coffin, but it was made of metal and warm to the touch. Tom ran his fingers around its edges, wondering if there was some way to open it easily, and then he thought of the gophers. They'd been darting in and out beneath the benching next to the cabinet, so he knelt and peered into the shadows.

There was a hole through which a gopher could slip inside, but that was it. Nothing more. No way for him to get in, nor to see what was there.

Unless.

He scouted the lab quickly, feeling Honey's gaze tracking him. "Not long," he said.

"Don't worry. I like watching you work."

"I'm not working."

"What's your job if it isn't to save me?"

Tom wondered again just how much Honey had changed during her shutdown, and then he spotted what he was after: a small mirror fixed to the wall above the wash basin in the corner. He tried to prise it from the concrete, failed, punched it instead. It shattered into the sink and he selected the largest shard. He grabbed a second piece as an afterthought — he'd need light — and then went back to the cabinet.

All done with mirrors, the Baker had often muttered as he performed some astonishing new scientific feat. Now Tom used mirrors as well. And for the briefest, darkest, almost human moment, the black magic he had never believed in faced him down.

He could see the pale hue of new skin even before he slipped the mirror into the hole. The leg was sheened with fine hairs, and they seemed to thicken and darken as he watched.

"What is it?" Honey asked.

Tom did not answer. He *could* not. Because he'd angled the second mirror to catch some light and bounce it up into the cabinet, giving brief illumination to what stood within, illuminating nothing... *because Tom could not understand.*

Why or how or when... *he did not understand.*

The naked man dipped its head and looked down at him.

He was looking at himself.

Paler, thinner, not quite *all there*... but himself. There was no real expression on the face. That made it worse. The light was feeble, but Tom could see some details he'd rather not. Like the fact that the simulacrum had no real eyes, only milky white jelly balls in its sockets. Or the way its hair seemed to be forcing itself through the scalp, twisting and waving like a million baby snakes, *hushing* against the inside of the cabinet as if the splash of light had agitated it.

Tom dropped the mirror shards and scrambled back on his hands and heels, leaving bloody hand prints on the floor.

"What is it?" Honey asked again, concern tingeing her voice.

"It's me," Tom whispered very quietly. "It's me...."

"What?" Honey hadn't heard, and now she was walking unsteadily across the laboratory and reaching down, swapping roles as she helped Tom stand and lean against the oak desk. "Tom... if it's that bad we can leave and shut it in."

Tom looked Honey in the eyes — they were full of life again now and their golden hue had returned, as mysterious and bewitching as before — and he realized that he didn't want to tell her. And he didn't *need* to.

That one crazy glimpse had seemed to lessen his own existence. For a second he'd felt... insignificant.

He was an artificial, after all.

"Do you love me?" he said.

Honey frowned and looked up at the ceiling. "Well, you know,

I'm a plastic bitch and I hear the word 'love' a lot… but then you did rescue me. And you have resurrected me. So yes, I suppose I do."

Tom was crestfallen.

Then Honey laughed and kissed him, and she held his face in her hands so that he couldn't look away. "Of course I do! Now, can we leave please? There's a place I need to go."

"Where?"

"The Slaughterhouse. Best club in town."

He was dumbfounded. Didn't she realize just how deep the shit was they were wallowing in? "Honey, we need to *leave*! Hot Chocolate Bob… we have to leave the city, get out, maybe up into the mountains—"

"There's a friend I have to say goodbye to. And it's near the city walls."

Tom looked around at the cabinet as it started to hiss. It was venting an opaque gas from a port in its head. He realized how this had been the first place he'd thought of bringing Honey for safety… and he wondered how much of that decision had been a subconscious wish to say a silent, final farewell to the Baker's memory. Was Honey's request so different?

"We have to be quick!" he said.

Honey kissed him once more, and then stepped back so that he could open the door.

The thing in the cabinet had shocked and disgusted him. Some of the Baker's equipment must have corrupted and gone bad, kick-starting the creation of some meaningless experiment as soon as he'd entered the rooms. The instant he and Honey found themselves out in the open Tom uttered the locking phrase, praying that he, nor anyone else, would ever have to go in there again.

And he bid the long-dead Baker a fond, final goodbye.

They hurried away from the business estate. Tom thought of the simulacrum of himself trapped down there forever, without benefit of memory or knowledge to keep it sane. He remembered the Baker saying that some things in those rooms were best forgotten. Now more than ever that was true. So he put a block on the image and memory, and he and Honey moved on.

The streets sang with the sounds of night. Sirens echoed between the tower-blocks like carrion cries in desert canyons. The flood of chopped humans turned the city into an extravagant nightmare, a place of evolution bastardized by enforced mutation. A thousand possible futures walked the pavements, waving their wings, whistling through gilled throats, scurrying spider-like or walking tall.

"He'll look for us," Honey said. "Hot Chocolate Bob won't give in. He'd have spread the word." She ducked into a boarded-up shop doorway as a feisty gang of teenagers ran by, trailing a sense of threat behind them.

"Going to a club is crazy!" Tom said. "Who is it you need to see?"

Honey turned to him and held his face. "You sound jealous," she said, smiling.

"I would be if others like us could love," he said.

"What?"

And then Tom realized for the first time that, as much as Honey's feelings for him were a surprise to her, the reason behind them would be more so. He should tell her. But he was afraid.

How to tell her that her love was caused by a virus?

"Nothing," he said. "And I'm not jealous. I've never felt like this before and I know it can't be false. You and I... we'll endure. If we're given the chance. And *that's* what frightens me, the idea that we won't even be able to try. If you've been to this club before, it's one of the places your pimp— "

"He isn't my pimp anymore," Honey said, quietly but firmly.

Tom shook his head. "Yes, but you know what I mean."

"The man I'm going to see... he's my only client that Hot Choco-late Bob never knew about."

Tom was confused. A lover? A sex partner for a hooker? Or was the Baker wrong? Had love existed for artificials all along, and only he, Tom, had never experienced it? The thought was chilling and belittling. He felt the world moving out from him, and Honey seemed to recede, forever beyond his reach, their separation confirmed by an awful, unbelievable truth.

"And you have to say goodbye?"

Honey nodded slowly. "He's a human. His name's Doug Skin. There were lots, hundreds, but he was kind, Tom. Not the first time; then he was just like them all — he fucked me, beat me, came in me and left. But the second time he'd changed, he was different. We never had sex again. *Ever.* And he said it was because he'd fallen in love with me."

"Do you love him?" Tom asked. Such complexities in four short words. The answer would make or break his existence.

"No," Honey said.

"*Did* you, once?"

She frowned. "No. I respected him, and I was grateful to him, and I *treasured* him. I still do. But no, I never loved him, even though he wanted it so much. It was never like that."

"Can we trust him?"

Honey merely nodded once, and Tom thought it was because she was angry at the question.

More people passed them by, a couple of grotesque manacled women stopping to hiss and laugh and piss at their feet. One man — chopped so that he was over eight feet tall — strode over and whipped the women around the necks and faces with his extended phallus, as long as he was tall and festooned with knotty lumps.

"Hope they're not going to this club of yours," Tom said as the three freaks sauntered away, laughing and crying together.

Honey raised her eyebrows. "Well, they're going the right way."

Tom sighed and followed, grabbing Honey's hand and enjoying the contact. They were both dressed in black, and really they didn't seem that out of place on the streets. But if Hot Chocolate Bob did have important contacts, and money to buy up-to-scratch surveillance equipment, then they would be found. No question. Chances were, if he worked in association with regional drug barons or the illicit chop surgeons, he would be tracking them now with a hijacked police satellite. Recognition software would have picked them up within minutes of leaving the Baker's unit.

Tom looked behind them, up, across the street, feeling eyes burning into him from every angle. He'd never felt so exposed, even though they were lost in a crowd. And each time he turned to Honey she was looking at him, smiling, eating him up with her resurrected eyes and holding his hand tighter every time.

"What?" he asked, half-smiling.

"I don't know. I'm just enjoying what's going on, loving that fact that I love. Maybe I caught life from one of the humans who had me."

Tom thought about that, about all the living stuff she'd had pumped into, onto and over her. In reality it wasn't life she'd caught, but something even less quantifiable and understood.

Yet again, he wondered whether he'd *ever* tell her the truth.

And that's when they were seen. Freedom, so fleeting and precious, was lost to them in the space between breaths.

Tom felt the instant change in atmosphere. One second they were part of a crowd, two black-clad night walkers with plenty of secrets to hide, and that was their camouflage. Next second, all attention was on them.

When he turned around and scanned the street behind them, he saw why.

"We've been found!"

Three people emerged from the steaming mouth of a subway station and ran straight at them. They were chopped. They had elongated legs to help them move faster, at least two extra arms for multiple weapon implementation, and their bodies were mostly hidden by a sleek, shiny protective coating. They looked like man-sized beetles.

"Mercenaries," Honey said. "One chance. Run with me!"

The crowds parted as Tom and Honey sprinted along the pavement. For a second Tom wanted to mingle with them, pressing away from the streetlights and melting into the dark. But he knew that would be pointless. The mercenaries had them now, they were locked on as surely as if they were all chained together, and the only chance of escape was to outrun or outmaneuver them.

And that was hopeless.

The street had quietened suddenly, all conversation and laughter and singing smothered by terror. The only sounds now were their own pounding footsteps and the regular, incredibly fast *slap-slap-slap-slap* of the mercenaries' hydraulically driven feet meeting concrete. The hunters closed in quickly, echoes bringing them even nearer. Tom knew that they would be caught within seconds.

He glanced at the people pressed against walls or huddled in alleys, but no one would meet his eye.

"Where?" he gasped, and Honey reached behind her and grabbed his hand, squeezing. Hours ago she had been shut down and deflated, and now here she was running for her life from three mercenaries, people so drastically chopped that they were more mutant than human, more machine than mutant. Her new charge must be draining quickly.

It wouldn't matter. Within a few seconds they would have either escaped — and Tom had a hunch now as to where Honey was leading them — or they'd be dead.

At least their deaths would be quick. The mercenaries were trained killers, and from what Tom knew of them they had no time for torture or melodramatic acts of vicarious vengeance. If they were hired to kill they killed, in the most effective and economic manner available.

They'd probably crush his skull under their feet to save on ammunition.

As if conjured by his panicked thoughts, a machine gun opened up behind them. He'd never been near to gunfire, and the sudden cacophony shocked him, the white-hot kiss of bullet trails across his skin sending him into a state approaching panic. Bullets thumped into the ground ahead of them, spinning shattered concrete slabs along the street. More impacted the façades of shops and buildings, and Tom was sure he saw indistinct shadows flailing and spinning, heard the surprised cries of innocent victims. The gun paused for a moment, and as Tom wondered why, something smashed into his ankle, taking his feet from under him and sending him across the concrete on his face.

"Grenade!" Honey hissed. She grabbed Tom, dragging him clumsily across the pavement and into the doorway of an old hotel.

It stank of piss and stale booze, and the pain from Tom's foot brought everything out clearly, even in the weak streetlight: the crumpled newspapers damp beneath him; Honey trying to hug the two of them into one; the smell, the stench, a miasma of everything that could show fear.

There was a surreal moment of utter quiet in the street before the grenade exploded.

They were protected from most of the blast by the reveal of the inset door. The ground shook, windows shattered and rained glass across the street, bricks burst into stinging powder, people screamed, the air was sucked from Tom's lungs by the blast, his outstretched legs were shoved into the brick wall, bringing more white-hot agony. He heard Honey moaning beside him, and he reached for her and cried out joyously as she squeezed his hand twice, a message that could only mean *I'm fine.* He squeezed back as he stared to get to his feet.

"We may have a second or two," he said. His voice sounded distant, eardrums ringing. The echoes of the blast still reverberated along the street, and now he could hear more cries, moans and screams of pain or shock.

And fading in as the explosion passed away, the *slap-slap-slap* of the mercenaries' continuing pursuit.

"Come on!" he hissed. "Wherever you were going, go!"

Honey stood, rubbed dust from her eyes and lead them back out onto the pavement.

The feeling of stepping into full view of the mercenaries was terrible. But it was their only chance. If they remained in the doorway the chopped warriors would be on them in seconds, and then it would simply be a matter of a bullet to the back of the head or a quick spray from a flame unit. At least in the open there was a chance. The dust and smoke from the blast gave a false sense of concealment, but Tom knew that the fighters' senses were paring in on them even now, radar and sonar, heat detectors and biometric scanners picking them out of the chaos.

Tom's ankle gave way and he fell to one knee, but Honey pulled him up and he staggered on. The pain was incredible — he'd never felt anything like it before — and he tried unsuccessfully to block it out.

Each second that passed, he expected the slew of bullets that would cut him in half.

"Here!" Honey said, darting left into a small alley. There was more gunfire behind them, a sustained burst accompanied by fresh screams. Ricochets echoed between the tall buildings, startling flocks of fat pigeons aloft. Bullets annihilated the walls either side of the entrance, exploding bricks, disintegrating corners, sending shrapnel cutting along the alley. Tom's jacket and shirt were ripped, his skin scoured by hot shards of stone.

"Run!" Honey shouted. "Ten meters!"

Tom heard the footfalls of the mercenaries slow, and a grind of metal on concrete as one of them stopped and pivoted at the alley entrance.

Next would come the grenade, or a hail of explosive-tipped bullets, or perhaps a shower in fire.

The alley ended with a blank wall holding a pocked, solid-looking door. Tom began to fear that Honey really had no idea where she was going — her headlong flight driven by panic, pure and simple — but then she stopped and punched a lever on the wall.

She turned to look at him, her eyes wide, breathing harsh and heavy. It sounded like something in her throat was broken; every time she breathed, it clicked. And as Tom noticed the scorched bullet trail reaching from just beneath her left ear to her mouth, so she glanced over his shoulder and her eyes widened.

A doorway opened in the wall next to them. It was camouflaged by moss, the green-grey growth on the scarred metal merging it in with the old brickwork.

Several black metal eggs bounced against their feet.

Honey fell sideways, pulling Tom with her, and they landed on the piss-stinking floor of an elevator.

The doors started to slide shut. Tom watched the grenades spinning in lazy circles as they came to rest on the alley floor… with one of them rolling slowly towards the closing doors. It rolled, the doors hissed together, Tom could not breathe… and he heard the tiny *tap* as the grenade struck the doors a second after they had finally closed.

Honey kicked up at the control panel and sent them humming downwards. She looked at Tom, seeing right into him and telling him so much, and he knew that this moment was life or death. In two seconds they would be alive to run some more, or dead, smashed bodies in a blasted lift, left to rot down here, food for rats, wild cats and perhaps a desperate, dying buzzed.

The grenades exploded.

The shockwave buckled the lift walls and punched Tom like a train. He cried out but could not hear, because his ears were already bleeding. Blood oozed from his nose, his eyes, his mouth. The lift must have been below ground level — otherwise the blast would have crushed it like a cardboard box — but the remains of the wall above showered down onto the roof, shoving it down faster than the lift could take. Something whined and screeched and then snapped. The lift jerked sideways, tilted ten degrees, grumbled for a few seconds and then stuck fast.

"No!" Honey shouted. She stood and leaned on the control panel, punching buttons, looking at the doors as if willing them to open. "Tom, we have to open these. Those bastards won't stop until they can see our corpses."

"Where are we?" Tom knelt by the doors and shoved his fingers in the warped crack, pulling both ways. He was ridiculously aware of Honey's leg pressed against his upper arm as she did the same higher up, its muscles tensing and spasming as she heaved.

He spat dusty blood and felt it dribbling from his ears.

"A hooker's got to know the city," she said and grunted as she pulled, gasped, and Tom closed his eyes to see her naked and writhing on his face the day before.

I'm more human than I think, he thought.

There was a continuous rattle and thud as detritus from the ruined alley rained down the lift shaft. And then came three louder impacts, regularly spaced, and time froze again.

The doors screeched open. Tom and Honey rolled out and crawled sideways so that they were away from the lift doors. Tom had a second to look around — they were in a long, dimly lit tunnel, service pipes ribbing the ceiling, condensation dripping onto the rusted metal walkway, fists of fungi pressing out between old bricks in the walls — and then the three grenades exploded. The lift disintegrated and splashed its metallic guts out into the corridor, wounding Tom's senses even more and stroking his outstretched legs with a brief tongue of fire.

He gasped in relief as the fire retreated... and then screamed as fresh flame leapt from the ragged hole in the wall, white-hot and stinking of intent. It flowered like a cloud of snowflakes gusting through an open door, twisting and wavering almost as if it were conscious. Service pipes burst apart, spraying water and gases which were heated and mixed by the chemical fires, turning breathable air into a deadly mist of poisonous steam.

Tom stood clumsily, favoring his good leg, and grabbed Honey under the arm.

"Where to?" he shouted, coughing and retching as the bad air clawed his throat.

Honey nodded along the tunnel and started running, Tom following on behind. His ankle had swollen and pushed the head of his boot out; his back was cool with shed blood; other bumps and cuts added their own song to his symphony of pain. And in front of him, leading the way, was Honey; her clothing soaked from her left shoulder down by the blood leaking from her gashed neck. The bullet had scored a line there without actually entering... but Tom was still terribly afraid at the damage it may have done.

The last thing they could do was stop.

From behind them came the sound of flames gushing through the lift wreckage, and a blast as another grenade was dropped. It wouldn't take the mercenaries long to realize that there were no dead artificials at the bottom of the shaft.

"Where are we going?" Tom shouted.

"It's a maintenance tunnel to the underground," Honey called back. Her hand went up to her gashed neck and pressed as she spoke. "The other way leads back into the station those things came from. This way goes to the river, branches out, connects into other underground networks. You can get from one side of the city to the other, if you put your mind to it."

"We may be able to buy passage downriver."

"The Slaughterhouse is this way," Honey continued, acting as if she hadn't even heard Tom's idea.

The noises behind them had stopped, and they paused in their flight. Tom found the silence more distressing than the sounds of destruction. It meant that the mercenaries were thinking. "I think we should get out of this tunnel."

"I agree," Honey said, "but I'm still not quite sure where we are."

"You're bleeding," Tom said. He moved to her and tilted her head slightly so that he could look at her neck.

"So are you."

He kissed her above the wound, tasting sweat and blood. He

couldn't believe that she still wanted to visit the club, but for now their priority was to escape. Where they went afterwards... that was something to think about later.

"I think that way," Tom said, indicating a door in the wall a few steps away. "If we do our best to get lost down here, we'll lose them as well."

"Well, that's original crisis thinking at least." Honey grinned at him, a bloodied plastic doll.

They opened the door and entered the corridor beyond. It was much narrower than the one they left, badly lit as well, and here and there on the floor were piles of ragged clothing which may once have contained people. Tom was glad for the bad light; it meant he couldn't see bone or desiccated flesh. Rats scurried around their feet, flies buzzed them, and fattened things crawled on the slimy walls.

"They say the buzzed sometimes come down here to die," Honey said. "Getting out of the sunlight soothes the pain. Or something."

Knowing whom the remains belonged to didn't help Tom one bit. The further they walked along the dank, damp tunnel, the more corpses they came across. At one point they had to step on brittle bones and shift piles of clothing aside with their feet to get by. Rusted chains jangled as they finally parted, spilling cheap imitation jewelry to the floor.

"Do you think we lost them?" Tom asked.

Honey stopped, turned and cocked her head slightly to one side. "Stop breathing," she said. They exhaled, and Tom could hear only the blood pulsing through his ears, whispering secret words to him, messages from his body saying, *run, this is all wrong, you're not built for this, this love, this fear and danger.* But looking at Honey he chose instantly to ignore them, because she was worth everything.

"I love you," he said.

"I think they're burning their way along the tunnels," she said. Then she glanced at him and smiled. "Love you too. What a strange thing to say."

"I mean it!"

"Not you, me. I never thought I'd ever say it to anyone. Never in my vocabulary."

"Well—"

"We're not built for it." Honey gave him a quick kiss, wincing as the movement stretched the wound on her neck. "But I guess we'll adapt."

They moved on and took the next exit from the tunnel. It was a hole smashed through a thick brick wall into the neighboring main sewer, its edges rough and festooned with an alarming swathe of spider web. Tom heard the web tearing as his arm brushed by, and he wondered whether it would serve as another fresh sign of flight for the mercenaries.

"We need to change tunnels again soon," he said. "As soon as we can, three or four times. They must have biometric scanners; they'll pick up our sweat from the air, our breath, our shed skin. We won't lose them by running fast. But hopefully we can confuse them enough to give them the slip."

There was a coughing explosion from somewhere far behind them and the tunnel lit briefly, softly

They jumped down into the sewer. It was disgusting. It stank; it was thick like congealed soup. Tom could even taste the filth in the air.

Another explosion rumbled through the sewers, knocking a drift of dust down from the curved brick ceiling. It was difficult to tell which direction the blast had come from.

"There!" Tom said, spotting a rotten wooden door leading off from a stone ledge.

Honey scrambled up and tried the door but it seemed to be locked from the other side. Tom joined her and together they smashed at it, groaning as the impacts reminded them of their various wounds. The wood gave after several attempts, and they spilled into another tunnel, this one lit intermittently from above through frosted glass paving blocks.

As they hurried along, Tom tried to think of where they could be. There was a pavement like this down by the river, spread along the main promenade road in front of the classier hotels. There was also a roller skating area back in the center of the city, a gathering place for junkies and buzzed when the lights went down. But there were probably a dozen more streets and roads and courtyards with glass paving... and Tom finally admitted to himself that he was lost.

Honey was leading them now.

For some inexplicable reason, this change of emphasis disturbed him. Perhaps it was a machismo thing, the idea that *he* had saved *her* and should continue to do so. But that was just so human....

"Do you know where we're going?" he asked. "I think we should try to go up top now, get out of the city— "

"We're going in circles," Honey said. "We'll lose them soon, then head for The Slaughterhouse. They'll have trouble finding us in there."

"How do you know?"

She glanced back and smiled at him, lit by dirty light filtered down from the city. "You've obviously never been there."

The tunnel dipped and they descended several flights of stairs, listening out all the time for the echoes of pursuit. After a couple of minutes they emerged onto an old, deserted tube platform. It was barely lit by sun pipes sprouting from the arched ceiling like the ends of severed arteries, the light weakened by every reflective elbow it had to travel. During the day it may have been light enough to read, but now, at night, the only illumination that found its way down was the borrowed glare of civilization: street lamps; neon signs; the city's nighttime glow reflected from the underside of low, pollutant-heavy clouds. It was a grubby light, well suited to what it revealed.

The platform and station must have been deserted for years. Tom had heard about these places, way stations on the old underground network, deserted rather than adapted when the trains were changed to monorail. And like any forgotten place it attracted the more feeble side of humanity, those wanting to find themselves lost. The junkies, the wretched homeless, the criminals... there was talk of whole gangs living down here, communing via old tunnels, rising to the surface to attack and rob and do whatever it was they imagined their purpose called for.

"Into the tunnel," Honey said.

"There's no light. Who knows what's in there!"

Honey hugged him and Tom could smell her, sense his brain's ecstatic reaction to her unique aroma in the rush of blood in his veins. They stood like lovers waiting for a train that would never arrive.

"You're so brave," she said. "Who'd have thought you'd have rescued me like that? Who'd believe I was worth rescuing, by anyone?"

"Nobody's ever loved you before, obviously." Honey shrugged slightly, but said nothing.

Tom thought of Doug Skin, her human customer who had supposedly fallen for her, and for a moment he was overcome by something bitter, new and shocking: jealousy. He hated the idea that they were going through this to say goodbye to someone else. They could have left the city and that would have been that.

"Why is your pimp trying to kill you for running? Girls must run all the time."

"On occasion they do. And Hot Chocolate Bob hunts them

down, or more likely has someone do it for him, and they die. Then he buys more plastic bitches on the black market as instant replacements. Gives him a good turnover of girls, fresh meat. Keeps the customers happy."

"Jesus," Tom muttered, hugging her tighter as if that would protect her more. "Why can't he just let you go."

"Face," she said. Or perhaps she said *fate*.

A *thump* passed through the station. It may have been a sound coming in from the distance, wending its way through tunnels and vents like a gust of air. Or perhaps they only felt it through the ground. A rat maybe, hidden by shadows, jumping from a wall onto the platform… or a violent grenade explosion five tunnels and a mile away.

"Let's get out of here," Tom said. "Into the tunnel like you said. If we hold hands we can never get lost."

"Romance," Honey said, arching her eyebrows. Yet again, she confused Tom even more. As they jumped down between the rails and out of the weak light, he wondered whether that was love all over.

They walked for two hours. Through the train tunnel, across another platform, into a long, rising corridor, through a set of iron doors that had been blasted open at some point in the distant past. The atmosphere was dank, damp, dangerous, and they held hands as often as they could. Most of the places they passed through had some form of illumination — weak emergency lighting, or more often borrowed light bleeding down somehow from the surface. Some were pitch black. These they traversed as quickly as they could, relying on senses heightened by fear. And deep inside, Tom tried to trust fate as well. He desperately believed that they would have never come this far if an unseen, pointless death down here was all that awaited them.

They heard and felt intermittent signs of pursuit, from a rattling explosion, to a subtly decreased pressure on their eardrums as a heavy door was opened in some distant tunnel.

Eventually, finally, Tom climbed a rusted iron ladder, shoved a manhole open with his shoulders and helped Honey up into the open air.

He stood panting in the deserted street, his right foot and ankle a heavy weight of pain, the cool night air kissing his bleeding wounds as if to soothe. Honey stood next to him and looked around, nodding and sighing quietly. She knew where they were. *A hooker has to know the city*, she'd said as they took the lift into the underworld. Tom wondered if she'd been a whore forever, but they'd have plenty of time to get to know each other properly. *Plenty*. The idea that they knew virtually nothing about each other, and yet they were fleeing together for their lives, seemed far too romantic to take seriously.

Looking around, diverting his attention outwards, seemed to ease the pain. They were at the very edge of the city. Tom could even see the enclosure wall, eighty feet high and well lit, its top spotted with bored guards.

Honey pointed across the street at a low, curved doorway set in the face of a blank concrete façade. The building was huge and square, more dismissive of aesthetics than any in the city. There were hardly any windows, and those that were there appeared to have been boarded up. Its bulk seemed to swallow the light. Even though a misty rain was falling, there were no reflections from its damp walls.

Above the doorway hung a glowing axe, dripping neon blood onto the heads of anyone who chose to enter.

"That," said Honey, "is The Slaughterhouse."

Tom had only been inside a few clubs in his time. Mostly they were visits marred by too much noise, too many drugs, too much drink, too much body chopping... just *too much*. Artificial he may be — cloned, grown, extruded, constructed and programmed — but Tom was not a man of extremes. The Baker had told him that those who resorted to extremities of existence had lost sight of the beauty at its heart. At the time Tom had found it difficult to understand, but after the old scientist died and the years went by he began to see the truth in the words. Most of those who wandered the streets at night, seeking enjoyment or satisfaction in the arms of mindless experimentation, had lost the simple ability to *live*. They needed more, and more, and more, without giving themselves the chance to get used to what they already had.

Tom's club visits had been out of interest in other people, not to find anything for himself.

He'd been to The Club at the End of Time, Fuck-Shit and Hell, among a few other. In one he was mugged, in another he was hit on, in the rest he was ignored. He'd hated every one of them.

The Slaughterhouse... it was as much a club as Krakatoa had been a slight pop. The Slaughterhouse was a *world*. The second Honey opened the main front door and they passed beneath the axe, that world launched its attack on Tom's senses.

They were in a corridor not unlike some of the tunnels they'd just been fleeing along. There were a few barred windows in the walls, payment booths, but more like viewing holes in prison doors. There was nobody behind them and Honey did not give them a second glance. The floor was uneven, and in the low light Tom could see what he thought were shattered bones forming its covering, the curve of a skull here, the ragged end of a snapped femur there. His balance was thrown and he held out his arms, staggering at every step. He tried not to look down. He was sure... *certain*... that the bones must be false. *Must* be.

Waves of smoke frolicked in the air, disturbed by mysterious drafts. A skein of rich fumes settled around Tom's head. He breathed in, unable to resist the spicy hint of forbidden pleasures, feeling the sense of them settling into his nostrils and setting his blood aflame.

"What's that?" he asked.

"What, the smell? It's a mix of everything the club stands for. They extract it, concentrate and vent it over newcomers. Gets them ready. Gets them hot. You're smelling drugs, fear, sweat, rage, sex and burning bone."

Burning bone. Tom looked down at the floor and an eye socket stared back.

There was a sudden explosion ahead of them, pounding through the air, hitting his already bloodied ears and stealing his balance. He sagged against the wall. It was slimy to the touch, and the slime smelled of sex. Unconsciously, still reeling from the blast, Tom touched his fingers to his tongue and closed his eyes. He could have been eating pussy. He snapped his eyes open again, wondering what was happening to him, why he was drifting away when those things were here, they'd found them, they would blast The Slaughterhouse until Honey and he were dead.

"*Buzz 'n' Chaos!*" Honey shouted. She turned to Tom, a crazy grin on her face. "You've never heard or seen live music until you've seen these guys."

It sounded more like inclement weather than good music to Tom, but he followed Honey through a pair of heavy doors and into the club itself.

Outside, in the corridor, they could have been almost anywhere. But anywhere was never like this.

The place was a riot of humanity, a deep sea of people, a swarm of experimenters indulging their most devilish whims, the air redolent of highs and sex and a vibrant freedom. The music of *Buzz 'n Chaos* stalked the air like a rogue dragon, setting glasses shaking on tabletops and teeth rattling in skulls. There was shouting, screaming, sighing and crying, arguing, talking, wailing and laughing. And there was movement everywhere. The designers of The Slaughterhouse had never allowed economics or gravity to hobble their decadent dream.

The room was the size of the building containing it, but it looked impossibly larger. There were no windows. There were no internal stories, only platforms, staircases, open lifts, glass slides, chains suspending swinging floors. On every visible surface people sat or danced or stood talking, sipping drinks and smoking and wiping exotic drug patches across their tongues or eyes, eating, climbing sleeping and fucking. Lots of fucking.

It reminded Tom of a giant ant nest, but here all the ants were seeking only one thing — enjoyment. And enjoyment, Tom realized within seconds of entering, came in all shapes and sizes.

"Holy shit!" he shouted above the cacophony. "Honey, what the hell are we doing here? These people are wasters, freaks, chopped because they can't— "

But Honey did not let him finish. "This is my thing, Tom, where I like to be when I'm not being fucked and beaten and spat on. I know I'm artificial so I can't be chopped, but these freaks as you call them make me feel... normal. I'm a whore but that's no worse than most of these. And much better than some. Love me, love what I do."

He didn't know what to say. A woman walked past with grotesque gashes across her body, a dozen inches long, their edges pouting around thick strips of cardboard to prevent the wounds from healing. She grimaced, and it may have been a smile. "Oh *God*, Honey." Even he was surprised at how much desperation and disgust came out in his voice.

"You told me you loved me," Honey said, moving in close so that she could talk into his ear, "and yet you don't know a thing about me. You don't know what I like to eat or do, whether I have religion, what books I read."

"You like to dance," Tom said. "You like to be held. You like puppets."

"Puppets," she said. She barked a hard laugh, stood back with her hands on her hips and Tom realized that she was *exasperated*. She looked up as if searching for someone in this multi-level altar to pleasure.

"It's what you told me," Tom said, trailing off. The band seemed to be between songs, but the volume in the place had not relented.

"We're all puppets, Tom," she said. "Especially us, the likes of you and me. Artificials. I don't like puppets, I like those who cut their strings and rebel. Watching that Chinaman's show outside the brothel... it makes me really look at myself. It makes me think about who pulls my stings, and how beholden I am to them. These people here — the chopped people and the lost artificials — they shed their strings long ago."

"We need to get out of the city," Tom said, uncomfortable and confused with where this was leading. They had to escape now, together, and then time would be theirs. "We can get to know each other when we're away."

Honey looked at him, her lips pressed tight and a frown hardening her face. She was about to say something. But the band started up again, and a veil of blue smoke wafted down from above, setting Tom's nostrils alight, his blood pulsing through his veins at twice its normal rate. Honey smiled and held out her hands, pulling him close and hugging him tightly. But there was something else there, a hesitance he hadn't felt before. Almost as if her thoughts hung between them, a weight requiring crushing before they could touch.

"Honey...."

"Come on," she said. "Let's find Skin, then we can move on. Get out of there. Finish all this."

"Leave the city, you mean."

"Leave the city," she said. At least he thought those were her words. But she'd already started turning away, and her eyes had left his.

As they started walking, Tom felt much lighter than before. His perception had widened, his senses apparently refreshed and enlivened by whatever chemicals he'd breathed in with the smoke. He could make out the band's individual instruments, the harmonies bouncing off each other, the rasp of the guitarist's rough skin against the strings, the clicks and sighs of the vocalist's breathing method between lyrics... even the volume seemed manageable now, rather than painful. He wondered what the drug had been and decided, against all logic, that he liked it.

Honey led him up onto an uneven platform welded together from what looked like panels of a ship's hull. There were even traces of a name along one side of the suspended floor, and star-shaped rust patches as big as fists which may have been where creatures had once clung. There was a group of people at one end of the platform, some of them dancing, others — mostly men — paying more attention to the woman hanging from chains above them. Meat hooks curved through the flesh of her shoulder blades, buttocks and calves, and the chains that rose into the gloomy heights were rusted, the color of dried blood.

She was grinning as she swung back and forth, her rhythm matching the fast beat of the music in some terribly soporific way. She was naked. Blood ran copiously onto the heads and shoulders of those below. One of the men reached up and squeezed her pendulous breasts, twisting her nipples and pulling hard, changing her direction of swing. Another shoved him aside and flipped into a handstand, his engorged prick flopping as he walked clumsily towards the woman on his hands, offering himself up to be sucked. His gang screamed and shouted and jeered. The woman nudged out with one hand, hitting him on the knee and sending him tumbling.

Her blood drew graceful arcs on the dark grey platform. Her swinging, twisting and rotating was all in time with the music, like some grisly metronome. She caught Tom's eye and smiled. He looked away, disgusted and embarrassed, as one of the men started to jump and bash his face between her thighs.

Honey passed by the group without a second glance, and Tom was pleased when they started climbing a ladder to the next platform.

"Chopped folks up here," Honey shouted down before she disappeared onto the floor above. Tom climbed faster, wondering what to expect. He'd seen people walking to and from these clubs, noticed the freakish adjustments many of the humans made to their bodies. He didn't think he could still be completely shocked. He thought he'd seen it all.

The couple had given themselves over, completely and utterly, to sex.

The man's prick had been hugely extended, thickened and distorted so that he could screw the woman at a distance, at any angle, and still dip his head to lick her arse or the other openings weeping and swelling across her body.

There were several other men scattered across the smaller platform, all naked and obviously recently sated. A couple of them glanced nervously at the rutting couple, and Tom guessed that they'd been at the woman until this grotesquely chopped man had appeared, someone with the same commitment to sex as she had. Normal men she could entertain by the half-dozen, but none of them wanted to pit their sexual prowess against this freak.

Tom and Honey walked by as the man withdrew and entered another hole, this one in the woman's side. She groaned and writhed, her extra sets of arms and hands doing their best to keep her other holes occupied, fingers obviously augmented such was their speed of manipulation.

"You like these places?" Tom asked, amazed. Honey ignored him, but one of the naked men glanced up and smiled sheepishly. The band cranked into another number. Its opening chords swelled out to the edges of the club, echoing back several seconds later, the echoes themselves forming an integral part of the music. This one must have been a favorite, because a roar went up that hurt Tom's ears and set the platform they were on swaying. The inhuman couple never stopped fucking.

"Skin's up there!" Honey shouted, putting one arm around Tom's shoulders and pointing up into the club's shadowy heights. There were at least a dozen levels to climb, and the far walls were obscured by a haze of smoke. Chains draped down, ladders snaked up, bridges strung across spaces, people swung on ropes... and Tom knew that they would be here for a long time. There was no quick way up that high, other than a long, exhausting climb. He really didn't believe that he could shin up a chain the way he felt now; his ankle was numb with pain, and he was beginning to think he'd lost more blood than was safe. The wounds had been sealed by his body's defence — he could feel the new skin setting already — but the bones in his ankle may have been crushed. Their knitting would take days, and rest was the best thing for it.

Honey was still bleeding from her neck. Tom wondered whether she'd allowed it to continue because of her visit to The Slaughterhouse, a weird pain perversion she revelled in herself when she came here. She winced whenever she turned her head.

They climbed. The band assaulted the club with its music, strafing the platforms with power chords that would have knocked a flock of birds from the sky. Sheets of smoke rose and fell, drugladen exhalations that set Tom's blood bubbling, steamed bubbles of viscous fluid from his pores, hauled up random memories to dart at him like forgotten ghosts. Some memories were good and these he smiled at, but some weren't so good. The drug, whatever it was, did not allow him to pick and choose. Between a warm memory of the Baker philosophizing, and the cold empty loneliness after he'd died, Tom had time to wonder at the sort of people who willingly submitted themselves to this. He thought he saw the platform where this drug haze originated. The people there were crying, laughing, smiling, weeping, shouting and raging at the visions the drugs were uncovering. Perhaps sometimes they found unwanted truths. Tom was afraid.

They passed many chopped people, some of them changed even

more drastically than the rutting couple they'd just seen. One woman resembled an octopus, a head and body with at least eight legs splayed star-like around her. Five men and women licked or fucked or suckled between her thighs.

Sex was the thing. To be chopped was to increase sexual performance and expand proclivities.

They took the easier routes up into the club, traveling between several platforms on a moving, rising walkway. Each level presented new surprises, greater mutilations, none of which seemed to surprise or bother Honey. Climbing eventually onto the highest platform, Tom could see the band. Four men and a woman singing, their instruments and an amplification system looking as if it came from thirty years before. They were surrounded by a jumping, stamping, waving throng, some of them gyrating so close to the edge that Tom was amazed they weren't sent tumbling... and then one of them *did* fall.

She spread out her veined, leathered wings, glided through a haze of drug smoke and landed clumsily on a platform near to the club's floor.

"She flew," Tom said mildly. *She had flown!* He'd never know, never believed that such a chop was possible. And officially, he was certain, it wasn't. It was the sort of thing the Baker had only ever dreamed of.

Tom began to wonder exactly what this place was, and why Honey had brought him here.

"He's there!" Honey shouted, grabbing Tom's arm and pointing at the band. "That's Doug, that's Doug Skin!"

"The drummer?"

Honey was smiling, a wide open smile that contained sheer delight. "No, silly. The guy standing in front taking the band's holo!"

Tom saw a tall, heavily built man right by the stage, not jumping with the rest of the crowd. He simply stood there and pointed a camera at the band as they pelted their way into another track.

Honey closed her eyes and Doug Skin turned to look at them.

She spoke to him with her mind, Tom thought. He'd heard it was possible... the Baker had mooted it once or twice... but not in an artificial, surely? And not a plastic bitch built specifically and exclusively for sex?

He felt the center of attention. The song was about him, the drugged-up clubbers were laughing at him, giggling as they fucked, writing tattoo poetry about his stupidity on each other's backs. Their eyes bore in, his skin was transparent, and he wished the Baker were here.

Doug Skin smiled at Honey and pushed his way through the crowd. He embraced her and kissed her neck. Once more Tom felt the uncomfortable rush of jealousy, but then he saw that she held back slightly, tensing as the big man displayed his obvious affection.

"That him?" he asked, nodding at Tom.

Honey's eyes shone, but Tom didn't know why. It could have been the lasers reflecting from walls, or ceiling lights filtered through the smoky atmosphere. Probably... perhaps... it was the twinkle of her love for him.

"Yes," she said. "That's him."

Skin eyed Tom up and down. "I expected him to be bigger."

What the fuck is going on here? Tom thought, and maybe he spoke it aloud.

He had no hope of finding out. Because right then hell broke loose, and there were screams and explosions and gunfire, and the sounds of people dying again.

Two minutes later, Tom would see himself dead.

Upon entering The Slaughterhouse, Tom had an inkling of what Honey meant about the mercenaries never finding them in there. They would, of course, given enough time and opportunity, but it would not be an easy search. The place defied the senses.

What neither of them had banked on was Hot Chocolate Bob's utter determination to find and kill them.

It was slaughter. As if in mockery of the club's moniker the mercenaries came in shooting, dishing out death at random. They must have known that their entrance would be noticed immediately, so rather than try to find Tom and Honey amongst surprised and angry clubbers, they introduced chaos and terror instead. It was obviously an atmosphere they were used to working in.

They strafed the whole interior of the club with gunfire. People span and danced and fell, screaming and shouting, tumbling from their platforms and hitting those below, or falling all the way to the litter-strewn floor. The band played on for a few seconds, adding a surreal theme tune to the massacre. Grenades popped from the mercenaries' armor like black eggs being laid, arching up and exploding in mid-air, shrapnel slashing visible swathes through the smoke. One explosion ripped out a ladder and set of chains, tipping a platform and spilling those cowering on it to the floor far below. They hit like rag dolls, limbs askew.

The band cut out as the power stuttered, flickering the lights and adding a stroboscopic effect to the twitching clubbers, the blood spraying the air, the corpses slipping down from platform to platform, bullets and shrapnel ricocheting through swathes of drug smoke, the three mercenaries advancing into the club like huge spiders, swinging their way from platform to platform, spreading out, leaving dead or dying people in their wake.

Skin had pulled Honey down as soon as the gunfire began, and Tom hunkered down next to them, staring over the rim of the huge platform. They were maybe a hundred feet from the floor, the mercenaries a few levels below them. At the rate the chopped warriors were advancing, they'd be on them in seconds.

One of the mercenaries suddenly slipped to one side, flame flowering from his midriff, arms flailing for a handhold. He tumbled from the platform but found a chain before he fell too far. The flames were already extinguished, but a rain of blood and insides was dripping from his dangling legs.

He brought up three guns and opened fire on a platform across from him. Tracer rounds directed his aim to a metal shield that had sprung up there, and Tom could make out a few people sheltering behind it, frantically fumbling with a some huge barrelled weapon.

The other two mercenaries paused to watch.

The fighter stopped firing for a second. The recoil had set him swinging, and the whine of chains was audible across the club. Reload springs lunged from his belt and fed magazines into the machine guns.

Two men stood from behind the barrier, aimed and fired.

The mercenary disintegrated, flames slewing outward as his ammunition ignited.

A second later the victorious attackers were torn to pieces by a five-second hail of fire from the two surviving intruders. Bullets, flame and grenades scattered their remains over what was left of their platform.

"We should have just left the city!" Tom shouted at Honey. "This is all for us!" But his anger was misplaced and useless now.

"Don't talk!" Skin hissed. "They'll be scanning for your voice patterns. Your one hope is to trust me and maybe I can get you both out of here. But we have to move, you have to follow me, *now!*" He turned and belly-crawled across the floor, shoving people aside with his big hands.

The gunfire and explosions stopped, but the mercenaries had initiated the panic they desired. Screaming and crying and moaning continued, almost as loud as the sounds of killing. Interspersed amongst them, the clanking impacts of metal-booted feet on ladders, chains and platforms, always coming nearer.

Maybe they'd already been spotted.

Honey was following Skin. Tom watched her go, and then followed her. He had no choice. To stay still was to die, to go after Skin was to submit himself to the man's mercy. He was helpless, useless... and he realized that he'd been almost totally ineffectual since leaving the Baker's old laboratory.

Honey had always been the one in charge. The strong one. Their only real hope.

People moved aside to let them pass. The band was cowering on the stage, trying to edge back but tangling themselves in power lines and the expansive drum kit. Skin crawled across the stage, Honey followed, and Tom was about to follow her when he heard a high-pitched shriek from somewhere else in the club.

It was not a human sound. It was a *fighting* sound, an angry shrill from vocal chords designed to communicate nothing but pain and terror.

He half-stood and hurried to the edge of the stage, from where he could see at least a third of the club's space. From the corner of his eye he spotted a dark shadow swinging and scampering along one huge wall, aiming at a place halfway to the ground. Another shape swung from rope to chain to ladder, heading the same way. They screeched in unison now, and Tom tried to make out their target.

And stared into his own eyes.

He was standing down there on a platform, surrounded by chopped people whose bodies were already punctured and torn, leaking blood around his feet. He was standing down there and looking up. From this distance Tom could not quite make out the expression in his eyes... but he recognized his own quiet smile.

"Holy shit...." Honey said, appearing at his shoulder.

The two mercenaries landed on the platform either side of the second Tom. Without pause they stretched out their arms, locked their weapons onto him and opened fire.

Tom watched himself come apart. The bullets tore him to shreds, blood and bone splashing into the air, skull splitting and gushing brain out across the platform. The gunfire only lasted for two seconds, but the thing that slumped down at the mercenaries' feet could never have been visually identified... had Tom not seen its face.

One of the mercenaries snatched a quick sample of blood. Then they used their flame units, and the sad remains bubbled black.

Tom crawled back from the edge of the stage, head down, feeling more cold and alone than he could have believed. Even when Honey came back to him, touched his face and slung one arm across his back, Tom felt abandoned. He'd just seen....

He didn't know *what* he'd seen.

"I guess they're just looking for you now," he said to Honey. His voice sounded shallow and vague.

"What happened?" Honey said.

"I think I died." Tom smiled at her. Already, the mysterious threads were coming together. "Let's go. If we escape, we can talk about it then."

"You could hide," she said. "You could leave me, let them come after me and catch me if they can— "

Tom did not even honor this with a response.

Skin led them to the rear of the stage and across a narrow metal walkway, connecting the stage platform with the blank outside wall. There was a flimsy handrail, the only thing between them and the floor a hundred feet below, but it had been distorted at several points by bullet or shrapnel impacts. None of them trusted it.

Tom felt naked and exposed, expected the intrusive kiss of a bullet at any moment. The way Honey moved ahead of him — shoulders hunched, arms pulled in, legs slightly bent — he thought she did too.

The Slaughterhouse had gone amazingly quiet since the mercenaries killed Tom's doppelganger. Tom could still hear the clambering, clanking footsteps of the hunters as they searched for Honey, but the clubbers had all fallen silent, either dead or shocked dumb. Perhaps they feared that now the killers had found and killed their target, any slight sound would merely set them on the rampage again.

Tom, Honey and Skin reached the wall. Skin led them through a door, cleverly concealed in the shadows of a concrete overhang. It emerged onto the head of a staircase. Tom stood on the landing and looked down, down, until the flights disappeared in a grey haze. It seemed far deeper than the club.

"It's the only way I can think of to get you out," Skin said. "It goes straight down to the basements. The theaters. From there you can get out onto the streets or down into the sewers and tunnels... just about anywhere."

"They're only looking for me now," Honey said. "Tom, who *was* that?"

"The Baker."

"I thought he was dead?"

Tom nodded, waved his hands to clear his confusion. "He is, he is! But... remember at the lab, that cabinet? Me. My clone. The Baker not only gave me love, but ensured it was protected as well. He knew that if I ever had cause to return to the lab it would be because I was in trouble. How he could have known... how he could have *imagined*...."

"You really meant the world to him, didn't you?" Honey asked. It was a strange thing to say. Tom didn't know how to respond.

"Don't mind me," Skin said, "but can we talk as we walk? It's very quiet in there...."

They stood silently for a few seconds, listening for sounds of pursuit, listening for *anything*. Maybe the two mercenaries were motionless now... standing somewhere in the club... listening... listening for the sounds of escape....

"Quietly," Skin whispered, slipping down the first flight of stairs. They'd descended eight flights before Tom spoke again.

"They think I'm dead."

"They'll probe the corpse," Skin said from in front. "Genetic tests."

"The Baker would have thought of that. It's a clone of me, it's... *me*."

"He really was a crazy old bastard, wasn't he?" Skin laughed, before turning and starting down another flight.

"What? What makes you say that?"

Skin stopped and looked back up past Honey at Tom. He didn't look any more welcoming than he had when they'd first arrived a few minutes before, but now there was a hint of humor in his eyes. Cruel humor.

"He's a bit of a legend, in some parts," Skin said. "Places like this. To people like us. And you, too. The artificial looking for love. Almost a fairy tale!"

"Skin!" Honey said quietly.

"Honey? What's he on about?"

She looked at Tom and shook her head, looking so sad.

"Honey?"

"Let's get the hell out of here," Honey said, not looking at either man. "Tom, the basements may interest you. It's where some of the chopping takes place."

Skin started on down again, followed by Honey, Tom bringing up the rear. Tom thought of making love with Honey, hugging her, being with her... and it all felt one way. He looked at her bloodied back and blood-caked head as they hurried down the stairs, trying to see inside. He wasn't sure he'd like what he saw. She hadn't changed, she'd *expanded*. She'd been right. He didn't know her at all, and any sense that he did was misplaced, a falsehood brought on by love and his *need* to love.

After a few more flights, when it looked as if they'd evaded the mercenaries, Tom asked: "You don't love me, do you?"

Skin snorted, but Honey turned and looked at him with wide eyes.

"How could I not love the man who risked everything to get me away from that bastard?"

"But you don't. Not *really*. Not *truly*."

Honey averted her eyes, looking down at her feet. It was answer enough for Tom, but she had to go and spell it out, had to destroy whatever illusion he could rescue from what had happened here. "Tom… I can't. I'm artificial. Artificials don't love. *You* know that."

"*I'm* artificial!" he said. "*I* love. The Baker made sure of it, he gave me a virus, and I've given it to you and— "

"You really are priceless," Skin said. He was standing on a landing looking back up the stairwell, a grin splitting his face. Tom couldn't tell whether he'd been chopped or not. If he had, it was internal.

"Why did you come to him?" Tom asked, nodding at Skin.

"I told you, to say goodbye."

"I don't believe you." Tom was flushed now, jealous, embarrassed at the rejection, angry at Honey's use of him.

"It's true!" Honey said again. "To say goodbye and… ask for his release. Skin and I are connected. Psychically. He likes to watch me sometimes when I'm working; it's his vice and he paid me well and that's it, I swear!"

"Swear all you want. You used me to escape, you lead me on, you told me everything I wanted to know. Fuck off. Fuck off with your human lover and — "

"Tom," she said quietly, softly. His heart sank. The Baker's virus had worked on him for sure, because he felt such an emptiness when he saw the lack of love in her, such a sense of abandonment. "Tom, I'm so sorry. I had to get away from Hot Chocolate Bob. You came along and offered me that, how could I not take it? But I feel like…. I *could* love. You. Maybe it'll take longer to have an effect on me. Maybe it's more than a virus. It'll grow, not like something fake or artificial."

"We could have been killed!"

"You already have," she said. "Thanks to the Baker, everyone thinks you're dead. So you're free."

Tom thought about this. And he thought about how the Baker's virus had had years to affect him. "The Baker told me it would be perfect," he said.

"Mad old fuck," Skin said, shaking his head. Honey spun on him.

"He may have been mad, but at least he sought the right thing. He found it in Tom. Let me go, Doug."

She turned back to Tom, and she was crying artificial tears from artificial eyes.

"So what do we do now?" Tom said. "Are you leaving?"

"Yes."

"I'm going with you."

"Tom, you're free…. Hot Chocolate Bob thinks you're dead, you can— "

"I'm going with you. I still believe in the Baker. That is, if…."

Honey smiled and to Tom she was beautiful, even after everything. Even her tears.

"How about planting a seed first?" she said. "I need a charge and… well, it's the least we can do."

"What do you mean?"

Honey turned back to Skin, who stood leaning against the wall like a petulant child. Tom could see now how he'd been chopped: dazzling blue eyes; perfect designer stubble; a squared jaw which did not suit his face. Vanity personified.

"Doug, does this place still have the buzz units?"

"'Course it does," he said. "Did you see the state of some of those artificials out there? Buzzed to fuck and couldn't care less."

"We need them."

"Honey, I can access the net anywhere, we don't need—"

Honey smiled up at Tom even though she was still leaking tears. She could stop, he knew that, she could control their shedding. But as she'd said before, she so wanted to be human.

"*Love's the answer,*" she said, "*whatever the question may be.* I heard that once. A stupid idea, especially for the likes of me, but it made me jealous." She stared up the stairwell, seeing nothing there and apparently liking that. "I've been a whore for as long as I can remember, Tom. The start of my memory is my creation. Imagine if love stopped the need for plastic bitches like me."

"The world would be a nicer place."

She nodded. "And that shithead pimp would be out of business."

"What the hell are you two robots talking about?" Skin asked.

Effectively dismissed by Honey, his anger was rising now, a red-faced attitude burning its way through his altered good-looks. *Robots* was as derogatory as he could have been.

"We need a buzz unit to bleed Tom's virus onto the net. And Doug, I need you to let me go. You've had your fun. Your time's up. Let me go."

Skin looked at Honey, at Tom, back to Honey. There was so much potential in his eyes — for violence, hate and betrayal — but in the end he simply sighed, pulled a small egg-shaped thing from his ear and crunched it under the heel of his boot.

Honey winced slightly, then smiled. "Thank you, Doug."

"Fucking robots," Skin muttered as he walked back up the stairs. Tom watched him go.

"Come on," Honey said, grabbing his hand. She pushed open a door and they entered a long, dimly lit corridor. "I've seen them used a couple of times... I'm sure I can find them."

Tom was lost. He felt abandoned and loved, led and in charge, alive and dead... artificial and human. He wished the Baker could explain, but he guessed that even the old man would have made little sense of all this. Honey was leading and he was following, and this wasn't how he had imagined it at all.

"What if the mercenaries find their way down here?" Tom asked. "If they catch Skin they'll make him talk in seconds."

"Don't know," Honey said. "I suppose that'll be it." And that's all she offered. She was, Tom realized, as out of control as he.

Honey's mention of needing a charge had started to make him feel weak, as if his muscles and byways and synapses had responded to her words, his bones thinning, his lungs withering. He could hook straight to the net and give them both a clean charge, but Honey's idea to spread whatever he had — virus, madness, disease — onto the net... well, it was what the Baker had always wanted. Spreading a fire of love. The old man could never have imagined that the smoldering stage would have taken fifteen years.

The corridor twisted and turned, opened up into wider areas, narrowed again, sloped up ramps and down steps dripping with condensation and slime. The basement was the guts of The Slaughterhouse, Tom thought, a maze of rooms which all had closed doors. He was glad for that. This was where the chopping took place, Honey had said. From the extremes he had seen in the club, Tom did not want to know.

"Can you find your way out again?" he asked. Honey paused and glanced back at him. She looked stunned.

"You mean you haven't been remembering our route?"

"Oh Jesus…."

"Come on," she said, "I think we're almost there."

They must have been way down now, staggering through the depths of the club's basement. And this far down the club must have felt safe… because some of its doors were still open.

Most of the rooms were empty, full of dank air and dark potential.

Some had rudimentary furnishings, beds in the center or equipment burnt into a congealed mass in the corners.

A few were occupied.

Tom wondered how they survived, these victims of chops gone wrong. He saw heads and feet and pricks and stomachs, insides outside, pieces enlarged or shrunk or missing altogether. He saw other things too: appendages he could not identify; globes of flesh with eyes and vaginas; spider-limbs stretched around a webbed parcel; eyes on stalks, ribcage exposed. One person had limp pricks sprouting from his nether regions like a porcupine's spines, dozens of them dribbling in profusion. A woman, startlingly beautiful where she lay uncovered in her bed, seemed to be fused to the bed itself, flesh and bone arms merging somewhere with the metal frame, legs overhanging and disappearing into the ivory tiled floor.

Honey seemed not to notice, or was unconcerned if she did.

They emerged into a well-lit room, larger than any they had seen before, and she paused.

"This is where it happens," she said, her voice neutral.

"I don't know why they do it," Tom said, staring at the three operating tables arrayed with all manner of arcane equipment. It reminded him of the Baker's lab. He tried to shake that impression but it stuck fast, and the more he looked the more he found similarities. He hated that that. He didn't consider himself chopped.

"Most of them choose what they become," Honey said. "Mistakes are very rare."

"Those things back there…?"

Honey nodded. "Even mistakes have a right to life. And maybe even some of those chose."

Tom shook his head, exhausted and amazed.

"So where's the buzz unit?"

"Through here, in a little room in the corner. If that's where they still keep them. If they're still working. If we've really escaped the mercenaries and have an hour to do it. If, if, if…."

They crossed the operating theater and opened the door in the far corner. The buzz units were in there, vast conglomerations of wire and capacitors and chip-hoods; other pieces of equipment tagged on seemingly at random. They were the machine equivalent of the people hidden away in basement rooms, except that these had purpose.

There was a bed with grubby grey sheets, on which the subject would lie.

"You first," Honey said. "You're the important one. Tom." She paused and looked into his eyes. "This might change everything. *Everything.*"

"The Baker always told me that change is good. It's how we evolve."

"Do artificials evolve?"

Tom merely shrugged. He thought of the chopped people he'd seen back there, and those who lived on the streets. He thought of himself, what he was, as an abstract idea rather than a familiar. And he supposed that evolution was a track that nothing could really escape.

He lay on the bed and let Honey hook him up. He resisted the temptation to open a route to the net himself, instead allowing the buzz unit to do so, a violent, painful connection that caused him to wince and tense his limbs. He felt the charge begin to leak in, and it was like drinking piss instead of fresh water. He was invaded rather than energized. But as with all buzz units, it was an exchange rather than a one-way feed. Some of him was leaking out as well, dregs of his essence drifting against the tide like a backflow against his pumping heart... and this is what they intended.

As the first rush of outside images smashed into Tom's senses, he closed his eyes and let fate carry him along.

Within seconds he knew why they became addicted.

A clean charge went one way. A buzzed charge was a vampiric symbiosis, demanding something of the user's essence in return. And once given — or taken — that shred of memory, experience or thought remained in the net, floating like a miniscule fish egg in a vast ocean. Waiting for someone else to enter and sweep it up.

Tom's veins and synapses tingled with the stolen charge, and at the same time his senses came under assault. He smelled rose and rust, tasted pussy and spice, felt a feather touch his eyelid and a weight crush his foot, saw a man on a barren hillside and a girl crucified on barbed wire, heard the soft pop of lips opening by his ear and the roar of a crowd. He gasped and thrashed on the bed, but something was holding him down. He opened his eyes to see Honey sitting astride his hips. She was smiling at him, and there were old lead connectors pasted to her temples and thrust into the slit beneath her breast.

This was a dual effort, a doubling-up. Tom had heard how dangerous this was, and a few times he'd seen artificials who had tried it. They were lost. Not hurt or damaged, but vacant. Missing. Gone somewhere else.

He closed his eyes and tried to buck her off, but the flow of input to his brain crippled him.

"Shhhhh," a voice said, and he saw Hot Chocolate Bob shafting someone from behind, taking out his prick and coming on her back, his victim's skin sizzling as the sweet blue acid spurted from his chopped cock and balls. The pimp laughed but he was somewhere else now, somewhere darker and more intimate. He offered Tom a drink and smiled kindly, dropping a gold ring into the glass just before Tom saw Honey's hand take it.

Tom struggled to open his eyes and there was Honey. She was smiling still, even though her eyes were closed, and he found a free second to wonder which of his memories she was experiencing.

He was pulled back in as his muscles rippled with renewed energy. And there was the Chinaman performing his puppet dance, each finger alive, every twitch of his hand communicating a desperate passion, a morbid misery. Silence then, and blackness, before the dark was filled with the muffled crashing of music from a long way off, seeping between floorboards and through walls, setting him moving to the rough beat.

"Shhhhhh," the voice said again, and Tom opened his eyes. The room was moving around him, the table tilting, the ceiling fluid and pocked with hundreds more memories yet to be seen. The only stillness in the room was Honey. She had loosened her clothing and tried to make herself naked. Dried blood speckled her breasts and stomach from her neck wound, and as her hand delved inside Tom's trousers and found his prick he went under again.

The room had velvet-lined walls and stank of stale sex. There was a naked fat man between his legs — Honey's legs, because it was her past history he was seeing and living in snippets — and his hand worked at her slit. He kept glancing up as if his rough assault was pleasuring her, and Tom heard Honey sigh and groan, felt her shifting her hips to maintain the illusion—

—and he opened his eyes and she was feeding him inside her, sinking down onto him and gasping out loud as the penetration matched some hidden memory leaked from his mind. She rose and fell, and Tom could see his wet length revealed and swallowed again like scraps of memory, never the whole picture. He snapped back again, eyes forced closed, and there was another room in that stinking whorehouse, two men at him this time, abusing Honey's body as if payment meant ownership, if only for a time. One of them fucked her, the other burnt her stomach with hot ash from a cigarette, and she writhed in fake ecstasy.

Tom shook his head to kill the memory and she was dancing on her own... and, finding respite, he felt himself penetrating her and being penetrated at the same time, two minds in one.

He hoped she was feeling the same.

Honey rode him, pressing down on his chest to steady herself, and Tom kept his eyes open for as long as he could. Her smile was constant, whatever fragments of his past she was living, and that had to be good. He pushed back, trying to stay deep inside in case he lost her. But she was in control. And inside their minds, finding each other in an impossible sea of a million strangers' memories, she let him feel how she felt, guiding him in and thrusting himself up.

And in that sex, blooming and bursting like an endless orgasm, something strange and unknown in Honey's mind... something very much like love.

Tom sat up and shouted, finding the strength in himself — strength of mind, of body, of purpose and soul — to snap off the connectors, plucking them from Honey's body as well, throwing them at the sizzling machine beside them.

They were leaking sweat from their pores and tears from their eyes.

"Holy fuck!" Tom said.

"Did you feel it?" she gasped. "Did you feel it go? Did you feel it leave? It's out there now, waiting for millions of people to come along and snap it up."

"It'll get lost, it — "

"Love can't get lost," Honey said. "Not even if it takes forever." She kissed him hard and heaved herself up and down violently. She was hot around him, and he didn't once think about the thousands of other men who had been there, the scum and the sad, the pathetic and the cruel. They made love on the dirty mattress, and when they had come they stayed that way, stroking and giggling and kissing as if it was the first time for them both.

She was a dream. Tom had dreamed of her once, but after their joint buzzing he could not know whether it was decades or minutes ago. Maybe it was when the Baker was giving him the virus, or perhaps it was just now. That did not upset him. In fact, he quite liked it. She was a timeless dream, and she was fleeing the city with him.

"Where can we go?" she said.

"The hills? Maybe north? Anywhere away from Hot Chocolate Bob."

"He won't live forever. Bastards like that have enemies."

They walked on quietly until they felt the cool kiss of fresh air on their skins, tasted it in their mouths. They struggled through a gap in the wall, barely wide enough to crawl through, emerging minutes later from a maintenance pipe on the riverbank. The river flowed into the city. It was so huge, wide and sluggish that its gravity seemed to pull them with the flow, urging them back, back home.

"I've never lived anywhere else," Honey said, looking at the lights behind them.

"I've never *been* anywhere else," Tom said.

"It'll be fun. We can discover things." She looked at him and smiled a mischievous smile. "And Tom, do I know some things about you!"

"Shall we go?" he said, heading off along the course of the river.

"Not forever," she said. "We'll come back one day. Not forever, Tom."

He nodded. They'd come back because he owed that to the Baker.

They'd return to see what they had done.

Story Notes

I love to read story notes, learning writers' inspirations, the thought processes that led to certain ideas or themes being explored. In fact, if you're anything like me, you're reading this before you read the stories! So the first thing I have to say is: be warned — **Here There Be Spoilers!**

I've talked about these tales in chronological order, without actually being sure which order they'll take in the collection. And here's another warning... I'm often unsure where a story came from, and why, even when I'm working on it. Writing these notes was like looking through a window at myself, back into the past when these novellas were being written. Sometimes it's sunny and clear and the view is unimpeded, but on occasion it's raining, water's running down the glass and the view is obscured. And sometimes, there's little memory of the inspiration at all. The window's frosted up and I'm little more than a shadow moving beyond.

It's almost six years since the first of these novellas was written, and their original inspirations may well have misted away in the fog of time. But for me a story is a living, breathing thing, and in time the root of its creation becomes less important than what it represents as a whole.

But there are always details... the things that make the world go around... and I'm sure I'll remember something.

"From Bad Flesh"
Faith in the Flesh — Razorblade Press, 1998

Writing this novella six years ago was the most intense writing experience of my life. I've yet to match it. I sat down one Thursday evening, stared at the thin blank screen of my Olivetti Jetwriter 900 electronic typewriter, and wondered what to write. It's a wonderful thing that blank screen, the virgin paper, the empty notebook... wonderful, but always daunting. From then until now, I'm thinking *How do I start? What do I write? Can I really cover this with anything worthwhile?* And that first line is always the killer. I usually know if a story's going to work for me from the first line on (and I mean writing here, not reading!) Sounds strange... but I can imagine painters knowing with their first brushstroke whether their new work is going to be something special.

So I sat there staring at the screen. I had files full of ideas and notes, and there were a couple of short stories I was working on. But I decided to let the mood take me. That first line, "Della is the only person I still listen to." appeared... and I was away.

I took the next day off work, and wrote all day and on into the evening. By midday Saturday I had a 23,000 word novella finished in first draft.

As to where it came from... I'd been on holiday to Zakynthos, a small island off Greece, a couple of years before, and that's the inspiration for the location. The disease, Della, the quest for a cure... don't know. They just... came.

I believe this was the first story in which I mentioned the Ruin, an ambiguous, nasty fate that has befallen society. It's used again in many of my stories, novellas and novels, and indeed all the novellas in this volume are intentionally, or could be set in this ruined world. A world where bad things are happening, and where there are worse things to come.

"The First Law"
Faith in the Flesh — Razorblade Press, 1998

This is a story I'd been wanting to write for a while, and it could be seen as one of my first forays into the Humankind versus Nature theme. This is something that still fascinates me, the idea that we have tried to disassociate ourselves from nature and, in the process, damaged our relationship with it. Damaged beyond repair? Who's to say. I guess we'll know in a hundred years or so.

In "The First Law," my unfortunate sailors find themselves in a place where humanity is already shunned. They think they're survivors, but they're little more than parasites. And the island, their Nemesis, is determined to exterminate them one by one. I enjoyed working on the relationships between the men, providing that internal conflict as well as the threat from without. It's pretty grim and downbeat, so I'm told... but from where I view the story, there's a definite note of hope and even triumph at the end.

Of course, if you're reading the story from the island's point of view, it's a virtual comedy!

This was also released as an excellently produced audio book from Elmtree.

"White"
White (chapbook) — MoT Press, 1999

I'd always wanted to write a siege story. In "The First Law" the men were under a form of siege — although they were mobile, there was no escape from the outside forces pressing in.

With "White" I wanted to create a real sense of claustrophobia, confusion and fear.

This originally started life as a science fiction novella, with a first line that went something like "Dave Smith was the first human being to die on another planet." The siege would have been set up there, the creatures purely alien instead of the more supernatural "things" the whites seem to be in the finished novella. But somehow I just couldn't get it to work. That first line didn't inspire me, the idea didn't sit right, and I put it aside to let the ideas brew.

And when I translated it to Cornwall, everything fell into place.

I had great fun writing this. It became more claustrophobic and intense as I went along, and setting it in a snowbound house added that bit of frisson I was looking for. The main character is under siege from the folks in the house as well as the creatures outside, and I hope that makes it something much more than simply a "stalk and slash" novella. Indeed, quite a few people seemed to like it. It was reprinted in *Year's Best Fantasy and Horror* and *The Mammoth Book of Best New Horror*, as well as being nominated for the International Horror Guild Award and winning the British Fantasy Award.

A complaint I had from a few readers was "So, what the hell *were* the whites?" My answer then and now is, *I don't really know.* An author under complete control is not allowing for the story to take over. My people in the mansion didn't know what the whites were, so why should the reader?

Hell, why should I?

Read it for yourself. *Decide* for yourself. And if you think you know, please drop me a line.

"The Origin of Truth"
Scifi.com, 2000

This is another story that came pretty much unbidden and unplanned. The idea that nanotechnology could run away with it-self had been with me for quite some time, and whilst I wasn't altogether clued up on the science, the images and ideas it con-jured were astounding.

I think it's my first truly science-fictional story, in that the sci-ence is researched and, hopefully, the premise is at least possible, if not (one hopes) probable. It's perhaps one of the grimmest stories I've ever written in that there really is little hope for sur-vival from line one, but when the "receiver of knowledge" idea crept in I did see a glimmer of light, the idea that knowledge is available to us all if we'd only be more receptive to it. Knowledge and capability. It's a pity that humans seem to fight more than forge ahead.

I had huge fun writing this. It was a real challenge because of the mix and blending of ideas, but that complexity made it very satisfying to work on.

And research... yes, I did research. It's not usually my strong point, but when I submitted this to Ellen Datlow for consider-ation for Scifi.com, her first response was... *prove it.* So I spent some time reading up on nanotechnology, merrily surfing the net, and I ended up presenting a report on the science behind the story. Ellen seemed happy with it, and it was fun to do.

If a little scary...

"Hell"
Original to this collection

How many times have you read a newspaper or watched the TV news and thought: "Wow, I'm glad I don't live there." I live in a country — Great Britain — where our changeable weather is rarely deadly, civil unrest is usually restricted to drunken gang-fights on a Saturday night, and the scariest wildlife is a vaguely poisonous adder. Even our spiders aren't that big, and our crime rate, though climbing, is positively pacifistic compared to some countries.

I'm lucky. I think I know that. I see news items about terrible floods in Bangladesh, famines in Africa, wars and plagues and conflicts I cannot comprehend... and I think myself lucky that my family doesn't live somewhere like that. What the hell have I got to complain about?

Of course, sometimes I do complain. Don't we all? But what if I could be made to *see* the people worse off than me, *feel* their agonies, *hear* their pain? Would it make me feel any better?

That's what "Hell" is. A place of nightmares where people are taken to be convinced that they really haven't got it so bad.

Like Nolan. His daughter has run off with a religious sect, his wife is dead and he's plunging into depression. Hell finds him (*you* don't find *it*!) and takes him on a journey... during which he sees his daughter crucified on barbed wire.

With "Hell" I wanted to write something fast-paced, full of adventure, a chase story with other layers to it. I hope you enjoy it.

Hope you have fun.

Hope you don't recognize anyone.

"Mannequin Man and the Plastic Bitch"
Original to this collection

Now here's a strange one, I'm sure you'll agree.

"Where do you get your ideas from?" is the question I hate the most, because a lot of the time I just don't have an answer. My favorite reply is "No idea," but that tends to piss most people off, they think it's flippant and dismissive... even though, mostly, it's true. Maybe they're expecting me to reveal a Source — a book, a website, alien intervention, a plane of consciousness — while in truth, every idea comes from somewhere different and unique, and usually mysterious to me.

This one... well it may sound shallow, but it came from the title. Mannequin Man and the Plastic Bitch... sounds like a line from a song. It has a musical lilt to it, something heavy perhaps, thrumming bass and smashing drums. Now what the hell can that be about?

It stayed with me for a long time until I decided to go literal!

This is a love story about two people who shouldn't be able to love, an action story, a tale with what I hope is a strong moral core. It also introduces The Baker, a wacky inventor about whom I hope to find out more in future tales. He doesn't play a big part here — it's his memory and his legacy that the Mannequin Man is interested in — but I feel he has many more stories to tell from this strange, near-future world.

And there's another interesting aspect to having little control over my own ideas. There's a definite new trend in my later work, especially the two original novellas herein: near-future, almost fantastical. "Hell" and "Mannequin Man..." could easily be set in the same world (in fact as I was writing them, that's just what I imagined). And a new novella I've just completed for a Cemetery Dance anthology, "In the Valley, Where Belladonna Grows," is equally fantastical.

Not intentional. It just happened that way.

Why? Where do these stories come from? No idea.

And still, however different the worlds may be, the Ruin is always there. The ills of society, perhaps. The inevitable future. The slide into chaos and decay which humanity faces as a race. Cynical and pessimistic, maybe... but what better places to tell stories about the triumph of the human spirit?

I hope you enjoy reading these tales as much as I enjoyed writing them. Please, let me know what you think.

And take care.